The Trout Whisperers

The Trout Whisperers

A NOVEL

Pete Bodo

STACKPOLE
BOOKS

Published by
STACKPOLE BOOKS
5067 Ritter Road
Mechanicsburg, PA 17055
www.stackpolebooks.com

Printed in the United States

First edition

10 9 8 7 6 5 4 3 2 1

Library of Congress Cataloging-in-Publication Data
Bodo, Peter.
  The trout whisperers / Pete Bodo.— 1st ed.
    p. cm.
  ISBN-13: 978-0-8117-0177-8
  ISBN-10: 0-8117-0177-8
  1. Fly fishing—Fiction. 2. Camping—Fiction. 3. Vacations—Fiction. 4. Middle-aged men—Fiction. 5. Male friendship—Fiction. 6. Montana—Fiction. I. Title.

PS3602.O333T76 2006
813'.6—dc22
                                                              2005027882

For Lisa:
My wife and partner on the longest and
most exciting float of them all . . .

Acknowledgments

Although authors rarely publish acknowledgments with a novel, I owe a debt to my core group of fishing buddies, whose personalities and passions, habits and experiences are the marinade in which *The Trout Whisperers* was soaked: Here they are, then, stand-up men and women who know there's no real need to ask for whom the bell tolls—it *always* tolls for the other guy (the one who's stuck in the office while the rest of us are out fishing).

So thanks, Richard Franklin, Frank Rodriguez, Glyn Vincent, Rick Warren, Chris von Strasser, David Blinken, Greg Hubert, Isabelle Fritz-Cope, and James Prosek; thanks Joel Aronoff, Lisa Lyons, Ollie Marshall, David and Shane Mann, and Billy Murray. You too, Billy Taylor, Jim Emery, Joan Wulff, Wayne and Anna Nordberg, George Semler, David Foster, Rich Epstein, Paul Nevin, Joe Maloney, Steve Renehan, Jeremy Frost, Jim Range, Billy McHenry, Jeff More, David Taylor, George Cooper, Lizzie Shuler, Eugene Garrity, Dave Berman, and Danny Byrd. It pains me to admit this, but I've never fished with Nick Lyons or Pat Hemingway, but it sure feels as if I have; and if I don't ever fish with Judith Schnell, I'll just have to learn to lie about it.

And a moment of silence for A. Tucker Cluett, presently bushwhacking along a bank the rest of us will walk one day, too.

Part I

"We were now about to penetrate a country at least two thousand miles in width, on which the foot of civilized man had never trodden; the good or evil it had in store for us was for experiment yet to determine, and these little vessels contained every article by which we were to expect to subsist and defend ourselves."

—APRIL 7, 1805,
The Journals of Lewis and Clark

1

Caw-caw-caw . . .

The magpie landed heavily in the cottonwood tree towering over the campground on the Beaverhead River and began to squawk, announcing another Montana morning. Well, almost. For the day was developing slowly, like a photo negative in a chemical bath.

Touches of pink appeared in the pale sky. A translucent moon still rode high. The air was crisp and cold, even though it was summer and likely to hit ninety degrees by the afternoon.

Caw-caw-caw . . .

The river slid along, running bankfull with a coppery tint. It wasn't very wide—perhaps sixty feet across here at the small, nearly empty campground just off the two-lane road leading to the town of Dillon. The camping area, where the odd visitors were much more likely to be sleeping off a hangover or making out than relaxing in the great outdoors, was bald dirt with no real amenities save for a rusted, empty trash barrel and a few burned-out fire rings containing charred, scrunched-up beer cans.

Caw-caw-caw . . .

On the far side of the river, though, the foliage was lush. The overhanging alders tippled the surface. Now and then, a swirl appeared under the branches. It was made by a brown trout of more than eight pounds that leisurely fed on the spent mayflies known to fly fishers as spinners.

The giant trout lived just downstream, in a deep pool at the base of a dramatic cliff of porous yellow stone. The pool was a miniature reservoir created behind an irrigation dam and pumping station that were just becoming distinguishable. Curlicues of mist rose from the calm surface.

Caw-caw-caw . . .

The trout lay in the depths of the pool under the cliff all day, unmolested, in water so deep that it was impossible to see the bottom even in bright sunlight. But each evening after dark, the giant leisurely swam up along the cliff to the alders, snacking on bugs and little fish along the way. Then it settled in to feed until shortly after daybreak, when it drifted back down into the deep pool with a full belly to rest for the day.

The trout had a safe haven. Even an experienced angler couldn't position himself to get a good, natural float with a fly under the alders. And because of the small dam, the many drift boats that plied the Beaverhead on a typical day, bristling with fly rods and jolly anglers dressed like aliens from tackle catalogs, always ended their float at a takeout half a mile above the campground.

In fact, only one person had ever caught that humongous brown trout, and he'd done so twice. On the first occasion, six years earlier, the fish had been just a foot-long juvenile. The second time, almost exactly a year later, it was a should-have-known-better sixteen-incher.

Now it knew better.

Caw-caw-caw . . . Caw-caw-caw . . .

A host of other birds began twittering and complaining as the light improved. Another mayfly spinner drifted under the alders and disappeared in a whirlpool with an audible *pop*.

Two vehicles were parked like toys left in the campground overnight. One, which had arrived in the middle of the night, was a maroon-and-gray pickup of uncertain vintage, with a few ovals of gray primer above the rear wheel wells and a bumper sticker that read, "Attention: Driver Carries Only $20 Worth of Ammo." An aluminum camper was mounted in the truck's bed, with lots of gear lashed to the roof with yellow plastic rope. Parked on uneven ground at a sloppy angle to the river, the rig listed perilously to the left.

Not far away, under the great cottonwood at the upstream end of the campsite, was an entirely different setup—one that, in the dim light, could have been mistaken for an entire village. This camp was discreetly screened by a muscular-looking, dark green SUV with Washington state plates and a handsome McKenzie drift boat on a trailer.

The SUV was jammed with camping and fishing gear in a bewildering if neat assortment of boxes and stuff sacks. Two float tubes were secured to the luggage rack like giant doughnuts. A dream catcher dangled from the rearview mirror, and the rear window was plastered with decals for organizations such as the Seattle Flyfishers and the Ironfeather Society.

The SUV belonged to Raul Mendoza, who was just beginning to stir in his one-man tent pitched under the cottonwood. Not far away, on a grassy knoll just a few feet from the river, was another one-man tent, a blue one.

The tent expanded and contracted, breathing like a giant blue lung. Inside lay B. Louis Traub, stretched out on his back, snoring prodigiously. The *B* stood for Bonaparte, a fact that Louis took great pains to hide. His hands lay placidly crossed on his mound of a stomach, and his eyelids fluttered like mad butterflies.

This was Louis and Raul's twenty-fifth annual fishing and camping jaunt in Montana. When they first hooked up as young men in their midtwenties, they had fished madly, carried minimal gear, shared a tent and even a single set of silverware. They drew the line only after a lengthy discussion on the pros and cons of using a common toothbrush.

Year after year, they fine-tuned their approach, seeking maximum efficiency and comfort, and when a conflict arose between the two—as it did after Louis, having put on a great deal of weight, became a vigorous snorer—comfort gradually had come to trump efficiency.

Over the years, these trips had become more important to both of them than any other activity, including vacations with their families.

This was but one of the reasons that neither of them had much in the way of family anymore.

Louis was snoring so mightily that his jowls trembled, and even the magpie perched on a bough over the tent kept cocking its head, trying to decipher the meaning of the strange and terrible puffings and blowings and wheezings emanating at regular intervals from the little blue cocoon of a tent. Agitated, the magpie let loose again.

Caw-caw-caw . . . Caw-caw-caw.

The bird fell silent at the loud squeak of a hinge. The back door of the camper truck opened, and a boy of about seven jumped to the ground. His bare legs were covered with lumpy mosquito bites. Despite the cold air, he was wearing just a T-shirt that said, "Grandma's Favorite Little Son-of-a-Bitch." The boy munched a candy bar while his father climbed out, backward, wearing heavy canvas chest waders and holding a cheap, stubby fishing rod.

The sunburned man had a blond flattop and a "Semper Fi" tattoo on his left bicep, partially hidden by a T-shirt sleeve that fit him like a sausage casing. He swooped the boy up with his free arm, took a few steps, and let him drop again, saying, "Let's get us a big'un son. Be quiet now so's we don't wake the neighbors."

The man's name was Earl. The boy was Just Ray. Until recently, Earl had always called his son Little Ray, but his wife nagged him so much about using just the boy's proper name that he took to calling him Just Ray—just to fix her wagon.

They walked the riverbank, past the campsite hidden behind the SUV and boat. Earl stopped, untangled the fishing line from around the rod, and slipped a fat, white maggot on the hook. He hoisted Just Ray onto his broad shoulders and waded into the river.

The current was so strong and the gravel bottom so unstable that Earl felt as if he were walking on marbles. But Earl had powerful legs, and soon he'd waded two-thirds of the way across the river—farther than any man could without the extra ballast provided by the fearless child on his shoulders.

Earl instructed Just Ray to drop the line in the water and pay it out, allowing the bait to drift downstream, bouncing on the bottom. The boy obeyed, squeezing his legs tighter around his father's neck.

A broad swath of thin, yellow light fell over the upper portion of the cottonwood and illuminated the top of the cliff. It would be a fine, fine morning.

The magpie flew off, discharging a wet gob of poop.

Caw-caw-caw . . . Caw-caw-caw.

Louis was vaguely aware of the guano landing on his tent with a soft *plop*. In his half sleep, he also heard Earl and Just Ray's muffled voices.

It had been a rough night for Louis. He and Raul had hooked up with Bowen Kiick, a friend they had met some fifteen years earlier on the banks of Idaho's Henry's Fork River during the famous brown drake mayfly hatch. That was, as Louis liked to say, back in the day—back before the Fork was overrun by the folks he described as "Redford's *River Runs Through It* crowd," along with the more recent menace, busloads of fly-fishing Japanese. The best you could say about the latter was that though they scarfed up all the expensive reels and trout-related T-shirts in Last Chance, they largely left the trout unmolested.

Louis, Raul, and Bowen—"feather throwers," as Louis, in his more fanciful moments, liked to describe fly fishers—bonded instantly that day on the Fork when Bowen showed them how easily medical syringes could be converted into handy dispensers. He used them for the various viscous substances that were of critical importance to feather throwers, including dry-fly floatant, hand cream, even commercial dishwashing soap—a product with many surprisingly innovative applications in fly fishing. From that day forward, half a dozen modified syringes dangled from the densely packed fishing vests that Raul and Louis carefully folded and placed at the foot of their sleeping bags every night on any given river. And that was many, many nights. For, like Bowen, the men loved fly fishing for trout above all other things.

Louis and Raul also appreciated that Bowen was a rebel. His father was some kind of Wall Street pooh-bah, but Bowen had dropped out of Wharton business school and moved to Bozeman, Montana. He wanted to spend his life casting flies to "big heads," thumbing convention, and burning through his trust fund before he drank himself to death. The outcome of that race was by no means decided, for though it once had been an awfully big trust fund, Bowen was both a gifted drinker and flagrant spendthrift.

Such proclivities ensured that Bowen invariably was described by his admirers as "a real stand-up guy" and by his detractors—mostly angry members of the opposite sex—as "just another swinging dick." Either way, he looked and acted the part. Bowen was handsome and built like a linebacker. He had wild blond hair, an impish gleam in his blue eyes, and a snaggletooth that he refused to have fixed. It lent him the air of a desperado.

Bowen had a squeeze in almost every trailer park from Helena to Ennis, and though he had nothing but contempt for the New York and Hollywood glitterati who were swarming all over Livingston and the Paradise Valley with their hand-painted cowboy boots, gelled hair, and three-picture deals, he was an intellectual. He had catholic tastes and read copiously. Fittingly, it was Bowen who, aware of Louis's love for Montana, bestowed on him the nickname "Big Sky Bonaparte"—eventually shortening it to "Sky."

In typical stand-up-guy fashion, Bowen had driven all the way out from Bozeman with his McKenzie drift boat to take his two friends for a float on the lower Beaverhead, and in typical swinging-dick fashion, he had brought along a bottle of Louis's favorite tequila, Herradura. This was a touching gesture, for while Louis perceived himself as, first and foremost, a mountain man, he also was a man of discriminating taste to whom there was no such thing as simple vodka, scotch, or tequila. There was only Absolut, Albemarle single malt, or Herradura.

The men had enjoyed a feast the previous night to celebrate this anniversary trip, with Raul making his special spicy fish tacos from scratch—habanero peppers and all. They made a great big fire and ate prodigiously. With a few beers and a fair amount of Herradura already under his belt, Louis decided to make one of the elaborate toasts that flowed like honey from his lips when he was well lit.

He rose and, losing his balance, sloshed a little Herradura out of his glass. "Bowen, Raul . . ." After a dramatic pause, he continued. "As we all know, this year marks the twenty-fifth anniversary of Raul's and my first, um, explorations of the Big Sky country. In light of that, I suggest that we all pause for a moment's reflection . . ."

Louis looked up at the sky, as if searching for words. Then he said, in his rich, nasal voice: "Here's to three old and great amigos and feather throwers. I suppose we are but relatively insignificant beings in what is commonly described as the *grand scheme of things,* yet, truth be told, we are bonded as brothers in the noble pursuit of a truly, um, aristocratic fish. A magnificent fish. This lovely fish—the trout. I stand before you, humbled by the good fortune that enables me to pursue this quest, year after year, through seasons and days, with such fine companions . . ."

"Hear, hear," Bowen cried, greatly enjoying this preface.

"Join me," Louis went on, "in partaking of the fruit of *Agave tequilana . . .*"

Louis took a long drink, as did Bowen, while Raul had a small sip. At this point, Louis digressed, pointing out to his friends that the plant commonly known as the agave was not, as even ardent tequila fans supposed, a member of the cactus family at all. It was, technically speaking, a succulent. Then he returned to the main subject, noting that the ancient civilizations of Mexico believed that the agave contained the mysterious power from which humans originally derived their ability to laugh.

He then speculated on the nature of ancient cultures, big heads, and stand-up guys, eventually finding his way back from the Mayan ruins and bloodied Aztec altars to the Rocky Mountains. He wound up his speech with the kind of exhortation that might just as easily have rolled from the lips of his hero, Capt. Meriwether Lewis, had the leader of the legendary outfit known as the Corps of Discovery at that moment been in Louis's unusually small size-eight shoes.

On a roll now, Louis switched to the archaic language he sometimes affected: "On the morrow, we embark for parts unknown, borne along on the streaming waters of yon Beaverhead. We will gaze upon vistas heretofore unknown to us, pursuing our quest with passion and a sense of purpose unknown to most men."

After a pause, he added, "Gentlemen . . . Here's to big fish—*and lots of 'em!*"

They roared and drank again, except Raul. A stream of tequila ran down Bowen's chin and shone in the firelight. Louis's rambling speech had so amused him that he shook with laughter and finally bellowed, "Damn all, Sky—isn't there *anything* you don't know?"

———

Now that morning had arrived, Bowen too was sound asleep. He was shacked up many miles away in a motel just outside Dillon, with a waitress named Amber, who had a pierced navel and worked at the Elkhorn Café.

The empty Herradura bottle lay on its side in the dirt near Louis's tent.

All was quiet, and then a shout rang out: "Whoooo-eeee, you got 'im! Reel on 'im, Just Ray!"

Just Ray lost his balance and fell into the river with an enormous splash. Earl grabbed him by the scruff of the neck before he was swept away, and together they wallowed and lurched toward shore as the giant trout bolted downstream, heading for the safety of deep water. As he dangled from Earl's grasp, the swift current pushed the boy from side to side on the surface, but he clung resolutely to the rod.

Earl and Just Ray hit the shore running. They scooted down the bank, the rod bucking in the boy's hands.

The big trout just kept going, right over the top of the dam. Father and son ran out on the narrow structure. There was no easy way around it; the bank was steep and the brush was too dense. As the big trout continued to take line, Earl had a thought: "This here's the difference between having a monster trout mounted above the sofa and just another story to tell."

Earl looked down at the seething water twenty-five feet below. "You hold on to him now, Just Ray," he said. "You hold on, no matter what." Earl ripped off his waders, held his nose, and jumped off the dam feet-first. He landed with a massive splash, lurched to the shore, and took off downstream after the trout.

"Daddy!" Just Ray cried. "You git 'im, Daddy!"

———

Raul, having emerged from his tent, hunched over the propane stove, patiently waiting to depress the plunger in the French-style coffeemaker. It was positioned in a pot of simmering water, ensuring that the coffee—a special blend of North Slope Kenyan and Sumerian lowland beans, with just a touch of chicory, that Raul had settled on after years of careful experimentation—would remain hot. Later, the hot water would be used for washing dishes.

He again read the hand-scrawled note that Bowen had left on the windshield of the SUV. Bowen wrote that he had some unexpected business to attend to and wouldn't be able to make the float after all. The boat fished better with just two anyway, and he promised to be waiting at the downstream takeout at the end of the day to drive his friends back up to camp.

Raul was dressed in a navy zippered fleece that was sold in a catalog featuring heavily tanned, blue-eyed alpinists. Raul was dark-skinned, as befitting his Dominican roots. He was a superbly fit, handsome man who stood just over six feet tall, with glowing chestnut eyes, a full head of glossy black hair, and a neat Zapata mustache.

Although he appeared imperturbable, Raul was high-strung and prone to stuttering when he was nervous. Those who just met him often were surprised to learn that before Raul dedicated himself to a career in dental hygiene, he had been a highly touted major-league pitching prospect.

Presently, Raul's thoughts were far from baseball—or molars. He was troubled by Bowen's note. As Louis or any of Raul's three former wives could attest, Raul did not take well to sudden changes and frequently expressed his revulsion toward "flying by the seat of the pants."

As the years slipped by, Raul had become increasingly devoted to routine and lost his urge to see what lay beyond the next bend. He liked that he and Louis knew exactly which rivers they would fish and in what order. Indeed, they often knew whom, among their many friends in the fraternity of feather throwers, they might rendezvous with along the way. And they always returned to their favorite campsites.

Raul frowned and gently depressed the plunger in the coffeepot. As he waited to pour his first cup, his mind drifted back to the first day of their trip.

Louis's nonstop flight from New York to Seattle had arrived on time. As usual upon meeting, the men performed the Shoshone embrace—the greeting the Indians had taught Lewis and Clark. Face-to-face, each man flung his right arm over his friend's left shoulder and clasped the small of his back so firmly that their chests met and cheeks touched.

Then they returned to Raul's home, where the camping and fishing gear was all laid out in the garage, neatly sorted, stacked, and ready to load. That evening, they made their ritual visit to the local Home Grown supermarket to stock up on essentials that might not be readily found on the trail—aged Kobe beef, cornichons, macadamia nuts, kippered herring, and such.

In the produce department, they'd had an encounter that even in retrospect made Raul wince. They'd come upon the manager, a guy named Bud, reaming out a scrawny, longhaired kid for smoking in the employee break room. Caught unaware, the embarrassed manager tried to engage Louis and Raul in pleasant conversation, while the kid returned to stacking grapefruit.

Bud recommended some choice plums that had just come in from the Klamath River Valley in southern Oregon. On hearing the name of the Klamath, Louis stopped squeezing peaches and turned to Bud. "I beg your pardon, sir—did I hear you correctly? Did you say the *Klamath* River Valley?"

Bud looked quizzically at Louis, who continued: "Are you aware, sir, that thanks to the sweetheart irrigation deal the fruit growers have down there—not to mention abject consumer indifference and irresponsibility among retailers—one of the last remaining strains of wild chinook salmon in the Pacific Northwest is presently endangered?"

Louis went on, lecturing Bud on the Klamath ecosystem and the lobbying powers of the nefarious California Fruit Growers Association. Bud began to twitch and turned whole-body red. He finally stormed off, sputtering, "Go ahead then, eat the lousy *California* plums if you're so gol-darned smart."

"Wow," the scrawny youngster had said, as Bud vanished around a corner. "That was, like, trippy."

"He da-da-da-doesn't mean to offend anyone," said Raul.

Louis, remembering that they still needed some scented hand wipes, left Raul to guard the overflowing cart. Raul conversed pleasantly about fishing with the kid, who had the sleek black hair and high cheekbones of a Native American. His name tag said Phoenix. Raul felt a spiritual affinity with the boy, even though he smoked cigarettes and appeared to have some kind of a dragon tattooed on his back and lower neck. The kid liked fishing, and Raul gathered from the brief conversation that, like himself, he came from a broken home.

Raul extolled the joys of fly fishing, and Phoenix seemed interested in Louis and Raul's trip. By the time Louis returned with the hand wipes, Raul felt conflicted about breaking off the conversation. He'd connected with the kid, and that left him with a certain feeling of responsibility. That's how it was for all the men who, like Raul, belonged to the male empowerment group known as the Ironfeather Society of Warriors.

Finally the coffee was ready. Raul poured a cup, added milk, and took a sip. He set it down to cool and picked up his rumpled brown fedora. He smoothed the jet black crow feather jauntily stuck in the band. Was he dwelling on the supermarket encounter because of the empathy he felt with the kid Phoenix or because it was the latest, embarrassing example of his fishing partner's increasingly imperious ways? Louis's authoritative attitude had always been okay with Raul, since he could back it up with knowledge and a high degree of competence. But even that went only so far—certainly not far enough to diminish Raul's anxieties about floating the Beaverhead without an experienced hand aboard.

Besides, they were flying by the seat of the pants just by being on the Beaverhead at this stage in their trip. That, too, was largely because of Louis. On the morning they'd pulled out of Seattle, Louis had a brainstorm, suggesting that they postpone their customary first stop at Idaho's Silver Creek.

Louis's logic was, as usual, impeccable. Silver Creek's famous *Tricorythodes* hatch was almost sure to be late because of a cold, wet spring. So Louis suggested bypassing the river he called Silver Crick and going straight to the Beaverhead, where they could hook up with Bowen. They might also spend a few days renewing their search for a mythic river known to veteran Montana hands as Little Gooseneck Creek. It was a stream cited in a handful of pioneer diaries and obscure fly-fishing tomes but never positively identified. Whether it even existed was a source of fierce debate.

Raul took a sip of the hot coffee, glad that he had vowed to put off addressing his growing physical and emotional dependence on caffeine until after this anniversary trip. Though sound, Louis's new plan had disappointed Raul, for Silver Creek was his favorite fishery. In fact, this very time a year ago, he was happy as a clam on Silver Creek, not far from Hailey, a town with premium coffee bars, health food shops, and civilized residents, including many attractive women who wore turquoise jewelry and walked around with their unencumbered breasts jiggling in halter tops.

Raul loved natural ways. And despite Louis's ritual grousing about noise from the highway and the crowded campground at Silver Crick, they almost always experienced great fishing there. The previous year, they had timed the Trico hatch on the Nature Conservancy water perfectly, and Raul had landed a twenty-two-inch rainbow on a minute size 24 midge pupa fly.

"Mornin', pardner."

The sound of Louis's voice snapped Raul back to reality. Crawling out of the blue tent, Louis stood and cleaned the round lenses of his wire-rimmed spectacles with a red bandanna. He was still in the black thermals that he wore under his neoprene waders, looking as if he were about to draw his sword and declare, "En garde!"

"How do you feel?" Raul inquired.

Louis issued a prolonged groan. "I wonder sometimes why I do this to myself."

"I wonder why you do it to yourself, too," Raul said.

Louis belched. He sat on a stump and made some additional noises of an unidentifiable nature. Forced to work around his stomach, he tried to insert his tiny feet into his fancy lightweight hiking boots. After much huffing and puffing, he was finally laced up, with the Velcro straps secured high above his ankles.

"Raul, where's Bowen's rig?"

"He's gone." Raul explained the situation in his raspy voice while he poured Louis some coffee.

"So he just split and left us with the boat?"

"Yep."

"Interesting. I see no reason to balk, do you? We have the collective skills to make this float."

They both understood "skills" to mean that Raul would do most of the rowing, for Louis was in pitiable physical shape. Raul didn't mind, though; he hadn't groaned and grunted through a winter of workouts in a gym under the supervision of a personal trainer for nothing.

"This is no undertaking for an empty stomach," Louis added. "What say you to one-eyed Connollys?"

"Louis, I really think if we're floating, we don't have time for all that cooking."

Louis made a carefree gesture that meant "Whatever." Louis was a man of many gestures, as befitting someone whose personal card proclaimed that he was a "Wordsmith and Public Intellectual." Although he did a little copyediting, wrote catalog copy, and churned out a high volume of letters to the editor, his principal occupation was running and providing the bulk of the content for his own website, Guardian of Grammar.

A great believer in technology and the power of the Internet, Louis had created the site to serve as the ultimate arbiter of English language usage. He fielded queries from citizens of all nations, including real stumpers such as "Why isn't *phonetic* spelled phonetically?" or "Is the expression 'fellow countryman' redundant?" One e-mailing reader had presented him with a conundrum that he still puzzled over, months later: "If someone is said to be modest, is it the ultimate insult or compliment to reply, 'He has a lot to be modest about'?"

Louis stood in awe of the power of words, and that's why he often enhanced their effect with an appropriate, well-timed gesture, such as the slow sweep of an arm across an imaginary landscape, beckoning a rapt listener to imagine some breathtaking panorama that existed in Louis's mind's eye. Likewise, he often presented observations with a slight bow and an unrolling of an arm until his hand was extended, palm up—a gesture that made his comment seem inarguable. Louis often ducked his head and leaned close to a listener before revealing a particularly juicy fact, knowing that this hint of conspiratorial kinship could be a powerful persuasive tool.

But Louis's signature gesture was involuntary. When he experienced a serious shock, he reacted with something his mother, Fern, had taken to calling a "spell": His head tilted back and his eyes rolled in their sockets, showing only white; simultaneously, his forearms shot forward to a position much like that of a clever Pomeranian that had been taught to sit up and beg. Thus positioned, Louis's hands would jiggle involuntarily, and his eyelids would twitch and flutter. A stranger might easily mistake one of these spells for a fit of petit mal. Thankfully, though, the spells weren't dangerous, and they rarely lasted more than a few moments.

Raul set about making some camp toast for Louis and a bowl of yogurt with kiwifruit, coconut, and toasted almonds for himself. Louis wandered over to the camp table, set aside his glasses, and ran a little water from their five-gallon plastic container into his cupped palm. He patted his cheeks and eye sockets with it. He peered into a pocket mirror, regarding his pleasant, plump oval face. Occasionally he grew a beard to hide his weak chin, but on this trip he was content with salt-and-pepper stubble. The striking quality of his gray eyes was somewhat muted by some corkscrewing eyebrow hairs.

Louis tamped down the thin tufts of graying hair protruding from his temples and the back of his head. Unlike his athletic companion, Louis actually looked his fifty-odd years—and then some. He mused, "Did you, perchance, notice Bowen's reluctance to engage in conversation about the Little Goose?"

"No, I did not."

"Hmmm, how do I put this? I found him . . . not exactly evasive but, shall we say, *unforthcoming?*"

Raul shrugged. "Maybe he's tired of the hunt. He's spent as much time searching for Little Gooseneck Creek as we have. More."

Louis mulled this over. The lore of the river was well established among the feather-throwing elite, but that only piqued the interest of some who still searched for it. The Little Goose was said to be teeming with huge brown and rainbow trout, and there were wild tales of the river having a brown drake hatch that was in the same league as the one on Louis's beloved Fork.

The sketchy details suggested that the Little Goose burst forth in full flow from giant springs in a kind of geological sinkhole buffered by vast, mineral-rich limestone deposits. The stream was rumored to flow only a short distance, although nobody knew whether it was a tributary of some other river, flowed into a lake, or fed a large wetland.

Though it was theoretically possible that the Little Goose was tucked away in some remote corner of the state or on a vast tract of land inaccessible to the public, to many the very idea of finding a significant, undiscovered trout stream anywhere in the Lower Forty-eight was preposterous. Awesome trout rivers were extremely rare; all of the great ones, whether they were in Patagonia, Croatia, Tasmania, or Montana, were known.

There was an entire school of savvy feather throwers who believed that Little Gooseneck Creek was nothing more than the original name of one of Montana's many widely known spring-creek fisheries. It could have been the original name of Armstrong's, Odell's, or DePuy's. Those in that school scoffed at the romantic souls who still carried the torch, characterizing them as hopeless dreamers.

But Louis also knew that if the Little Goose did exist, whoever discovered it would assume his place among the great fly-fishing pioneers— men like Ed Tryzcinski, the first feather thrower to descend the Willow Canyon stretch of the Clark Fork of the Columbia in just a float tube. Or Marco Capobianco, the machinist from Fair Lawn, New Jersey, who was fishing near Allentown, Pennsylvania, when he happened to discover a previously unknown mayfly during a hatch of puny olive-and-black flies that everyone had always taken for the insects known as Tricos. The astonished—and humbled—entomologists at New York's Museum of

Natural History had no recourse but to name that insect in his honor, *Ephemerella Marcocapobianco.*

"When we eventually head south, perhaps we should take a ride through the Centennial Valley," Louis suggested. "We haven't been there in years, and it's about as pretty a place as there is for a wild goose chase—no pun intended."

"Oh my," Raul gasped. "Oh my, oh my, oh my . . ."

Louis looked up from his toast and saw Earl and Just Ray straggling back to camp. The boy's arms and legs were scratched and covered with blood. The father's clothes were muddy and torn, but he had one hand hooked under the gills of a monster brown trout. The fish was so big its tail dragged in the dirt. Father and son disappeared behind their truck.

By the time Louis and Raul made it down to the riverbank, Earl was squatting on the gravel bar, washing down the freshly gutted trout. The sight of the big, dead fish immediately plunged Louis into one of his spells. Earl, concentrating on the task at hand, saw the jiggling wrists out of the corner of his eye and asked, "Is everything okay there, mister?"

Raul, who was already attending to his partner, said, "He's fa-fa-fa-fine. It's the fa-fa-fa-fa-ish did it. That's an enormous trout—just enormous."

Earl rose, wiping his forehead with the forearm of his knife hand. "He's sure a bruiser, in't he? My boy here got 'im. Right acrost from your camp. That's a mighty nice setup you got there, mister."

Just Ray, a shy boy, cast covert glances at the strangers as he skipped stones across the big pool that was no longer the home of the magnificent brown trout.

Louis's eyelids fell still, and he came out of his spell. His arms dangled at his sides. Staring at the fish, he said, "What a magnificent example of *Salmo trutta.* Are you aware, sir, of how long it takes a brown trout to attain such proportions?"

"We're goin' to have him mounted," Earl said, ignoring the question. "That's why we killed 'im. I don't even like to eat fish. Nobody in our family does."

The words hit Louis like a blow. He sputtered, "Did you even, for a moment, consider taking accurate measurements and a photograph? Even a, um, mediocre image from a disposable thirty-five-millimeter camera would have sufficed. These days you can make perfectly lifelike replicas of trophy fish out of epoxy—as do our enlightened bonefishing colleagues in the Florida Keys."

"What are you gittin' at, mister?"

Earl stood up slowly. Just Ray moved very close to his father, staring at the intruders.

"Excuse us," Raul said. "My friend here, he's ja-ja-ja-just a little ah-ah-ah-ah-upset."

"Yeah, 'cause we caught the fish an' he didn't."

"That isn't quite accurate, sir," Louis said. "If I am upset, and indeed I am, it's for one reason only. In this day and age, we can ill afford to kill fish in the same way as did our hunter-gatherer forebears. In order to maintain genetic diversity, we need to protect superior specimens such as this one. I, for one, have no problem if an angler in the right circumstances chooses to kill a small to medium-size fish for a meal . . ."

"I already tole you," Earl growled. "We don't eat fish."

Louis plowed on, making his point about the relation between size and genetic diversity in fish, but then the boy interrupted. "Did we do something bad, daddy?" Just Ray looked puzzled. He held his right hand over his brow to shield his eyes from the sun.

"We ain't done nothin' wrong, Just Ray. Now go get in the truck."

"But—"

"You heard me. Git."

Earl grabbed the giant trout and sloshed it around in the water. A vein in his temple was throbbing. He took a step toward Louis, growling, "You got some nerve, mister . . ." Earl turned and, lugging the trout, stomped off to his truck. He drove off so quickly that as he turned out of the lot, it looked as if the vehicle would topple.

Louis and Raul watched the truck vanish, the deep rumble of its damaged muffler audible for a long time. "Bonaparte." When Raul was truly upset with his friend, he sometimes addressed him by his proper first name. "I don't like that they killed that fish either. But you spoiled it for that little boy."

"They're scary, people like that . . ."

Regarding his friend closely, Raul asked, "People like what?"

Louis thought for while before he calmly replied, "Regular people."

Raul said nothing. As an Ironfeather man, Raul was intensely aware that he needed to be sensitive to the needs of *all* men and boys. That was one thing that Darby Wingo, the founder of Ironfeather, made crystal clear in his magnum opus, a collection of maxims called *The Virilian Protocols*. Raul quietly recited the 11th Virilian Protocol: "The healer lies buried in every warrior, as the warrior lies buried in every man—to help your fellow man to grow is all."

Louis ignored the mantra; he was distracted and upset. Some gum wrappers and other litter lay about where Earl had been parked, and the dirt was marked with a large, dark stain where water had leaked out of a cooler. He pondered the stain and finally muttered, "The despoilers. They're everywhere."

Louis might have been even more dejected had he known that the big trout Earl killed had been the one Louis himself, some years ago, had caught and released—twice.

———

At about the same time that the giant trout made a last, involuntary spasm in the bottom of Earl's cooler, Nathan Nuckel sat down on the edge of a bed covered with a boldly flowered spread in a clean, beige room in the Bozeman Best Western motel, some two hours' drive east of the Beaverhead. Nuckel was crane-like, with a pencil-thin neck, hazel eyes, and brown hair, strands of which he carefully separated and spread out each morning to get the maximum comb-over effect on his bald dome.

Nuckel had dallied over coffee in the Best Western's breakfast buffet room, reading *USA Today*, a paper he did not often see but always enjoyed because of the profusion of colored pie charts and graphs sprinkled through it. Now, after a shower, he was adjusting the garters he wore to hold up his hose under casual but neatly pressed khakis.

Nearby, a pair of lace-trimmed, sky blue panties lay on the brown Naugahyde seat of the armchair by the window, but nothing else in the room suggested the presence of another individual, much less a woman.

The television was on, tuned to an all-morning sports show. Nuckel's red pin-striped pajamas were neatly folded on top of his black carry-on suitcase, which lay open at the foot of the bed.

He snapped the last button on his garter, rose, and crossed to the TV sitting on a low dresser against the wall.

He peered at the crawl at the bottom of the screen until the score came up: The Colorado Rockies had bombed the Phillies at Coors Field the previous night, nine to one. "Way to go, fellas," he thought.

Nuckel picked up the photograph lying next to the holstered revolver atop the TV and went over to the good light at the window looking out on I-90. A native of Butte and a private investigator, he carefully examined for the umpteenth time the picture of the man he was hunting.

The fellow could easily be mistaken for a Montana boy. Like a truculent buffalo, he looked simultaneously unkempt and well fed. His police record included multiple drunken-driving arrests, outstanding emergency-room bills from the hospital in Great Falls, two restraining orders, and an unusually high number of citations for trespassing. He could have been Joe Elk Hunter from Billings, Kalispell, or Helena.

But when Nuckel's contacts in law enforcement had finally come through a few days earlier, they only confirmed what Nuckel had suspected with every bone in his experienced sleuth's body. His quarry was no Montana boy, not at all; he was a transplant, like so much of the rest of the riffraff from down around Bozeman.

Nuckel had no use for Bozeman. Like Missoula, it had grown thick with tree huggers, vegetarians, backpackers, fudgepackers—the whole stinking works. This only made Nuckel more determined to bring the fugitive to justice, and now that the chase was heating up, he once again felt the thrill spreading into his every pore.

It was time to move, time to tighten the noose.

Nuckel went over to the chair and picked up the blue panties, folding them carefully after he examined the label. He picked a fresh Ziploc bag out of the box in his suitcase and put the undergarment into it, squeezing out the excess air as he sealed the bag, and placed it in his suitcase.

"These out-of-state hell raisers and troublemakers," Nuckel thought. "They don't know enough to pour piss from a boot, most of them. They think they can just come here and act as if . . . as if anything goes. We'll see about that, mister, mister . . . Kiick."

"Kiick," Nuckel thought. "Bowen Kiick. Hail, that name don't even sound like it belongs to a Montana boy . . ."

2

Louis sat basking in the molten morning light on the gunwale of Bowen's drift boat at the primitive launch site almost a mile below the Beaverhead campsite, waiting for Raul to return from parking the SUV. He drank in the scent of cold, pure water mixed with the bitter fragrance of sagebrush. Nearby, willows whispered and swayed while the Rockies loomed dark blue in the distance, contrasting sharply with the brilliant, pillowlike clouds overhead.

Louis examined the tan nylon painter attached to the bow. It certainly was a far cry from the rough, elk-hide ropes used on the pirogues of the Corps of Discovery when Lewis and Clark traveled this very body of water. Surely, Louis thought, the explorers would have appreciated the lightweight, ultrastrong rope now made from polyethylene and similar petroleum by-products.

"Did you leave the War Pony in the shade?" Louis asked.

Raul was carrying the folding aluminum beach chair in which he liked to sunbathe in his briefs. He leaned it against a rough, hand-painted sign proclaiming, "Caution at Squawfish Hole—Portage Advised," and asked, "What do we make of this?"

"It's some sort of warning for inexperienced canoeists."

Louis hated Raul's sunbathing chair—it would be totally out of place on board the elegant, wooden McKenzie boat. The craft, named for the wild Oregon river on which it was developed, was heavy but extremely stable thanks to its ample width and upturned ends. It looked like a giant slice of cantaloupe.

"Check this out," Louis said. "This is interesting."

Raul joined Louis in studying one of the miniature brass pulleys that was part of the anchor-line rigging. They agreed that it was a deft bit of engineering.

Louis rose, groaning. His fully loaded fishing vest added considerably to his already top-heavy construction. Myriad doodads, including a camera, surgeon's forceps, thermometer, clippers, syringes, magnifying glass, and insect net, dangled from the vest, clinking as he walked. He also wore a fishing hat—one of those legionnaire jobs developed for equatorial climes. It was shaped roughly like a tuna fish can, with flaps that rolled down in the back to protect his neck from the sun and an extralong duckbill made of semitranslucent, dark green plastic.

"Captain Mendoza?" Louis gestured toward the boat. "After you."

Raul climbed in and stowed the duffel, a cooler, and the beach chair. They carefully slid three rigged fly rods into racks built into the sides of the boat.

"Would you mind rowing the first mile, Louis?" Raul asked. "I'd like to get organized."

"Not at all, pardner," Louis said.

The center bench seat creaked as he settled in and took the oars. Raul shoved the craft off the beach and into the current. The boat turned this way and that as Louis flailed with the oars, but he soon got the nose pointed downstream and found his stroke. The men looked at each other. They grinned. It was always like this—always like the very first time they had ever gone fishing.

"This is exciting; I'm g-g-g-glad we decided to do this," Raul rasped. He took off his fedora so he could catch some sun and adjusted the red bandanna that he wore, rather flamboyantly, around his neck.

"Check out that dwarf cypress," Louis remarked, gesturing toward the bank with his chin. "The boughs are so symmetrical. It's so feminine—like a chick's pineapple."

Raul did not think the little tree looked anything like a woman's pudendum, so he just went, "Hmmmm."

"I dig the way the most fundamental forms in nature repeat themselves," Louis added.

Beyond the tiny tree lay classic short-grass prairie—brome and cheat, with some sagebrush here and there. Finches twittered in the wild rose and willow bushes lining the bank. Louis didn't have to do much rowing, just a bit of correcting with either oar, to steer clear of the brushy banks of the swift, even-flowing river.

They traveled in typical drift-boat fashion, leading with the bow of the craft so both oarsman and angler had a clear view downstream. The rower could then position the boat so that the caster, who stood leaning against a special brace in the bow, had more time to put his fly over rising fish or attractive lies. And if the rower wanted to slow the boat down, all he had to do was row normally.

Louis gazed at the riverbed sliding by under them. Despire the coppery tint, the water was extremely clear; every detail was visible in the jumble of multicolored rocks. Louis never tired of looking into trout water. Sometimes he grew transfixed and experienced vertigo, until he shook his head to snap out of the trance.

"Heartbreak Hill," Raul said, noting the hillock that marked the farthest downstream they had ever hiked, perspiring in their waders, to fish. He opened the largest of the seven fly boxes he carried in his vest. The flies were arranged in rows according to size and color, although only a fly fisher could readily discern the subtle differences among them. With their tan and gray wings, the various mayfly and caddisfly imitations looked like tiny jets crowded together on the deck of an aircraft carrier.

"*Oecetis disjuncta?*" Louis liked to call flies by their proper Latin names. Most other anglers knew the fly in question as the little tan caddis.

"They should be starting up. But I expect to see some PMDs later—just like yesterday," Raul said. He was referring to pale morning duns, mayflies that often emerged on the same days as the little tan caddis. The challenge for feather throwers lay in determining whether the fish were keying on the caddis or PMDs.

"The PMDs didn't start until right around four yesterday, no?" Raul asked Louis.

"Closer to three, I'd say."

Raul snapped one box shut and began to tidy up another, nudging the flies this way and that with the tip of the same hospital-grade forceps he used to remove hooks from fish. Their boat shot through a riffle and passed another drift boat anchored in the backwater at the tip of a gravel bar poking like a long finger into the pool below. An angler with a guide by his shoulder was flipping a nymph—a fly imitating the larval or nymphal stage of an aquatic insect—out into the foam line where the stillwater met the fast water. About three feet above the fly was a hank of red fluorescent yarn, greased up so it would float and plunge under if a trout grabbed the fly as it bounced along the streambed.

"Bobber fishermen," Louis muttered. He purposely averted his eyes.

Louis and Raul were dry-fly men; they fished exclusively with floating flies for trout feeding on the surface on freshly hatched or expiring insects. In their ethos, fishing below the surface with nymphs or the streamer flies that imitated small baitfish was pedestrian—never more so than when the fly or line was weighted and used with a strike indicator. For then the angler didn't even have to swish his line to and fro in the casting technique that was the essence of their sport.

Feather throwers knew that the real art of fly fishing lay in selecting the correct fly to match the hatch and presenting it with a skillful cast. Any knuckle dragger could flip or pitch some weighted nymph that looked like a tiny tarantula out into the current, where it landed with a graceless *kerplunk* and bounced along the bottom, invisible to the angler, until the garish strike indicator plunged under and the hapless trout was hooked.

"Look left," Louis called out. "Bank feeder!"

"Copy," Raul cried.

About thirty-five yards below, a pile of large rocks spilled from the bank into the water, propping up a weathered fence post that still had barbed wire on it. Just downstream of this structure was a deep, swirling eddy about the size of a bathtub. Both men had seen the nose of a big trout poke up in the eddy as it sipped in an insect. Louis rowed furiously, trying to move the boat upstream so that he could pull over to the bank well above the rising fish.

"It's a good fish." Raul lurched forward as the boat spun sideways. "A really good fish."

Louis finally wrangled the boat into the slow water at the shore, well upstream of the fence post, and dropped the anchor. "It wasn't pretty," he said, "but here we are."

"There he is again," Raul said. "Wa-wa-wa-wa-war council."

The men watched the spot below them. They sized up the situation as the fish rose again. "Interesting impedimenta," Louis noted as he studied potential angles of approach. He concluded, "I see no solution but to approach from downstream."

"Agreed." Raul drew the rods out from the racks. He propped two in the stern and selected his trusty 5-weight rig. "I think it ca-ca-ca-ca-calls for a real bender of a curve cast to the right. That's *if* I can wade out far enough to keep the backcast out of those willows."

"A not insignificant 'if,'" Louis said gravely. "The spinners appear to be over, and I'm not seeing any caddis yet. What do you think he's on?"

"Blow-in," Raul said, meaning ants or grasshoppers from dry land. He reached for the box on which he had neatly written, "Terrestrials."

"Small hopper. Maybe a flying ant."

"I'd go with the ant."

Raul finished Louis's thought: "Smaller splashdown in that tight spot. Good choice. Okay . . . It's sh-sh-sh-sh-sh-showtime."

"Showtime," Louis repeated.

Raul clambered over the side of the boat and up onto the steep bank. He walked downstream, well back from the edge of the river, so he could approach the fish from below. He would have to make a tricky curve cast that landed the ant right below the fence post and within a foot of the bank, while avoiding the three rusty strands of barbed wire tethering the fence post.

Louis had confidence in Raul, for he had taken the highest of the high roads open to feather throwers, becoming a man devoted exclusively to stalking the wiliest of all trout—the bank feeders. These were trout positioned very tight to the shore, beneath overhanging foliage or obstructions like this one. Such impediments presented the ultimate challenge in presentation, but they often sheltered the largest trout.

Raul loved the implicit challenge; to him, it was the ultimate refinement of the fair-chase ethic. He was a bank-feeder fanatic who refused even to cast for fish that were less than twenty inches long—the informal dividing line between a good fish and a *great* fish.

Embracing such limitations gave Raul great cachet among fly fishers, many of whom referred to him in hushed tones as the "trout whisperer." But Raul's lofty ethic also put him in a curious position. He was an angler of supreme skill, he fished many of the best rivers in the world for weeks at a time, but he rarely caught a trout anymore—not even on those days when his companion Louis or benighted nymph fishermen all around him were hauling in fish hand-over-fist, gleefully crying out, "Jeez, he hit like a freight train!" or "Whoooo-eee, just another day in paradise!"

Furthermore, on the rare occasion when Raul did manage to hook one of the giant bank feeders that lay like alligators along snags or undercut banks, waiting for juicy grasshoppers to fall from the sky, it usually busted up his gear and left him trembling in his boots, with the last few feet of his severed leader tippling in the breeze.

Raul, though, had no regrets about renouncing the typical angler's infatuation with shrieking reels and bucking rods. The way he saw it, this was all part of his "personal journey," in the course of which he had already learned that the glory of fly fishing lay somewhere other than in catching fish. This was a wise attitude and a convenient one as well, for in the previous two years, Raul had landed exactly *seven* trout.

Some fly fishers would have trouble understanding how Raul could bear to have such a low catch rate and still keep fishing. But there was another component to his discipline. Raul placed a high value on personal hygiene. By exclusively pursuing large bank feeders, he had hit upon a way to avoid the most unsanitary aspect of fly fishing—getting stinky, sticky hands from handling all those gorgeous but slimy trout.

Louis studied Raul as he got into position, full of admiration for his friend's heron-like patience. Raul methodically stripped line off the reel, measuring out by feel the exact length he needed to cast. Then he waited.

When the fish rose again, he began to cast, slowly and rhythmically, until he had the proper amount of pale green line in the air. The sun glinted off the line as it traveled in a smooth, tight loop, back and forth.

Raul made four or five casts that were off the mark by mere inches. He probed with a foot and stepped out into the powerful current until he dared go no farther. Louis understood his problem. A right-hander, Raul couldn't get quite far enough out from the brushy bank to make the cast he wanted. He had to worry about his backcast hanging up in the bushes.

Then Raul did something unexpected. He stripped off even more line and made another cast. At the peak of the power thrust, he transferred the rod to his left hand and gave it a violent shake just as the cast straightened out. The shake brought the line back sharply toward Raul, filling it with slack.

The fly fluttered down and wrapped itself around the upper strand of barbed wire. But as the current ate up the S-curves on the water, the leader on the barbed wire tugged the wraps and the fly unwound and plopped into the eddy—alighting as gently as any natural.

"My God," Louis muttered. "Brilliant."

The trout rose, exposing a giant snout, dorsal fin, and tail. It inhaled the ant.

"He's on," Raul cried, lifting his rod.

The heavy fish raced upstream, audibly ripping line through the current. At the end of the run, the fish abruptly changed direction and bolted downstream. It kept going, with Raul in hot pursuit and Louis chasing them both. The fish rocketed past Raul and swam through a massive, half-submerged deadfall at the head of the deep pool below. When Louis finally caught up, Raul was standing just above the downed tree in a narrow run of swift water. The rod was deeply bent, and the fly line plunged into the water at a sharp angle, disappearing into a mess of roots.

"You appear to be hung up," Louis observed.

Raul grunted. "I th-th-th-ink we may still have a shot at landing the fish—if we can pass the rod through."

"I should be the one positioned on the downstream side, where it's shallower."

"Okay, Louis. But please—don't do anything when I pass the rod through. Just try to hold the fish, if it's still on. It's the bank feeder of a lifetime."

"Certainly, pardner."

Louis went downstream of the snag. He stripped off his camera, vest, and shirt. Then he inched his way into the swift river, clutching a branch in case he should slip. There was no telling what might happen if he plunged in. The shore gave way to depths quickly, and the current was strong.

"Be careful . . . easy does it," Raul muttered, working his way into the water as well, but on the upstream side of the snag. "Your safety is worth more than a fish. Even this big a fish."

They got into position on opposite sides of the snag, water lapping at the tops of their waders, ready to pass the rod through. "Let's do it. Ready?" said Louis. Raul plunged his arm under and, with surgeonlike delicacy, probed and pushed the rod tip through the same gaps where the line went. Louis also submerged his arm. The water was tingly cold. After groping around, he felt the very tip of the rod. "I've got it! I've got it!"

"Here it comes, then."

It was do or die. Raul kept pushing the rod through until his hand was all the way down the butt end. He felt sick as he gave it one last, gentle shove and let go. Louis simultaneously pulled, and the rod miraculously slipped through the maze without getting hung up. By the time Louis had it up and out of the water, Raul was beside him; he had shipped quite a bit of water, but it was the last thing on his mind.

The waterlogged reel made a funny growling sound as Raul cranked up line. But lo and behold, when he took up the slack, he was still tight on the fish. He walked downstream, gaining line. The trout was holed up about thirty yards below, in a pocket in the middle of some broken water.

When Raul got opposite the fish, he began to apply pressure with the rod. The fish was just twenty-five feet away and stubbornly holding. But by keeping the pressure on and pumping slowly, Raul gradually gained line and tired the big fish. The giant trout finally became exhausted by the tug-of-war. It dropped slightly downstream and swam indolently toward the shore.

"The worm has turned," Louis said. "He's licked now."

"We'll see." Raul continued to work the fish, wishing they had a net. Occasionally a dull flash of butter yellow was visible through the amber water. Agonizing minutes passed.

"Now L-L-L-Louis, get down below me. I think he's ready. I want to turn him toward the bank."

Louis stationed himself. Raul slid his left hand up the rod for leverage and slowly swept it around toward shore. The fish followed docilely. Louis plunged in his arms, grabbed the trout, and tried to lift it clear, but the big fish heaved and cartwheeled out of his grip. It hit the water with a huge splash and bolted downstream. Louis almost fell over; he could barely see, for the fish had sprayed water on his glasses.

But what luck! The monster was still hooked.

Once again, Raul led the trout back toward his friend, who waited, kneeling. When the fish came in, Louis calmly grabbed the leader and pulled it close, then hugged the exhausted fish to his chest. He spat some water and hollered, "Done deal, pardner!"

Raul splashed ashore, lay the rod down, and ran over to Louis, who was already admiring the prize. Raul could barely speak. "Great job, Louis. Thank you, thank you, thank you."

"Kudos, pardner," Louis said. "This is as fine a specimen of *Salmo trutta* as I've ever seen."

Louis relinquished the fish and retreated to the bank to catch his breath. He flopped down, knowing that precious few men could have handled the job so expertly or worked so smoothly together. They had been pitted man against trout—man against nature, as it were—and they had prevailed.

Raul held the fish, semisubmerged, above a bed of bright green weeds. It was more than two feet long and a solid five and a half pounds. On a dry fly, that was the fish of a lifetime anywhere in the Lower Forty-eight. The brown trout's belly was the color of fresh cream, and it had deep yellow flanks with a profusion of small black and orange spots that became dense on the olive back, head, and snout. The fish gulped air, trying to regain strength.

"He's so beautiful," Raul said. "What a trout."

Louis regained his composure and began to fumble with his camera. "Okay, look natural now."

Raul held the fish with both hands, grinning at the camera, stooped like a man having a bowel movement.

"Perfect. That's a classic shot. Tilt the fish a little toward me—I want to get the full palette of his, um, vermiculations." Louis snapped off three more frames. "Pull your bandanna around a little. Now hold the fish up again and toward me . . . that's right."

"Hurry up." Raul was getting anxious. He didn't want to stress the poor fish too much longer. Louis wouldn't rush, though. This was a potential cover shot for any number of the magazines to which he regularly submitted photographs, including *Upper Midwest Fly Fishing and Fly Tying* and *American Rod Builders Quarterly*.

"He needs to go . . . we're done," Raul said. Still kneeling, he moved the fish back and forth in the stream, gently pushing water through its gills to help it recoup strength.

"Look how beautiful this fish is," Raul said. "It's just like . . . like a little person."

It was after eleven by the time Louis and Raul finally resumed their float, with Raul at the oars. There was no reason to dally—no insects hatching or fish rising—and they wanted to make it past the Farnsworth Bridge, a rickety wooden structure that was the only crossing of the Beaverhead for the length of their float, before they stopped for lunch.

Raul felt elated and alive. Catching that trout once again helped him get in contact with things more elemental and valuable than anything the deadening, so-called "civilized" life offered. The experience underscored themes touched on most recently in Raul's life by Kiku Ma, a Santa Fe–based shaman who conducted seminars on male centeredness. Raul and some fellow Ironfeather members had attended a Ma event called "Embracing the Chi of the Great Fathers," and after learning much, the men ended up frolicking naked in a wallow of hot mud. The experience had left a lasting impression on him.

Raul set aside his fedora, stripped off his fishing vest and shirt, and rolled down his wader tops. He dunked his red bandanna in the cold river and retied it around his neck. Then he continued rowing, bare-chested.

"Raul, you should apply sunblock," Louis said firmly. "You need UV protection, even with your dusky complexion and sun-worshiping proclivities."

"That's a good point," Raul said without moving. Over the years, he had developed ways to reject Louis's directives without overtly challenging his bossy friend.

They drifted on a broad, slow stretch of river. A breeze off the high prairie ruffled the water. High overhead, an osprey rode thermals of light, cool Rocky Mountain air.

"I hope those pictures turn out," Raul said. "I want to send one to Sedona."

"We should have excellent images. Look." Louis pointed into the water as they passed over a large rock with embedded specks of glinting quartz. "Rhyolite. It must have been deposited along with all this schist—perhaps by a resurgent caldera or some similar volcanic phenomenon."

After a few moments, Raul said, "Thank you for pointing that out, Louis."

It was nothing, Louis gestured. He enjoyed sharing his vast stores of knowledge, whether the subject was English grammar, high-end stereo equipment, or geology.

"How old is Sedona now?"

"Twelve. And she adores me," Raul rasped. "You're not supposed to play favorites, but she's my favorite granddaughter."

Raul was nineteen when he hooked up with the first of his three wives, a Connecticut girl who changed her name from Helen to Willow when she ran away to San Francisco, a flower child. Raul and Willow had two daughters, the eldest a girl they named Briese. Sedona was the first of Briese's three children and the first of Raul's total of five grandchildren, all of them girls.

"You used to feel somewhat, um . . . ," Louis propped his hand on his thighs and rolled his eyes skyward, searching for the word, " . . . traumatized about having become a grandfather."

"Yes, Louis. It was a confrontation with my own mortality. Seems long ago, doesn't it?"

"It was the year we discovered Three-Can campsite," Louis recalled, referring to the secluded spot they had found on the Boulder River. They had named the site for the three rusted tins they found in an old fire ring there, and they used the camp on and off for almost ten years. Then the easygoing rancher who had always allowed them to camp on the property had to subdivide for tax reasons. The new owner of the parcel, a contractor from Minneapolis, posted it to keep out trespassers.

Feeling mellow, Raul quoted from Darby Wingo's Virilian Protocols: "The wisdom of the buffalo is of the ages; the vanity of men is of the moment."

Louis was not a big fan of Wingo-isms, despite his fondness for buffalo and most things Indian. Though he respected his partner's keen interest in male empowerment and Native American spiritualism, Louis preferred to think of Indians in a more realistic fashion—as pagans and horse thieves, unbowed if syphilis-ridden lords of the Great Plains who tried their best to halt the advance of the pale-faced settlers and schemers who would despoil the West.

"Our first night at Three-Can, Louis . . . you caught that monster rainbow. Remember?"

"It took a size 18 tan caddis pupa with a Sparkle Yarn trailing shuck, dead drifted in the surface film," Louis said.

"I think that was the first year we tied our flies with Sparkle Yarn."

"Rachel would have been about eight then," Louis mused, talking about his only child.

Raul looked over the side of the boat but saw nothing in the surface film. "What's Rachel doing this summer?"

"I gather from her mother that she's taken an internship with some sort of, um, financial institution." Louis uttered a pained laugh. He still didn't fully understand where he'd gone wrong with the little girl who used to enjoy catching sunfish with her daddy—other than separating from her mother, Naomi, when Rachel was nine.

Rachel was now a college student who had more or less shut her father out of her life. Her goal was to work on Wall Street because, as she once remarked, practically spitting the words in his face, "I need to make shitloads of money so I can finally have what I want. For me."

Granted, Louis had never made any real money with his various writing projects. He had never even made unreal money. But then, he wasn't a crass, materialistic go-getter. He had inherited a tidy little stock portfolio and managed it cleverly, so that he was always able to avoid having to take an actual job. Supporting a family on his stock dealings and meager income was challenging, but Louis was up to the task.

In fact, Louis had raised the role of a thrifty, creative provider to an art form. At the meat market, he would take his time selecting the choicest of the choice cuts of beef or pork and firmly instruct the butcher to trim off the fat *before* weighing and pricing the meat—a clever ploy that left many a butcher red-faced, with his cleaver hand trembling.

Unfortunately, this turned out to be not quite good enough for Naomi. When they had first met, Naomi was a skinny, nail-biting chain smoker, forever waving blue clouds away from her intense black eyes. Naomi fell for Louis's bohemian aura—he did, after all, live in a Soho loft—as well as his broad knowledge and mastery of the English language. And unlike her wishy-washy father, Louis had an appealing authoritative manner.

At first Naomi found Louis's passion for fly fishing a real turn-on. But over time, she grew discontented and impatient with his angling obsession and his prudent ways. She resented that Louis spent six or seven weeks each year in Montana, yet their family vacations were limited to one-week sojourns to a grim, rented cottage on Cape Cod.

Gradually, Naomi developed a smoldering anger and came to view Louis as a lazy, self-centered gasbag and cheapskate. He put all that down to her high-strung nature, which he had always accepted with equanimity. But he felt bad that Rachel had taken after her.

"My daughter inherited all of her mother's neuroses and none of her assets," Louis said, feeling a sentimental pang at the memory of Naomi's pendulous breasts.

"It's probably just a rough patch she's going through," Raul observed.

"You're lucky to have such a large and close family, Raul."

"Thank you, Louis. That's very supportive. I've paid the price, though. Three marriages' worth."

"You know, I'm not into self-help tomes. But perhaps there's some truth in that theory about men being from Mars and women from Venus."

But Louis knew Raul didn't drive his wives crazy because he was from Mars. In fact, despite his handsome looks and Latino charm, Raul was very much in touch with his Venusian side; it was the best explanation for the way women trusted and fell for him. Although his three wives all considered themselves progressive, even feminist, they were not able to handle the way Raul put them to shame as a cook. He made them cry when he inspected and found particles of rice or spinach on the pots and pans they had volunteered to wash—often from the sheer desire to contribute after Raul had whipped up yet another fabulous meal.

In addition, Raul's personal grooming was impeccable, and he was a whirling dervish with a dust mop. He cleaned in places—including the top of the fridge and around light switches and doorknobs—that escaped his wives' notice. He was also nothing short of a magician with geraniums. And on top of all that, he was a well-endowed and skilled lover with an inordinate fascination with the velvet mousetrap.

In short, Raul proved to be more man than any of them could handle, and twice the woman any of them ever hoped to be. His spouses all ended up feeling like hapless bystanders.

Louis wondered how Raul had managed to be so fruitful. Two daughters and five grandchildren. That was something to crow about—even if none of them were boys.

Raul studied the river as it carried them along, requiring only the occasional correction with an oar. The breeze had died down; it was suddenly very still and blazing hot. There were no caddis to be seen, nor any PMDs. Louis knew that the river was full of trout, but at the moment it seemed devoid of life.

"Pardner, we've loved and lost . . . and lived to fish again."

Raul noticed the ribbon of dirt road snaking down out of the distant mountains to the left, toward the river and Farnsworth Bridge, which lay just another mile or so downstream. They hadn't seen much shade in this last stretch of river and hoped there might be some below the bridge, where they planned to pull over for lunch. A vehicle made a plume of dirt on the road, heading for the bridge.

Louis had fallen asleep in the bow seat, facing Raul. He slumped to the side, chin resting on his chest. The sun was strong. Dark stains of sweat were starting to show through the shirt on Louis's chest.

Raul was worried about Louis. Although he was no athlete, Louis had been in reasonable shape at twenty-something when they first met. Now he was corpulent, his largely gray hair was almost all gone, and he had a pasty pallor except on his forearms and hands—the only parts of his body that were ever directly exposed to the sun. Raul never could understand Louis's aversion to the sun. All the years they had fished together, Louis had never been moved to strip down, dive into a cold river, and bask, drying, on a warm boulder in the sun.

Raul softly began singing the Native Song of Praise to the Great Spirit: "Wee-ohhh, Wee-ohhhh-ho-wee-ho-way." He repeated the words with a slightly different inflection: "Wee-ohhh, Wee-ohhhh-ho-wee-ho-way."

Raul knew that like all warriors—for the warrior lay buried in *all* men—Louis would have to find his own way through the smoke that stings all eyes, to healing. Perhaps the Great Spirit would hear his words and bless Louis with vision. "Wee-ohhh, Wee-ohhhh-ho-wee-ho-way." Wavelets tapped rythmically against the hull until Raul's voice again broke the silence: "Wee-ohhh, Wee-ohhhh-ho-wee-ho-way."

Eventually Louis stirred, smacking his lips. He stretched and craned his neck to look downstream. "What on earth . . . ?"

Raul stood and took in a puzzling sight—a dozen fly fishermen lined up on either side of the river just above the bridge. "What the hell are they doing here?"

Louis groaned. "I suspect one of our local rancher friends has experienced a change of heart about allowing public access to his road. This is truly unfortunate."

Raul eyeballed the swifter water coming up, trying to choose the drift line that would least disturb the fish within casting distance of the wading anglers. The boat picked up speed, the water in the faster flow slapping against it. Louis stood as the boat slipped past the first of the anglers and called out, "Howdy!"

The feather thrower was wearing a black ten-gallon hat with an enormous peacock feather thrusting out of the band. His eyes were hidden behind wraparound sunglasses. He ignored Louis's salutation. As they drifted by, Louis commented on the fellow's rod: "That's a nice TLS, sweet rod!"

Just below them, an angler called across the river to a friend who was netting a fish: "What'd he take?"

"I'm not sure. One of those caddis things, I think."

Louis cupped his hands around his mouth in order to be heard. He called to the men, "Probably *Oecetis disjuncta,* the little tan caddis. We haven't seen too many yet, but it should start happening." As the boat shot by the anglers, Louis turned; they would be out of earshot soon. "The fish will be on the pupae first. We'll probably have PMDs later, too."

"What?" one of the men shouted.

Louis made a gesture indicating that he couldn't hear and flopped back down into his seat. They were approaching the bridge, where a substantial number of vehicles were parked. One angler was stuffing money into a steel box mounted on a fence post. "It looks like someone's made it a park-and-pay deal," Raul said.

The bridge, made from black rail ties, spanned a dramatic choke point of swift, deep water. A few anglers flailed away in a big eddy just above the span. The McKenzie boat picked up speed and shot under the bridge, where it was momentarily—and deliciously—dark and cold.

There were plenty of anglers downstream of the bridge as well, but they thinned out about two hundred yards along. The boat was almost past the line of fishers when Raul noticed a hunchbacked angler in a rumpled, gray Stetson. He called out, "Hansy! Is that you, Hansy?"

"Who's that?" The wader turned.

Raul back-rowed briskly, turning the bow. He got the boat to shore not far below the man wading toward them, who called, "Raul, Sky. . . where's Bowen?"

The drifters greeted their friend and filled him in on how they had gotten the boat. Like Louis, Hansy was a New Yorker, an owlish-looking forty-year-old who wore glasses with thick, unfashionable frames and parted his dense mat of unkempt brown-and-gray hair on the side. He was an ardent feather thrower who stood in awe of Louis's formidable stores of knowledge.

"I'm impressed that you found this access," Louis said. "Neither Raul nor I knew about it."

"Thanks. It's been a rough day."

Hansy explained that he'd inadvertently left his favorite fishing reel back home in New York. Then he'd locked the keys in his rental car— with the engine running—back in the Bozeman Best Western's parking lot.

This was not exactly surprising. Among elite feather throwers, Hansy's carelessness was legendary. He had never been known to switch off a light, close a drawer, or refasten a gas cap after tanking up. He couldn't go a week without losing his wallet. Fittingly, even the part in his hair wandered this way and that. But then, he was a bona fide count who had been raised by a gaggle of nannies and professional "aunties." You couldn't expect him to retain a dry-cleaning ticket or turn off the range after boiling water.

The most serious downside to Hansy's ways was that fly boxes virtually leaked from his vest and duffel bag. Over the years, any number of anglers had fished out a blaze orange box bobbing along in the current or picked one up along some forsaken railroad tracks and read the name on the box: Hans von Strouser. Occasionally, once even mailed it back.

Hansy compensated for his absentmindedness in effective ways: He was a fearless wader and a bold, instinctive angler armed with a silky, powerful casting stroke. On a good day, he could fish with the best of them.

Hansy told Louis and Raul that he had come to Montana on the spur of the moment for a long weekend. He pointed to an angler waving a fly rod around in the turtle water about a hundred yards downstream. He explained that the obvious beginner, Ubaldo something or other, was his companion on the trip and the brother of a Paduan princess Hansy had been dating.

Raul suggested that they all pile into the boat and drift down another mile or so, far from the crowd, where they could have a leisurely shore lunch. Afterward, Hansy and his pal Ubaldo could take their sweet time, fishing their way back upstream to the parking lot, while Raul and Louis continued their float.

The three men dog-walked the boat downstream to Ubaldo. Making the introductions, Hansy mentioned that Sky was the very man he had described to Ubaldo on the drive over the mountains that morning.

"Howdy, tenderfoot," Louis said, tipping his legionnaire's cap.

"Ciao." Ubaldo was tall and stork-like, with something like a Euro-Afro. He had wire-rimmed glasses, and everything he was wearing or holding appeared to be new, including his handsome, waxed-cotton Filson hat. He added, in a heavy accent, "Nisze to meet you. Do you prefer Szky or Louis?"

"Whatever."

———————

As they drifted downstream, scouting a good location for lunch, Raul told Hansy about his big catch of the morning. Hansy cried out gleefully as Raul described the rod transfer through the root ball. Meanwhile, Louis had somehow gotten onto the subject of his hero, Bob Dylan, and was giving Ubaldo an earful. Eventually Hansy turned to Louis: "Been to the Fork yet, Sky?"

Louis held up his hand—he was just telling Ubaldo the story about Bob Dylan going electric at Newport.

Hansy gave up and closed his eyes. He began dozing off to the soothing nasal tones of Louis reciting some of Dylan's most memorable lyrics. He woke with a jolt a few minutes later as Raul grounded the boat near some skinny pines that created just enough shade on the bank for a good lunch spot. Out of the corner of his eye, Raul also saw a fish rise.

Louis and Raul quickly unpacked the boat, working in silent but perfect unison. Louis located the plastic bag containing their cognac-soaked mesquite chips, while Raul fished around in the cooler and came up with the venison steaks they had been marinating for two days. Raul then put together the rest of the meal: a loaf of multigrain bread, chèvre and Zaragoza cheeses, olives stuffed with anchovies, and various condiments.

There was plenty of wood along the shore for building a fire up on the bank, near a long, sun-bleached log on which they could sit. Louis made a quick firewood run and then dug out a shallow pit, added some dry grasses and kindling, and positioned the folding wire grill over the pit as Raul prepped the steaks.

Hansy and Ubaldo sheepishly took sandwiches out of their vests—ham and cheese on white, with yellow mustard—and warm beers out of their wader tops.

"What's that about?" Raul rasped. "We've got plenty of food for everyone, and Oktoberfest beers. I'd be honored if you ate some of this deer—it's special." The deer, he explained, had been killed by a long-bow hunting fanatic who made his own buckskin clothing and often wore it to the Ironfeather Society study groups.

"We have a saying," he added. "The spirit that gives lives in the spirit of giving. This is the way of the people."

"I approve of that sentiment," Louis said. "This once was the land of the Shoshones, Oblado."

"Ubaldo," Hansy corrected.

"Ubaldo," Louis repeated amiably. "Of course, the Shoshones were the tribe of Sacajawea. Raul?"

Raul rose and advanced toward Louis. They demonstrated the Shoshone embrace, and Louis explained that it was somewhere near this very place that the Corps of Discovery finally encountered the Shoshones—where Sacajawea miraculously recognized not only her people, but her brother, Cameahwait, and her childhood friend Jumping Fish.

"Sheeesh—I think I lost my Swiss Army knife," Hansy muttered. "Do you guys have a bottle opener?"

They all sat on the log but for Hansy, who lounged in the coarse grass on the ground, one hand propping up his head. Raul studied the fire. It was time to introduce the mesquite chips and put on the steaks. Soon the venison was sizzling. Raul saw another rise—the slashing rise trout made when they were chasing caddis.

"What about Little Gooseneck Creek?" Hansy asked. "Are you putting some time into that?"

Louis said he thought the Little Goose was a myth.

"I wouldn't be so sure," Hansy said. "I'm coming back for two weeks. I may poke around a little. See something different."

Raul went to get beers from the cooler. Squatting, he studied the surface of the stream. He saw numerous dimples, much like tiny raindrops, where caddisflies were breaking through the surface from below. Occasionally he saw individual caddis emerge and commence to zoom around like berserk little powerboats in the surface film, trying to wriggle free from the nymphal shucks in which their wings were still folded.

It was starting to happen. It was starting to happen in a pretty big way.

Raul returned and passed out the beers. He looked out over the prairie and the succession of blue hills that rose in layers in the distance to become mountains. Far away, a few antelope grazed, little black stick figures. He drank in the smell of burning mesquite and cooking venison.

Raul suddenly felt a pang—the long-suppressed, collective spirit of the warrior that he knew lay buried within all men, including those gathered around him now. In recent years, he had learned to recognize and listen to the voice of his inner warrior. It was like the whisper of a best friend, sharing moments like this one. It was amazing how attuned he had become to all things male.

Ubaldo remarked on the great natural beauty of the river. He had never seen rocks quite like the variety that lay in profusion in the bed of the Beaverhead.

"Oblado," Louis said, "what you've noticed is not insignificant."

Raul and Hansy exchanged glances. They knew what was coming, and it wasn't conversation—at least not the pedestrian kind in which two people, perhaps ill informed but usually amiable, exchange haphazard thoughts and opinions punctuated by commentary like "Oh, really?" or "I never knew that."

Louis looked their Italian guest in the eye and began: "Unlike the Alps towering in the north of your sunny native land, the Rockies were formed in the Mesozoic and Early Cenozoic eras. To be more precise, during the Cordilleran orogeny."

Hansy pushed his glasses up on his nose and repeated, in disbelief, *"Orogeny?"*

Louis cast his eyes skyward and folded his hands on his stomach. His oval face was serene. "The word defines the folding and, as it were, *uplift* of the earth's crust to form mountain ranges. Orogenies are almost always accompanied by volcanic and seismic activity." He continued in layman's terms, explaining how the earth was like an enormous peach. The pit at its center was surrounded by a thick mantle of peridotite, dense black rock comparable to the flesh of the peach. Because of the intense heat in the mantle, the peridotite constantly changed shape. It even flowed.

"Afaszinating," Ubaldo muttered.

Louis explained how the outer sixty miles of the mantle was relatively cool, with a crust that he urbanely likened to that of a freshly baked Italian panna. He went into the theory of plate tectonics while Raul began pulling the steaks from the grill. Ubaldo and Hansy listened, rapt, as Louis told them how the uplift that created the Rockies involved a series of pulses that occurred over millions of years.

Louis poked around the steaks piled on the tin plate, identified the choicest cut, and dragged it onto his plate. He carved off an enormous hunk of Zaragoza cheese and tore off a hunk of bread, musing for all to hear: "All this occurred not thousands of years, or even hundreds of thousands, but *millions* of years ago. It's quite mind-boggling, is it not?"

The plate came back around to Raul. He took one of the three remaining steaks and quickly cut a sample bite. It was succulent, infused with the flavor of Louis's new cumin and guava marinade.

Louis dabbed a piece of bread in the steak juice and popped it into his mouth. He licked his fingers before he continued. "Bear in mind, however, that since those early times, the Rocky Mountains have been significantly eroded. This has exposed various ancient, crystalline cores and still other sedimentary rocks." He set down his plate. "If you want to see the ultimate assortment of those younger and older crystals and rocks, just walk right down to the river's edge."

He paused and took a long drink of beer, then said to Ubaldo, "So, you are quite perceptive, my European friend. Those are no ordinary rocks in the Beaverhead. Not at all. They are nothing short of a geological, um, glyph, worthy of display in any museum."

The party sat in a stunned silence. Finally, Ubaldo volunteered in an awestruck voice, "I did not realize this is so compli-cato. Thank you."

"I told you," Hansy said, to no one in particular.

They finished eating in silence.

"Louis," Raul said, setting his plate aside, "look at the water."

Louis, who sat hunched forward with his palms on his thighs, burped. He swiveled awkwardly on the log. He saw the rising fish, all over the river. He could tell from the riseforms—a combination of violent slashes and subtle bulges—that the fish were feasting on emerging caddis.

"Look at those fish!" Hansy was so excited that he fairly jumped up and down. "The river's boiling."

"It's sh-sh-sh-showtime," Raul declared.

The rods were all laid up against the far end of the log. Hansy and Ubaldo scrambled back into their waders and donned their vests. Louis rose slowly, groaning and stretching. He was feeling logy from the rich meal and beers. Raul had no desire to join them. Later, he thought, he might take a leisurely stroll downstream to see if he could spot a bank feeder or two. But for now he would be content to slip into his red Speedos, get out his beach chair and book, and do a little sunbathing.

He was just getting settled into his chair with a copy of *Killing Father: Non-Traditional Approaches to Male Self-Actualization* when he heard a whoop from the river. Hansy held his deeply bent rod high over his head. He seemed to be doing quite well, despite having left his polarized glasses in the grass near the smoldering fire.

"There he is," Louis called out, striking a fish. "He took the Sparkle Pupa—the one with the Antron head!"

"Way to go!" Raul shouted before returning to his book.

Hansy and Louis eventually gravitated to each other, as old friends are apt to do, and worked their way downstream. They caught fish and kept up a running dialogue on subjects ranging from the relative merits of chemically sharpened Japanese dry-fly hooks to the lubricated cork drag mechanism on Louis's $700 Franklin fly reel.

Left to himself, the tenderfoot Ubaldo soon made a mess of his leader and, unable to sort it out, retreated to the bank. Raul laid down his book and walked over to Ubaldo. "Do you need help?"

"No, I am quite happy, thank you."

"Are you enjoying fly-fishing? It's quite a wonderful sport."

"I am learning. Is more dee-fee-coolt than I thought." Ubaldo added, affably, "Your friend—Louis. He look like the American president Neex-on when he szpeak."

That thought had never occurred to Raul, but it was true—something about the way Louis shook his head and jowls for emphasis was decidedly Nixonian. "It's ironic," he said. "Louis hated Nixon. But you know, that crook had a very enlightened policy toward Native Americans."

Ubaldo pondered this, then blurted out: "I have a question. I am a big fan of baze-a-ball, a fanatic of baze-a-ball—since I was little boy in Ee-taly. I notice your family name is Mendoza. You are not *the* Raul Mendoza, the relief pitcher who was heet in the face in Szacramento?"

"Wa-wa-wa-why, yes . . . I am." Raul's face lit up. "How wonderful of you to know."

"Of course, I know. You still have the triple-A rookie record for szaves, no? Twenty-two."

"That's incredible," Raul said.

Pressed by Ubaldo, Raul told his story—a tragic saga known only to a few connoisseurs of the game. Raul, an extremely promising pitcher, was on the cusp of going to the majors when he was struck by a line drive that shattered his cheekbone and ultimately ended his career on a fine, sultry night in Sacramento.

Raul once again shivered at the memory—the mixture of terror and relief he felt when he came to, lying on an operating table, with a ring of masked faces peering down at him. It was that experience that led him to dedicate his life to helping others in pain.

Ubaldo asked Raul, "And the baze-a-ball? You never play no more?"

Raul explained that after having his cheek shattered, he could still throw fine in the bullpen or on the sideline. But when he stepped on the mound to face a batter, he came unglued. He was lucky to get one pitch in ten over the plate—at any speed. He'd lost it. Just like that.

"Yes, that is story I read. You went to the psychologist, every-thing . . .

"I was going through the motions," Raul reflected. "I see that now. I knew deep down I wasn't going to play anymore, but I was fearful of what that implied. I rebelled against myself."

Given that Raul was a twenty-two-year-old high school dropout, quitting baseball wasn't easy. But over the months while he pursued his comeback, he worked on his GED. He also discovered his calling. He quit the game cold in order to enroll in a training program for dental hygienists in his hometown of San Francisco.

As a profession, dental hygiene wasn't hugely popular with career-minded men or struggling ex-ballplayers. At first this made the handsome former pitcher something of a curiosity, and those who knew his story whispered about him. But soon, as gay men—including many dentists—began flooding into the city by the bay, Raul suddenly became a hot commodity.

Raul's popularity as a hygienist had less to do with his sex appeal than his soothing bedside manner. He was a wonderful caregiver. Many a groggy waiter or modern dancer emerged from the fog of anesthesia comforted by Raul's dark soulful eyes, gleaming smile, and the obvious, heartfelt concern in his voice as he said, "Welcome back to the world. Would you like a nice mug of peppermint tea?"

Finishing his tale, Raul said, "May I tell you something, Ubaldo? I only played baseball because I was afraid to disappoint my father. He pushed me into baseball. And he wasn't even a good father. In fact, he was an abusive drunk." He added, "I'm sorry. It's an intimate detail, I know."

Raul explained how he eventually earned a college degree and used his savings to start a small company that specialized in providing male hygienists for dentists all over the West Coast, called Dent-A-Men. In fact, it was through Dr. Richard Epstein, one of his first clients, that Raul came to fly fishing. As an introspective, shy boy, Raul had spent many days fishing with eels and such for bottom feeders off the jetties and docks in San Francisco Bay. But Dr. Epstein opened up an entirely new, exciting world to the angler within—a world filled with speckled trout, jewel-like reels, delicate flies, and elegant hats.

While Ubaldo and Raul talked, the shadows lengthened. It was nearly five and the hatch was petering out by the time Louis and Hansy finally came staggering up the bank. By then Raul felt a kinship with Ubaldo. He gently said, "Thank you. This was a very special moment for me, Ubaldo. I feel that I made a new friend today. Thank you very much."

"This was a true pleasure for me," Ubaldo replied. "And alszo an honn-orr."

On an impulse, Raul pulled him close and engaged him in a Shoshone embrace.

———————

"Nice fellow, that Oblado," Louis said, waving one last time as they drifted out of view of their friends around a gentle bend. "His casting was quite mediocre, and he didn't seem very eager to improve. I was disappointed to see him leave the water so soon. He probably doesn't have the right stuff."

"Well, you and Hansy didn't help. I think he got discouraged."

"You know how it is at showtime," Louis said. "Every man's own fishing comes first."

Raul, happy to be floating again, let the subject drop. The high bank on one side was dramatically eroded, the red soil drilled with cliff swallow nesting holes. They drifted by a handful of brown cattle that gazed longingly at the river from behind a gray wooden fence. The air was cooling and smelled sweet. The rods were standing by, propped up in the bow.

"This is one of those mellow moments when I wish I could still smoke a cigar," Raul said.

"Not me." Louis drained a beer and burped. "Do you know, I've never smoked a cigar—not once in my entire life."

"Really?" It was novel to learn something new about Louis. "Not even at a bachelor party?"

"I always associated cigars with people of a certain ilk. People who lack, um, *sensitivity*. How many artists have you known, or know of, who smoke cigars?"

"You make a good point. I never thought of it that way."

"Now if you asked me what I would most want after a day such as this—a special float, a venison feast, big heads up on caddis for two solid hours . . . I think you already *know* what I'm about to say."

"Okay, go ahead," Raul said.

Louis leaned forward, shaking his jowls: *"Poontang."*

"Are you aware, Louis, that when you do that, you resemble Richard M. Nixon?"

The boat slipped along a slow, wide stretch. As the sunlight waned, copper and gold highlights danced on the surface. The banks on either side were gently sloped, with arborvitae and grasses growing right down to the water's edge. The two men passed a collection of bright white bee boxes stacked along the edge of a meadow.

Louis was at the oars, but the boat required almost no rowing. Raul slowly dozed off, leaving Louis to his own thoughts. Those thoughts inexplicably turned to work. As always, before leaving for Montana, Louis had his website designer create a cute little "Gone Fishin'" graphic to post on the home page at Guardian_of_Grammar.com. A visitor could still get access to the archives, however, including Louis's most significant work, his weekly essays on usage. In those, he gamely took on "Myths, Misconstructions, and Malapropisms."

The last essay he had posted, just before leaving, bore the saucy headline "Personal Beefs." In it, he went after the chronic abusers of the word *personal*—as if a person could have anything but *personal* friends, *personal* opinions, and *personal* prejudices. What were you going to have, *impersonal* convictions? The habits of *others?*

Louis looked downstream, where the river appeared to gradually narrow. His mind wandered to a trend growing like a cancer even in literate society: the use of *reticent* as a synonym for *reluctant.* Then he contemplated the mangled grammar in the chorus of an old pop song, *I Think I Love You,* by—if he remembered correctly—David Cassidy.

> I think I love you,
> So what am I so afraid of?
> Afraid that I'm not sure of
> A Love there is no cure for . . .

Ugh, Louis thought—those dangling prepositions. He wondered what could be done about that, working out lyrics as he went. Suddenly, a solution dawned him. Why, it was as plain as the nose on his face . . .

> Afraid that I'm not sure of
> A love *for which* there is no cure . . .

It worked, by golly! Louis sang the chorus to himself, over and over. In fact, his version, in addition to being grammatically correct, boasted an added element: The extra words forced the singer to incorporate an almost scat-like change of inflection that made the rather mundane lyrics more interesting.

Louis looked up, but it was too late. Panic flooded through him. Preoccupied, he hadn't noticed how quickly the river had become swifter and narrower. He had failed to move out of the main flow in time, and the craft was now firmly in the grip of the maelstrom, plunging toward a chute at the bottom of which the river made a sharp right turn and crashed against a massive tangle of logs and branches. They had arrived at Squawfish Hole.

Louis leaped into action, waking Raul as he hammered the oars into the water. It was useless. The boat flew into the chute, twirling as if it were a leaf. Then they were sideways. Raul made a mad grab for the rods in the bow as the boat crashed heavily into the logjam.

Raul raised his arms just in time to ward off the blow of a heavy limb, but he was knocked out of the boat. With a horrible noise, the boat hung up in the nasty timber. Raul grabbed a gunwale and tried to haul himself back in. The boat was rocking and semisubmerged, with water pouring in over the sides and through a gaping hole the size of a basketball on the left side near the bow. Raul was unable to hang on in the powerful current. He let go and bobbed downstream, flailing away for shore.

Louis struggled to push the craft free from the snag. He looked down to see one of the oars drifting away, and he knew he had no option. He rolled heavily over the gunwale, into the water, and bobbed downstream after the oar.

Raul sloshed to shore, clutching his wet fedora. He ran toward Louis, who was having trouble reaching land. He waded out, grabbed his friend by the scruff of the neck, and pulled him onto the beach. They lurched up the bank and collapsed in a heap, water draining from their waders.

"A-a-a-a-anything broken?"

"No," Louis gasped. "Look . . ." Upstream, the river was peeling the swamped boat out of the deadfall with a grotesque scraping noise. Suddenly Louis's eyes rolled back. His elbows were pressed to his sides, and his wrists began to jiggle madly. It was another spell.

Raul grabbed him by the shoulders and tried to comfort him: "It's going to be all right. We're fine now. Calm down . . ." Gradually, Louis's eyelids ceased twitching; the spell was over. "Phew," Raul said. "That was close."

"Thank God for neoprene," Louis muttered. "We both would have drowned in the old canvas waders."

While Raul attended to his friend, the current pushed the boat all the way to shore. It now lay half submerged in calmer water.

"We were totally out of control," Raul said. "One minute I was reaching for the rods . . ." Their eyes met. They said simultaneously, "The rods!" Leaping up, they raced to the boat.

The backup rod lay inside, submerged but miraculously intact, along with most of their other equipment. Louis's rod had gotten hung up high in some branches in the logjam, also unharmed and close enough to reach. There was no sign of the third rod, Raul's favorite stick. Raul was beside himself.

Louis knew just how his partner felt. A feather thrower without his preferred 5-weight was like a pop music collector without a Dylan album. On top of that, this particular stick was a real classic—an Eagletech XTC model designed by the *enfant terrible* of rodmakers, Ted Blinken.

"We can replace it," Louis said. "I'll just call Ted."

"We can't re-re-re-re-replace it," Raul hissed. "That rod was steeped in dharma. How can you replace that?"

Louis had never seen Raul snap like this—he had to talk him down off the emotional ledge. He grabbed his friend by the shoulders. "*Raul.* I understand how you feel. Any angler would. But try to get a grip. The rod is replaceable, pure and simple. Raul Mendoza is not."

"It's four years old," Raul protested. "They don't even make that exact XTC anymore."

"Raul, I know what that specific rod means to you. But the only alteration they've made to that rod since you bought yours is the windings on the guides. They went from the maroon wraps with black tips to the green with chocolate tips. They wanted a more subtle but still hot look."

"That's not true," Raul said petulantly. "They went from the stainless to the smoke-colored snake guides."

"I stand corrected. But those were aesthetic improvements. They have no effect on the, um, fishability of the rod."

"I thought you hated that word—*fishability.*"

"Well, I'm not thinking too clearly at the moment."

Raul sighed. Deep down, he coveted the smoke-colored guides and had been toying with the idea of splurging on another $900 XTC for that very reason.

"Look, pardner, Ted told me at the Denver Expo last year that if I ever visited the shop, he'd give me a substantial discount on any rod I wanted. First chance we get, I'll call Ted and tell him I want to swing by Eagletech and take him up on the offer."

"Ra-ra-ra-ra-really?" Raul seemed heartened. The idea that he might end up with a brand new XTC 5-weight with smoke guides, at a discount price no less, certainly was appealing.

They turned to their larger, more immediate problem. It was getting toward six-thirty, and they had to get Bowen's boat down to the take-out ramp. They still had a way to go—at least three river miles, Raul reckoned—in a boat that would barely float. And if it got dark, they could easily miss the ramp and float all the way down to the Jefferson.

They stripped off their waders and laid them out, inside out, to dry. They got their backup clothing out of the waterproof duffel and picked up bits and pieces of gear that had washed up on shore. Then they bailed out the boat. Luckily, the gaping hole near the bow was above the waterline. But when they replaced all the gear and climbed aboard, the boat sank almost to the point of taking water again.

"As I weigh slightly more than you, perhaps I should sit on the gunwale opposite the hole," Louis suggested.

"That means I row," Raul said. He added, miserably, "How did we mess up so badly? What are we going to do about Bowen's boat?"

Unfazed, Louis answered, "Don't despair. Remember, the inestimable Charbonneau tipped and nearly lost the white pirogue—and all its contents—on the upper Missourah. Meriwether Lewis didn't even discipline him. He merely noted in his diary that the trapper was 'the most timid waterman in the world.'" Louis paused to let this encouraging comparison sink in before adding, "Granted, Squawfish Hole got the better of us today. But consider it a learning experience. It makes no sense to dwell on the what-ifs or berate each other."

"I'm still worried about Bowen's boat," Raul said. "It looks like some Charbonneau fired a cannon through its side."

"Yes, it may be a challenge to restore the boat to its original condition, but we'll address that later. Shall we?"

Soon they were afloat again. The boat listed steeply to the right, where Louis sprawled uncomfortably with his back against the gunwale.

He quickly fell asleep. Raul struggled with the oars to keep the craft tracking properly. It was all he could do to get the boat through the occasional sweeping bend or reach of fast, rolling water.

It was a beautiful evening, though, with atomic clusters of insects dancing in the shafts of fading light. The boat passed three mule deer, including a handsome four-by-four buck, that had come down to the river to drink. Raul woke Louis, who then kept close watch on the left bank, looking for any opening in the brush that might mark the takeout ramp.

Darkness was falling fast and the air was cold. Even though their damp waders had the insulating properties of a wet suit, they both shivered. Finally Raul saw an open spot along the bank—and headlights shining through it onto the water. "He's going to kill us," Raul muttered, pulling hard with his left oar to turn the bow toward shore. The boat hit nosefirst with a heavy thump.

The person who appeared in the headlights was not Bowen. It was girl of about twenty, dressed in Teva sandals, olive pants with cargo pockets, and an oversize jean jacket. She had a fine gold ring in her nose and dark, spiky hair with orange tips. She hugged her body with both arms for warmth.

"Hi, y'all," she said. "I'm Amber."

"Where's Bowen?" Raul asked her.

"He's like really, really sorry, dudes. He had to split—on business. But he sent me down to give y'all a ride back."

"Amber?" Raul asked. The name rang a bell. "From the Elkhorn Café in Dillon?"

"Yeah. I kind of remember you."

Raul looked at Louis. "What now?"

"Wow," Amber said. "Like what happened to the boat?"

"We-we-we-we put a hole in it. We'll fix it, though. Gosh, I wish Bowen were here. Where's his rig?"

"It's just me, in my Jetta."

The Jetta didn't have a trailer hitch. Louis would have to stay with the boat while Raul went back for the War Pony. They were only about fifteen miles from camp, but it would still be an hour round-trip. Amber went to the Jetta and got Louis an old wool dog blanket. Louis wrapped himself in it and stood watching as the Jetta's taillights went winding out of sight, leaving him alone.

Suddenly it was awfully quiet—and pitch black. But the sky was carpeted with stars, and Louis looked up at them until his neck hurt. He went back to the boat, strategically placed the seat cushions, and lay down. Gazing at the stars, he let his thoughts drift. That Amber, he thought, she was a quite a number. Did she, perchance, also have a pierced nipple or perhaps a tattoo—a leaping dolphin or pentacle—in an intimate place?

On the ridges nearby, the coyotes began singing. Their plaintive yipping and howling underscored a sudden feeling of loneliness that fell upon Louis. It was not an unfamiliar feeling for Louis, who grew up an only child in Brooklyn. His father, Arthur Traub, had a business manufacturing mannequins for the Seventh Avenue garmentos. His mother, Fern, had higher aspirations for her son, hoping he would grow up to be a writer, perhaps, or a painter. He was different from the other kids, that was for sure. He was a poor physical specimen and a bright if lazy, undisciplined student who did not make practical use of a formidable gift, a nearly photographic memory.

Louis's only serious adolescent interest was collecting and studying bugs and reptiles. He could recite the Latin names of most of them, including the lowly cockroaches that sometimes appeared on the Traubs' gas range. At age eleven, though, Louis went off to camp in the Catskills. There, on the camp's ten-acre lake, he experienced his first rural landscape and discovered fishing. It immediately gave his life the purpose it had previously lacked.

By the time Louis was fifteen, he had discovered, read, and reread—six times over—*The Journals of Lewis and Clark*. He also knew, from the fishing magazines on which he spent every extra dime, that the best trout fishing in the world was in that enchanted state whose very name rang musically in his impressionable mind and evoked exciting images right out of the journals: Montana.

It was only natural that a fantasist such as Louis would be attracted to the dreamy life of a writer. And this proved to be a fortuitous move, for it ensured his upward-striving parents' unconditional support. Louis did not need emotional support, however; by the time he was fifteen, his hide was as thick as that of an elephant from incessant teasing about his woeful performance on the athletic field and his collection of South American tree frogs.

What Louis did need, though, was Art and Fern's material support. He secured that quite easily. Fern certainly was not going to be short-sighted and demand that her only child go to work as a lowly journalist, copywriter, or anything else that might interfere with his chance of writing the Great American Novel—something, she shrewdly noted, that Philip Roth, Bernard Malamud, and even the great Saul Bellow and Norman Mailer had not yet achieved.

Louis was in no danger of following in the conventional footsteps of those authors. Instead of attending Yale or the University of Chicago, he opted for Hofstra on nearby Long Island. He became a hippie of sorts and spent weekend nights hanging around Greenwich Village, hoping to bump into his idol, the angry troubadour Dylan. He dabbled in all kinds of writing and, while under the influence of LSD, wrote a song that repeated the word *sunshot* thirty-four times.

When it became clear to Fern and Art that Louis was not destined to be a conventional wage earner, his parents took some of their savings and got him a loft in Manhattan's Soho. Louis persuaded them that he also needed a car—not just some ordinary American model, but a sporty, well-engineered, foreign coupe. So for graduation, they bought him a blue BMW.

A week after graduation, Louis and his friend Greg Hubert loaded up the new car with Louis's dog, a shepherd mix called Pomp; eight-track tapes by, among others, Bob Dylan and Country Joe & the Fish; camping gear; nearly a pound of pot; and a mountain of fishing gear. They lit out for Montana and didn't return until after Labor Day.

When Fern inquired why Louis and Greg had spent the entire summer fishing in Montana, he explained that a writer did his real work in the winter, when he could gaze out the window with his hands wrapped around a cup of hot tea and contemplate the somber skies and dead leaves; the summer was for collecting grist for the writer's mill.

Thirty-plus years later, as Louis lay in the bottom of Bowen's drift boat in a remote dirt parking lot reviewing his history in Montana, he wondered, "What if?"

What if he had, say, married the skinny, violin-playing, flat-chested, and knobby-kneed heiress Tara Rabinowitz?

What if he had gone to work, like some eager-beaver editor or newspaper reporter?

What if he had never met Raul?

None of it seemed to matter much, because in the end it all came down to the fishing. It was all about the fishing. It always had been, since he caught his first sunfish.

Louis's teeth began chattering. He reasoned that it was shock of some sort. He probably was suffering from a mild case of hypothermia.

3

Caw-caw-caw. Caw-caw-caw.
Caw-caw-caw!

The magpie perched in the cottonwood would not relent. Louis sat up inside the blue tent, wakened from a deep slumber by the smell of bacon. He was ravenous. By the time they'd gotten back to camp with the boat the previous night, Louis barely had the strength to strip off his waders and damp fleece tights before tumbling into a fierce sleep.

He poked his head out through the flap. The trees were dappled with morning light, and the morning air was sharp with fragrances that would soon be displaced by pure, dry heat.

Raul was preparing a breakfast of one-eyed Connollys, using an inverted whiskey glass to press out the holes in four individual slices of seven-grain bread. The first piece was already browning in bacon grease in the skillet, and he was about to crack the egg into the hole.

"Mornin' pardner," Louis growled. Still on all fours, he sniffed the air. "Is that the braunschweiger bacon we got from the Dusseldorfer butcher?"

"It is indeed," Raul replied. "It seemed a good morning for Connollys."

Each year, the men made a special stop at the butcher's to stock up on bacon, knockwurst, kassler ripchen, and head cheese. The man was an emotional misfit who had fled Dusseldorf to set up shop in Spokane.

The bacon, already cooked and lying neatly in strips on sheaves of paper towels, was the uniform color of brick. Louis had never known anyone to cook bacon as evenly and perfectly as did Raul. He always brought it right to the point where it almost turned crumbly.

Though Louis appreciated the unstable German butcher's perfectionism—his stuffed pork chops undeniably were a work of art—he was skeptical of the man's latest, lavish claim. This new bacon, the butcher had asserted, was made by some special, secret process that sealed the taste of maple syrup right into the meat. Louis asked for Raul's verdict on the matter.

Raul lovingly savored a piece of the bacon. He pronounced it "sweet—definitely permeated with essence of maple, but with a kind of salty joie de vivre."

That was all Louis needed to hear. He backed into the tent and began rooting around for clothing. The prospects for the day were improving by the moment. He also looked forward to the leisurely drive that would take them to West Yellowstone via the Centennial Valley, passing the Ruby River, Blacktail Creek, and myriad gems tucked away on sprawling, private ranchland.

"West," as Louis liked to call it, was the home of Eagletech Tackle and its brand new factory outlet store. He looked forward to visiting it, as well as working a deal with Ted Blinken to get Raul a new 5-weight XTC. Then they could pick from among three or four custom drift-boat builders who were equally qualified to repair Bowen's craft.

Louis emerged, dressed in rumpled blue jeans and a lightweight khaki shirt with a plethora of pockets. He pulled on his hiking boots and followed his usual routine at the water jug, patiently cleaning two sets of glasses and patting down his face with cold water. Although they'd been fishing only a few days, Louis's face was already turning tan everywhere outside the area shielded by his sunglasses. He was getting the ardent fly fisher's trademark raccoon eyes.

"Better be quick," Raul said. "The Connollys are almost all ready."

"So this girl, Amber—are we to believe that Bowen is engaged in some sort of, um, serious relationship with her? She's barely of college age."

Raul shrugged. "Insomuch as Bowen is capable of engaging in any serious relationship, I suppose. She told me she teaches snowboarding at Elk Mountain."

"We can address that with Bowen at a later date."

Louis loathed ski areas. All those condominiums and ski lifts desecrated a mountain. Worse yet, drawing water from local streams for snowmaking purposes usually left them low and vulnerable to deadly freezes that killed insects and fish.

Louis began to dry his sunglasses with a blue bandanna. "What manner of 'business' do you suppose Bowen would put ahead of us—ahead of a prearranged float trip during PMD time?"

"It's a good point," Raul said. He reminded Louis that many years earlier, the three of them had floated the Big Hole on the very day that Bowen's first wife, Janey—the one he now referred to only in an impersonal way, as Wife Number One—gave birth to their first child.

"Ah, yes. We had that great stonefly hatch that day, if my memory serves?"

"That's right." The trip was to have been a half-day float, because of Janey's pending delivery. But the fishing had been so hot that they didn't get off the river until after eleven that night. When they finally got back to the launch ramp, Bowen's brother-in-law was waiting, pacing, with the news—Janey had delivered a boy!

It all came back to Louis. "Those were the days, I reckon. It was great to share that special moment with Bowen. It's the kind of thing you can't possibly forget."

Raul dryly added, "Wife Number One certainly never forgot it."

They discussed Bowen's complicated life. He had three ex-wives and five children of school age, and he had never, as far as any of his friends could tell, earned a nickel or saved one he could spend. Bowen's profligate ways baffled Raul, who shared Louis's frugality. In fact, the pleasure he felt at the prospect of buying a coveted Eagletech rod at a deep discount was offset by concerns about the costs of the side trip and fixing the boat. This was exactly the kind of thing that happened when you started flying by the seat of the pants.

"Say what you will about Bowen's free spirit," Raul said, "I'm amazed he hasn't turned up to check out the damage. It's almost like he couldn't care less."

"I hear you." Louis knew what Raul was thinking. If only Bowen came around, there was a very good chance that he would survey the damage and cavalierly wave it off, forbidding his friends to pay a dime for repairs.

"If he doesn't show up before we break camp," Raul suggested, "we could backtrack to Dillon and stop by the Elkhorn. I think Amber said she was working today. Maybe he's around too."

"That would work for me," Louis said. "Perhaps the Elkhorn will feature a freshly baked huckleberry pie."

Satisfied, Louis fitted the temple stems of his glasses back into the soft, pink grooves on either side of his head. He was now ready for breakfast. The two men sat down, so hungry that for some time they ate in silence.

"I've been thinking," Louis said, licking his fingers as he started on his third one-eyed Connolly. "You know that brass pawl gear in the braking mechanism in the Franklin reel? What if they replaced it with one made from a lighter metal, perhaps titanium? That might solve the inertial start-up problem that hinders the performance of that reel's drag."

Raul thought this an excellent idea, and for the next fifteen minutes, they sat in their folding canvas camp chairs, carrying on a lively discussion about the innovative braking mechanisms found on better reels. Raul declared it ironic that fly reels, while maintaining a simple profile, had become complicated instruments. He fondly recalled a simpler time when reels didn't have all those bells and whistles. He suggested that fly fishing had been more of a macho sport in the past.

"*Raul.* One of the enduring glories of our sport is the evolution of the equipment. I would submit that fine engineering actually enhances our appreciation of nature. After all, isn't the brown trout—in its own way—also a marvel of engineering?"

Raul conceded that Louis had a point, although for his own part he had some trouble comparing an inanimate object with a glorious trout. And while he was loath to ignore issues of quality, there also was something to be said for simpler ways of engaging nature. It was something invaluable that he had learned on a recent Naked in the Desert retreat that the Ironfeather Society sponsored.

Louis, who was somewhat uncomfortable with the idea of male nudity, was hard put to reply. He thought the Ironfeather Society of Warriors was a cult, and out of earshot of Raul, he often joked that his friend had "drunk the Kool-Aid."

Raul was slightly hurt by the fact that just mentioning the Ironfeather Society to Louis was always a conversation stopper. It was the same way that Christians felt when they publicly expressed their belief. He believed that Louis could only benefit from coming face-to-face with the spiritual frontiers of his maleness.

Thankfully, Darby Wingo had presciently laid out guidelines for the way warrior males ought to deal with indifference, hostility, or even outright ridicule toward Ironfeather principles. Raul recited the 4th Virilian Protocol to himself: "The warrior seated closest to the fire listens not with his ears, but his heart. The male sitting farthest away listens not at all, but only the fire itself can draw him near."

Consoled, Raul cheerfully steered the subject back to drag components. This refired his friend's enthusiasm, and the two amicably debated further nuances of drag for quite some time, until their coffee went cold and they realized it was getting toward ten-thirty—the time they had targeted for breaking camp.

"If we don't find Bowen, what are we going to do around West while they fix the boat?" Raul stretched as he rose. He stroked the jet black feather in his fedora, which was almost completely dry.

"Interesting question." Louis knew that as anglers, they had outgrown the Madison River, which the feather-throwing elite sneeringly called "the world's longest riffle." Sure, it was stuffed with legions of fat, gullible rainbow trout that happily rose to take almost any old caddisfly you threw out there. But Louis and Raul both preferred more challenging fishing—the "technical" angling that almost always happened in slower water.

They continued the conversation as Raul cleared the breakfast dishes and Louis went to take his ritual morning leak behind the big cottonwood. "We could make inquiries about the Henry's Fork," Raul said loudly enough for Louis to hear. "With the hatches so screwed up this year, the Fork may not be too crowded."

"There's also Goat Crick," Louis countered, poking his head out around the tree. Goat Creek was a small stream with surprisingly large brown trout that flowed through rough canyon country in the shadow of the Absarokas near Jardine, not far from the north entrance to Yellowstone National Park. They hadn't fished the Goat for years.

"That's an excellent suggestion, Louis. I remember it had a lot of undercuts and bank feeders. Thank you for thinking of that."

It was Louis's turn to do the dishes. Meanwhile, Raul began packing sundry kitchen items into their proper cardboard and plastic containers. The men had proven methods for consolidating boxes and nesting articles in order to save space. Each item was like the piece in a giant puzzle that always fit somewhere, often inside something else.

Raul rolled a dishrag tightly around a large carving knife, and the whole works slid handily into the hollow core of a roll of paper towels. The carving board fit perfectly under the lid of the camp stove, which could then to be slipped under the front passenger seat—but only from behind the seat, or else it wouldn't sit quite right.

Yet for every ounce or square inch spared by shaving down the handle of a wooden spoon, drilling holes in the blade of the spatula, or storing liquids in collapsible backpacker's water bottles, their ever-growing kit continually created new challenges. It was one thing to add new fishing gear, such as the unwieldy but highly practical float tubes. It was quite another to travel, as they did, with "ergonomically advanced" pillows made from dense foam that was approved by NASA for sleeping aboard the space shuttle. Their spice collection was comprehensive—it took up an entire container the size of a breadbox and included fresh garam masala, coriander, and two different kinds of Hungarian paprika.

Aware of the growing space crunch, Raul and Louis had agreed to go fifty-fifty on a roof-mounted storage container. The one Raul selected after careful research was a tan, square box with a hinged lid that allowed easy access. But Louis was so put off by the resemblance of the box to a McDonald's Big Mac container that he vetoed the purchase. They eventually found a longer and thinner box in graphite gray, with a streamlined nose and only slightly less storage capacity.

They each had so many fishing rods that Raul had designed a special overhead rack made from titanium to accommodate all the aluminum tubes inside the SUV. That was in addition to the long, tubular rod carriers—or, as they preferred to call them, "scabbards"—attached like rocket launchers to the roof rack on either side of the vehicle. Each scabbard was a length of PVC pipe with an inner sleeve of soft foam pipe insulation, enabling Louis and Raul to travel with fully assembled 9-foot fly rods at the ready. If, perchance, the travelers were wending their way along a river with a full-blown hatch in progress, they could leap from the vehicle and have the rods drawn from the scabbards in seconds.

Raul, who was more conscious of personal hygiene than Louis, had discovered the Sunshower—an ingenious device made from a large vinyl bladder that, when filled with water and hung from a branch in direct sunlight, enabled a man to have a good, hot shower almost anywhere.

Yet for all their planning, they still encountered logistical problems, including Louis's stubborn resistance to transferring premium alcoholic beverages out of their original containers. Louis's latest discovery was Dalaigophraig Dew, a fifteen-year-old single-malt scotch. The handsome bottle had a leaping Atlantic salmon etched into it, but it was so heavy and oddly shaped that they had to get a whole new "whiskey box" to make room for what Louis already had dubbed "the delightful Double D."

Finally, though, all the duffels and bags and containers and boxes were loaded, the trailer was hooked up, and the float tubes and Sunshowers were lashed to the roof rack. The SUV now sat a few inches lower, and even Louis would have been hard-pressed to deny that it looked less like the war pony of a bloodthirsty Comanche than the overloaded wagon of a snake oil salesman. The SUV strained under the load as Raul pulled away.

"Wait," Louis cried. He popped out and went to the rear of the SUV, making a last-minute adjustment that would prevent the sun from beating directly on the whiskey box. As he shut the tailgate, he patted it and declared, "Move 'em out!"

As the men sped toward Dillon on I-15 north, they reviewed their kit to determine what they needed in the way of fresh supplies. They were looking forward to the Elkhorn's scrumptious pie, Bowen or no Bowen. According to Amber, the Elkhorn now also served mochaccinos.

"We could look up Al Troth while we're in town," Louis suggested. "That might be an edifying visit." Troth was the tackle-shop owner and fly tier credited with inventing the most popular of all imitations of the ubiquitous *Brachycentris* caddisfly, Troth's Elk Hair Caddis. He towered over the fly-tying landscape.

"It's late," Raul said, a mite testily. "It's either pie or bullshitting."

"In that case, let's make it pie, pardner."

Louis's amiable retort left Raul feeling guilty. He realized what was really bothering him: the overloaded state of the SUV, for which he somewhat unfairly blamed Louis and his stupid whiskey box. In Iron-feather terminology, Raul knew he was "refusing the spear"—sublimating the *real* source of his discontent from fear of having a confrontation.

A giant bug smacked the windshield like a rock, leaving a greenish yellow mark just below the rearview mirror. Raul flashed on a truth: Despite all the years he had fished with Louis, he was *still* intimidated by his partner's imperious ways. And that was his own fault.

"I'm sorry," Raul muttered.

The apology didn't really register, as Louis was busy thinking of a way to improve Troth's Elk Hair Caddis. He thought it might benefit from the addition of a trailing shuck of Sparkle Yarn and a pair of realistic antennae, which could be created easily enough by folding forward two strands of the elk-hair wing. Louis fantasized that such a fly might come to be known as Traub's Horned Caddis or some equally catchy name, an honor that would immediately catapult him into the company of other angling immortals who invented flies that bore their names, such as the Griffith's Gnat or Royal Wulff.

But Louis knew nobody could ever create an elk-hair caddis that would not automatically be classified as a variation on Troth's ubiquitous pattern. He said, "Troth may be an exceptional angler, but let's be frank. Artistically speaking, isn't there something disappointingly, um, coarse about his Elk Hair Caddis? Isn't the fly just a wee bit . . . simplistic?"

"His Elk Hair Caddis was a stroke of genius," Raul said flatly. He added, "It's like Kleenex or Velcro. Anything remotely like Velcro, ever, is always going to be called Velcro. That's as it should be."

This was an uncharacteristically definitive statement by Raul and a somewhat bitter pill for Louis to swallow. He was preparing a response when a vehicle on the opposite side of I-15 caught his eye. "Hey, that's Feigenbaum—Jeff Feigenbaum!"

Raul looked in the rearview mirror. Sure enough, the rapidly vanishing rig was trailing an inflatable Avon boat with a subtle camouflage pattern—just like Feigenbaum had painstakingly applied to his craft. Feigenbaum, like Bowen, was an old hand from back in the day on the Fork. He was a big-time New York pistachio importer who spent all of July and August toting his camo Avon around the northern Rockies.

"I'll bet he's on his way to the Missourah," Louis said. "He probably stopped for lunch at the Elkhorn. It appears we just missed him."

They were soon in Dillon, where only a few vehicles were parked on the small, nearly deserted main street. An ancient, raw-boned yellow Lab agonizingly pushed itself up on its haunches, then onto all fours. The dog walked toward them, staying in the shade cast by the two- and three-story brick and wood buildings.

"Powder," Louis said, rubbing the dog's giant head.

Powder's eyes were crusted; Louis wiped them clean with his fingers and then ran them over his jeans. "It's good to see you, pardner. I reckon you're looking for a little piece of something or other."

Louis opened the tailgate and fished a slice of the Dusseldorf butcher's bacon out of the cooler. He dangled it before Powder, who snapped it up and sucked it down. Louis felt a pang of nostalgia for his old dog, Pomp. He had made three western trips with Louis before he got electrocuted while chewing up a metal junction box in the loft.

Powder, still standing, watched the men cross the road. Louis fell into his Montana gait, puffing up his chest, swinging his shoulders from side to side. Back when Louis and his ex-wife, Naomi, had taken their one and only trip to Montana together, he used to hooked his thumbs in his belt loops while he walked. The habit had once led Naomi to coo, after a passionate interlude in the sleeping bag, "The way you walk . . . you're just like John Wayne—only smaller."

Louis was almost hit by the door as it flew open from the inside.

Before him stood a woman with eyes like chestnuts and pouty lips. She was wearing a flimsy, low-cut sundress. Her arms and legs were lean and tanned, and her short, brown hair was gathered in an unusual top-knot that resembled the stem of a pineapple.

"Excuse us, ma'am," Louis intoned. He touched the brim of his legionnaire's cap, the flaps of which were tucked up underneath for traveling, and bowed deeply.

"No, excuse me." The woman had a husky voice and she drawled her words. "I shouldn't be in such a big hurry all the time."

Louis stared at the freckles liberally sprinkled across the woman's chest, just below her neck. She had no need of a bra; her breasts were small but firm and perky.

"Did you get the pie?" Raul asked, regarding the Styrofoam container in the woman's hands. "They're famous for the pie here."

"Actually, it's a cheeseburger platter," the woman replied.

"Oh."

"Well, excuse me, then. Have a nice day."

Louis watched her walk to a generic, beat-up-looking Japanese sedan parked down the street. Finally, Raul said, "Come on. We don't have all day."

Raul removed his fedora upon entering and said, "Greetings."

"Howdy, ma'am," Louis said.

"How's the fishin', boys?" The waitress was a thin, frazzled woman in her late fifties, with frizzy hair.

66

"Great. Both the fishing and the catching," Louis replied. He walked up to the counter and sat on a red stool, then removed his hat and glasses and ran his fingers over the thinning hair at his temples.

The only other customers were two old geezers in cowboy hats who sat in a corner booth over cups of coffee in plain, white mugs. One of them was smoking a cigarette, whose stench offended Louis. The smoking man had to be eighty, yet he had ruddy skin and clear, ice blue eyes.

Louis eyed the men warily. They looked like ranchers—the old breed, the type he and other environmentalists had been battling for ages. They were arrogant men who thought nothing of dewatering a trout stream for irrigation—as if the water, like the public land on which their cattle grew fat at taxpayer expense, belonged to them.

"So where you boys from?" asked the waitress.

"Seattle," Raul answered. "My friend is from New York. You must be new. We stop here a few times a year for pie à la mode and coffee."

"Good," the waitress replied, setting down two glasses of water. "We can use some more Democrats out this way. I been here about seven months."

Louis leaned toward the waitress and confided, "Actually, I consider myself a Montanan, not a New Yorker, despite my liberal sensibilities. I know this country like the back of my hand, ma'am."

One of the geezers craned his neck, checking out the strangers.

Louis pointed to the pie rack and said, "So how's about you fixin' us up a nice piece of that famous Elkhorn huckleberry pie—with a scoop of vanilla."

"You mean the blackberry pie, hon?"

Louis considered the question. "I'm all for colloquialisms, ma'am. But I feel obliged to note that we're talking about two distinctly different fruits, alike as they may appear and even taste—the blackberry, genus *Rubus,* and the huckleberry, genus *Gaylussacia.*"

He paused to let this sink in, then added, "Of course, if you still prefer to use the words synonymously—well, that's fine by me too. Either way, it makes for a heck of a slice of pie."

"You sure sound smart, hon. Is that a yes?"

"My friend is a wordsmith," Raul muttered. "We'll *both* have the blackberry, with a scoop of vanilla—and a mochaccino for me. I'm Raul, and this is Louis."

"I'm Elda. Pleased to meet you." She turned back to Louis. "What're you drinking, hon?"

Louis, still in a jocular mood, read the $2.75 price of the fancy coffee drink from the menu. "At that price for a cup of joe, I reckon I best stick to my usual. Cherry cola, please."

As Elda started off, Raul asked, "Any sign of Amber today?"

"Called in sick. Something about her fella and some boat."

Louis glance at Raul. "Someone named Bowen, perchance?"

"Got me."

Elda hit the old chrome plunger on the cherry syrup dispenser, then set the glass under the gooseneck soda spigot.

She set down their pies and drinks, and the men temporarily forgot all their troubles. The pie was indeed blackberry, but Louis's disappointment vanished with the first tasty forkful. They ate with their heads bowed, focused on the pie.

"I'd say the Elkhorn has outdone itself, ma'am," Louis said. "This just might be the best pie I ever had—blackberry or huckleberry."

Elda, washing dishes, didn't hear.

"I wish Amber were here," Raul said. "Something just doesn't feel right."

"Like what?" Louis pressed his fork onto the last flakes of piecrust and swabbed up some melted ice cream with it.

"I ba-ba-ba-ba-bet Bowen's in trouble."

Louis suggested that they call Bowen's home in Bozeman from the road. They could also leave word for Amber that they could be reached at Eagletech, as Bowen also was a friend of Ted Blinken's.

The old-timers were leaving. The smoker stopped and asked, "Did I hear you say you fellers are blacksmiths?"

"No, no," Raul replied. "*Word*smith. That's him."

"I'll be goldarned." The man's blue eyes lit up, but he looked baffled.

Raul savored the last of his mochaccino.

"I'm quite content as a wordsmith, sir," Louis said, defensively. "I haven't the slightest interest in spending my days hunched over a roaring fire, pounding out a horseshoe or ax head. I take it you're a rancher."

"Hell, I ain't no rancher. I'm an in-shurance broker. Got an office just down the street."

"Oh," Louis said. "I'm pleased to meet you. I'm B. Louis Traub, and this here is my pardner, Raul Mendoza. Would you mind holding that cigarette to the other side?"

The smoker apologized and introduced himself as Lamar. They had a friendly conversation in which Louis told them about the Guardian of Grammar website and Raul described Dent-A-Men. The Montanans professed interest but changed the subject to the insurance industry—something about which neither Louis nor Raul cared much.

Eager to get going, Raul said, "We'd better settle up, Elda. Separate checks, please."

"As you're from here," Louis said, addressing Lamar, "you surely know the story behind this vintage soda fountain."

Lamar said he'd heard it had been brought down from up around Deer Lodge.

"You should be aware of this, too, Elda." Louis explained how the entire fountain setup—counters, stools, and all—had been built under commission in the late 1950s by the owner of a mine near Anaconda, who missed the soda fountains of his youth in California. When the mine and its owner went bust, the original proprietor of the Elkhorn bought the fountain and reassembled it in Dillon.

"That would have been old Rick Warren," Lamar said.

"Yes, I believe you're right. The name rings a bell," Louis said.

Raul looked at his bill. It was $4.25. He gave Elda a $5 bill and asked for a quarter back. Louis had the exact change to cover his bill, including an equally meager tip.

They left the café and lingered for a moment before the Elkhorn, exchanging parting pleasantries with their two new friends.

———————

At about the time that Louis and Raul got pointed in the right direction again, on I-15 south, Nathan Nuckel was poking around the campsite they had vacated just hours earlier. The entire campground was now deserted. Nuckel had driven up from Bozeman, having learned from folks that Bowen Kiick had mentioned something about friends camping up on the Beaverhead, near Dillon.

Nuckel enjoyed his job as a private investigator more than ever, although he had endured some bleak times since his primary focus, investigating workers' compensation cases on behalf of mine owners, had dried up. Nuckel was not a fly fisherman—quite the opposite. He was a major-league baseball fan whose idea of a great summer day was lounging in his air-conditioned basement rec room, watching the Colorado Rockies wallop some big fancy East Coast team, like the New York Mets or the Philadelphia Phillies.

For a score of reasons, Nuckel had it in for environmentalists and other out-of-staters—the folks who sneeringly referred to his hometown of Butte as "the armpit of Montana." Everywhere Nuckel turned, he found more motivation for pursuing Kiick with ardor. The transplant had a log home in Bozeman that made Nuckel's own low-slung ranchette look shabby. And the sweet-talking felon had been through a handful of wives—all of them lookers, too—while Nuckel, who was timid around women, had trouble getting them even to part with a pair of their underpants. That was how he had begun collecting them, as wistful tokens of what might have been.

Nuckel returned to the task at hand, examining the immediate area with the aid of a steel rod that looked like a putter, which he used to sift or scratch soil. He had designed it himself over the long All-Star weekend of 1998. He was nearly done combing over the area where Earl and Just Ray had camped.

Slowly, painstakingly, Nuckel came to the conclusion that this campsite had been occupied by a male adult and a child, with a three-quarter-ton pickup truck that leaked oil as well as water and also needed a wheel alignment. He looked around. "What a godforsaken place," he thought. "Why the hell would anyone want to come out here?"

Nuckel moved over to a fire ring, but he could tell from the dirt and grass that nobody had used it recently. He walked in a series of ever larger circles, scanning the ground, and eventually came across a footprint.

Unlike the other prints, this one had been made with a boot with studs. His heart beat faster. Native Montanans didn't wear cleated wading shoes; they wore pull-on canvas waders.

He found more sign, including an oddly compressed patch of grass under a large cottonwood—a logical choice for a campsite. And the trash barrel nearby contained, among many other items of interest, an empty bottle of Herradura—the very bottle Kiick had bought in a liquor store just outside Bozeman, as Nuckel had already established. No Montanan in his right mind would spend fifty-plus bucks for a bottle of hooch.

Little by little, Nuckel's patience and eye for detail paid off. Over the next ninety minutes, he pieced together a fairly complete picture. A party towing a boat in a relatively new vehicle, with top-of-the-line tires, had camped near the cottonwood, independent of the man and boy, for at least four days. Furthermore, whoever it was had lived in relative luxury, making use of camp stoves, propane lanterns, folding chairs, and other fancy items.

He stood, scratching his head. There appeared to be impressions and distinct stake holes left by *two* tents. Yet everyone who had positively identified Kiick on the road over from Bozeman had insisted that he was traveling alone.

"Son of a bitch," Nuckel thought. "This makes no sense."

The mysterious second tent might have been that of a backpacker or some other itinerant without a vehicle, but it was more likely that it belonged to someone with whom Kiick had a prearranged meeting. What better place for a secret rendezvous than this off-the-beaten-path campsite?

Nuckel dropped to his hands and knees and turned his face parallel to the ground. He was able to make out tracks left by the boat trailer and determined the direction of travel based on the orientation of the squashed vegetation.

He jumped up, ran over near the road, and checked from ground level again. The pieces began to fall into place rapidly in his mind. "A-ha! . . . you devil, you . . ."

This was what he lived for—the good old-fashioned dick work. In this case, the mystery posed by the second tent.

At the campground entrance, Nuckel straddled the track left by the left wheel of the trailer as it had pulled away. He raised his hands and formed blinders on either side of his face. He followed the track for some distance.

"That's it!"

Kiick had turned right out of the campground and headed north, toward Dillon. His tracks crossed over all the other ones, including the pickup, so he must have been the last to leave. And there were no additional footprints to suggest anyone had walked away from the campground after Kiick left.

Whoever had been in that second tent had to be traveling with Bowen Kiick in the SUV toward Dillon. Just as clearly, Nuckel would now be heading for Dillon, hot on Kiick's trail. While there, he thought, he could grab a quick bite of lunch at that place—what was it called? The Buckhorn, the Staghead, something like that . . .

Part II

Sah-cah-gar-we-ah our Indian woman was one of the female prisoners taekn at that time; tho' I cannot discover that she shews any immotion of sorrow in recollecting this event, or of joy in being restored to her native country; if she has enough to eat and a few trinkets to wear I believe she would be perfectly content anywhere.

—JULY 28, 1805,
The Journals of Lewis and Clark

4

Raul sat behind the wheel of the SUV, his hair slightly damp against the headrest. His eyes were closed. The sun baked his forearm as it rested on the open window. Each car on I-15 passed with a percussive *whoomph!* that made the War Pony rock.

They had killed some time in Dillon, getting gas and supplies, poking around town on the off chance they might bump into Bowen or Amber. Later, they pulled over a few miles south of Dell so that Louis could make some calls, including one to Bowen and another to his daughter, Rachel.

Trying to reach Rachel had become something of a formality, as she often didn't even bother to pick up when Louis was with Raul in Montana. It went back to when Rachel was a little girl and Louis had told her that in Big Sky country, they were far removed from civilization and its many bedeviling apparatus, like phone booths. She never forgave him that exaggeration.

Louis and Raul were near the Idaho line, en route to the Modina Pass, where they would pick up the gravel road that ran through the Centennial Valley, along the Red Rock River, before it joined Route 20 to take them into the tamer precincts of West Yellowstone.

Raul was tempted to close the power windows and run the air conditioner, but they had a pact to use the device as little as possible because of the association of Freon with global warming. They set aside their ecological concerns only when they were barreling down big inter-states like I-15, roads on which doing seventy-five or eighty with the windows open turned conversations into shouting matches.

Raul started as Louis opened the door.

Under way again, Louis explained that he'd left a message on Bowen's machine telling him what had happened and promising to take care of the damage to the boat. He could get in touch with them via Ted Blinken at Eagletech over the next day or so.

Gradually they gained speed and were soon cruising along at sev-enty. "I don't like the way this rig handles towing the boat," Raul said, glancing in the rearview mirror. Buffeted by the breeze, the drift boat wallowed slightly on the trailer. "The trailer wants to swing side to side; I can feel it."

"We'll have to drive prudently on the gravel," Louis noted.

They drove on in silence until Raul asked, "So how are things at home?"

"Rachel was very sarcastic," Louis admitted. "Somehow this trip trig-gers the same component of, um, jealousy as it always did in her mother."

"Hmmm . . ."

"You remember how Naomi used to try to sabotage the trip, always exaggerating and blowing things out of proportion on the off chance that she could induce me to jump on a plane home?"

Louis thought for a while. Then he mimicked Rachel's scolding tone: "If you hadn't been goofing off—*fishing*—all those years, I might have gone to Collegiate or Columbia Prep. I might have gotten that Jetta instead of the stupid . . . Hon-*duh!* And I might have had par-ents—*two* of them. And real vacations instead of stupid fishing trips!"

"I'm sorry, Louis. That sounds like a terrible conversation. It's a shame she doesn't understand about fishing."

Louis looked out the window. "She's a city girl: What does she know from fishing? What's wrong with a Honda? It's one of the most environmentally friendly vehicles on the road."

Louis proceeded to tell Raul horror stories about teenagers in the city, about tongue posts and pagers and what the twelve-year-olds now knew about sex. The discussion evolved into a lengthy speculation on whether humans were monogamous. It was the kind of rambling conversation they often had during high-speed, hypnotic, six-hour blasts along some dull interstate. As the mile markers, exit signs, and towering signs for "easy-on, easy-off" service stations whizzed by, blurring into one, the men would find themselves discussing for long periods whether Hitler was mad or evil, how the United States might have been different if the Italians had been more aggressive colonists than the British, or what male-female relationships might have been like in the age of dinosaurs.

They often spoke in a kind of shorthand, for either could just about complete the other's thoughts. While they certainly disagreed on some things, they respected each other's opinions and avoided confrontations. They made their respective points and moved on. They never listened to the radio for anything but a weather report.

They sped along in the shadow of the Tendoy Mountains, past Lima, into the broad valley of the upper Red Rock. It was late in the afternoon. Giant pillars of sunlight streamed through gaps in the clouds and fell across vast fields of alfalfa, stretching toward mountains that rose gradually on either side in melancholy shades of blue. The men were overcome by a sense of well-being and good fortune.

"Look at that rubble around the base of that rock formation," Louis said, gesturing toward an odd mound of rock erupting from the land. "Dig how it forms an, um, aureole."

Raul glanced at the structure but saw nothing that resembled any aspect of a mammary gland. He made a noncommittal sound. They were coming up on the turnoff for the Centennial Valley Road, at the most spectacular time of day.

———

As neither Louis nor Raul were experienced boat haulers, they were shocked at how badly the War Pony handled under the load on a rough road. Right from the start, the road was washboarded; it also had many tubular cattle grates that, when crossed, threatened to shake the fillings loose in their teeth.

Thankfully, though, the valley was at a high elevation and the road ran relatively flat, heading east. The land on either side of the road was grassland, tawny and sage green with islands of box elders, cottonwoods, and willows marking water. To the north, the valley turned into a series of gray-green swells that already were partly in the shade—the foothills of the Gravelly Mountains. To the south, the rugged Centennial Mountains—officially, the Continental Divide—tore up the horizon on the border with Idaho, their snowcapped peaks tinged amber by the late-afternoon sun.

The SUV shuddered again, and Raul felt it might shake into pieces.

"It's the same as always," Louis said, drunk on the vistas. "One of the last untouched places."

"I'm having trouble enjoying this," Raul confessed, through tight lips. "We're really beating up the rig."

Louis was silent. He didn't like it when Raul got all stressed out about material things. Raul had made plenty of money with Dent-A-Men. He was comfortable, if not filthy rich. A little wear and tear on his SUV seemed a small price to pay for the opportunity to behold this glorious piece of country.

Within minutes, they caught a glimpse of the upper Red Rock River, meandering like a dark blue ribbon through the high prairie.

"Did you know that this valley comprises critical habitat for more than two hundred bird species?" Louis asked.

"That's very nice, Louis," Raul replied tersely. "That's good information."

"There's no point in ruining the best part of this drive for yourself," Louis said. "I'm concerned about the rig, too. Remember, though, it's just a vehicle."

"Yes. But it's *my* vehicle. We always use my rig on this trip. *Your* car is parked with a special cover over it—in your uncle's garage."

"It's parked at a *friend* of my uncle Abe's," Louis corrected. "He's glad to have the extra cash. Social Security doesn't go that far . . ."

"Forget about it. It's just that this whole drift boat thing has been a bad, bad idea."

Raul braked, hard. The entire rig shuddered over a short stretch of washboard again.

"What we ought to do, one day, is throw all caution to the wind," Louis said. "We should take a chance and float-tube the Red Rock between Lima Reservoir and Lower Red Rock Lake. It's supposed to have humongous browns and some sort of a drake hatch."

This tantalizing idea distracted Raul. They calmly discussed whether the drake in question would be the brown or green, given the Red Rock's water temperature, bottom composition, gentle grade, and slow flow. They knew pathetically little about those issues, since the ranchers who owned most of the valley resolutely kept anglers out. One had even strung up barbed wire across the river to prevent anyone from floating it.

"What's that up ahead?" Louis asked.

The road ahead went downhill at a gentle grade, crossing a small, brushy creekbed half a mile away. Then it started uphill again, and far in the distance, a dark shape loomed on the side of the road.

"It's a bear!" Louis cried. "It could be a grizz!"

"That's no bear," said Raul. He had never worn glasses and took great pride in his eyesight.

They watched the object carefully as they rolled on. The clear air and epic scale of the sparse landscape played tricks on their eyes. They first decided the object was a large boulder. Then a tree. But soon enough it became clear that it was a vehicle, with the hood up. And somebody seemed to be sitting on a pile of goods near it.

"I think that's a woman sitting there," Raul said.

"I'll be, pardner. I believe it's that same woman we encountered briefly at the Elkhorn."

"That's exactly who it is," Raul said. "Car problems."

He slowed the rig and pulled over. Louis got out while Raul fished around for his sandals. The woman sat on a duffel bag atop a suitcase, knees akimbo, with an open book in her lap. As Louis approached with his John Wayne gait, the woman squinted and rose, clutching the book to her chest. Her loose sundress, clogs, and peculiar topknot combined to create a waifish effect.

"Howdy, little lady," Louis said. "You appear to have gotten yourself into a bit of trouble."

"I remember you! I can't believe someone finally came along. Oh my God."

She recounted how her car had suddenly quit. She had been waiting for hours, without a single vehicle having passed. She was worried about the coming night. Her voice rose and cracked, and suddenly she went slack-jawed and rapidly shook her head from side to side, mute.

Raul tried to calm her, saying, "Easy, now. It's just the stress—the prolonged stress. Everything is going to be fine."

She regained her composure and apologized. She issued something between a sob and a laugh, asking Louis, "Did you just call me . . . *little lady?* Did I hear right?'"

"Yes, ma'am. Did I offend you?"

"No. It's weird, that's all. My father used to call me that."

"Permit me to introduce ourselves formally. I'm B. Louis Traub." Louis removed his legionnaire's cap and made a sweeping gesture with it as he bowed. "And this is my partner, Raul Mendoza."

"Hi," the woman said. A weak chin and full lips combined to give her a pouty look. She drawled. "My name is Lottie. Lottie Moffo. You sound like you're from New Jersey . . . not that there's anything wrong with that."

"I suppose in some official way I am indeed from back east. New York, to be exact. But this is my spiritual home. I consider myself a, um, naturalized Montanan."

"I can see why. It's so beautiful here. It's like I imagined when we had to read about the pioneers and Lewis and Clark, in school."

"Ah, yes, my namesake . . ." Louis gestured. "A distant relation of sorts."

Raul looked at his friend, dumbfounded by his boyish fabrication.

"In fact," Louis continued, "Raul and I are fresh from the Beaverhead country ourselves—sacred country that was first explored by Captain Lewis and the Corps of Discovery some two hundred years ago."

"I'm more of a tourist than a history buff," Lottie confessed. "But I always wanted to come here." She flopped back down on her luggage and bit her lip. Her eyes welled up, and a single large tear rolled down her cheek.

Raul said, in a soothing voice, "That's good, Lottie—let go of the tension, just get it out. Off-load the bad. Just let it go."

She sighed and smiled weakly. "I was hoping to, I don't know . . . get in touch with nature a little. You know, see the bears in Yellowstone Park, experience the real West. I've got just a few days before I start a job, but now my car and cell phone are dead. What am I going to do?"

"You have a job out here?" Raul asked.

She nodded. "Up near Helena. I start in three days. I drove out from New York two weeks ago. It's supposed to be my vacation—my grand tour of the West."

"I approve of your interest and personally welcome you to Montana," Louis said. "Despite this minor setback, I guarantee you won't be disappointed." He offered to get Lottie a cold Fanta from the cooler and some tissues, which she gratefully accepted.

"We'll get you all fixed up shortly, Ms. Moffo," Louis said as he turned toward her vehicle. "Not to worry."

"That's very . . . gallant." When Lottie smiled, her eyes became tiny slits. "But please, call me Lottie. Do I have raccoon eyes from my eyeliner?"

"Not at all," Raul lied.

He figured Lottie to be about forty, although she was one of those people who would seem forever young. She was very fit, slight with lean, tan limbs and bony knees. If it weren't for her topknot and jaunty breasts, she easily could be mistaken for a fifteen-year-old boy.

Raul wondered just what Louis meant by "fixing her up." Louis certainly knew about vehicles. He was a performance aficionado and devoted subscriber to various automotive magazines, including *Road and Track*. But Louis was lost under the hood. He had never even changed his own oil or spark plugs, preferring to leave such menial tasks to those whom he called "service professionals."

As Louis was about to open the driver's side door of her car, Lottie cried, "Wait!" But it was too late. A tiny dog burst out, leaped up, and clamped fiercely onto Louis's bicep.

"Jack, Little Jack!" Lottie jumped up and raced toward them. "Stop!"

Louis howled. He whirled like a dervish in the dusty road, shaking his arm as he tried to dislodge the small but muscular creature. The dog hung on, all the while emitting a deep, guttural growl.

"Oh God, oh my God!" Raul shouted. "It's your casting arm!"

Lottie lunged forward and got hold of the dog. She repeatedly screamed "Jack!" as she struggled to pry open his jaws. Finally they all pitched over together, landing in a pile, with Lottie at last dislodging the dog from Louis's arm. As they struggled to sit up, Louis was overcome by a spell. His forearms worked like tiny flippers and his eyes rolled back. When Lottie saw him, her mouth fell open and her head began to vibrate again.

"It's all right, it's all right!" Raul called. He was standing on the trunk of Lottie's car. "It's just one of his spells. He gets them from stress."

"A spell?" Lottie grabbed Louis by the shoulders. "Are you all right? I feel terrible. Oh my God, what have I done?"

"I'm telling you, he's fine," Raul said, regarding the truculent little dog, which was looking up at him, growling and making a strange clicking sound with his gums. "This happens quite often. It's something like petit mal but not nearly as serious."

"Everything is going to be fine," Lottie said in a soothing drawl. "We'll take very good care of you." She gently patted Louis's brow with a tissue and plucked a smidgen of dirt off his temple.

Coming out of his spell, Louis was surprised to see Lottie's face so close to his own. He was accustomed to freaking people out with his spells. When his former wife, Naomi, had first witnessed one, she'd started crying and fled the room.

"Your words were reassuring," Louis muttered. "Thank you."

"It's okay. I used to be a trauma nurse. Jack, come here, boy. *Now.*"

The little dog ignored Lottie until he was good and ready to trot over and climb into her lap, a perch from which he continued to eyeball Louis. He was old, with two small splotches of black and brown on his pale gray hide. His eyes were going milky, and his muzzle was nearly white. Little Jack began to pant; he looked like he was smiling.

"This is Jack M. Russell," Lottie declared.

"We've met," Louis said.

Lottie stared into the dog's eyes and kissed him squarely on the nose. "He's practically deaf, but he's very protective of me. I have to tell you, I can't remember the last time he showed this much energy. "

Louis sat, rubbing his arm. There was neither blood nor lacerations, just a few dents that would become purple bruises.

"Thank God he doesn't have teeth anymore," Lottie added. "He can't bark much, either. Poor baby. He's just old."

Louis said, "Well, he must have been some ratter in his day."

Lottie smiled proudly.

"Should we try to do something about the car?" Raul asked.

Louis rose and dusted himself off. All three of them gathered around Lottie's disabled vehicle, a Korean Kuntsui. Jack, still in Lottie's arms, regarded Louis, faintly but steadily growling.

The backseat of the car was messy, piled with bags and plastic milk crates filled with files and books. The vehicle had a decal on the rear window for the Guy S. Hayes College of Peace and two bumper stickers: "Pro-Family *and* Pro-Choice" and "I Brake for Unicorns."

Louis reached in through the driver's side window and flicked the key. The engine barely turned over. Frowning, he muttered something about the battery or starter motor.

"That's not the problem," Lottie said. "I ran the battery down trying to start the car again."

Louis twisted the stem of the windshield wiper mechanism. The wipers moved, slowly clearing a fine layer of dust off the windshield. He muttered, "Wipers work."

Lottie turned and smiled at Raul, her eyes slits. "He's not really a mechanic, is he?"

"Oh, he knows his cars. Really, he's very na-na-na-na-knowledgeable."

Louis poked his head under the hood. He located the original vehicle identification number plate on the firewall and cried, "Ha! Now I get it. I should have known."

He emerged and summarized the contents of an exposé he'd read years before in *Car and Buyer:* "This is one of those *pre*-1993 Kuntsui Vivendis. The vehicle was assembled at an offshore plant—I believe it was in Indonesia—where quality control is, at best, a dubious enterprise. These vehicles were notorious—and I mean *notorious*—for using rubber gaskets and hoses of poor quality. The rubber went soft and degenerated from the heat. Look, you can see where the leaking fluid stained the engine compartment."

"So I need a stiffer hose?" Lottie asked.

The men agreed there was no recourse. Lottie would have to get the vehicle towed to the nearest town, West Yellowstone, although Louis doubted there would be a Kuntsui dealer anywhere within a thousand miles. They leaned against the fender of the car, deciding what to do. Raul suggested that things weren't really that bad—parts could be air-shipped to West Yellowstone in a day or two, max.

A large mayfly spinner flew overhead and landed on the windshield. Raul carefully trapped it under his hat. He got hold of the insect and held it tenderly; Louis joined in examining the creature. Like all mayflies, it had a long, gracefully tapered body and gauzy, upright wings that were shaped like sails.

"You need to see this, Lottie," Louis said. When she drew close, he muttered, "Isn't that an absolutely elegant brown drake?"

The wings of the mayfly were nearly transparent, with faint brown mottling and fine veins like those of a leaf. The insect had a tiny, oval face with two minute, lustrous black eyes.

"This," Louis said solemnly, "is the reason we're here."

"This bug?" Lottie's laugh was a forceful cackle that seemed unusual coming from a woman of such small stature. "Pardon me, but isn't that just a teensy little bit . . . *weird?*"

Louis chuckled. "You sound like my ex-wife."

"We're fly fishers," Raul interjected. "It's what we do. It's who we are."

"Ouch!" Louis jumped, for Jack had darted in and nipped his ankle.

"I'm sorry!" Lottie grabbed Jack by the scruff of the neck and gave him a shake, saying, "Now you leave Louis alone. You hear? I'm really sorry. He gets *very* jealous."

"You know, Louis, I'm not sure this is a brown drake," said Raul. "I'm not so sure at all. Look at the pronounced rake of the wings and how far back they begin. The coloration, too—I've never seen a thorax this dark."

"Hmmm."

Curious, Lottie stood on tiptoe, placing a hand on Louis's shoulder for balance.

Further study revealed that the segmentation of the abdomen was far more pronounced and bulbous than on the brown drakes found on the Fork and elsewhere. This was curious, indeed. They decided to keep the insect and solicit the opinion of Ted Blinken, who really knew his western mayfly species and subspecies. Raul went back to the SUV for an empty film canister in which to store the insect.

"I'd give anything to be yonder," Louis said, indicating the line of willows beyond which flowed the Red Rock River. It was a mere three hundred yards away, but it might as well have been in Antarctica. "Imagine the fish whacking these giant mayflies—it's a fly fisherman's dream."

"You guys must love to eat fish," Lottie remarked.

"Sacre bleu!" Louis was horrified. "That would be sacrilege. We love trout. We love them more than anything. To paraphrase the great Lee Wulff, a great gamefish is too valuable to catch just once. We release *all* the fish we catch."

Lottie wondered why, if they loved the trout so much, they were so fired up about hooking them and dragging them in and out of the water. She had seen plenty of images of the poor, terrified fish, leaping around, desperately trying to get free.

Raul returned, canister in hand.

"Are you guys, like . . . etymologists?" Lottie asked.

"I believe the word you're looking for is *entomologist*," Raul said. "Someone who studies insects."

"Actually," Louis interjected, "in my case, either word is appropriate. Etymology, the study and use of words, is my stock in trade as a writer."

"Wow!" Lottie exclaimed. "You're a writer?"

"I believe that would be an accurate description. Wouldn't you say, Raul?"

"He's a wordsmith," Raul said dryly, putting the film canister in a breast pocket. "I'm sorry, I think we need to make a move here. It's almost six—and we're still a good couple of hours from West."

Raul lay on his belly, half immersed in the SUV, tugging at various boxes and containers as he tried to clear room for the jump seat to fold back properly. They were so jammed for space that most of Lottie's things had ended up in the drift boat. All they needed now was to make room for Lottie and Jack. Under his breath, Raul cursed the stupid Double D and the whiskey box.

Lottie was curious about the partially inflated float tubes. Louis explained that they were also known as belly boats or personal watercraft, clever variations on the old inner-tube flotation concept, enabling anglers to settle into harnesses that kept them upright, waist-deep in the water, while they used scuba-type flippers for propulsion. He also explained about the Sunshowers, secured like giant botas to the roof rack.

"Very clever," Lottie said.

"Shit, shit, shit!" Raul wiggled out of the SUV, into a kneeling position on the road. He seemed on the verge of tears. "Now I can't fit the wader bag." He cursed again when it became obvious that he would have to repack and probably transfer the cooler to the boat as well. Eventually, though, they were ready to go.

"Jack, go make poopsy." Lottie's voice was stern and she pointed. The dog trotted away obediently and laid a little pipe at the edge of the road. Lottie shrugged. "It's the only trick he knows."

They all piled into the SUV. As soon as they pulled out, the pile of bags on which Jack rode alongside Lottie toppled. The dog disappeared into the back with the luggage.

"Phew!" Raul exclaimed, happy to be under way at last. In the distance, the lilac tint of evening already infused the air. The distant mountains looked darker, like bruises on the horizon.

They had been on the road only about ten minutes when Lottie poked her head between the two front seats and said to Raul, "I'm dying to know this, okay? Are you by any chance that guy who's been in all those movies by the Spanish director Almondóvar?"

"No, no, no," Raul said. A film buff himself, he knew the famous director, as well as the actor to whom Lottie was referring—a Cuban by the name of Diego Batista. In fact, she wasn't the first to notice the striking resemblance. "Thank you for the compliment, but no. I am a big fan of Almondóvar, though. He's in an interesting place, creativity-wise."

"You must get asked that a lot," Lottie said. "It's probably annoying."

They chatted about Almondóvar and the dark, sexy comedies he made, featuring cross-dressers and philanderers and religious hypocrites. Raul rued the fact that unlike the artistic Almondóvar, mainstream moviemakers always relegated talented Latino actors like Batista to stereotypical roles as drug dealers or pimps. He joked, "It's automatic: a full head of hair and a mustache—bingo!—you play the *traficante*."

"Yes!" Lottie cackled. She said he was too funny.

Louis didn't really see what a full head of hair had to do with anything. While Raul and Lottie bantered about the cinema, he looked out the window.

Suddenly, Louis cried, "Raul, pull over!" He jumped out and walked back along the road, then returned to the SUV with a long-stemmed, flowering plant he had plucked by the roadside. "What's your opinion?"

Raul examined the plant closely. The thin, pale green stem had sparse limbs, each of which ended in a pretty, pink flower about the size of a golf ball. Raul finally broke the silence: "Spotted knapweed."

"You think?"

"What else could it be?" Raul said as Louis got in. Raul pulled away. "It's not Canada thistle, I'm certain of that. It has to be knapweed."

"Lottie." Louis turned in his seat and explained. "The Nature Conservancy people recently identified and isolated several species of invasive weeds in this valley." He paused, thrusting the long stalk at her. She reluctantly took it. The plant had a strong, bitter odor.

Louis continued: "We suspect that this one is the most prevalent and, um, insidious of the invasives. Spotted knapweed, or, if you will, *Centaurea maculosa*. Is that right, Raul, or is it *Centaurea repens?*"

"*Repens* is the Russian knapweed, I think."

"Anyway, Lottie, seeing these invasives is a real drag. It would be impossible to overstate the danger they pose to the biodiversity of the grasslands here."

"Wow." Lottie examined the plant she was holding. It certainly didn't look very menacing. "I think I've read something about this. Man, you guys are, like, really smart!"

Louis explained how the invasives upset the natural balance. They had no value as habitat for native animal species, and they weren't used as food, so they flourished. They eventually crowded out the native species, forming unstoppable, sprawling, useless, single-species tracts that Louis termed "insidious green wastelands."

Lottie felt ignorant. She loved hiking but admitted that, had she come across *Centaurea maculosa* on one of her regular hikes in New York's Shawangunks, she probably would have thought it a pretty flower and left it at that.

"Ah, the 'Gunks," Louis said, nostalgically. "I know them well. I went to summer camp in the 'Gunks. Of course, that was before the bird-watchers, rock climbers, and other urban recreationists flooded there."

"Well, we all love nature, right?"

"Lottie." Louis weighed his words. "I approve of your, um, sensitivity to the intrinsic beauty of nature. I'm the first to admit that the hip thing about nature is that very beauty—even when it's expressed in a plant as potentially harmful as *Centaurea maculosa.* It's important to remember that even the noxious knapweed has its place in the natural order of things, but bear in mind that the operative phrase is 'natural order.'"

Louis continued, explaining how a plant like *maculosa,* though held in check within the boundaries of its native ecosystem, can radically transform a differently ordered environment. Here in the Rockies, for instance, *maculosa* has had a profound impact on the hydrology of the valley simply through the amount of water that, as a relatively "thirsty" invader, it draws out of an ecosystem that is already at the borderline of moisture deficit.

"And let's not forget," Raul interjected, "altering the hydrology can change the entire nutrient cycling regimen . . ."

Lottie said, "You sure know your botany."

"What's that smell?" Raul asked.

"Oh, Jack." Lottie smacked her lips, explaining, "He gets gas sometimes."

They all opened their power windows at once. Cool air rushed into the SUV.

The stalk of knapweed fell over in Lottie's hand, as if hinged at the center. Lottie squeezed the stem and was surprised to see how much moisture it contained. But she didn't know quite what to do with the stalk. If it were such a demon plant, she certainly wouldn't want to just throw it out the window. Besides, that would have been littering, and she thought of herself as an environmentalist. She donated money every year to Greenpeace and the Mother Earth Fund for a Green Planet.

Raul slowed to a crawl. About fifty head of cattle—giant, brown-and-white-spotted beef cows, many of them horned—milled about in the road before them.

Jack emerged from the mass of baggage in the back of the SUV. He propped his front legs on the rail of the side window and appeared to bark, although the only noise that came out of his mouth was a kind of strangled cough. The cows stared idly at the little dog.

Creeping forward, Raul eventually bumped a cow. It lurched out of the way. Others reacted, moving reluctantly. Gradually, Raul opened a lane through the cattle, while those on the perimeter stared blankly.

"Jack, down." Lottie said, almost shouting. "Why are they just standing there?"

"I reckon there's a cattle grate in the road just up here a little ways," Louis said. "When a piece of fence goes down, the cattle usually get on the road and start walking. That's why they install cattle grates. The cows are afraid to cross them."

One of the cows bellowed plaintively.

"Aw, quit your bellyachin'," Louis called out.

They rumbled over the grate and left the cattle behind. Lottie watched the cattle recede in the distance.

"Who cut the cheese?" Louis said.

They reflexively reached again for the power windows.

"I'm so sorry," Lottie drawled. "I'm mortified. Why don't you pull over? Jack can ride in the boat." When Raul expressed reservations, Lottie told him that Jack had spent plenty of summer weekends riding in the bow of a motorboat on Pennsylvania's Lake Wallenpaupack. "You just watch; he loves it."

Sure enough, little Jack was soon riding happily atop a duffel bag in the bow of the McKenzie boat, his tiny, muscular legs braced against the prow. Thus stationed, he looked like the figurehead on an ancient sailing ship.

They came to a rough, two-track lane that meandered away from the road toward a large wooden building of weathered gray wood and, beyond it, the river.

"Coyote!" Raul cried. He stopped the SUV.

The critter slunk along the lane toward the river. It looked like a small, mangy German shepherd with a big, fluffy tail.

"Wow," Lottie said. "That's the first one I've ever seen. It's just like a little wolf!"

"It *is* a little wolf," Louis said. "*Canis latrans.* In some places, the coyote was even called the brush wolf."

"Do they ever attack humans?"

Louis chuckled. He explained that coyotes were harmless omnivores, subsisting mostly on rodents, berries, rabbits, fruits, and ground-nesting birds.

"They say they'll take deer and lambs," Raul interjected, "and beef calves, too. Ranchers hate coyotes with a vengeance."

"That they do," Louis said. "But their odium is born of ignorance. Coyotes are no real threat to calves or lambs. Remember that the Native Americans worshiped the coyote as 'God's dog.' He was known in some tribes as 'the Trickster.' But white men of western European stock have always harbored an irrational hatred for wild canids, starting with the Trickster's larger cousin, the wolf . . ."

The coyote vanished in the tall grass. They sat looking at the old barn. It was in an advanced stage of collapse, with nothing left of the windows but black holes. Much of the siding was missing, and the roof, covered in splintering shingles, sagged in the center.

"It's part of the old Nevin homestead," Louis said quietly. "A hundred years ago, I reckon, it occupied almost the entire valley. I've always believed this building must have been the combination barn and bunk room, situated at the eastern end of the vast ranch to save cowboys riding time."

Behind them, the setting sun caught on some peaks and flared. Soon the entire valley lay bathed in dense, reddish light. Like some old paintings, it was simultaneously dark and illuminated. All three travelers gazed at the scene without speaking, as the old Nevin bunkhouse was transformed from a desolate ruin into something sublime and glowing. The listing walls and sagging roof flowed gracefully, creating an overall impression of majesty defeated.

The light was fading by the second.

Lottie quietly drawled, "I can see why you guys keep coming out here. This is . . . special."

———

Shortly after dark, they rolled into West Yellowstone, a rinky-dink town of tiny wooden houses, souvenir shops, neon signs, and Wild West–themed steakhouses. They drove straight to Laddie's Auto Repair and Body Shop to see what could be done about the Kuntsui. Ladislaus "Laddie" Feher, a Hungarian emigrant and feather thrower, was a mechanic and competitive caster whom the men knew from back in the day on the Fork.

The lights were still on though the shop was closing down. Laddie was away at a casting tournament, but Louis and Raul knew the mechanic on duty, Chuck. He was a fishing nut who had dropped out of college in Arizona and moved to West Yellowstone, initially supporting himself by running drift-boat shuttles for the esteemed guide Bob Jacklin. He was now working full-time for Laddie and complaining that he didn't get enough time to fish anymore.

Louis explained the situation, and Chuck promised to send a wrecker out first thing. He felt confident he could get hoses or gaskets for the vehicle from the NAPA dealer on the other side of town. He could probably get Lottie back on the road the following afternoon.

The next order of business was finding a place to stay. Lottie insisted on staking her rescuers to a room in town, where they could have a proper hot shower and sleep in a real bed. It was, she said, the least she could do.

Driving through town, they marveled at the bewildering number of chain-saw sculptures, fake totem poles, and novelty shops that specialized in Kodachrome film, New Age music, and T-shirts featuring wolves, bald eagles, and corny spiritual homilies attributed to noble savages.

"What a tourist trap," Lottie said.

Raul was anxious about towing the boat around the crowded town. He worried about sideswiping someone's pickup or that some reprobate would jump into the drift boat while they were at a light and rip off some of their stuff.

The No Vacancy signs were lit everywhere, for it was the peak of tourist season. Lottie kept trying, though. As a last resort, they pulled into the crowded dirt lot of the Cowpoke Motel—a long, narrow, one-story joint built of dark logs in the heart of town. Lottie, with Jack close on her heels, disappeared into the office.

Raul broke the silence. "There's something I need to discuss with you, Louis. How could you lie about something like your name and imply you were related to Meriwether Lewis? Your namesake? I've never heard you lie about *anything*—not how much you earn, not even about the size of the fish you catch."

"I was just being facetious." Louis chuckled. "You must admit, there was a measure of, um, verisimilitude in the situation." Feeling lighthearted, he launched into a playful reverie. "There we are, far, far, far from the well-trodden path of ordinary men, in the shadow of the Centennial Mountains . . ." He waved his hand as he painted a picture with words: "As evening descends, a lonely coyote howls. And yonder, we encounter a kindred spirit—another soul meant, like ourselves, to live in another time, another place. One who ought to be traveling in a pirogue, not an Indonesian-made, two-door Kuntsui, and wearing colorfully beaded buckskins and a festive buffalo robe."

"You see," Raul cried, growing animated, "you think you're joking, but you're in communion with the warrior within! You're trying to connect with the ancient ways!"

Louis, accustomed by now to the way Raul was forever reading into things and trying to promote his Ironfeather agenda, ignored his friend's earnest pitch. He made little wriggling motions with his fingers and continued in a hushed tone: "Glowing eyes regard us from behind every bush; signals of smoke rise in the clear night on the ridges . . ."

"Louis. Hey. Here she comes."

Lottie stopped just outside the office. She set Jack down. The dog immediately ran over and lifted his leg on the tire of a parked car.

Louis gazed at her and softly said, "I'll bet she's wearing a thong."

"I wouldn't go there, Louis . . ."

"Why not? I'll bet the thought has crossed your mind, pardner. You can admit it. It would be quite easy for you; she's under the impression you're some kind of movie star."

Raul was uncertain what to make of his friend's words. In any event, though Lottie had an attractive face and a lithe, boyish body, he felt that her cackling laugh, the curious topknot, not to mention the stinky little dog, were all turnoffs. He preferred women who were more demure, as well as fair-haired and large breasted.

Lottie squirmed into the jump seat. She sounded upset. "Ixnay. I don't know what to do next. I feel terrible."

Louis suggested that they camp together for the night and figure things out in the morning. He offered to let Lottie and Jack use his tent while he slept in the War Pony. "Let's all just stop obsessing over every little thing. Let's backtrack to the Grizz for some vittles. You aren't, perchance, a vegan, are you Lottie?"

"Ha!" She brightened up. "Not on your life, bub. What's the Grizz?"

Louis explained that it was the Hungry Grizzly, a restaurant and gathering place for many anglers who fished out of West.

Raul was amazed by his parsimonious friend's extravagant suggestion. "What about the stuffed pork chops? We were planning on making them tonight, with the rosemary-and-Roquefort mashed."

"They'll keep until tomorrow," Louis replied, segueing to his western accent. "I reckon it ain't too often that a couple of mountain men venture down this way. We may as well kick up our heels a bit."

"Stop!" Lottie cackled. "That cowboy accent—it just kills me."

Raul was on the verge of panic at the prospect of shelling out twenty-five, thirty bucks for a meal. But out of the blue, the 12th Viril-

ian Protocol popped into his mind: "When the quiver of the true warrior is full, he takes pleasure in bowing to the wishes of others in things
of the moment and the world."

Raul had always struggled mightily to embrace the 12th Protocol;
he knew he wasn't much good at "letting go." He was spared further
anguish, though, when Lottie declared that the only condition for her
joining them at the Grizz was that she pay for their meal. "What a very
generous offer, Lottie," he said. "If you insist, sure. And thank you in
advance."

The parking lot of the Grizz was crowded with camper rigs, RVs,
and pickups, many of them towing boats. Lottie took Jack from the
drift boat and locked him in the SUV.

The Grizz was a huge, multilevel log building with a few faux hitch-
ing posts out front. It was a cheery place with lots of stained glass,
mounted game animals, and antique objects, including gold-panning
articles and tin signs featuring scenes from the Wild West.

They were lucky. In no time, a pleasant hostess wearing a lawman's
badge for a name tag led them into the main dining room. It featured
an enormous salad bar, over which hung a massive chandelier made of
intertwined elk antlers. Strains of country music filtered in above the
din from the bar.

"Phil!" Raul said.

They stopped for a moment to exchange pleasantries with Phil Pic-
cione, a former plant supervisor from Minneapolis who had started his
own successful fly-line manufacturing company in his garage. He was
having dinner with a large, boisterous party that included many well-
known feather throwers: David Foster, John Randolph, Sid Evans, and
Paul Guernsey, all magazine editors and literary men of the first order;
writers, including Dave Whitlock, Monte Burke, Tom Rosenbauer, and
Nick Karras; and a maverick entrepreneur, Bill Klyn, the former mar-
keting man who was the mastermind behind the new Patagonia waders
with the built-in urination bladder that enabled anglers to pee without
having to get out of the river and undress.

After exchanging pleasantries, Louis and his party were seated at a
roomy table with a red-and-white-checked tablecloth. Louis waved at

two hefty, blond young men clad in pastel fleece across the room. They were guides for Bob Jacklin.

Raul leaned forward and whispered, "Don't turn around right now, but I think that's James Prosek right behind you—he's dining with Nick Lyons."

Louis arched his eyebrows. He leaned over to Lottie and whispered, "Nick is a true man of letters. I assume he's making an offer on Prosek's next book."

Louis explained that Prosek was an *enfant terrible* among wildlife artists. He specialized in semiabstract watercolors of trout. "They're really hip," Louis said. "Unfortunately, the field is dominated by ultra-realists and other uptight conservative types."

"I'm not very familiar with the issues in wildlife art," Lottie mumbled apologetically.

Louis went on: "Well . . . I, for one, am sick of images of guides on poling platforms, pointing at giant silver tarpon leaping in the tropical air. And I certainly have no use for yet another painting of a lion wandering around the veld with its jaws locked on a bloody impala fawn. Who needs such literal images? To me, that's mere *poster* art."

They ordered drinks and made for the salad bar. Louis was highly solicitous, providing commentary on many of the offerings, although Lottie was naturally inclined to avoid canned beets, imitation bacon bits, and marinated hearts of palm. When the two returned to the table, Louis's double scotch and Lottie's whiskey sour were waiting. Raul had already started on a meager, appetizer-size Caesar salad.

"To like-minded friends," Louis said, hoisting his whiskey glass. "New as well as old."

They all clinked glasses.

Lottie regarded Louis's mountainous salad. "It looks like a volcano," she said. Louis's salad was indeed a conical pile of broccoli, garbanzos, red pepper, carrot shavings, cherry tomatoes, jalapeños, cheddar pellets, sunflower seeds, melon balls, and marshmallows, with peppercorn ranch dressing studded with croutons and kernels of yellow corn oozing down its sides. Louis had topped it all off with a bulbous dollop of red Jell-O with fruit cocktail.

"I'm not a big lettuce fan," Louis allowed. He signaled to the wait-ress that he was ready for another scotch.

Lottie expressed some interest in the catch of the day, halibut, but Louis dissuaded her from ordering fish so far from the ocean. She switched to the queen cut prime rib, while Raul went for the herb-roasted chicken. Louis also ordered a pitcher of the local microbrew, Rattlesnake Creek Amber Ale, which he called "the Snake."

They were just digging into the salad when Louis blurted, "So tell us, who is Lottie Moffo?"

Lottie colored. She looked down and mumbled, "Who is anybody? I'm not very good at the concise summary."

"He's not, either," Raul said. "In case you hadn't noticed."

"In that case, I apologize," Louis said, with a gesture. "In truth, we aren't accustomed to running into a woman as conspicuously, um, *refined* as yourself in these parts. I couldn't help but notice that in addi-tion to your Sierra Club silver anniversary keychain, you have a copy of the contemporary novel *The Corrections*."

"Oh? You like Jonathan Franzen?"

The waitress appeared with their meals. Parts of Louis's twenty-two-ounce porterhouse steak, which lay half buried under spicy curly fries, hung over the edges of the plate. He caught Raul's eye and nodded toward the A1 sauce. Once they started eating, Raul asked about Lottie's roots.

She explained that she had been raised in a loving Italian family. Her father, whom she adored, had died just three years earlier. She had degrees in nursing, psychology, and speech therapy, and she was a certi-fied yoga instructor.

"Really?" Raul said. "I do yoga, too."

Professionally, Lottie explained, she had started out as a trauma nurse. After a brief, ultimately unsuccessful stint as a medical instru-ments saleswoman, she became a yoga disciple, supporting herself by waiting tables in Greenwich Village and working as a live model for art students.

"Nude," Louis thought. "That always means posing nude."

After returning to school to earn a degree in psychology, Lottie found her true calling: She developed a yoga-based approach to therapy that became fashionable and even got her written up in a few upscale magazines. Her clients ranged from people suffering from stress disorders to children with learning disabilities.

"I have to tell you," she confided in a low drawl, "I'm actually *Doctor* Lottie Moffo. I have my PhD."

"She must have posed nude," Louis thought.

"That's won-der-ful," Raul said, dragging out the word the way he always did when he meant it. "So you're a healer, Lottie. I come from a dysfunctional family, so I know firsthand about difference makers. I know what people like you can do."

Lottie basked in the compliment.

Catching the waitress's eye, Louis held up his empty scotch glass and jiggled it back and forth. He said, "My own learning disability, quite frankly, was that I never could spell . . . *dyslexia.*" Louis laughed at his own joke while Raul and Lottie exchanged knowing glances. A moment later, he blurted, "Have you, perchance, ever married?"

"Once. I was married to a basketball player. It didn't work out."

"Basketball," Louis said. He thought, with horror, of Wilt Chamberlain, the NBA star who claimed to have bedded more than two thousand women.

Raul said something about Lottie being in good company, and they were starting on a discussion of their respective marriages when the waitress showed up with a round of drinks—compliments of the two guides across the room.

Raul then asked about Lottie's work with children—specifically, about some of the developmental research conducted by a psychiatrist named Wankenfuller, a man whose seminal work purported to establish a link between stuttering and familial dysfunction. Lottie, it turned out, was quite the fan of Wankenfuller.

Louis studied Lottie as she spoke. She had nice, even teeth. Her dark eyes were large and lustrous. He wondered if she had a man back in New York. Somehow, he doubted it. No woman in a serious relationship would just up and light out for Montana, alone, for the better part of the summer.

They were just about finished eating. Louis helped himself to another quick glass of the Snake. It was a shame to see the pitcher go to waste, and neither Lottie nor Raul had made much of a dent in it. He asked Lottie about her pending job.

"I'm going to work for a man named Adolph Seebold," Lottie replied. "He has two children. They're both, well . . . challenged."

"*The* Adolph Seebold?" Raul asked. "The entrepreneur?"

Lottie nodded.

Louis, too, was impressed. Seebold was one of the wealthiest men in America. He also was a collector of trophy ranch properties. The crown jewel of his properties was Crooked Butte Ranch, an eighteen-thousand-acre spread on the Clearborn River, a tributary that entered the upper Missouri near where Louis and Raul customarily fished, between Helena and Great Falls. Louis had read a review of a best-seller written by Seebold that dubbed him "the world's most egomaniacal Christian entrepreneur."

"Interesting," Louis said. "I reckon we'll be neighbors shortly, up on the Missourah. Excuse me, I think I need to visit the little boys' room." As he pushed back from the table, Louis realized he was half in the bag. He suppressed a belch.

On his way back from the men's room, Louis stopped to thank the two guides for the drinks. They had some interesting intelligence for him on the Fork, which Louis absorbed while casting glances back at the table where Raul and Lottie were deep in conversation.

The guides told Louis that a study commissioned by the Friends of the Fork Foundation had determined that the puzzling decline in the trout fishery in recent years had been traced directly to dewatering to meet the needs of Idaho potato farmers. The drawdown was inefficient and wasteful. Curiously, though, when the biologists approached the farmers with their findings, it turned out that the potato growers were appalled by the harm they were inadvertently causing and more than willing to work with the foundation to redress the problem.

When Louis returned to his table, he interrupted the conversation. "Well, pardner. I've got some mighty good news about the Fork."

He turned to Lottie. "Excuse us for talking shop, but this is quite a pressing issue."

Lottie listened as Louis related the story. His jowls shook as he said, "Unbelievable, isn't it? There's a real lesson in this, for *all* of us. All it really took to get the deal done was for the two sides to sit down and have a rational, reasonable discussion, driven by solid science."

"Communication," Lottie said dreamily. "It works."

They ordered pecan pie for desert and asked for doggie bags, then spent the rest of the meal talking about agricultural pollution and how it affected western rivers. When it was time to leave, Lottie shielded her credit card invoice as she calculated a 20 percent tip that would have shocked her companions.

Leaving, Louis paused before an animal mount on the wall. He asked Lottie if she could identify it. She studied the jackrabbit with small antlers but was unable to come up with the name for the critter.

Raul came to her rescue. "It's a jackalope," he said. "It's kind of a regional joke played on strangers. There's no such thing, of course. I never understood why people found it funny."

"Okay, okay," Louis said.

Outside, their proximity to a commercial, KOA-style campground called Papa Bear's suddenly seemed very appealing to Raul. Their old campsite near West was quite a drive and perhaps no longer even accessible. Raul also liked the idea of taking a hot shower in the morning. Louis announced his loathing for camping with "the Wal-Mart crowd," but he was exhausted and ready to sleep.

In less than fifteen minutes, they were registered at Papa Bear's main office—identified as the Welcome Den—and in possession of their complimentary bundle of firewood. As they drove around the narrow, twisting road looking for their campsite, RVs loomed all around, their generators humming and lights blazing. But the weary travelers lucked out—their site was at the end of a cul-de-sac in the dirt road. The site was relatively secluded, though they were just across and up the road from the Play Den, a large, common cabin where patrons could shower, do laundry, or while away time—and quarters—in a video arcade. The best feature of their site was the way it backed onto the woods.

Raul adroitly positioned the SUV and boat to form a screen that would adequately shield them from overly friendly senior citizens waiting for the conclusion of the spin cycle, as well as the prying eyes of bony-kneed urchins who had run out of quarters. Then he got out the propane lantern and set it up on the picnic table. Lottie, watching from inside the SUV with Jack, admired how ably Louis unrolled the tent and assembled the shock-corded support poles. He was feeling his drinks and not exactly athletic, but there was still something decisive and adroit about the way he went about his business.

Lottie felt embarrassed about sitting in the heated vehicle while the men set the tents. But she was scantily clad, and the temperature had dropped some thirty degrees since the afternoon in the Centennial Valley. Plus, she was so tired she could barely see. She felt secure and cared for. Little Jack was curled up, sleeping on the driver's seat.

She ran a hand over the goosebumps on her lower thigh. She wondered if Louis had a woman back in New York. Somehow, she doubted it. No woman would have a serious relationship with the kind of man who would just up and light out for Montana, with his buddy, for the better part of the summer—and certainly not for twenty-five consecutive years.

When Louis had the tent up, he courteously shook out and fluffed up his sleeping bag before laying it out for Lottie to use. He even lit and hung a candle lantern, which was about the size of a beer can but gave off a lot of light because it was made of panels of mirrored glass. Raul declared that he was going to reconnoiter and vanished into the night.

Lottie saw Louis approaching and got out of the SUV, still wrapped in Raul's fleece jacket. "My bedroll smells of wood smoke," Louis told her. "I trust you're okay with that?"

"Yes! You're so sweet. I feel guilty, making you sleep in the car."

"I'll be fine."

Louis insisted on holding the flashlight and walking Lottie to the Play Den to wash up. She was surprised to find him waiting when she came back out. Walking back to the War Pony, Lottie felt groggy and cold. She slipped her hand behind Louis's arm for support, stammering that she was freezing.

Lottie collected Little Jack, and they walked over to the tent. Louis explained how to put out the candle lantern. They stood before the tent awkwardly.

"Louis?" Raul called. He was standing in the yellow light on the porch of the Play Den. "Can you please come over here with the flashlight?"

Lottie hastily said good night and vanished into the tent.

At the Play Den, Louis helped Raul find the toenail clippers in the grass. Then he staggered back to the SUV. He was knackered. He barely had the strength to clear room for himself and roll out some blankets. Once situated, Louis glanced out the side window at the tent, which was illuminated from within. Lottie's silhouette was perfectly etched on the thin nylon wall. She was sitting in the lotus position. Suddenly she pulled the sundress over her head, and Louis saw the perfect curve of her breasts. Then she stood up and snuffed the candle. He could see nothing more.

He lay there for some time, thinking about Lottie Moffo. He found himself wanting to know so much more—about her past, her passions, her favorite things. He wondered, Was she wearing a thong?

5

It was almost daybreak when Louis woke, rubbed the vapor off the inside of the window of the War Pony, and peeked out. Moisture rose in wisps off the pine boughs and the green tin roof of the Play Den. The rough-hewn picnic table, chained to a pine tree into which numerous campers and lovers had carved their initials, was glazed with dew. Soon the campers with their fat, sunburned children would be up and about. But for now the campground slept peacefully while birds and red squirrels frolicked in the trees.

Most mornings, Louis was happy to let Raul rise first. He enjoyed waking slowly, to the sound of Raul puttering around camp and the inevitable aroma of a rich coffee brewing. Today, though, he popped out of his bedroll and pulled on some clothes. He set about starting the fire and making coffee.

Raul, shocked by this burst of energy from Louis, emerged from his tent and inquired whether everything was all right. About twenty minutes later, Lottie unzipped the screen of the blue tent. Little Jack darted out, ran at Louis, growling, and locked onto his ankle just above the hiking boot.

"Owwwww . . ." Louis started hopping on one leg, trying to shake the dog off.

Lottie screamed and Jack let go. He scooted over to the drift boat and jumped in, with Louis in pursuit. Louis caught Jack, yanked him out of the boat, and wrestled the dog onto his back on the ground. Jack kicked his legs furiously while Louis put his own face right up against the dog's and made ferocious growling noises.

"Don't hurt him!" Lottie cried.

Little Jack fell still. Then he began whimpering, until Louis finally released his grip.

Lottie crawled out of the tent and stood up. She was still wearing the sundress, but she had a blanket wrapped around her for warmth. She went and stood before the fire. Raul was prepping their breakfast of crepes filled with apricot jam and sprinkled with cinnamon confectioner's sugar. He poured Lottie some coffee. She savored it, commenting on its flavor.

Lottie enjoyed the crackling blaze, even though the sun had already broken over the treetops and the chill was quickly dissipating. She sat down on the giant, strategically placed "fire-watching log" that was a major amenity and selling point for the Papa Bear's Campground chain. This was roughing it, sort of, she thought, despite the giant RV that hemmed them in on one side like the Great Wall of China and the hand-painted sign nearby that warned against radio playing after 10 P.M.

When Louis returned from the Play Den, he was freshly showered, clad in a pale yellow-checked fisherman's shirt with multiple pockets and brand new blue jeans. Raul whistled, arching his eyebrows. He rarely saw Louis in new jeans.

"That's a nice shirt," Lottie said. "You remind me of Ernest Hemingway. He was quite the fisherman, wasn't he?"

"Yes, but not a feather thrower," Louis replied. "He was a blue-water man."

"Thank you very much for making a fire, Louis," said Raul. "It's been a while since we've had a chill burner in the morning. I'm with Lottie, Louis—you do look rather . . . Hemingway-esque."

"You sure are early risers," Lottie said. She set down her coffee and gathered sundry things from the drift boat. She hugged them to her chest as she shuffled off, ducklike, to the Play Den.

Lottie showered, shaved her legs, and washed and dried her hair. She left it unbound, for it was still cool. She donned a white turtleneck and fresh khaki hiking shorts, with thick ragg socks and clogs. She carefully applied eyeliner and a little blush. By the time she returned, the crepes were just about ready.

Lottie took her plate and sat on the fire-viewing log. Louis and Raul had their folding canvas camp chairs, complete with cup holders, set up on either side of her. While they ate, Louis tossed small pieces of crepe to Jack.

Lottie wasn't interested in seconds. She set her plate down at her feet and said, "I've been meaning to ask . . . I've heard of fly fishing, but I never heard of—what is it, *feather throwing?* It has kind of a poetic ring."

"Actually," Louis replied, "it's quite a realistic description of exactly what we do."

Jack gave up on begging from Louis and began to lick Lottie's empty plate, pushing it around in the dirt as he tried to scarf up every bit of maple syrup.

"That's enough now." Lottie jumped up to retrieve the plate.

"As you know, our flies are fabricated mostly of feathers, although they frequently incorporate other equally light materials—sometimes a plethora of them—both natural and synthetic." Louis clasped his hands and rolled his eyes skyward as he organized his thoughts: "But the thing that most laymen fail to understand is the *essence* of the cast. And Lottie, I'll be the first to admit that it is indeed, um, counterintuitive . . . Bear with me."

Lottie nodded. Raul excused himself. Louis continued, explaining that with other kinds of fishing gear, a cast consisted of hurling an object of substantial weight—a lure or sinker—that pulled line off a reel until it lost momentum and fell to the water. But because an artificial fly was virtually weightless, the only way to throw it any distance was by using the flex of the rod and weight of the line. This was why the line made such an elegant, smooth arc in the air as the fly fisherman swished it back and forth.

"Curiously enough, we are really casting the line, not the fly. This makes the fly fisherman more like a cowboy throwing a lasso than a conventional angler. And if a cowboy throws rope, isn't the fly fisherman throwing . . . feathers? Voilà!"

Lottie sat, rapt.

Louis paused, chuckling, then went on: "Frankly, though, it sill amazes me. All the mystique. All the obfuscation. All the mumbo-jumbo that has catapulted fly fishing to such a preeminent place in our culture . . . And what's it all about, in the end? Throwing feathers. I like the term because it, um, rings of existential truth. One might ask, what is it that we're doing with our lives in general, most of the time? *Throwing feathers.*"

"Jeez, Louise . . . I never thought of it quite like that. You express yourself so well, Louis."

Louis waved off the compliment. "Words are my stock in trade. Perhaps you'd like to give casting a try yourself? We could arrange it at Eagletech."

"Try what?" Raul asked, appearing from behind them. He was bare-chested, with a towel wrapped around his midsection, holding his toiletries kit and a change of clothing.

Lotttie turned to him. "Throwing a fly . . . No wonder you're into this—you having been a baseball player and all."

"Baseball," Louis thought, wondering when Raul had told Lottie about his ill-fated career. "He *never* talked about that with strangers. When did he tell her about that?" Raul left to shower.

Louis cleared his throat. "I reckon I'll go start sorting some of the gear in the boat."

"I'll do the dishes," Lottie said.

Later, Lottie walked over to where Louis stood with his forearms resting on the gunwales of the drift boat.

"I have to tell you, I'm very interested in feather throwing," she said. "It seems like quite the art. I admire men like you and Raul."

Louis scowled. After a while, he said, "Raul's a good man. They don't make many like him anymore. It hardly matters what his ex-wives might say about his, um, inability to sustain a serious relationship."

Lottie was puzzled by this observation. She said, "Yes, I'm fond of Raul. Will you really teach me how to cast?"

"We'll see." Louis frostily added, "We've got a lot of ground to cover today. Your car may even be ready by the time we're done at Eagletech."

"I guess that's right," Lottie mumbled. "Jack, get down . . ."

The little dog was up on the picnic table nosing among the newly washed dishes that Lottie had spread out to dry in the sun.

"I need to fish," Louis said. "I guess it's a, um, *man* thing."

"I understand, Louis. I respect your passion."

Raul reappeared, fully dressed, and tried to shoo Jack off with his fedora. But he went about it so gingerly that the little dog easily held his ground.

"Jack!" Louis thundered. He strode over to the picnic table and pointed to the ground. He commanded, "Get down, Jack. *Now.*"

The terrier obeyed immediately.

"Wow," Lottie said. "He's never responded to anyone like that."

"Well, it seems that Little Jack needed to be reminded that there's just one alpha dog around here."

Raul's wet hair glistened in the sun. The comb had left heavy tracks in it. "You mentioned before that you're certified in yoga, too. I've been hearing about this new approach, it's called something like . . . NIA? I forget what the letters stand for."

"Neuromuscular integrative action. It has a little bit of *everything*— tai chi, yoga, tae kwon do. It even incorporates some principles of Feldenkrais and Alexander techniques. I love it."

Louis walked away, saying nothing.

Lottie and Raul continued, discussing various wellness programs that promised spiritual as well as physical benefits. He said he had been looking into a NIA-like practice, Stolt Praxis active meditation. Lottie said she'd tried SPAM but found it quite disappointing. The conversation drifted to Raul's work with the Ironfeather Society of Warriors.

Louis eventually returned. "I hate to break this up. But we need to get over to Eagletech—Ted will be waiting."

"We're talking about the Ironfeather Society," Lottie said, trying to draw Louis in. "Are you involved in the male empowerment movement too?"

Louis looked off into the distance, toward Targhee Pass. He said, "No, I reckon I don't know much about that."

Lottie added, "I thought that, as a wordsmith, you might have some interest in it. Wasn't the writer—what's his name, Robert Bly? Didn't he write a famous book, *Iron John* something?"

"*Iron John and the Male Mode of Feeling,*" Raul chimed.

"I always found Bly's poetry rather jejune," Louis said. "Are you ready?"

———

Louis remained in a funk on the twenty-mile drive west to Eagletech, in Idaho. He stared out the window at the magnificent peaks of the Yellowstone country and half listened to Raul and Lottie's conversation. "Movies," Louis thought, contemptuously. "Nothing but a series of flickering images that rarely lived up to the prose works on which they were based." He could bring nothing to the conversation; it was beneath him.

But Louis's spirits quickly improved as they came around a sweeping downhill curve and he spotted the Eagletech complex sprawled beside the highway about half a mile away. To him, the soaring windows of the outlet store, which was based on a log home design, were like those of a cathedral. Inside, he knew, they would find the finest examples of man's aspirations and vision when it came to quality fly-fishing gear and clothing.

"That's some bird," Raul said, looking up at the enormous hand-carved Eagletech logo, a giant osprey taking wing with a trout in its talons.

Louis told Lottie that Ted Blinken was like a mad genius of rod design. He even looked the part, with his wild, brown hair and owlish, wire-rim glasses. He was bearishly built but invariable dubbed "the Blink." Even the impertinent young guides who teased him at the Denver Fly-fishing Expo about his puffy, crepe-soled Ergowalker shoes all stood in awe of the Blink's skills.

The trio had trouble finding a space in the enormous lot. Hordes of anglers and tourists were milling about, tearing into their shopping bags, comparing their purchases, and talking shop. Louis and Raul got sidetracked discussing the new line of Eagletech reels and forgot about the mayfly in the film canister on the dash, but Lottie grabbed it from the console cup holder as they all piled out of the War Pony.

They went to the office and manufacturing portion of the complex, where they sat listening to a piped-in song, "I'm Holding Out for a Hero," while the receptionist in the lobby talked on the phone.

Louis whispered to Lottie, "Isn't this Muzak horrendous?" He told her that he shared some countercultural musical bloodlines with Ted, who often played the role of Jerry Garcia in a Grateful Dead clone band. Louis respected the Dead, but he was a Bob Dylan diehard.

"I love Dylan," Lottie declared.

Finally free, the receptionist said that Ted was expecting them back in the research-and-design module. They followed her down a long hall, past many people working in cubicles at computers.

Louis whispered to Raul, "They call the design space a 'module.' That's hip, isn't it?"

The module was like a Bucky Fuller geodesic dome, with exposed steel-frame members and a giant, circular skylight. "You can wait for him here," the receptionist said. "He's the only one around today. The rest of the rod team is at a three-day sales conference in Jackson."

Moments later, Ted emerged from the hallway to the toilets. Louis did a double take. His friend must have shed fifty pounds since they were last together at the Denver Expo. He was still hulking, but just a few modest folds of flesh hung over his tight jeans. His trademark beard was gone, replaced by a mustache, and he had an out-of-character, mullet-like haircut. He wore a giant turquoise belt buckle and pointy-toed cowboy boots instead of Ergowalkers.

"Sky," Ted said. He threw his left arm over Louis's shoulder and pulled him cheek-to-cheek. "How are you, man? Sorry to hear about Bowen's boat. I haven't seen or heard from that dude in months."

Louis introduced Raul and Lottie, who complimented Ted on his blue lizard-skin boots. Then Louis asked Ted how he had been doing.

"Dude, It's been busy here—*stupid* busy. Personally, it's been even crazier. I didn't want to get into it on the phone, but Peggy—my wife, Peggy, you know, the Pitfall? She walked out on me, man. Took off with another guy. Can you believe that? What a trip."

"I'm sorry to hear that," Louis said. He turned to his companions and explained, "Pitfall: Pain In The Frickin' Ass Linda Lee."

Ted continued, at a mile a minute: "I know the guy, too. That's the bitch of it. Roger Kekhauser. I fished with him a bunch, man. Dude can cast, but he's a little weak on the fine stuff, Tricos and all that. You know the type—a regular cowboy. Still . . ." Ted momentarily got a faraway look in his eyes. "We hung some big trout on the Madison together—*stupid* big trout."

"The name rings a bell," Louis said. "Didn't Kekhauser tend bar over at Buffalo Jump, that place in Ennis?'

"Right on . . . So get this, Sky—Peggy said this breakup was inevitable because I was 'all about the fishing.'" Ted paused. "'*Hell yeah,*' I told her. 'And you knew going in that I'm all about the fishing. You still married me, right? So what do you think Kekhauser is all about? Harvey wallbangers? White Russians? Foreign movies with subtitles?'"

As the words poured forth, Louis noticed that Ted had a few flakes of white powder on his mustache.

"Sky. When I said that, she threw the friggin' *DustBuster* at me . . ."

"It sounds pretty bad."

"It was bad—at first. Man, it was *real* bad. But then it got good, and it's been good. Yeah, good. Mostly. So-so to good, I'd say . . ." Ted turned to Raul. "*Dude.* I've heard so much about you. Sky told me—you're like his main man."

They all welcomed this abrupt change of subject. While Raul and Ted said what great things they'd heard about each other and went through a laundry list of mutual angling acquaintances, Louis took Lottie aside and gave her a brief introduction to the process of graphite rod manufacturing.

He explained how the graphite fibers were initially set into a blanket, or scrim, made from a fiberglasslike compound. The scrim was then wrapped on tapered rods called mandrels and baked at extreme heat to produce the hollow blanks that ultimately would be fitted with guides, ferrules, reel seat, and cork grip to create a rod.

"Hey, man," Ted interrupted. "So I've got this new lady, Wanda. I'm kind of thinking of taking her on a float next week—for her birthday present. What's the Beaverhead fishing like?"

Raul filled him in.

Louis asked Ted what he thought of the rival Orvis company's new Smartflex technology, but Ted excused himself and went to the bathroom.

"Did you see his mustache?" Louis whispered.

"Peruvian marching powder," Raul said knowingly.

"Jeez, Louise . . . I sure hope Wanda likes fishing."

"Poor guy," Louis said. He turned to Lottie. "He's quite obviously a mess. This really isn't him. I wish we could do something."

When Ted returned, Louis brought up Smartflex again. Ted raced to the freestanding blackboard and, illustrating his comments with fancy equations and parabolic drawings, proceeded to demonstrate that it was impossible to make a rod that adjusted to the casting ability of the user, as Smartflex technology claimed to do.

"It's much as I suspected," Louis said, stroking his chin. "The kinetic energy—as expressed in that flex coefficient equation on the lower right—simply cannot be unleashed below a baseline value . . ."

"Bada-bing," Ted said. "You can judge for yourself. Compare one of theirs and ours. You'll see."

Raul, who was getting itchy because nobody had broached the subject of buying rods at a deep discount yet, diplomatically asked if they might take the conversation to the casting pond. Ted gathered a bunch of the rods loosely stacked in bins by the door. On their way out, Louis started to tell Ted the amazing saga of how the Henry's Fork Foundation had hammered out a win-win situation with the despoilers and polluters of the potato-growing industry, but Ted cut him short in the middle of the story and went off to the men's room again.

Soon Raul was fussing over a demo 5-weight XTC almost identical to the one he'd lost on the Beaverhead. He became perplexed when he found that he slightly preferred the Smartflex equivalent. He told Louis as much while Ted was making another bathroom run but conceded that the Eagletech still beat the crap out of all the other popular models.

Lottie was awed by the way the feather throwers bandied around complicated terms and principles of physics and higher mathematics, but she knew her chances of getting a casting lesson were slipping away. She decided to go check out some fleece jackets and sweaters in the factory store.

"I'll have to walk you through," Ted said. "Security doors."

Ted apologized for not being able to extend a company discount, as he had maxed out his monthly allowance. Lottie took this better than did the men, who saw their hopes of walking away with a few Eagletech reels, and perhaps a handsome belt or rain jacket, dashed. But they were mollified when Ted assured them he could still do something on the rods.

Walking over to the retail store with Ted, Lottie remembered the brown drake and gave him the film canister. He seemed curious about it and promised to examine the insect. By the time Ted returned to the casting pond, Raul had made up his mind. He declared that he wanted to buy the 5-weight Eagletech. He was ecstatic when Ted, unprodded, offered a 40 percent discount.

"Tell you what, man," Ted said. "You like the one you're casting, the demo? Give me two hundred bucks, cash, and you can have it. The offer goes for you, too, Sky."

"That's more than generous," Raul replied. "But I think I'll go with the brand new one. I like having the rod tube, the warranty card, all that . . ."

Ted told him they had all kinds of extra tubes lying around, but Raul stuck to his guns. He wanted a brand new rod, not a demo. Ted gathered up the rods and said he needed to be somewhere soon. He directed them to the accounting department, where Raul could pay for the rod, and buried them in an avalanche of *dudes* and *great to see yas*. They traded soul shakes and bear hugs all around this time.

At the last moment, Louis remembered to ask about boat builders in West who might be able to repair the drift boat.

"Ostopchek relocated to Missoula," Ted said, turning and walking backward as he spoke. "McAtee's closed down—I think. The only one I know right now, man, is Mike Varney. His place is in West, at the end of that street with the Yamaha dealer up top. You know the one . . . Dudes—happy trails."

Lottie caught up with Louis and Raul at the customer service desk of the factory store, where Raul had to go through yet another round of paperwork to get his rod. Leaving him, Louis and Lottie went to look around. He noticed that she had put her hair back up in a topknot and complimented her on the look. Lottie colored and showed Louis her purchases: a periwinkle fleece pullover featuring Eagletech's logo, a set of coasters depicting various trout flies, and buffalo jerky doggie treats. "The fleece was expensive," Lottie admitted, "but 5 percent of the price goes to the Nature Conservancy."

"I approve of your conscientiousness, Lottie. But don't you think the jerky treats are apt to aggravate Little Jack's intestinal disorders?"

"I couldn't help it," Lottie drawled. "Jack just *loves* jerky."

They went to the reel department, where Louis showed Lottie the latest Eagletech wide-arbor reels with interchangeable cassette spools. He pointed out fine engineering details that only a discriminating eye might appreciate, like Eagletech's use of Allen screws rather than common Phillips heads, and the beveled edges on each of the many aeration holes in the back of the reel cage.

"Look at this," Louis said, forcing Lottie to examine the discreet Eagletech logo on the backside of the reel. "See how this abstract squiggle merely, um, *insinuates* a fish of some sort clutched in the osprey's talons? It's very Paul Klee. That's hip."

"You have an amazing eye for detail, Louis. But what exactly is a 'pawl gear'?"

Louis patiently explained, and then offered to give her a guided tour of the fly section, in which thousands of flies were on display, sorted by type and size, in a row of handsome, antique wooden cases with glass-topped drawers.

"This is quite a comprehensive selection," Louis said. "It may be confusing, but keep this in mind: There are two important insect genera for trout in all of North America—mayflies and caddisflies. If you prefer, the exquisite *Ephemerella* mayflies and the more mundane but considerably more ubiquitous *Trichoptera* caddis." He leaned close and added, "*Tricops,* in the patois."

A college-age youth came over and asked if they needed help. Louis leaned back slightly, eyeballing the clerk as if he were a bug. "Buckaroo—you need to learn that it doesn't behoove an employee in an establishment of this nature to harass or stalk the clientele. If I were in need of help, I would have sought you out. Or did you mistake me for a rank beginner or some other easy mark?"

Mumbling apologies, the kid retreated.

Louis turned back to Lottie. "I have a real thing about pushy sales clerks." He then went on to explain that in contrast to the lovely mayfly, the caddis featured a delta-shaped wing that it carried folded like a teensy pup tent when it wasn't flying. Caddis also tolerated warmer and marginally less pure water, and they tended to be drab and almost dusty looking. Such differences made it child's play to tell the insects apart, and that was of great value to anglers, particularly novices. In general, though, the *Tricops* was a far, far less sexy insect than the *Ephemerella.*

Lottie spotted Raul in the distance, talking to a tall, thin, gray-haired man in the shoe department.

"Besides," Louis said quite seriously, "when it comes to the critical environmental issue of water quality, the mayfly—not the black rhino, the greater kudu, or the minke whale—is the threatened creature from which we *Homo sapiens* ought to be taking our cues. These ineffable creatures are the canaries in the gold mine of industrialized, polluting society."

Louis poked around. "Ah, now here's a foam ant—clearly the same creature as the common carpenter ant."

"What's the Latin name for that one?" Lottie said, testing him.

"*Camponotus.*"

She didn't let on how impressed she was. But she also felt she knew about as much as she wanted about carpenter ants, so she changed the subject before he could get started. "What did Ted keep calling you? Sky?"

"It's an affectionate nickname that some of my friends use. You may have noticed that the Montana license plate says, 'Big Sky Country.'"

"Oh."

Louis explained that the phrase derived from the title of A. B. Guthrie's famous novel *The Big Sky*. He wanted to return to the fly case, as they had only gotten through the top drawer, but Lottie suggested that they check in with Raul. He was over in the shoe department, engrossed in a conversation with a man he introduced as Ian, a former dental-floss salesman who used to call on Raul at Dent-A-Men. Ian had wispy hair, watery blue eyes, and some kind of flaky red rash on the tops of his hands.

He had just finished telling Raul about his midlife crisis and the dramatic career change that resulted in his becoming one of the top bonsai tree growers in the country, with a flourishing international business. He had plenty of time now for his new hobbies of backpacking and spelunking and had just built a new log home on the nearby road to Madison Junction. He invited Louis and Lottie to join Raul there that evening to "break bread."

On the way out, Raul explained that Ian had expressed an interest in the Ironfeather Society. He had confided to Raul that for years he had been the victim of spousal abuse. Raul wanted to "be there" for Ian and planned to take him up on his dinner invitation.

Louis, thinking *he* needed to be in camp for some pork chops and a good night's rest, said, "This isn't really my bag, Raul. But you need to do what you need to do. You go, and have a good time."

Now they had to deal with the boat. They tried Bowen again from a pay phone. Louis told the answering machine that they planned to arrange for the repair of the boat and leave it for Bowen to pick up at Varney's shop.

The day had flown by; it was already late afternoon. They decided to drop the boat and collect Lottie's Kuntsui so Raul wouldn't have to drive them all the way back to the campsite, which was in the opposite direction from Ian's.

———

Mike Varney's house was a modest one-story building with the name of the business—Mike Varney's Custom Drift Boats—painted on the side of an old double-ender McKenzie sitting on the lawn. The shop was a converted garage behind the house at the end of a long, narrow driveway.

When Raul pulled over, a wiry redhead who looked about sixty came out of the house. He was holding a work boot. He sized up the visitors and carefully took a bite out of the bologna-and-cheese sandwich that he managed to hold, along with a can of grape soda, in his free hand.

"Better bring Little Jack in the car," Louis told Lottie as they got out.

The man sat down on the edge of the porch, set down his soda with the sandwich on top, and pulled on his boot. He sauntered over.

"What in tarnation . . . ?" He had trouble speaking because he'd taken a big bite and the freshly made sandwich was chewy, like gum.

"As you can see, we experienced a mishap of sorts," Louis said.

The man walked over to the puncture. "Shit, you could stick your goddamned head through that sumbitchin' hole."

"But why would you want to?" Raul muttered.

"Looks like somebody shot a goddamned cannonball through her is what it looks like."

"We struck a particularly nasty deadfall," Louis said. "On the Beaverhead."

"Useless goddamned river." The man's forearms had a fine coating of white spray paint. He took out his pocketknife and poked the blade around the splintered wood. "That sumbitch ain't nothin' but a boat killer."

"It gets worse," Louis said. "It's not our boat. That's why we're here, Mr. Varney. We have to get it repaired."

"I ain't Varney," the man said. He whistled. "This sumbitchin' gunwale's all shot to hell, too."

When pressed, the man explained that he was just painting the interior of the house. Mike Varney was up floating the Smith River, although he was due back any time now. The painter lost interest and wandered back into the house.

"I can't ba-ba-ba-believe it," Raul said. "I'm sa-sa-sa-sa-so sick of this. I'm sa-sa-sa-sa-sick of towing this boat around. What're we going to do now?"

After conferring, Louis and Raul decided that it was silly to wait for Varney. They would return and drop off the boat in the morning on their way to Goat Creek.

———

By the time they got back to Laddie's garage, it was almost five. Chuck explained that the Kuntsui was ready to go. It turned out there was nothing wrong with the hoses or gaskets; the fuel pump relay switch had failed and blown a fuse. He told Louis that the ignition system had blown the new ten-amp fuse he put in as well, so he put in a fifteen-amp one and that seemed to do the trick. There were a few others for backup in an envelope in the glove box. He asked if Louis knew where the fuse box was.

"Refresh my memory."

Chuck pointed out the small, black box mounted under the dash near the steering column.

Lottie was relieved that the total bill was a mere $80, including towing.

"Well, I guess this is good-bye," Lottie said to Raul, standing by the drift boat as they waited for Chuck to pull the Kuntsui around. "You know I can't thank you enough, so I won't even try. But thank you." Lottie dabbed at tears in the corners of her eyes, laughing. "I get too emotional, I know."

"Tha-tha-tha-tha-tha-thank you," Raul said. "You're a highly evolved woman. Perhaps we'll see you again in a few weeks' time—up in the Missouri country."

Chuck pulled up in the Kuntsui.

Lottie took a sheet off Raul's dash-mounted notebook and scrawled her cell phone number, the main number at Seebold's Crooked Butte Ranch, and her address back in New York. She added a smiley face. "I have to tell you, Raul," she said, "I don't think you have to search anymore. You've found the warrior within. I can tell. He's gentle—but oh, what a warrior." With that, she flung her arms around his neck.

Louis had a queasy sensation. His mind drifted off and he pictured himself sitting on a handsome Appaloosa horse, looking down at Raul and Lottie, who were standing arm-in-arm on the porch of a rustic homesteader's cabin in a picturesque Montana valley. Louis held the horn of his saddle with one hand, leaned forward, and lightly touched an index finger to the brim of his Stetson. He told Raul and Lottie, the homesteaders, that he'd best be moseying on. He wished them luck, gently spurred the horse, and rode off.

When the reverie passed, Raul was already getting into the SUV. Pulling out, he told Louis to keep the home fires burning—he ought to be back by ten or so.

"Ready?" Lottie asked.

Louis had trouble squeezing into the small Japanese sedan's passenger seat. With much fiddling, it proved adequate.

"Oh, Jack!" Lottie cackled. "Shame on you. It must be the buffalo jerky treats."

Louis noticed the fine down on her thighs. He suggested that she also fasten her seat belt and gave her elaborate driving directions.

Little Jack jumped forward, into Louis's lap.

"I can't believe it," Lottie said. "Jack just loves you."

"Well, I don't love lapdogs," Louis replied. He returned Jack to the backseat, commanding, "Now stay . . . Good boy."

Jack whimpered and Lottie muttered, "You don't have to be that stern, Louis. He's just a little old dog."

"No dog knows it's little."

Lottie had a curious driving style. She drove at breakneck speed, wrapping both arms around the wheel and nearly touching it with her chin as she leaned way forward. She used body English liberally when steering.

"I hope you're okay with my driving," she drawled. "I didn't even get my license until just three years ago."

"I'm fine," Louis said, feeling mildly nauseous.

———

Lottie could feel Louis's warm breath on the back of her neck. It made her feel all tingly inside. He was an exciting man to be around, the type who never asked directions. He stood behind her, reaching around her chest with both arms, much like the proverbial tennis or golf instructor teaching an innocent beauty the intricacies of the swing.

They were on the neatly mown grass out behind their Papa Bear's campsite. The pork chops were marinating, and the water for the mashed potatoes was heating on the grate of the fire pit. The bottle of Double D sat on the picnic table.

Scalloped clouds filled the western sky, tinged pink. It was a still evening, without even a hint of breeze. The smell of hamburgers cooking wafted on the air.

"Now . . . pause . . . lift sharply . . . pause," Louis said. "That's right, now . . . pause, thrust . . . shoot the line. Remember, the key to the cast is a brisk take-up. You want to shoot that line. Now try it again. Just you."

Louis stepped back, watching Lottie cast. He was pleased. She had the fundamentals down pat.

"Don't wave the rod," he cautioned yet again. "Thrust it, with command. Remember, load it, thrust it, shoot it. Load, thrust, shoot . . . Excellent. That's terrific. You're a natural, Lottie."

"You're just saying that . . ."

"Of course not. You have a definite knack."

Lottie was glad that casting wasn't nearly as difficult as she'd imagined. In fact, it seemed quite simple. She felt competent and proud; all her life she had tried obsessively to please teachers. She wondered if Louis found it sexy that she could cast.

Now that they'd been going at it for about forty minutes, thrusting and shooting, she was exhausted. She told Louis she'd had enough.

"I'm glad you decided not to leave," Louis said, breaking down the rod. "It doesn't make sense to drive this beautiful country at night."

They repaired to the campsite. Lottie was happy with another Fanta, while Louis poured himself a jumbo Double D and prepared to cook. He asked Lottie to gather and stage the ingredients that would go into the rosemary-and-Roquefort mashed potatoes.

Louis was surprised how easy it was to be alone with Lottie.

As she followed his detailed instructions, she was half humming, half singing the song she couldn't get out of her head since they'd been at Eagletech, "Holding Out for a Hero."

"You have a lovely voice," Louis said. "Have you done any work on stage?"

Lottie laughed and shook her head no. "I don't even like that stupid song. It's just stuck in my head." She hummed again, then softly sang a snatch:

> "Racing on the thunder and rising with the heat,
> It's gonna take a superman to sweep me off my feet.
> I need a hero . . ."

"Lottie?"

"Yes, Louis?"

"Oh, nothing."

They worked separately. The evening air was warm and soft, without the chill that descends in the high country.

Lottie broke the silence: "So what exactly is it that you do on your website?"

Louis took a long sip of the Double D before he replied: "Various things. I monitor common usage and grammar in the various media, and then I post corrections, critiques, commentary . . . anything that strikes my fancy. I also post a regular weekly essay. I like to think that were it not for me, uncouth journalists, second-rate academics, and literary poseurs of all stripes could have their way with the English language and never, ever be held accountable. Any hack could get away with, say, describing squash as a legume, when in reality it's a gourd. Nobody would ever be the wiser."

"I would have guessed that squash was a legume, too," Lottie confessed.

"I reckon most folks would. That's why my site exists." Louis set down his whiskey glass. "Case in point: Earlier today, I heard you ask Raul, 'Does everyone bring their tent?' You realize, of course, that you used a plural possessive pronoun—'their'—to modify a singular noun. To the astute grammarian, this is an egregious error; it's on the magnitude of saying, 'I haven't never been there before.'"

"I'd *never* say that," Lottie protested, coloring. "That's a double negative. *Everyone* knows that."

Louis rose from the bench. He paced as he spoke, waving the basting brush for emphasis. "True enough. But I wasn't trying to embarrass you. I merely wanted to alert you to a critical weakness in the English language—let me qualify that—in *American English*. Our singular possessive third-person pronouns, *his* and *her,* are gender specific."

He explained how the British solved the problem this presented by incorporating into their language the indefinite personal pronoun, as in "Everyone must bring *one's* tent." And the French have the equivalent in the pronoun *on*. "But we colonial upstarts," Louis continued, "we disdain the effete British construction and pooh-pooh all things French, except, of course, French wines. The price we pay is confusion."

The fire was roaring. Louis knocked down some of the logs to create a bed of hot coals, waving the legionnaire's hat in front of his burning face.

"I have exciting news, though, on that front," he said. "I may have hit upon a solution to the dilemma of the indefinite possessive pronoun." He rose and backed away from the flames. "In fact, I posted my solution on the website just before heading west. I have a strange feeling I may find myself in the midst of a literary firestorm upon returning home."

"You mean you won't go online for weeks, while you're out here?"

"Never," Louis said. "Work is work. Fishing is fishing."

"I don't mean to be nosy," Lottie drawled, "but can you actually make a living doing just that?"

Louis told her about the modest stock portfolio he had inherited and how prudent investing had enabled him to supplement his admittedly meager earnings from the website and various freelance writing jobs, such as writing copy for catalogs. One of his catalog lines, in fact, had recently won an esteemed Best Hook award from the American Society of Catalog Copy Writers. Describing a clever folding cot for an outfit called Home Solutions, Louis had written this hook: "Just think—you won't ever have to make grandma sleep on that blow-up mattress on the floor again."

"It was a dilemma everyone could relate to," Louis said. "Apparently I touched a nerve that triggered a windfall for Home Solutions."

Lottie poked the potatoes with a fork and pronounced them soft. Louis directed her to remove, drain, and partially peel them. Then came the tricky part—co-coordinating the grilling with the blending and mashing.

"I like it when you tell me exactly how to do things," she muttered. "I'm not even sure why."

After a little while, she added, "I'm dying to hear what your proposal for the indefinite personal pronoun was. Are you comfortable telling me?"

"I'd be delighted." Louis began laying the chops on the grill, letting the suspense build. The chops sizzled and created dense, billowing clouds of smoke as the olive oil and other highly combustible, exotic ingredients in the marinade caught fire. Louis backed away, his eyes burning. He removed his glasses and wiped his eyes with his red bandanna.

"I proposed that we adopt . . ." He broke off, coughing from the smoke as dark pillars spiraled upward.

"Wow," Lottie said. "I can really smell that burning coconut."

"I proposed that we adopt the word *om* as our indefinite personal possessive pronoun. That's the *famous om*—the syllable so frequently chanted by Buddhists and other practitioners of the meditative arts. So it would be "Everyone must bring *om* tent.'"

He waited for a reaction, but Lottie merely looked puzzled. As the chops sizzled, the smoke intensified. When the wind shifted, they took refuge upwind by a pine tree.

Louis continued, stopping now and then to dispel the miasma with his legionnaire's cap. The reasoning behind his proposal was simple. These days, you needed something catchy and of-the-moment just to get on the cultural radar screen. He felt that people who fancied themselves political progressives, as well as tattooed, earringed, crystal-worshiping slackers, would love the *om* idea. And because of that alone, the mainstream media would pick it up and run with it.

"Besides," Louis said, "while I'm a Darwin man myself and, as such, have no great use for formal religion, I'm all for incorporating some enlightened Buddhist principles into our materialistic culture . . ."

"Yes!" But a moment later, Lottie's idealism melted away. "But don't you think it sounds a little funny? 'Everyone must bring *om* tent'?"

"A-ha!" Louis barked as they returned to the grate. "Not at all. Here's why."

As he poked the chops and Lottie worked on the potatoes, Louis pointed out the familial relationship between the syllable *om* and the familiar British and French words, *one's* and *on,* that presently served the same purpose. "Nobody ever complains that they're funny," Louis said. "It's merely a matter of familiarity—conditioning, if you will."

"Okay, I'm sold," Lottie said. "And there's no doubt that everyone is trying to get more in touch with . . . *om* . . . spiritual side these days."

"Precisely."

Suddenly a pickup with a flashing blue light on the dash roared up and came sliding to a stop at the campsite. A man leaped out, toting a fire extinguisher. A moment later, a small army of senior citizens appeared on foot.

"What's going on here?" the man with the fire extinguisher demanded.

"We're rustling up a little grub—much as it appears." Louis took measure of the seniors, who had walked right into the camp. "And what, pray tell, is this? Some sort of pensioneer posse?"

The seniors, including two blue-haired ladies in pastel terry-cloth warm-ups, shrank back in fear. An old fellow with giant, liver-colored spots on his bald pate stepped forward. He said, "We're from the American Nomads RV Club. We saw your smoke, young feller, and thought *fire.* So we called Harley here."

"I'm Harley Little," said the man with the fire extinguisher. "Your camp manager."

Louis explained that they were just cooking a specialty dish. He remembered the chops and scampered over and began to drag them off the fire.

"We were concerned about losing our rigs in an inferno," the leader of the Nomads said. He threw a condescending glance at the Kuntsui before adding, "These RVs aren't like tin-box automobiles. You can't just up and drive off in one in case of an emergency. You'd have to remove the levelers, disconnect the hookups . . . We are at risk."

"I'm well aware of how your land yachts operate," Louis said, cutting him off. He sarcastically added, "You needn't fear an *inferno.*"

One of the old ladies, getting a whiff of the rosemary-and-Roquefort potatoes, made some comment on the cheesy aroma in the air. Lottie showed her the pot of mashed and invited the nosy senior to taste the spuds.

"You'll have to excuse us now," Louis said politely but firmly. "We appreciate your concern and thank you for stopping by."

The ersatz fire brigade melted away. Most of the smoke had dissolved by then anyway. But fine fingers of blue haze lingered in the still air over the campsite. When they sat down to eat, Louis produced a bottle of red wine from the whiskey box and declared, "Surprise!"

"Louis! What's the occasion?"

"Your first experience of Montana," Louis replied. "Ample cause for celebration, to my way of thinking." He slid the chops onto their plates, then poured two glasses of wine and raised his in a toast: "Dr. Lottie Moffo . . . To the success of your trip. Welcome to the Big Sky country. It's a pleasure to have you in my stomping grounds."

Lottie giggled and self-consciously added, as they clinked glasses, "To you and Raul. My knights in shining armor."

"I'll hear none of that." Louis went at his blackened chop. It splintered with an audible crack. He said, "The outside has *caramelized* in an interesting way."

Lottie took a bite, careful not to cut herself on a piece of pork. "It's tender inside, anyways. How do you like the mashed?"

"Perfectly executed," he said. "The cheese-to-butter ratio is perfect."

They made small talk about the meal and reviewed the visit with Ted, eventually getting around to clone bands and one of Louis's favorite topics, Bob Dylan. He was amazed that Lottie didn't know all about Dylan going electric at Newport or his motorcycle accident near

Woodstock. Louis quoted some of his favorite Dylan lines, shaking his jowls as he adopted Dylan's phrasing: "The light ain't yellow, it's chicken . . ."

Lottie gave him a searching look. "What does that mean, anyway? I always wondered."

"It's a *traffic* light Dylan was talking about. A yellow light means caution, right? But being yellow also means being afraid, or *chicken*—get it?"

"Well, I know *that*." Lottie still looked puzzled. "So the traffic light is afraid? How can that be? I'm sorry. Traffic lights don't experience emotions. I don't get it. I just don't."

"*Lottie*. It's the *sensibility*. The combination of Dylan's rebelliousness . . ." Louis clasped his hands, rolled his eyes skyward. ". . . And this poetic, Dada-istic thing he does with the language."

Lottie had one of her speechless moments; her head quivered from side to side. She finally said, "I get it. At least, I think I get it."

"Perhaps you need to be a child of the sixties to fully appreciate it." Louis was just about finished with his second chop. When he tried to pour Lottie more wine, she covered the glass with her hand. Suddenly the silence was awkward.

"Dylan, Schmylan," he said. "It's funny, isn't it, how life throws people together?"

They talked about fate and relationships. Louis asked how long Lottie had been married, and she told him seven *long* years.

"So this *gentleman*—your husband—he was a basketball player, I believe you said? Was he especially, um, *tall?*"

"Oh, no. He was five-ten."

"Interesting. Did he have a colorful name—Jamal, perchance, or Carmelo?"

"Dirk." Lottie laughed. She explained that her short ex-husband had been of Irish ancestry. He was a big star as a Catholic prep school player in New Jersey and a solid, small-time college player.

Louis felt relieved. "So he wasn't in the NBA?"

"NBA? Jeez, Louise—don't talk to me about NBA." She leaned over and drawled, sotto voce, "I'll be happy if I never hear that word again for the rest of my life."

Lottie explained that when she met Dirk, he was already a few years out of college but still clinging to unrealistic hopes of becoming an NBA pro. They got married after a whirlwind courtship, before Lottie fully understood that all Dirk really wanted to do was play ball—not coach ball, not sit on the sofa on weekends watching ball. He wanted to *play* ball. So for the seven years that he flailed about in the basketball minor leagues, rarely bringing in enough of a paycheck even to cover the rent, Lottie quietly supported them both.

"Why did you put up with it?" Louis asked.

"Because he really loved it." Lottie shrugged. "I mean, he *loved* it loved it. That can be very sexy."

They fell silent.

She continued: "I have to tell you, eventually it became ridiculous. His idea of a vacation was a trip to the Basketball Hall of Fame. But I learned a lot. Dirk introduced me to yoga. He got into it because he thought it would make him a better athlete. He tried hypnosis, too. And Scientology. He left no stone unturned, but the real problem was simple: He was too short."

"I myself recognized that I was too short for basketball," Louis offered. "But beyond that, I was interested in the life of the mind."

"And bugs." Lottie shivered. Dusk was falling, and so was the temperature.

"And bugs." Louis reminisced about youthful days spent capturing frogs and lizards and various insects that he kept in makeshift cages fabricated from empty creamed herring or gefilte fish jars. "I reckon that was one of the first points of kinship I felt with Meriwether Lewis, a like-minded penchant for collecting and cataloging."

Louis broke the ensuing silence. "Did you and Dirk have any offspring?"

Lottie sighed. "Dirk was enough. I had my hands full."

She picked through her mashed potatoes, locating little nuggets of bleu cheese. She added, "All my life, I've been busy taking care of other people."

"You appear to be freezing," Louis said. "Shall I make a campfire?"

"Yes!" Lottie stamped her feet rapidly. "I have to tell you—I brought some marshmallows. I've never roasted them on a campfire, but I vowed to myself I would do it on this trip."

"Consider it done," Louis said, bowing.

———————

The flames intertwined and rose skyward from the fire pit like twisting orange ropes and gradually dissolved into countless sparks, corkscrewing skyward until they burned out. Louis and Lottie sat side by side on a neatly spread blanket, leaning back against the fire-viewing log, close enough to feel the intense warmth on their faces.

Lottie pulled a flaming marshmallow from the blaze, blew it out, and waited for the black, gooey ball to cool off sufficiently to eat. She was impressed by the woodsman in Louis—he had gone into the forest in the pitch black to cut her a special roasting stick. "Yummy, yummy," she said, simultaneously blowing and contorting her lips as she addressed a hot tidbit. Her eyes were moist and shone darkly in the firelight.

Louis wasn't much of a roasted marshmallow man. He nursed his Double D. He was half in the bag already and vaguely aware that he was starting to slur his words. He tried extra hard to speak normally. In a pensive mood, he opened up about his bohemian college years and his first clumsy thrashings as a writer, telling Lottie about the novel he had started back as a senior at Hofstra, one provisionally titled *The Corrections*—just like the book Lottie was now reading. The success of Franzen's more recent version confirmed Louis's feeling that he had been on to something.

In truth, the books had little in common, for Louis's book, had he ever finished, would have been an extraordinary epic. He wrote 672 pages, barely denting chapter 2—but this was back when, after happily ingesting some sort of psychedelic drug, he could easily write for twelve or sixteen hours at a clip.

The Corrections, by B. Louis Traub, was to be the story of how fame, fortune, and women ruined the life of a proofreader and part-time musician who finally makes it big as a rock star. Louis had modeled his protagonist on Bob Dylan, but there were many autobiographical elements in the tale as well. For example, Louis had been the proofreader for the campus newspaper for two years, until he resigned to protest U.S. involvement in the Vietnam War.

"You really do have a thing for Bob Dylan, don'tcha?" Lottie said, picking up the conversation again as she nibbled at the last marshmallow.

"I even played a little acoustic guitar back then," Louis confided, jocularly adding that, unlike Dylan, he never did go electric. He performed mostly covers of popular songs such as Arlo Guthrie's paean to a pot smuggler, *Coming into Los Angeles.*

"But I changed the famous lines in the refrain," Louis explained. "I went from 'Don't touch my bags if you please, Mister Customs Man' to 'Don't touch my bags if you please, Mister President Nixon man.'" He chuckled. "The crowd ate it up."

"Wow. So you were part of the student protest movement?"

"Those were heady days, indeed." Louis was overcome by a wave of nostalgia. "We believed in all the right things, and we fought for them. We thought we could stop war, poverty, racism . . . I reckon we were a mite naive. We even started a 'free university' for the surrounding community, and it turned out nobody in the community wanted to have anything to do with us. It was a black neighborhood. Most of our neighbors hoped we'd all die in a fire. But so what?"

Lottie, too, felt wistful. "I have to tell you, all my life I wished I'd grown up in the sixties. I wanted to have a Volkswagen beetle with flower decals and peace signs plastered all over it."

"The Volkswagen was indeed a practical vehicle, if somewhat underpowered."

Each of them drifted off to private thoughts, gazing at the fire.

Lottie began humming the tune to the song "If You're Going to San Francisco." She savored her last bit of marshmallow, peeling scraps off the roasting stick. "You haven't told me a thing about your own marriage," she said. "Are you comfortable talking about it?"

"Sure," Louis said uncertainly.

Lottie waited and finally asked, "What was she like?"

"Who? Oh. Naomi. Let me see . . . A pit viper comes to mind." Louis laughed and waved his arm. "I'm being facetious. Sort of. Naomi was a lively, fun-loving, hippie chick. At least, she was when we met. She soured considerably as time went on. Especially after the birth of our daughter, Rachel."

"Did she work?"

Louis explained that Naomi had ambitions as a hatter and speculated that he probably chose her as a subconscious act of rebellion against his mother's lifelong obsession with the Rabinowitzes, acquaintances who lived on Manhattan's Upper West Side and represented everything that Fern Traub aspired to. They had an apartment overlooking Central Park, they had season subscriptions to the opera, they ate Szechuan take-out at least twice a week, and besides being filthy rich, they were outspoken socialists.

The Rabinowitzes, Louis explained, also had a violin-playing daughter, Tara. Fern was obsessed with the idea that Louis and Tara might marry. But Louis never liked Tara. He told Lottie that Tara lacked personality but discreetly left out that she was thin as a stick and flat-chested. Naomi, by contast, had boobs like luscious melons and a flamboyant streak. Louis described her fondness for colorful peasant skirts, above-the-knee boots, and flamenco dancing.

"Above-the-knee boots?" Lottie asked warily. "She was tall, wasn't she?"

Louis nodded.

Louis told her how Naomi had learned to cast, bought her own fishing vest and waders, and even gone west with him the first year they were married. She loved Louis's downtown loft and expected to be friends with tortured poets and other fascinating bohemians. She envisioned taking vacations in places like Florence, where they might rent a villa for a month and immerse themselves in the study of art.

"Naomi didn't really understand that I had no interest in being part of the glitterati. And I wasn't the type to be up by nine-thirty every morning, like some ambitious bond trader. Italy? Why would I want to go to Italy?"

"Because she wanted to?" Lottie said.

"But there aren't any mayflies in Italy," Louis joked. But he turned serious. "Do you want to go to Italy?"

"I have to tell you, I went twice. But mostly to meet family. I never wore those high boots, though. And I never studied art."

"Good for you." Louis added, "Naomi was high-maintenance."

Lottie said nothing.

Louis explained how quickly Naomi had grown disenchanted with the kind of social life he preferred. For he felt that his feather-throwing comrades were more interesting than a bunch of surly, leather-jacketed painters or attention-craving performance artists. "What a bogus art form," Louis declared. "I'd rather watch cloggers than performance artists. But that's just me."

Lottie asked him to help straighten up the blanket. Louis took advantage of the break to pour himself just a snitch more of the Double D. As there was just another finger or so left, he drained the bottle.

"Now Raul has one less thing to complain about," he thought.

When they settled back in, their hips were touching.

"Go on," Lottie said. "I like hearing about your life."

"Well, I have lived, if I shay show myself." It was too much effort, trying to mouth the words properly. "But it wasn't always easy."

"So you took family fishing trips?"

"Yesh. For a brief period, anyway. Day and weekend trips near home. They were fun. But once we got married, Naomi didn't want to pull on the waders."

Louis's head was spinning. He groaned and stood to get away from the heat. He sobered for a moment in the cooler air. He explained how fishing became a symbol for Naomi of all that was missing from her life: the Connecticut country house, Saturday night dinner parties, vacations in palazzi, interesting and perhaps even famous friends. It only made it worse that her own career as a hatter never took off. Instead of a attracting movie stars and other affluent clientele, she was besieged by exhibitionists and other weirdos from Brooklyn and the East Village.

"Louis, you're weaving a bit. Are you all right?"

"Itsch nothing," Louis said.

He sat back down on the log and looked at the fire. He was hot again and felt a little sick. He told Lottie about the night it had all come to a head. After watching Naomi grow increasingly miserable through nine years of marriage, despite their lovely daughter, he couldn't take it anymore. In the course of a horrible domestic squabble, Naomi called him irresponsible and said that somewhere along the line he had stopped growing.

"You shoulda heard her," Louis said. "She looked at me, hishing, 'You've shtopped growing. You're jusht half a man.'"

Louis fell silent.

"It must have been awful," Lottie said. "I have to tell you, I'm not sure I need to hear any more."

"Ha," Louis said. "You know what I did?"

He popped up.

"I jumped up out of the chair where I was shitting, and I jusht shaid, 'But *that* half is mountain man. And that half, *he* jusht keeps growing bigger.'"

Before Lottie could say anything, Louis started making frantic, circular motions with his arms, trying to keep his balance. Then he toppled backward, over the log and onto his back in the dark.

Lottie went slack-jawed, her head quivering from side to side.

6

A red squirrel scampering in the pine above the picnic table let loose a robust call, sounding like a drumstick dragged over a wooden washboard. Another squirrel began chasing it. Lottie sat on the picnic table, Little Jack between her ankles, with a cup of coffee. It was morning and growing warmer by the moment.

Raul approached her. "I'm afraid I have some bad news. There's no hot water or showers until after noon. We need to be on the road well before then."

"Jeez. I need to shower."

"Not to worry," Raul said. "I can hang one of the Sunshowers in the woods for you. It's secluded back there. Are you okay with that?"

"Sure," she said, smiling. "Nothing like roughing it."

Louis was still sleeping in the blue tent nearby, occasionally issuing strange noises.

Lottie filled Raul in on the events of the previous evening—about the pork chop inferno and the senior brigade, about how Louis finally passed out, leaving Lottie to trundle him off to the blue tent, which they ended up sharing for the night. She said, "He was so drunk, I had to take his boots off for him. He was like a giant baby."

"Yes," Raul replied. "He can be quite childlike."

Lottie cackled. She planned to head north later in the morning, hoping to do some wildlife viewing and general exploring. She still had two full days before she had to report at Seebold's Crooked Butte Ranch.

Raul described his visit with Ian. It had been quite a posh dinner party, attended by a fascinating group, including an importer of medicinal crystals and a man who described himself as a wizard. Ian, it turned out, was contemplating scaling back the bonsai business to devote more time to his growing interest in shamanism.

This was a subject about which Raul knew a thing or two, thanks to an Ironfeather Society seminar he once attended. Raul and a dozen other men sat around naked in a sweat lodge, frequently flogging each other with switches, banging on homemade drums, and sucking on specially selected desert herbs and roots that were said by some to give men visions—something Raul could not verify, as the bitter roots he ingested gave him only an annoying case of heartburn.

Suddenly the squirrels raced down the tree trunk and began dashing about. Little Jack leaped off the bench and commenced to whirl in place, as if possessed. Lottie grabbed and held the panting dog still.

Raul held up a gift from Ian, a translucent plastic jug full of thick, olive green liquid. It was some kind of nutritional supplement made from organic spinach, molasses, various herbs, and other secret ingredients—and two tablespoons of squid ink. Raul unscrewed the lid, sniffed the contents, and made a face.

"Shall we try it, Lottie?"

"I don't know." Lottie was skeptical. "This guy, Yoshi, who used to cut my hair? He was into squid ink. I tried it once, and I have to tell you—it was pretty yucky. I experimented with tons of this stuff when my father was sick. Trust me, I know about bark extract, shark cartilage, marrow, whatever."

"What was wrong with him?"

"Cancer."

Raul winced. "I'm sorry."

Lottie's eyes welled up. She exhaled heavily. "I have to tell you, I still miss him so much. It's been four years since he died, and I'm still in mourning. I can't help it."

Raul put an arm around her shoulder and comforted her. He asked what Lottie's father had been like. Lottie explained that Aldo Moffo's life had revolved around three things: family, work, and faith. Lottie, the most sensitive—and youngest—of his six children, was especially attached to him.

"He was a short, wiry man," Lottie said. "But in my eyes, he was a giant."

Aldo was diagnosed with cancer shortly after Lottie left her husband, Dirk. It was a double whammy, but Aldo's illness brought out the best in Lottie and helped take her mind off her busted marriage. She became Aldo's primary caregiver—and a rock for the entire Moffo family, including her meek mother, Graziela.

Lottie applied herself to her mission so fiercely that she became the scourge of every cancer specialist in New York. She had no problem waiting on the phone, on hold, for hours. She would show up at any hour on the doorstep of some posh suburban home with a list of written questions for the doctor who lived there. She rode the subway at all hours with armfuls of esoteric medical texts, culled from special bookstores and libraries.

The upshot was that Aldo ended up living for six years rather than the initially projected eighteen months. But the downside was that through all that time, Lottie neglected all her other significant relationships and formed no new ones.

"We have an Ironfeather saying," Raul said softly. "The warrior who neglects to lay fragrant grasses on his own fire soon finds himself with no strong flame to share."

"That's beautiful," Lottie said. "I *am* learning to take care of myself. At last."

"It's an important step."

Lottie brightened. "It was just so hard, for so long. Nobody ever took care of me like my father did. He always knew the answers—to everything I wanted to know."

"Thank you for sharing that with me, Lottie."

Louis poked his head out of the blue tent, muttering, "Mornin', pardner."

When he emerged, Louis was holding his legionnaire's cap, ready for his morning water-jug routine. His complexion, though, was gray-green. He growled, "Hmmm . . . java. Good. I reckon Lottie filled you in on the festivities of the evening?"

"Yes," Raul said.

Louis walked over, unsteadily. His hand shook as he unscrewed the top of the water bottle. He made odd growling noises as he patted his cheeks and eyelids with water. Then he took a long swig and commented that the exquisite taste of Rocky Mountain spring water almost made it worthwhile having a vicious hangover.

"Lottie's volunteered to make French toast for breakfast. Oh—there's no hot water or shower."

Louis diligently set about cleaning his various glasses as Raul told him about Ian.

Then Raul told Lottie that he was going to hang the Sunshowers; Louis could walk her through the preparations for making French toast. Louis continued to futz with his sunglasses while Lottie went about firing up the camp stove and digging out the maple syrup, vanilla extract, and the critically important almond paste that the men liked in their French toast.

Lottie broke the silence: "I have to tell you. That was fun last night."

"Yes," Louis replied. "I reckon I was due to bust loose. I wonder . . ."

After a polite interval, Lottie asked, "Wonder what?"

"Did I, perchance, engage in any, um, unduly forward behavior yesterday evening?"

"Not at all." Lottie looked at the ground, embarrassed.

Louis sat down on the bench, knees akimbo, and rested his weight on his arms. Noticing the way she handled the skillet, he suggested his own method for melting butter to coat it evenly. Then he said, puzzled, "I seem to remember you fumbling with my shirt."

Lottie colored. "I was just getting you undressed for bed!"

Louis began stammering something about being a gentleman, but she cut him off: "Louis. Stop. Just stop, please."

Louis stood up. He noticed a large tear rolling down Lottie's cheek. At a loss, he retreated to the blue tent and began to break it down. He suddenly felt weak and put it down to his hangover. By evening, he and Raul would be fishing Goat Creek.

Raul came back from the woods. He set about making more coffee while Lottie finished browning the last piece of toast to Louis's specs. He had told her, "Imagine a yellow drop cloth amply speckled with tan paint . . ."

"Very nice," Raul observed. "You're a quick study, Lottie."

On his knees nearby, rolling up the tent, Louis tried to ignore their banter. She said something that caused Raul to throw his head back and laugh. The fantasy Louis had experienced the previous day returned. He saw himself tipping his hat and riding off into the wild, leaving the homesteaders, Raul and Lottie, on the porch of their cabin. This time, she was wearing a red gingham dress.

"We're all set, Louis," Lottie called out. "Breakfast!"

Louis took a deep breath and struggled up from his knees.

He steered clear of the breakfast conversation about the shortcomings of formal religion. Raul admitted to being a lapsed Catholic and described the nuns in the Catholic school he had attended as "torturers."

"They ta-ta-took every opportunity to crack some poor child on his fa-fa-fingertips with a blackboard pointer. I remember Sister Ba-Ba-Boniface made us push all our desks aside. She lined up the entire fourth-grade class against one wall and tha-threw a piece of candy onto the empty floor. We ran and fa-fa-fa-fought to get it!"

"Wow," Lottie said. "That's not a school, that's a zoo."

"I got a ba-black eye once," Raul said, still sensitive to the memory, "diving for a piece of sa-sa-sa-sa-saltwater taffy."

Lottie confessed that her parochial school experience was much more positive and that she still had a very strong faith and frequently attended church. It would have been particularly hard for her to renounce her Catholicism, because Aldo and Graziela Moffo were such an old-fashioned Italian couple.

Louis ate in silence as she went on.

In fact, Aldo had built a small shrine to the Virgin in the Moffos' front yard, which he decorated lavishly every Christmas with a crèche and assorted alabaster figures—the three wise men and the little drum-

mer boy, as well as some personages not usually associated with Christmas, such as St. Ignatius Loyola and Pope Pius XII.

Raul said, "Lottie's father passed away a few years ago, Louis. She's
been through a lot—and look how she's come through."

Lottie colored at the compliment.

"My parents were agnostics," Louis said. "They perceived themselves as intellectuals. At least, my mother did."

If Lottie was curious to know more about the agnostic Traubs, she
lost her chance to inquire when Raul began to vent about his abusive,
alcoholic father. They talked about Raul's childhood learning disabilities
and various other components of his troubled youth, throwing around
acronyms—ADD, DST, MRL—like confetti.

Louis set his plate down on the ground next to his chair and asked,
"Where's Little Jack?"

Lottie started. "Jack?"

They jumped up and began to search. Lottie sensed that something
was wrong. Raul, over by the boat, reported, "He's not here."

"Oh my God, oh my God, oh my God." Lottie was overcome.

"It's okay, everybody, I've got him," Louis shouted. He was kneeling, unrolling the tent. There was a conspicuous lump where Louis had
rolled Jack into it.

Liberated, Jack bounced up and down like a jumping bean, obse-
quiously licking Louis's hands and face. Lottie rushed over and caught
the dog up in her arms. She murmured little nothings in his ear.

As Raul gathered dishes, he told Lottie where to find the Sunshower, hanging some thirty yards along a path in the woods behind
camp.

"Let me help clean up first," she said.

Raul said he was going to gas up and get some ice and antacid
tablets at the convenience store just up the road. If they were on the
road in an hour or so, they'd have plenty of time to drop off the drift
boat and make Goat Creek by around five—plenty of time to make
camp and make the most of the prime evening fishing hours.

"Sounds like a plan," Louis said amiably.

Lottie excused herself to go shower. The men huddled over the map to double-check the route to Goat Creek. Satisfied, Raul left to do the errands.

Alone in camp, Louis surveyed their gear. It was in pretty good order. He wandered toward the woods, thinking he might urinate. But at the fringe of the forest, he heard Lottie humming the tune to "Holding Out for a Hero."

Louis tiptoed along the margin of the woods and found a trail of sorts; the brush all around was dense but not impenetrable. He crept toward a pine tree, beyond which—somewhere—Lottie was showering. Crouching, Louis peered through the sun-dappled undergrowth and pine boughs. He could see the lower portion of Lottie's legs. His heart was pounding in his chest, and his mouth was dry.

The pine needles allowed Louis to move soundlessly. He slowly worked his way around the pine, reaching a spot where he had a more open view. There stood Lottie under the Sunshower, utterly naked, with a little puff of white soap on her mound of Venus. She was lathering her boobs. Her face was wet and shiny.

Suddenly Louis heard a whimper. He saw Jack, but it was too late. The little dog raced toward him, whining. Lottie crouched, looking straight at him. A strangled cry issued from her throat. Louis rose, then everything went black.

By the time Lottie reached Louis, his eyes had rolled back and his arms were in the kangaroo position, hands working like flippers. Louis heard her pleading, "Are you all right? Louis? Louis, please—tell me you're okay?"

"I'm okay," he muttered. Lying there, staring up through the boughs at the Big Sky, Louis felt ashamed. He was aware of Jack licking his face.

Clutching a towel to her chest with one hand, Lottie knelt beside Louis and helped him into a seated position. The ground beneath him was soft. He drank in the soothing, fresh scent of pine needles. Still dazed, Louis leaned back on one arm.

"You don't have to say anything, Louis. Really."

Louis tried anyway but only stammered.

Lottie had one of her slack-jawed moments, head quivering. Then, in an acrobatic move, she rolled, shed the towel, and suddenly knelt before Louis naked.

He sat there transfixed.

Lottie opened her arms wide and shook them, making her boobs jiggle. In a smoldering voice, she said, "Take me, you mountain man. Take me here and take me now."

Panic flooded over Louis. This had to be some kind of hallucination. This was not well thought out or reasonable. But there he was, lying flat on his back, with Lottie naked as a jaybird, perched somewhat precariously on his giant stomach, tearing at his shirt. She was muttering something about fragrant grasses.

———

When Raul got back to camp, he was puzzled to see how little had been accomplished. Neither Louis nor Lottie said much to Raul at first; they went about their little chores, cleaning, packing, asking where this or that went, almost somberly.

"How did you like the Sunshower?" Raul asked.

"Delicious," she said, adding a banal observation about the pleasant water temperature. Then she excused herself to go use the restroom.

When she was out of earshot, Louis said, "Raul. We have to talk."

The two men walked over to the War Pony. Raul leaned against the front fender and asked what was up.

"I've asked Lottie to join us tonight at Goat Crick. She's demonstrated reasonable, um, aptitude for casting. And it would give us an extra hand around camp."

"You have the ha-ha-ha-hots for her, don't you?"

"It's more than that," Louis blurted. He took off his legionnaire's cap as if he had come begging for a favor. "She's, she's my . . . *Sacajawea*."

Raul looked distressed. He could see it now—the three of them on the river. Lottie would need constant advice and guidance, while Louis would be even more inclined than usual to pontificate about every little stinkweed and mica-flecked pebble on the trail. They would be noisy. They would put down every bank feeder within fifty yards of them.

And of course, one of them would forever need to be helping Lottie out—that's just how it was with novices. Someone would have to tie on her fly, take her arm while wading, untangle the leader from around the tip of her rod with a jolly crack: "Oh, it's nothing. It's easier for me to do it, and I'm in no hurry to fish myself . . ." And Raul knew that he would somehow end up being that someone.

And then there was the prospect of that stinky little dog, always getting into the tents, taking a dump by the War Pony, running up and down the bank, scaring the fish.

Raul was on a slow burn. He asked, "How can you do this to me? I thought we were partners. *You* and *me*."

"That we are." Louis magnanimously swept an arm. "This doesn't change very much."

"This ch-ch-ch-hanges everything."

The color drained from Raul's face. Agitated, he began pacing. "And who do you think is going to be the one who teaches Lottie how to tie a blood knot while you fish? Who's going to take charge of her casting?"

"The same person who takes charge of everything," Louis said in a calm voice. "Me."

"You, Mr. Pillow-hugger? You, Mr. Wake-me-when-it's-time-for-coffee?"

"Yes, me." Louis paused. "And frankly, I always thought you took special pleasure in making the java. You needed to be, um, in charge of *something*."

"Oh, really?" Raul crossed his arms and glared at Louis. "Well, Ba-Ba-Ba-Bonaparte—Mr. In-charge-of-everything. Whose vehicle do we use every year? Who has to keep waiting for Mr. Out-of-shape to catch up every time we have to climb an anthill? What about that stupid special crate you make to protect your beloved Double-whatever-it-is whiskey? Who's in charge of lugging that around?"

"Raul." Louis spoke calmly. "You may wear size thirty-two jeans and bear a vague resemblance to some Latino movie star, but who always makes the call when we have to decide about our itinerary? Who assumes the burden of suggesting a new river to fish or exploring for a new campsite? Who invariably steps in to do the cooking?"

"I do *more* than my share of the cooking," Raul protested.

"What about the Missourah cookout with Graham and that crowd? Whenever we happen to have a particularly large slab of meat to cook—a rack of lamb or a succulent crown roast—who always takes over?"

Raul glared at Louis. He kicked the SUV's rear tire and snapped, "Well, I'm sick of flying by the seat of my pants. That's it for me."

In the ensuing silence, they both heard the screen door slam as Lottie emerged from the Play Den.

Finally, Louis said, "It just isn't the same between us."

"No, it's not," Raul replied. "We don't really communicate anymore."

"This isn't really about Lottie," Louis said. He watched Lottie veer off, on her way to refill the water bottle from the nearby pump. "But maybe I should just throw my gear into her vehicle. Maybe it's high time we just moseyed on our separate ways."

"If that's wa-wa-what you wa-want, fa-fa-fine."

Louis felt a pang of remorse. He would so much prefer a roomy SUV to that old beater Kuntsui.

"Remind me to give you the special whiskey crate," Raul said, his voice dripping with sarcasm. "I'd like to see where that will go in a two-door midsize."

"Hey, you two," Lottie said. But her radiant smile clouded over as she realized something was terribly wrong.

"Lottie," Louis said. "I'd like to have a few words with you—in private?"

He took her arm, and they walked to the edge of the woods, out of earshot. Raul closed his eyes and leaned back against the War Pony. The idea of camping and fishing alone at Goat Creek—or anywhere else, for that matter—was highly disconcerting. He couldn't even imagine being in Montana without having Louis decide where to fish, or pitch the tent, or park the SUV.

In the distance, Lottie and Louis stood face-to-face.

Louis made his points with a liberal dose of the body language that was all too familiar to Raul—the outstretched arms, the panoramic sweep, the emphatic shaking of the head and jowls. Lottie stood there, hands on her hips, listening.

"I ca-ca-ca-can do this," Raul told himself, over and over. He closed his eyes and took a few deep breaths. Then he softly began to sing the native song of praise for the Great Spirit: "Wee-ohhh, Wee-oh-ho-wee-ho-way . . ." Perhaps the Great Spirit would hear his words, help him find his way through the smoke that stings all eyes. "Wee-ohhh, Wee-oh-ho-wee-ho-way."

Raul focused heavily on his chanting; he didn't notice that Lottie and Louis had returned until she spoke, briskly. "I'm sorry, Raul. I created this mess. Can we talk?" Louis stood off to the side, looking away.

Lottie took Raul's arm and walked him away from camp. Louis leaned back against the War Pony, closing his eyes. He began to relive the carnal glories he had recently experienced. But his delicious memories were displaced by a growing dread of continuing on without the partner whose values and sensitivities so complemented his own.

"She is my Sacajawea," Louis told himself. "She's my Sacajawea."

Yet as fully as he believed that, Louis wondered how they could possibly fit his gear—the fly-tying kit, the extra waders, the float tube, and the Sunshower—in the Kuntsui. They would have to buy one of those ungainly boxes that attach to the roof, and they would look like out-of-state greenhorns, plodding along in a vehicle festooned with bumper stickers but barely able to pull the hills on I-10 near Helena and Great Falls.

Lottie returned alone. She took Louis's big paw in her hand. Her eyes were moist and shining. She looked at his oval face and bit her lip. "You're a wonderful man, B. Louis Traub. You are wise and witty and knowledgeable—and about so many things it makes my head spin. And what we shared—it was a beautiful and precious thing . . . But I have to tell you, I can't—I *won't*—destroy a great relationship. I am no, no . . . Yoko Ono."

"But—what about us?"

"Here is what we are going to do," she said with authority. "You and Raul are going to proceed as planned. I am going to follow you to Goat Creek and camp with you. But I'm not fishing, and first thing in the morning, I'm leaving for Crooked Butte Ranch."

"Really?" Louis could hardly believe his ears. He couldn't imagine a woman being so open-minded and selfless. He had at least one more night with his Sacajawea without having to give up his friendship—or the comforts of the War Pony.

"I yield to your wishes," Louis said gallantly. In an urgent, hushed voice, he added, "I am yours."

"And I am yours," she whispered, quickly giving his hand a squeeze before she turned and gave Raul an all-clear signal.

Raul advanced toward Louis. Louis walked out to meet Raul. They met halfway, face-to-face. And then they performed a Shoshone embrace, holding each other tight and close for a long time.

Little Jack trotted with anxious, mincing steps from the Kuntsui to the drift boat to the SUV and back again, clearly confused about what to do, as the travelers prepared to roll out of camp.

Louis flicked the key on the Kuntsui to fire up the radio and listen to the weather report. It was favorable. He walked over to Raul, who was just attaching the Sunshowers to the SUV. Lottie volunteered to walk their black plastic trash bag over to the campground's big green Dumpster.

"Louis, would you be kind enough to dig out that piece of parachute cord?" Raul was being even more polite than usual. "The one we always use as a backup to the tie-downs?"

"Sure, pardner," Louis replied amiably. He passed Raul the parachute cord and said, "I'm looking forward to us fishing Goat Crick again. It's one of the first places we fished together."

"I am too, Louis."

An RV now sat idling alongside the Kuntsui, clearly waiting to take over the campsite, for it was just past checkout time. Irritated, Louis remarked under his breath, "I reckon these camping octogenarians figure they'd better make the most of what little time they have left."

Raul jumped down off the rear tire, and Lottie reappeared, ready to go. Louis got into the Kuntsui on the passenger side, and Lottie climbed behind the wheel and turned the key in the ignition. The radio came on and the engine started. So did the wipers, at top speed. Then the seat-belt shoulder harnesses began madly sliding in their tracks, and suddenly the dome light came on while a horrific, acrid smell and blue smoke filled the cab.

"Jeez . . . What's going on?"

"Shut it down!" Louis cried.

It was too late. Every accessory in or on the vehicle was going berserk: The emergency flashers were blinking, the horn was blaring, and sparks sputtered and crackled under the hood as a great, white bolt of electricity shot around the cab of the Kuntsui.

"Abandon the vehicle!" Louis shouted. "Get out while you can!"

"Oh my God! Oh my God!"

Lottie managed to get her seat belt unbuckled; she flung open her door and rolled out. Louis did the same as the Kuntsui was fully enveloped in a haze of stinky smoke. Raul ran over, and Jack, who had leaped from the Kuntsui at the first sign of trouble, now stood in his favorite spot in the bow of the drift boat.

A young man with a mullet haircut, in a sleeveless T-shirt advertising "Stone Cold Steve Austin," appeared out of nowhere. He stood by watching as the smoke billowed upward.

"What happened?" Lottie asked.

"We seem to have experienced some sort of electrical malfunction," Louis said.

The young onlooker interjected: "Dude—you burned out the 'lectrics is what happened. Probably a fuse."

Lottie looked to Louis for confirmation. He experienced a pang of guilt. For a moment, he thought to tell her that upon getting back to camp from Laddie's, he had replaced the fifteen-amp fuse with one of the backup twenty-amp jobs. But he just said, "I believe this young man's analysis is correct."

The kid approached them, saying that he worked as a mechanic at an Iowa Harley-Davidson dealership and knew a fair amount about electrical systems. He cautiously lifted the hood, waving a hand to dispel the smoke and stench still trapped underneath. "Whoa, dude. Tell you what. You got no 'lectrics left—you got zilch."

Lottie looked at Louis for confirmation. Louis looked at Raul. Raul shrugged.

"My guess is that somewhere along the line, a fuse that should've blowed didn't. The system was overloaded." The helpful young man wagged his head at the sad sight of the engine. "Smell that pukey odor? That would be the plates in your battery. You couldn't fry it better at KFC. What's them tubes on the SUV?"

"Rod scabbards," Raul answered.

"What am I going to do now?" Lottie asked. Tears were welling in her eyes.

"Come with us in the SUV," Raul said wearily. "Your car is officially dead."

"She's dead, all right," the youth agreed. "She's about deader than a doornail."

Lottie was forlorn. "You try and you try and then—this!"

"Don't beat yourself up," Raul said with conviction. "It's not your fault."

Louis looked at his hiking boots. "Electrics are very tricky. Especially on foreign vehicles."

"It's going to be all right, Lottie," Raul added. "We'll make sure you get to Seebold's—one way or another."

Lottie dabbed the corners of her eyes with the bottoms of her sleeves. "You are both so supportive. I don't know what I would do without you. You don't really have to take care of me, honest."

They quickly conferred. It no longer made sense to drop off the drift boat; they needed it to store gear. And neither Raul nor Louis was eager to have Little Jack's atomic farts wafting through the SUV's cab every five minutes. They could deal with the drift boat after parting with Lottie. And they could arrange for Laddie to tow away the car and see if it could be salvaged.

When they were done transferring the gear from the burned-out car, Louis asked, "Goat Crick?"

"Goat Creek," Raul replied, accelerating as he pulled onto the highway leading to West Yellowstone.

The joys and rewards of being on the road again helped dispel Lottie's blues. As they left West behind, she regarded the new vistas in the bright, flat midday light. Now and then, Louis pointed out an interesting feature of the landscape or the flora and fauna. He noted the enormous exposures of basement rock and contended that even more than Precambrian Belt formations in southwestern Montana, they told of a planet about which we know so little that it may as well be in a different universe. Some of the rocks in the Beartooth Plateau, he pointed out, were thought to be more than 3.3 billion years old.

Lottie asked what basement rocks were, and Louis explained that they were the various minerals that, cooked and scrambled by volcanic activity and shifting tectonic plates, became massive formations of granite. He reached behind his seat, found Lottie's thigh, and gave it a reassuring squeeze. She briefly kneaded his hand.

"Look, a bunny!" Lottie cried.

"Jackrabbit," Louis corrected, as a hare the size of a poodle bounded from the roadside into the brush. "To a coyote, that's like a thirty-two-ounce sirloin."

Louis explained all about the terrible campaigns waged for generations against the coyote, including the wholesale poisonings and den burnings. Yet the coyote not only survived, it actually flourished. And loath as he was to credit someone he considered a fascist with anything, Louis admitted that President Richard M. Nixon had passed landmark legislation to outlaw the widespread, inhumane use of poison against coyotes and other forms of wildlife considered vermin by ranchers and the despoilers in the beef industry.

"Somebody once told me that Nixon also did good things for Native Americans," Lottie said. "I didn't believe him."

"He did, though," Raul interjected.

"He probably did the right thing for the wrong reason," Louis said. "It was probably some kind of payback for his corporate friends. Perhaps he saw casino gambling or the tax-free cigarette industry on the horizon."

"Maybe he just did the right thing for the right reason," Raul reasoned. "Even though he was Nixon."

"Raul is more conservative than I am," Louis confided.

Lottie slumped back into the seat. They drifted off to their own thoughts. Raul savored the imminent prospect of a new river to search for bank feeders. He glanced in the mirror. Jack still rode proudly, a figurehead in the bow of the drift boat.

After an hour, Lottie said, "Raul? This is embarrassing. But I really need to pee."

The men laughed. Louis asked, "Badly?"

"Yes! Do you think we'll come to a restroom soon?"

Raul said that might be a while. He offered to pull over at a place that afforded reasonable privacy.

"Up ahead, by that old shed," Louis said a few moments later. "Do you need paper, darling?"

"Louis!" Lottie cried.

They pulled over by the rough run-in shed for cows and horses. Raul shut down the engine. When Lottie was out of earshot, Raul said, "You really are head over heels, aren't you?"

"Raul." Louis looked around, as if someone might be spying on them, then whispered, "She's hotter than a two-dollar pistol."

Just about ten miles north, a rugged belt of mountains towered behind the rolling, tawny foothills. Goat Creek began way up among those dramatic peaks, tumbling fourteen miles down into the valley below.

Few anglers knew the great secret of Goat Creek. Once you got above the canyon through which the river fell, pell-mell and virtually unfishable, Goat Creek was a lovely, meandering meadow stream with undercuts and bank feeders. It slipped through a high plateau, and it held a lot of water.

"These posted signs are an unfortunate choice," Louis said, regarding the proliferation of harshly worded, hunter-orange signs nailed to every fence post and scraggly tree along the dirt road leading sharply up through the Goat Creek canyon. "Montana has been, um, inundated with outsiders," he told Lottie. He described the woes wrought upon the Big Sky Country by California celebrities, survivalists, and Redford's "River Runs Through It" crowd.

"Raul and I, we'd never dream of leaving a cattle gate open behind us or a vehicle blocking access to a hay field. But it's a different crowd now. And they're ruining it for everybody."

Raul agreed. He added, "Since it's been a while, maybe we should stop at the Barker homestead—make sure we still have permission to camp and fish."

"An excellent suggestion."

While Louis launched into a detailed account of how they had discovered Goat Creek, Raul concentrated on the narrow road climbing and winding through the canyon. Hundreds of feet below, the only sign of the river at the bottom of the steep slope was the density of brush and trees—willows, cottonwoods, box elders—hiding it from view.

They finally emerged onto the broad valley at the head of the canyon. A brand new, massive, honey-colored log home occupied a commanding position on the high ground across the valley. Raul and Louis groaned simultaneously.

"Another prime example of the Californication of Montana," Louis complained. "See what I'm talking about?"

They drove on, passing some towering formations of pale gray stone on the right. Soon Louis recognized the meadow in which they had camped when they last fished Goat Creek. It looked the same; you could drive off the road on fairly flat ground, make camp, and then walk a few hundred yards to the river.

"It's beautiful," Lottie said, gazing at the meadow with its heathery grasses and tiny blue, white, and yellow wildflowers.

Raul kept driving; it was another two miles to the Barker homestead, a sprawling, low-slung dwelling made of stone. Beyond it, the road petered out to a rough track.

They pulled over next to a carelessly parked old pickup. The place appeared to be deserted, but Louis went up and knocked anyway. There was no answer. By the time they backtracked and made camp, it was almost six.

Lottie, sensitive to being the third wheel, insisted on going along with them purely as a spectator. She might try throwing feathers in the morning, when they had more time.

The men seemed to be in a great hurry as they scrambled to rig up.

"Do you always get so eager?" Lottie asked.

"Look in the air," Raul said tersely. "Da-da-da-da-do you see those insects? There's a full-blown caddis hatch under way." He stood up, folded a bandanna into a triangle, and tied it around the lower half of his face, bandit-style. Then walked away toward the War Pony.

"Raul has this phobia," Louis explained. "When there's an intense hatch, he likes to make sure nothing flies into his mouth or nostrils."

This sounded perfectly reasonable to Lottie, who began to fold her own kerchief. But Louis shook his head and made a circular motion around his ear with his finger. She realized she didn't have to follow suit.

Soon they were walking toward the river, with Raul periodically lifting his bandanna to gulp air, and Little Jack obediently trotting beside Louis. They traversed a long, gentle berm of brush parallel with the river and hit the creek in an open area with a good view in either direction. They were by a swift, shallow run between pools, where a few small fish were slashing at caddis.

"Okay," Louis said. "I guess it's about that time."

"Showtime," Raul said emphatically. "Good luck and adios—I'm heading upstream." He walked briskly to the tailout of the pool above, then dropped to a crouch and adjusted his bandanna. He sneaked along the grassy edge of the river, now and then getting on all fours and parting tall grass. Soon he had scooted out of sight.

Louis and Lottie went downstream a short way to the head of the next pool, where the river came up hard against the far bank and made a sharp turn, creating a deep, black channel. Fish were rising all over, especially in the seam of the current. Picking out a fish, Louis said, "Yes, indeed-y. It is *showtime.*"

The light was ripening; the sun was about to drop behind rock formations that towered like the pipes of a giant organ across the river. A chill rose from the water. Lottie was glad to be wearing an extra layer under her new Eagletech fleece. She sat down on a bleached log on the bank, Little Jack in her lap, while Louis waded into the water.

Louis dropped the first fly he selected into the river. He stabbed at it a few times, lurching downstream, but never recovered it. He looked back at Lottie and shrugged. She laughed; he looked so sheepish.

Soon he had a fly tied on. When the fish he had targeted rose within casting range, he pointed his rod tip at it, gave Lottie a thumbs-up, and began to sneak into position.

When the fish rose again, Louis was all set. He dropped into a crouch, his jaw thrust forward, concentrating fiercely. He held the loose coils of line in his left hand and began to false-cast.

Lottie watched carefully, for Louis had taught her the simple key components of the casting stroke. His own stroke was full of flourishes and embellishments, with a good dose of added body English. "He's so expressive," she thought, "it's almost like modern dance."

"There he is!" Louis called out, lifting his rod as the trout took the fly. The fish immediately cartwheeled from the water and raced downstream. "Whoa, there!"

Lottie jumped up and scrambled down to the river. She watched Louis battle the trout. He handled the rod with authority, putting maximum pressure on the fish without breaking the thin leader. All the while, he was wading back toward Lottie. Three minutes later, he was kneeling at the edge of the water, displaying a gasping, foot-and-a-half-long trout.

"Oh, put him back! Put him back in the water!" Lottie cried, jumping up and down.

"He'll be fine," Louis said. "I just want you to fully appreciate your first Goat Crick rainbow." He pointed to the spotted back of the fish: "Note these handsome vermiculations . . ."

"Put him back," she implored, clasping her hands together.

A thunderous gunshot rent the air.

Little Jack leaped out of Lottie's lap and ran off. Louis lost his grip on the trout, which flopped back into the creek and made a wake as it beelined for deeper water.

Two more shots—heavy and booming—resounded through the valley.

"Jack!" Lottie cried. Terrified, she scrambled into the lee of the tall bank.

"What in tarnation . . . ? It's okay, Lottie. I reckon that's just one of the Barkers, popping an innocent coyote or hedgehog."

Lottie stood up. She knew Jack couldn't be far.

Louis waded back into position. But before he cast again, there was great crashing in the brush upstream. Moments later, a magnificent mule deer buck bounded into view, not fifty feet away. It saw them and veered off sharply toward the road.

Then a fat, little black bear cub the size of an ottoman burst from the brush and raced right by Lottie. She screamed.

Before the echo died, Raul popped out of the bushes at a dead run, holding his red bandanna in one hand and rod in the other. "Run!" he cried. "Ra-ra-ra-run for your life!"

Louis splashed toward shore. Lottie grabbed Raul. He gasped as he spit the words: "They tried to shoot me! I saw the ba-ba-ba-bullets hit the water."

"Who did?" Louis yelled.

Suddenly they heard engines and two ATVs came bouncing over the berm from the roadside. They pulled right up.

"Just what the hell do you think you're doing here?" said a lean, red-haired man, ripping a shotgun out of a scabbard as he dismounted. He wore a black NRA gimme cap, with yellow military braiding on the brim. "Can't y'all read a posted sign?"

Raul began stammering an apology.

"This here is private property. No fishing. Now, what part of '*no*' don't you folks understand?"

"Now just a moment, here," Louis said.

"Shut up, fatso." The lean man poked the barrel of the gun into Louis's belly.

Lottie gasped. Her mouth fell open, and her head quivered from side to side.

"This is a misunderstanding of some sort," Louis said. "Me and my pardner here, we go back a long ways with the Barkers . . . And whom do I have the pleasure of speaking with?"

"Well, this ain't the Barkers' land no more. I've owned it for three years now."

"I see." Louis made a flourish, suggesting that he was willing to let bygones be bygones. "This is an unfortunate situation."

"You bet."

Louis stroked his chin and did nothing to hide his disdain as he asked, "And that structure . . . that, um, log home down the valley a piece—is that yours?"

"That's none of your goddamned business. You got all of ten minutes to get clear out before I shoot you or have you arrested." The man jerked his head toward his companion, who still sat on his ATV. "Armstrong here's the local deputy sheriff."

"Neither you nor citizen Armstrong need feel alarmed," Louis said reasonably. "It was an honest mistake."

"No," the man said. "It was a big, stupid mistake."

"May I ask, sir—are you a native Montanan?"

The lean man ignored Louis's question. "That's your rig up near the road, right? Just make sure it's gone by sundown."

"We can do that," Raul promised.

The landowner sheathed his shotgun and fired up his ATV. He and Armstrong blasted off back the way they'd come.

"Are you all right?" Louis asked Lottie.

"I guess so," she replied, subdued. She was pale, clearly shaken.

"Well, that's that," Raul said.

They stood there for a few moments in silence. There was movement in the brush, then Little Jack emerged, whimpering, and ran over to Lottie. They started back. Raul, the most discombobulated among them, forged ahead, double-time.

Louis ran a suggestion by Lottie. They could head up toward Livingston, just a few hours' drive. They had plenty of places to camp along the Yellowstone River. In the morning, they could head for the Missouri via Bozeman, stopping by Bowen's en route.

"I'd rather that you saw the Absaroka country at its best, in the day-light," Louis said, "but we're somewhat pressed."

"I don't mind," Lottie said. She walked beside him silently for a little ways.

"I have to tell you, Louis, I admire the way you handled that situa-tion back there. You were one cool customer. I'd freak if someone pointed a gun at me."

"Shucks," Louis said, adding in a western accent, "it waren't nothin'."

Lottie squeezed his hand, then made him walk faster to catch up with Raul.

———

Darkness was descending by the time they were loaded up and ready to roll. They were very hungry but unlikely to find any place to eat soon. Although Raul wasn't thrilled by the idea, Lottie talked him into allowing Little Jack to ride in the War Pony. She was worried about how he would react to further gunshots and promised that at the first sign of Jack breaking wind, she would dangle him out the open car win-dow to dissipate the odor. They were under way for only a few minutes when Lottie first was obliged to make good on her promise.

The Goat Creek canyon was dark, and piloting the combined weight of the SUV and the boat down some of the steeper grades was treacher-ous. A few times, the whole rig began to shake and slide sideways under heavy braking. Raul clutched the wheel with both hands and, bug-eyed and perspiring, recited Darby Wingo-isms pertaining to courage and the warrior code.

Once they were clear of the harrowing canyon, the going was easy on the wide dirt road descending the last few miles to the highway. They were almost at the blacktop when the headlights of the SUV picked up a pair of eyes just across the roadside ditch. Raul slowed and aimed the SUV toward the shoulder, flicking on his brights.

Lying down, a coyote was feasting on the entrails of a freshly killed lamb. Its snout and gray face were smeared with fresh blood that glis-tened in the lights.

"Interesting," Louis said.

Blinded, perhaps, the coyote seemed unfazed and unwilling to leave his kill.

"Yuck," Lottie said, shielding Little Jack's eyes. She drawled, "I thought you said coyotes just ate grasshoppers and huckleberries."

"I did, indeed," Louis said. "I suspect that Mr. Latrans here simply had the good fortune to stumble upon an unfortunate creature that had succumbed to some other ailment—foot-and-mouth disease, perhaps, or one of the numerous forms of ovine tuberculosis."

Raul turned the SUV back toward the road and accelerated, leaving the coyote to its feast.

They started north. It was a beautiful night, cool but soft. The sky was carpeted with stars, and open range stretched toward distant mountains on either side of the broad valley. The land lay awash in creamy moonlight so strong that the small buttes and solitary trees cast shadows. Occasionally a pale yellow dot marked the light of a ranch or bunkhouse, usually well back where the valley rose to mountain slopes on either side.

It was a good hour before they rolled into the small town of Pray and, famished, pulled up in front of the Round Up Inn. Lottie read out loud the legend on the portable electric sign in front of the joint: "Eat Here Now or We'll Both Starve." Below, in smaller letters, it said: "Square Dancing Tonight with Fiddler Jake Tait and the Silver Spurs."

It was crowded inside, with almost all the tables filled. Groups of cowboys and roughnecks were gathered around the pool and foosball tables. The sconces on the wall had colored lights, bringing a touch of Christmas in July to the Round Up. The main theme, though, was railroad. In addition to the obligatory moose, deer, and elk mounts, replicas of railcars, equipment, and posters hung from the walls and ceiling.

The band was on a break, but the jukebox was blaring country music. The weary travelers took their seats at a Formica table off to the side from where the Silver Spurs were set up. A passing waitress tossed down some plastic-covered menus produced on an old typewriter that left no holes in the *o*'s.

The pale haze of cigarette smoke hung in the air. The cowboys all had facial hair, and their gals were dressed in gingham, denim, fringed skirts, and other staples of western wear. Lottie felt self-conscious, sensing a message being sent: Real women don't wear fleece.

Louis said something, but Raul pointed to an ear and indicated he could not hear above the noise. Both men ordered buffalo burgers and a pitcher of beer, with a double scotch to start for Louis. Lottie went for a glass of red wine and, with the men unable to hear and veto her choice, she asked for the seafood Newburg.

"How's this for a taste of the true West?" Louis shouted.

Lottie smiled, nodding her head to the beat.

Louis squeezed in an order for another whiskey before their food arrived.

Lottie tried to make herself heard, asking Louis if he square-danced.

"Do I believe in romance?" Louis heard her say. He nodded yes, making a suggestive gesture with his eyebrows.

"Good," Lottie said, sitting back.

While they ate, Raul waved away the smell of smoke, frowning each time. But his spirits soon improved. The band returned, launching into a number, and couples flooded the dance floor.

Raul found himself mesmerized by the band leader, Tait. He looked about seventy. He had a leathery, chestnut brown face, ice blue eyes, and brilliant white dentures. He had cheeks like a chipmunk. He sounded like an auctioneer as he called out instructions to the square dancers, pausing now and then to fiddle.

Raul signaled to Lottie. He leaned over to make himself heard. "I can really feel this old fiddler's chi. What an amazing man."

Lottie nodded. "Yes! He radiates spiritual energy."

She took a last sip of her wine, leaped up, and dragged Louis onto the dance floor. Lottie was quite the square dancer. She expertly placed Louis's arms and hands in the proper position around her waist or on her shoulders and counted out the beats, thus enabling him to get the hang of the orchestrated maneuvers.

Lottie strutted and high-stepped with tango-esque flair. She flung her head back at just the right moments, threw in a pirouette here and there, and added a sprightly little leg kick at the end of each dance move.

Raul watched wistfully. His friends clearly were enjoying themselves.

Inspired by Lottie, Louis lost his inhibitions. He mimicked moves of other dancers and began to improvise. He threw his arms in the air and wiggled his palms, added a hip bump, and even made a whimsical bunny hop out of a quarter turn that all the unimaginative wranglers performed in identical, restrained fashion.

Soon Louis was perspiring heavily. A continual stream of people flooded the dance floor while many stood at the perimeter, watching and smoking or taking sips from long-necked beers or strawberry daiquiris.

The tempo picked up. Like a puppeteer, Tait goaded the men to spin their partners with increasing abandon as he commenced to fiddle like mad. At the very peak of the mayhem, Louis spun Lottie with so much gusto that her clog flew off. It hit a tall, fiftyish blond with a bouffant hairdo like a brick—right smack in the middle of the forehead. The woman shrieked, just as Tait cut off the music with a dramatic flourish.

The entire joint fell silent.

"You little dago bitch," the blond said as she went into a swoon. Her partner, a cowboy built like a walking stick, tried to catch her. But she slipped through his arms and hit the ground with a thud.

The cowboy glared at Louis, lunged, and took a swing. Louis ducked, and the punch caught another wrangler just behind him. Louis grabbed Lottie, and they hit the deck as cowboys poured onto the dance floor, hooting, hollering, and punching.

Somebody rapidly fired a few shots in the air; smoke and the acrid smell of gunpowder filled the air.

Louis and Lottie, clinging to each other, made it to the fire door and ran out, happy to see that Raul was already waiting in the War Pony with the engine running.

Harley Little, manager of Papa Bear's Campground near West Yellowstone, was trying to listen and work at the same time, fiddling with the blue emergency flasher that he was trying to mount on the brand new light bar on top of his pickup. He grunted and slammed the roof with an open palm. "I just can't git that damned wire through the hole whiles I keep the durned fixture in place. I need a couple-three more fingers."

"Tell you what you do." Nathan Nuckel examined one of the fingernails on his nicely manicured right hand. No point getting it dirty with someone else's do-it-yourself project. "You take a foot of string, pass it through both holes, and tie the wire to it. Then you draw it all back through the holes while you hold the fixture still with your other hand. I got string in the car, if you need it."

Little grunted. It was a clever idea. He swiped the sweat from his forehead with his upper arm. He had long, glossy black hair, combed back in a massive pompadour, which is why the campground employees often called him the Fonz. Little's arms were covered with faded tattoos.

Little was growing irritated with this storkish, well-scrubbed know-it-all, Nuckel. He was asking way too many questions about the customers—particularly those folks with the boat who had just pulled out a few hours earlier after one of their vehicles had burned up. Little didn't like investigators or lawmen of any kind. On the other hand, his string idea was a good one.

"Who did you say you was working for?" Little asked.

"It's confidential," Nuckel said, winking. "Nature of the business."

Little was proving a tough nut, unlike the elderly couple Nuckel had interviewed at one campsite, the Bungholzers. Nuckel had won their complete confidence with a bogus business card, complete with an embossed logo, identifying him as a claims adjuster for a fictitious insurance company. Within moments, the nosy Bungholzers were singing like birds, offering information as well as speculation and opinion.

Nuckel had a lot more respect for fellows like Little, but it was folks like the Bungholzers who made his life easier—as long as you took nothing they said at face value. The Bungholzers had exaggerated wildly, taking credit for saving the entire campground from going up in roaring flames after that couple—the fella who talked fancy and the girl with the odd topknot—lost control of their campfire. Nuckel knew

Little's version was more likely true: The folks were just easterners who had funny notions about barbecuing.

One thing puzzled Nuckel, though: The Bungholzers had been unable to identify Bowen Kiick from his photo. But Velma Bungholzer did remember a mysterious third man camping with the couple. They thought he was some kind of Mexican; Nuckel wondered if it were Kiick wearing a serape or some other clever disguise.

He had a gut feeling that the burned-out second car was the key to the whole shooting match. Clearly it belonged to the last person to join the gang—the woman with the topknot. They must have picked her up after leaving Dillon, for there was no sign of a female presence at the campground on the Beaverhead—no dainty footprint, discarded tampon wrapper, or ball of hair stripped from a brush.

The burned vehicle wouldn't be hard to find in a town as small as West Yellowstone. The Bungholzers swore all over creation that the car was an old Chevy Vega, and Nuckel had to take their word on that. The only trace left at the campsite was a large, black oval of charred grass.

Nuckel covertly studied Little until it dawned on him—the camp manager resembled that guy, that TV actor Henry Winkler.

"No offense, Mr. Nuckel. But I ain't no snitch."

"I'm not asking you to be," Nuckel said. "What makes you think these folks did anything wrong?"

"Well, it just don't feel right."

Nuckel said, "Here, let me get you some of that string."

Before Little could decline, Nuckel was into the glove box of his Oldsmobile. He fished out some thin twine and gave it to Little, repeating his instructions.

"Well, I'll be . . ." Little drew the wire through the hole. "You were right, Mr. Nuckel. It works."

"I'm glad," Nuckel replied. "Say, you mind if I have a look at that burned-out vehicle?"

"I sure don't mind. But you'll have to git over to Laddie's garage in West Yellowstone to do that. They hauled it off from here about an hour ago."

Yes, Nuckel thought. It was always like this with the Harley Littles of the world, the working stiffs and straight shooters. They wouldn't rat out anyone, but they'd give you the shirts off their backs if you so much as offered them a smoke—or a piece of string.

"Thank you, Mr. Little. I'm much obliged. Yessireee." Leaving the camp manager, Nuckel muttered to himself, "Damn, you're good."

Part III

"But on the other hand it is a noble river. . . in addition to which it passes through a rich fertile And one of the most beautifully picturesque countries that I ever beheld, through a wide expanse of which, innumerable herds of living anamals are seen, its borders garnished with one continued garden of roses, while its lofty and open forests are the habitation of miriads of the feathered tribes who salute the ear of the passing traveler with their wild and simple, yet sweet and cheerfull melody."

—June 8, 1805,
The Journals of Lewis and Clark

7

Louis lay fully stretched out on his back, hands clasped on his stomach, inside the sleeping bag. He felt pensive, watching the strange shadows cast on the ceiling of the blue tent by a moth zinging around the candle lantern. He closed his eyes momentarily, listening to the crickets chirping and the rush of the river. They were camped on a side channel of the mighty Yellowstone River.

"There are so many things I have yet to accomplish," Louis confessed to Lottie. "I feel a hankering to leave a, um, footprint in these shifting sands, as it were. It may be destined to dissolve in the mere blink of an eye—at least in terms of geological time—but so be it. I still feel that urge."

"I love listening to you talk," Lottie drawled softly. She lay in her own bag, parallel with Louis in the tiny tent. She too was looking straight up. "You have a beautiful way with words."

They had arrived at the campsite, a hidden gem on the floodplain of the Yellowstone River, a few hours after their experience at the Round Up. The rich bottomland in the darkness beyond camp was teeming with bears, coyotes, mountain lions, deer and other game, and upland birds. Spring creeks and meanders off the main river, like the one on which they were camped, threaded through the valley. It was a rare lush habitat for the West, thanks to the Yellowstone.

Louis had pitched the tent on the bank above the side channel because, as he explained, he wanted Lottie to have an experience much like that of the Corps of Discovery when it first explored the Yellowstone on the return leg of Lewis and Clark's expedition. He also wanted privacy, despite Raul's prudent suggestion that they keep the tents fairly close because of grizzly bears. As this was the last night Louis and Lottie would spend together for who knew how long, Louis didn't want Raul privy to the wild cries of passion or guttural noises that might emanate from the tent. For Louis had spent a good part of the previous day on Goat Creek fantasizing about just this moment.

He had pictured himself and Lottie, lying in the blue tent, listening to the sounds of the river and the owls, grasshoppers, and various other creatures of the night. He visualized her compliantly extending her arms upward as he slipped her fleece up over her head, exposing her breasts in the rich candlelight.

Now, though, he felt curiously immobile—more in touch with the innermost recesses of his soul than with appendages and organs situated further south. Although Lottie lay flank-to-flank with him—albeit in her puffy sleeping bag—Louis was abstracted, curiously unable to act on his desires.

"I sometimes wonder, what's the use?" Louis continued. "I don't even have a dry fly named after me. By my age, the incomparable Lee Wulff had originated and made famous the entire *series* of flies that bears his name. To tell you the truth, I'm not even an Al Troth. He's the opportunist in Dillon who created the ubiquitous Elk Hair Caddis—an inelegant, if effective, dry fly."

"But Louis—you're not just a feather thrower . . . not that there's anything wrong with that. You're a writer. A wordsmith. Not long ago, you told me that language matters. I have to tell you, Mister B. Louis Traub—Mister Guardian of Grammar—it does matter. It matters so much."

Louis sighed deeply. "I suppose it really would be preferable to be remembered as a wordsmith—perhaps as a man of letters. The man who brought the pronoun *om* into the language."

"Yes!"

"Are you always so, um, supportive?"

Lottie wriggled in her bag and said, "It's pretty simple for me. I try to give other people the things that I most want myself. That makes sense, doesn't it?"

"Yes—that's a fine sentiment."

"I have to tell you—it doesn't always pay off. But so what? Life isn't perfect."

Louis thought for a while before he spoke. "You know what I find depressing? Lefty Kreh, David Foster, Flip Pallot, John Merwin, John Randolph, Jerry Gibbs, Al Caucci, Monte Burke—all those so-called *experts*. They get to fish full-time."

"If that's what you want to do, go for it. Why not?"

"Oh, do I wish Naomi could hear that!"

It was quiet for a bit.

"You have to let that go, Louis. It's been what, ten years?"

"Twelve. And she's still an unhappy person." Louis paused. "Do you know the definition of an 'expert'?"

He chuckled and finished before she could reply. "A guy more than twenty miles from home with a slide show."

"Louis. Forget Naomi. That was then. This is now. Life goes on."

They lay there for a while without speaking.

"I reckon my big crime was just being myself," Louis said. "She always tried to make me choose, between fishing and . . ."

Lottie waited, but he just said, "This is our last night together."

"I know that, Louis." Lottie sighed. She wriggled again. "Louis?"

"Yes?"

"When you were a campus radical, did you, did you believe in free love?"

"Yes," he replied tersely, "I most certainly did."

"Wow. Did you live with someone?"

"Actually . . . I lived with my parents. Hofstra was primarily a commuter school. May I ask you a question?"

"Yes?"

"What kind of men have you been most attracted to?"

"In high school, I had a thing for geeky boys. Especially skinny ones—with red hair."

"I see. It's funny how people change."

After a while, she said, "What's the matter, Louis? You seem troubled."

He groaned.

"Lottie. I have a confession. Don't be alarmed. This has nothing to do with STDs or anything of that nature."

She waited.

"I lied to you," he blurted. "I'm hoping you might forgive me."

Her alarms went off. She remembered the time she caught Dirk necking in the basement laundry room of their apartment house with the superintendent's sister, a hefty Croatian brunette who fancied red pumps and dramatic embroidered shawls. Bracing for the worst, she asked, "What lie, Louis?"

"My name," Louis said. "It's not really spelled with a *w*, like Meriwether Lewis. It's an *o-u*. As in . . . Joe Louis."

She absorbed this information and said, "That's it? . . . You're sweet, Louis with an oh-you."

"So you're not hurt?"

"Oh-you," Lottie murmured. She popped into a sitting position and stripped the sleeping bag down to her waist. In one motion, she tore the hair thingy out of her topknot and stripped off her nightshirt, flinging it to the side.

Louis gaped at her.

Lottie cupped a hand under each of her boobs and growled like a tiger.

For the next ten minutes, the little blue tent trembled and shook at the edge of the overhang, so forcefully that small fissures opened in the soft soil.

Then it was quiet.

Lottie was the first to speak. "I felt the earth move, Louis. Honest I did."

Louis was panting too heavily to reply, but slowly he got hold of himself. He rolled over, emitting an unusual noise just as the ground abruptly gave way, and the tent and a large portion of the bank slid down to the river twenty-five feet below. The tent finally came to rest at a crazy angle in a pile of dirt and brush at the water's edge. Lottie somehow made a soft landing on top of Louis.

———

Raul woke shortly after daybreak.

After applying some soothing eucalyptus skin lotion, he pulled on his clothes and soft deerskin driving slippers and crawled from his tent. He let Little Jack out of the SUV. When he looked around and saw the caved-in bank, he panicked. Shouting his friends' names, he rushed over and scrambled down to the tent.

"Raul—is that you?" Louis sounded groggy.

"Whhhhat?" Lottie asked sleepily.

Raul tore madly at the zippered entry flap of the tent. He peered in and saw Louis, sprawled naked, with Lottie curled up alongside him.

"Whoop-sy," Raul said, releasing the flap. He took a step back. "So sorry . . ."

"Don't go," Louis said. "We need to get out of here."

Raul stood outside, watching the tent move this way and that as Louis struggled. Eventually he poked his head out. His hair was sticking out every which way. He had scratch marks on one ear and a big hickey on his neck. But his eyes shone and he looked twenty years younger.

Louis winked at Raul. He made an imaginary gun with his fingers and blew on his index finger. They grinned like schoolboys.

When Lottie finally emerged, she had already done her makeup. Her topknot was like a wild fountain, but she was radiant.

They all went up the bank and sat down on the naked tree trunk lying at the perimeter of the campsite.

"I could use a short stack and sausage, drenched in maple syrup," Louis said. "We aren't even prepared for coffee."

"Let's do a full-on breakfast," said Raul. "We have so much to celebrate—after all we've been through in the past twenty-four hours."

"For sure," Lottie chimed in. "But I have to tell you, I'm feeling a little queasy right now."

"It's probably hunger pangs," Louis said. "We'll take care of that."

They relaxed in the sun. They had no more pressing concern than getting to Great Falls by early evening—a cinch.

The campsite provided a great view of meadows pocked with dark patches of woods that stretched all the way to the base of the mountains. The sun glistened on the dew still clinging to the cheatgrass. In the other direction lay the river bottom, with brushy ravines filled with wild grape, plum, and chokecherry.

"I'm glad you're feeling celebratory, Raul. I was concerned that the traumatic events of last night might have impacted you, um, adversely."

Raul nodded, but he didn't explain about the epiphany he had experienced when he saw the joy on the faces of his friends down by the tent. He had thought automatically of Darby Wingo and recalled the 9th Virilian Protocol: "The warrior who draws his bow on fate is doomed to lose an arrow better used on an enemy that he has some hope of defeating."

The wisdom of those words was amazing, he realized. For the romance blossoming between his fishing partner and this sunny, wholesome yoga instructor seemed fated. Who was he to interfere? It was something to which he not only would have to yield, but wanted to yield. He felt a surge of warmth for his companions and focused on sharing their joy. His own role, he knew, as a veteran of the romantic wars, was that of an elder, a counselor in the ways of love.

"Louis? Lottie? I have a fa-fa-fa-favor to ask." Raul waited until he had their full attention. "How would you all feel about calling me Yo-Yo-Yo-Yo-Yova?"

"Yova?" Louis repeated. "Your name is Raul. What's this Yova?"

"It's Ha-Ha-Ha-Ha-Hindu. The closest English word would be something like *elder* or *patriarch*."

"Yova," Lottie repeated. "Hmmmm."

"I don't know, pardner. You're, um, cognizant of the fact that this is Montana, not the Hindu Kush?"

"Yes . . . But please. It would mean a lot to me."

Lottie rose from the log and paced, familiarizing herself. "Yova. Yeah. It has a nice ring . . . Yova. Yova. Yova. There's something gentle and knowing about the word. Yova. It's kind of Zen."

Raul nodded. Obviously Lottie understood.

"It sounds like some sort of dairy product," Louis observed.

"Don't be such a stick-in-the-mud!" Lottie cried. "Besides, it's not really that different from Raul."

The men looked at her quizzically.

Lottie had one of her speechless moments, head quivering. Then she said, "Don't look at me like I'm crazy, Mister Guardian of Grammar. Think about the language. Both names, Raul and Yova, have two syllables. And four letters—two vowels and two consonants."

Louis bowed and made a sweeping gesture: "Yo-va it is."

"Uh-oh," Lottie said, shifting her weight from leg to leg. "I need a restroom. I need it right away."

Before anyone could reply, she shuffled quickly and stiffly toward the brush. She disappeared over the lip of the bank.

"Did you notice how green she looked?" Raul asked.

"Yes . . ."

Lottie called Louis's name from the bushes.

"I'm coming, Lottie. I'm bringing you some paper."

Louis retrieved a roll of toilet paper from the SUV and went to assist Lottie. When they emerged from the brush several minutes later, Lottie clung to Louis's arm, hunched over. He gently led her back to the log and lowered her to a seated position. She melted to her side and lay there, rocking gently and moaning.

Little Jack whimpered. He turned circles at her feet and finally lay down in a tight curl. He groaned and buried his nose between his paws.

"She's really sick, Raul."

"Yova," Lottie said weakly.

"Yova," Louis repeated. "Try to be quiet, Lottie. Save your energy."

She lay there, perspiring heavily. She rolled over and retched.

Louis signaled to Raul, and the men walked away to allow her to be sick in peace. They discussed her condition. It had be some kind of intestinal ailment, perhaps a delayed reaction to her imprudent choice the previous night of seafood Newburg. Now they were in trouble. Louis and Raul had scant medical resources; they were better prepared for a venomous snakebite or severed limb than a stomach bug.

Louis took charge. He decided that they would make a fire and a bed so that Lottie could rest comfortably. He instructed Raul to set up the stove and boil water while he contemplated an appropriate treatment—perhaps the application of a poultice, a remedy favored by mountain men.

"Medicine has changed a lot since then," Raul noted cautiously.

"Yova. I'm a rational man—you know that. So you—of all people—know that I've never been seduced by phony spiritualism of any kind. I have no use for cockamamie superstitions like channeling or Roman Catholicism. But Raul, I know this . . ." He paused, entwined his fingers, and looked up at the sky, as if searching for the words. "I know there's something supernatural occurring right here in my life. Do you recall that the Corps of Discovery almost lost Sacajawea just as they were approaching present-day Great Falls?"

"Really?"

"Lewis managed to save her, but just barely. He treated her with sulfur water from a nearby spring and poultices of Peruvian bark and opium."

"Louis!" Raul rushed to his friend. "It's synchronicity!" The men met in a Shoshone embrace. It was a particularly emotional moment for Raul, as he had just about given up on Louis's ever recognizing that there was far more to life than science and cold reason. There were supernatural realities. They were inexplicable, but they couldn't be ignored. In the crux, life was not a scientific quest but a spiritual one.

Raul cried out, "Your inner warrior lives!"

Lottie had stopped vomiting, but they could her moaning.

Louis was determined. "We can't afford to lose her, Raul. Yova. We have to bring her back to health."

Raul welled with emotion. "I'll do whatever you ask."

Louis instructed Raul to boil water. Lottie didn't need anything as dramatic as a poultice made of opium, or even Peruvian bark; she didn't have a giant, pus-filled abscess or even an infected liver. Intestinal disorders had been the most common illness on the Journey of Discovery, and Meriwether Lewis usually treated them with a very strong tea, often made from whatever herbs and plants were at hand.

Louis decided to make his tea from the leaves and twigs of the abundant chokecherry. While foraging, he also decided that a poultice, though not strictly required, might make Lottie more comfortable and hasten her recovery. It would be easy enough to make one from wheatgrass and watercress, perhaps even some crushed aspirin, all bound together with mud from the river.

By the time Louis returned to camp with all his ingredients, the water was boiling. The fire was roaring, and Raul was softly singing the native song of praise for the Great Spirit as he sprinkled grasses over the flames, praying for healing: "Wee-ohhh, Wee-oh-ho-wee-ho-way."

Lottie leaped to her feet and staggered toward the bushes for a third time. She didn't quite make it. The men graciously walked away.

Next, Louis dispatched Raul to find a spring—preferably one discharging a sulfurous odor—while he brewed up the chokecherry tea in a ceramic bowl. The concoction was nearly black, with bits of organic matter floating in it, including an unfortunate cricket that he plucked out.

Lottie scrunched up her nose at the sight of the beverage, but she propped herself up on an elbow and obeyed when Louis told her to drink.

"It's yucky," Lottie complained.

The fire helped, but she still suffered bouts of the chills. She had convinced herself that she was going to die out there in the middle of the wilderness. She was worried about Little Jack, and in her somewhat delirious state, she asked over and over if Louis was prepared to take care of Jack in the event that she died on the banks of the Yellowstone.

Louis ignored the question, insisting that she was going to be fine—and soon.

"But if I do die," Lottie said for the umpteenth time, "will you make sure Jack is okay?"

Flustered, he finally said, "Yes. Of course I will."

"You see! I *am* going to die," Lottie wailed. "I know you were lying!"

Raul reappeared, toting a filled water bottle, while Louis was trying to calm Lottie. Louis waved him toward the SUV. He ordered Lottie to keep drinking the tea and promised to return shortly. When Louis went to the War Pony to confer with Raul, Lottie crawled away to retch in the weeds again.

Neither Louis nor Raul could tell by smell whether the spring water contained sulfur, but they decided to force Lottie to drink a lot of it anyway to stave off dehydration.

"She's somewhat delirious," Louis observed. "We may need to get her to the hospital in Livingston if she gets worse. First I'm going to apply a poultice."

"Ah-ah-ah-are you sure?" Raul was terrified. "Ma-ma-ma-maybe we should just go to the hospital ra-ra-ra-right now."

"This will help. I'm sure of it . . . So is my inner warrior."

Louis set to work, laying out the ingredients of the poultice on the hood of the car. He kneaded them into a thick, oval pancake, but even the mud and long strands of wheatgrass did not hold the works together. Louis added some Natural Jane's organic blueberry pancake batter, and that seemed to do the trick. He rearranged Lottie's bed and gently laid the poultice on her forehead, explaining that it was a traditional remedy, without spelling out the exact ingredients.

"It feels so nice and cool." Lottie lay on her side, panting lightly.

"Rest now, Little Squaw," Louis murmured.

"Yes . . . I think I feel a little better."

Louis plucked a speck of blueberry out of the batter. He worried that Lottie was so close to the fire that the poultice might begin cooking into a pancake.

"Talk to me, Louis."

Louis told Lottie the story of Sacajawea's illness and how, to this day, tourists could visit Sacajawea Spring, the place where Lewis got his sulfur water for the cure. He said he was a big believer in the curative powers of the waters of the Yellowstone. It had, the Shoshones knew, Big Medicine.

Lottie asked, "What was wrong with Sacajawea?"

"It was probably a severe pelvic inflammation brought on by gonorrheal infection." He hastily added, "I'm sure that we're dealing with something different here." Louis sought to further comfort her by noting the most remarkable aspect of the Journey of Discovery. Only one man had died on the entire trip—and he succumbed to a pedestrian burst appendix.

Lottie, who'd already had her appendix removed, found herself much comforted, and her sickly pallor was fading. The tea seemed to be doing its job, although it had stained her lips and tongue and teeth a curious purple.

She sighed, feeling she was in good hands. She curled into a fetal position and fell sound asleep.

"Yova. Look at the interstices in those clouds."

Raul looked at the white clouds above the Absarokas. They were long and narrow, with fine ribbons of blue visible between them. It was around noon, and they had a lot of ground to cover in the War Pony if they were to make Seebold's Crooked Butte Ranch at a respectable hour.

Lottie sat in the back, wrapped in a blanket. She was still weak but diligently sipped the last of the chokecherry tea. The road atlas was open in her lap. Now and then, she read out a name that struck her fancy.

"Lolo," Lottie said aloud. "Lo-lo-lo, Merrrrrrry Christmas."

Raul laughed, adding, "How lo-lo can you go?"

"I like that," Lottie said. She'd loved this silly map-reading game as a child, sitting in the backseat of the family's blue Ford station wagon. You called out the names of towns on the map, and everyone, including Aldo and Graziela, would try to make a pun of it or use the word in some funny context.

"What's special about those clouds?" she asked idly.

"Those are cirrus clouds, Lottie. They play a critical role in the way our planet stores and circulates water."

Louis explained that cirrus clouds existed between elevations of seventeen thousand and nineteen thousand feet. Like most clouds, they were formed by a phenomenon called wave formation, an energy transfer that occurred at the molecular level. Louis traced the life history of a bead of rainwater—Mister Raindrop, he named it—from the time it began to form to the point where its gravitational properties were so enhanced that it became heavy enough to fall to earth to disperse its energy in the form of rain.

Lottie whistled. "So that's where rain comes from."

"Yes, but where does lunch come from?" Raul asked.

"I'm hungry as well," Louis said.

"Noxon," Lottie read. She cackled. "President Noxon."

"The school of hard Noxon," Raul suggested.

"That's funny. You're good at wordplay, Raul."

Lottie felt a pang of nostalgia for the Moffos' old family Ford, and how the wind howled through the windows back in those pre-air-conditioning days while she tried to fold up a cumbersome road map. She thought about Aldo. She still thought of her father every day.

They decided to stop for lunch in Livingston. Raul rued the fact that they wouldn't have time to visit the wonderful art galleries. Louis wished they had more time so they might call on any number of the literary men who had ranches nearby—Jim Harrison or perhaps even Tom McGuane.

"Do you know him?" Lottie asked. "He used to go out with Susan Sarandon. Or was it Debra Winger?"

"Tom and I haven't actually met. But I would feel no more compunction about calling on someone like Tom than, I presume, he would have about calling on me. Ours is a tightly knit fraternity."

"I think Tom Brokaw just bought a big ranch out here," Lottie interjected. "I read that somewhere."

"I'd like to stop at The Mild, Mild West," Raul said. "Lottie, they do wonderful crepes and latte and serve real gelato. Perhaps some ice cream might help settle your stomach."

"I don't know," Lottie said. "I'm still feeling a little delicate."

Louis said that if they stopped for gelato, they wouldn't have time to visit Dan Bailey's fly shop and Lottie would miss her chance to see the legendary Wall of Fame. The wall was covered with homemade plaques bearing the outlines of giant trout and hand-scrawled statistics relating specifics of their capture. The only conditions for getting on the Wall of Fame were that the trout be fly-caught and weigh over four pounds.

"Do either of you have a plaque up there?"

"Technically," Louis said, "that answer would be no."

"The Wall is from another era," Raul added. "You pretty much have to kill the fish to trace it on a board."

"That's right," Louis said. "Of course, we've both caught plenty of Wall-class trout."

"Of course," Raul added.

"Over four pounds?" Lottie asked.

"Well, yes. In that, um, ballpark." Louis paused. "But Raul and I both eschew scorekeeping of *any* kind when we fish. Angling is a contemplative pastime, almost Zen-like in its serenity. Still, either of us could fish the pants off most of the anglers represented on the Wall. Am I right, pardner?"

"Most certainly," Raul mumbled. "But I still vote for gelato."

Lottie wasn't all that interested in ogling fish tracings. She suggested that they save the Wall of Fame for another time. Louis didn't mind; he enjoyed the occasional focaccia con panna chocolata as much as the next man did.

Lottie regarded the scenery flying past. There seemed no end to the beauty. There was almost too much of it, bathed in clear and crisp light, soaring skyward in the massive, unfinished disarray of cliffs and buttes and forested mountainsides that made the Rockies so impressive.

"It's all like some giant postcard," she said.

"Actually, it's a snapshot," Louis interjected. "I like to think of it as comparable to the photographic image of a wave breaking. These mountains do not stand still for the camera any more than a wave does. They just move far more slowly, at the pace of geological time. They're changing, though."

Lottie viscerally felt the truth of his observation. It was an amazing thing to contemplate, and she was thankful that Louis had made her aware of geological time.

These were exciting thoughts, but the combination of illness, exhaustion, and the squish-squish-squish of the tires over the expansion joints mesmerized Lottie. She read, "Thompson's Driveway," but before

Raul could come up with a pun, the road atlas slipped from her hands; her head rolled to the side, and she was asleep.

———————

The Mild, Mild West lived up to Raul's advance billing. The chokecherry tea had done wonders; Lottie was sufficiently recovered to consume a hot-fudge sundae with rainbow sprinkles. They left the establishment with Louis carrying a large bag filled with sandwiches for later and a to-go cup of hazelnut gelato for Little Jack.

They walked down Livingston's picturesque main drag, where cars were parked at an angle, noses to the curb, facing two- and three-story brick and wood buildings, many with ornate trim, just like in western movies. Because of the drift boat, they were parked a block off the main drag. When they got there, they found a skinny hippie with weathered skin and long, straight, blond hair loitering by the War Pony, examining the rod scabbards.

Lottie uttered a friendly, "Hi."

"What are these sinister instruments?" the hippie asked, gently laying a hand on one of the scabbards. "Would you be military men?"

"Not at all," Raul replied airily. The mistake was understandable, given the olive paint and yellow markings so similar to those found on bazookas or rocket launchers.

The hippie turned to Louis. "Well—you can't blame me for asking. You bear a resemblance to that baby killer Richard Milhous Nixon."

"Beg your pardon?" Louis said, incredulous.

"They're just fly fishermen," Lottie interjected. "Feather throwers."

"I see. Nimrods."

"Little Jack," Lottie cooed, tapping on the window of the SUV to wake the dog.

"I don't see what's so great about this nation. The military sucks, man."

"That may indeed be true, sir," Louis replied. "But examine, if you will, that amazingly accurate, affordable, virtually bulletproof watch on your wrist. Without the miniaturization technologies spawned for NASA, that would likely still be a heavy and cumbersome analogue wristwatch. In other words, it would not be capable of chiming on the hour or acting as an alarm clock. It couldn't tell you the day and date, or the precise time the sun will set, or when the tide will hit dead high."

The hippie seemed to weigh this information seriously before he said he didn't really care what day it was. He wandered off, briefly turning to suggest, "Blow it out yer ass."

In no time, they were again rolling down I-90 toward Bozeman. The men returned to the subject of the Wall of Fame and the feather throwers' ethic, expressing their aversion to crass, commercial enterprises like tournaments, team competitions, big fish derbies, and contests of the kind in which knuckle draggers of every description raced around trying to catch a ten-pound lake trout or walleye with a giant fluorescent tag streaming out of its back—all in order to claim a fancy powerboat, a year's worth of free car washes, or some other prize.

Louis maintained that even when the proceeds from such contests went to worthwhile causes involving children with inoperable tumors, they besmirched the good name of the honorable angling tradition.

"That's pretty militant," Lottie ventured. "I have to tell you, you can't do too much for the children."

"I'm sure Louis meant that metaphorically," Raul said.

"Yes," Louis said. "But it would be more accurate to say I didn't mean that *literally*. *Metaphorically* is a grotesquely overused word." He delved into the nuances of those two words, and the conversation soon evolved into an interstate episode, a high-minded if not entirely focused contemplation of man's capacity—or lack thereof—for communication.

Raul posed a rhetorical question: Was the urge to communicate rooted in the survival instinct, or did it spring from man's nature as a social animal and just happen to help him survive?

Because of her vast expertise in learning disabilities, Lottie brought to this conversation a degree of hard knowledge and scientific evidence to which her more philosophically inclined companions were unaccustomed. She argued that communication was primarily a social function with great survival advantages, not the other way around.

But Louis remained adamant. He dramatically declared his allegiance to Darwin and the facts of evolution, insisting that *all* human characteristics sprang from the struggle to gain survival advantage. "Your interpretation is pleasantly, um, romantic," Louis said. "But it's a tad naive when you consider man's development in the truly big picture."

"I have to tell you, I don't get too involved in the 'truly big picture,'" Lottie conceded. She was suddenly gripped by the irrational fear that she might be missing something or failing to think in sufficiently grandiose terms—much like she had been thinking before Louis introduced her to the concept of geological time. But she stuck to her guns, adding, "I just focus on how people learn—and how they can learn to learn better."

"Bozeman approaching," Raul said, relieved to change the subject.

The town sprawled on a large, golden prairie in the shadow of the mountains, fanning out from the small cluster of mostly brick buildings and railway sidings that constituted the original settlement. Lottie, expecting to find Bozeman quaint, was disappointed when they left the interstate and rolled by a mishmash of strip malls, car dealerships, and housing developments.

Eventually Raul turned onto Wapiti Lane, a road winding back toward the mountains. The houses soon thinned out, and the road ended in a cul-de-sac with three homes heavily shaded by towering pines. "That's Bowen's, the one with the trout weather vane," Louis said, pointing to a dark brown, chalet-style house.

"Doesn't look like anyone's even living there," Raul remarked.

The shades in all the windows were drawn; a sprinkling of pine needles lay over the gravel driveway. Pennysaver newspapers in plastic bags were piled up by the storm door, which had some kind of notice on it. Bowen was the sort who always had stuff lying around—empty dog kennels, aluminum rowing frames, half-pitched tents . . . But the place looked cleaned out.

Louis got out and approached the house to investigate. Little Jack jumped out of the boat and trotted along beside him.

"I don't like this," Raul said. "Not at all."

"It's a pretty house," Lottie observed. "I like those white flower boxes."

Louis got back into the car. "This is quite disturbing," he said. "The notice on the door is for a foreclosure sale. Apparently, there will be some sort of auction of Bowen's home—and all its contents."

"Poor Bowen," Raul said. "We had no idea."

"He had a few Payne rods. I wonder what they would bring?"

Louis and Raul discussed the idea of filing a missing persons report on Bowen but soon came to their senses. In some way or other, Bowen had been AWOL all his adult life. Right now, he could be fishing hoppers on the Green River or dragging waking dry flies for summer-run steelhead on Idaho's Clearwater River.

"What do we do with the boat now?" Raul wondered. "Technically, it probably belongs in the sale."

They decided to play dumb and take the boat up to the Missouri. If they got it repaired quickly enough, they might even get some use out of it. The Missouri between Helena and Great Falls was an easy float, with no canyons or dangerous rapids.

But as Raul pulled around the cul-de-sac, he felt anxious. He sensed that Bowen was in real trouble this time.

Shortly, they were back on I-90, heading for Great Falls. As they neared Three Forks, Louis thought it might be nice to show Lottie the historic place where the Jefferson, Madison, and Gallatin Rivers met to form the Missouri. He quickly forgot about Bowen as he recounted how Meriwether Lewis beheld the confluence early on the morning of July 27, 1805. The Corps of Discovery camped that morning just a short way up the Jefferson, on gravel bars amid cottonwood groves just like the ones that were there this very day.

The men of the corps had been surrounded by rich fields of sweetgrass and other flora that flourished in the lush valley formed by the three rivers. Sandhill cranes chuckled from the sandy bottomland, and pinyon jays screamed at Lewis's men as they made their campfires for a splendid evening repast that included fresh venison and tender blue grouse.

By the time Louis finished, Raul was pulling into the parking lot of the Headwaters viewpoint and nature trail. At the lookout, Louis removed his legionnaire's cap and held it over his heart as they somberly watched the newly formed waters of the Missouri stream by. Lottie began to ask a question, but Louis raised a finger to his lips and shushed her quiet.

The river was brown and strong; boils as big around as manhole covers blossomed on the water and immediately disappeared. The Missouri surged against the sides of towering cliffs the color of caramel and formed small whirlpools that made sucking noises where the currents clashed.

Louis suggested a quick visit to Lewis Rock, the very knob of limestone that the great explorer had scaled to survey the countryside. As they walked, he stopped, stooped down, and pointed at some insects building a pyramid-shaped mound of sand and gravel.

"Western harvester ants—*Pogonomyrmex occidentalis*," he said. "One of but *three hundred* plant and animal species first identified by the men of the corps."

Walking back to the War Pony later, Louis explained how Lewis had decided to split up the corps into two parties at Three Forks, with Clark designated to travel up the Jefferson while Lewis marched on an overland route, looking to make contact with natives.

"Lottie. Given your recent, um, travails, you'll appreciate the fact that Clark became terribly ill before they set out."

"Really?"

Louis stopped. "However, his disorders were quite the opposite of yours. He was severely constipated—"

"Louis!" Lottie colored deeply.

Raul, who had been largely quiet, said, "Louis, thank you for showing us this."

"Not at all. By the way, there's some controversy among scholars about the wisdom of splitting up the corps at Three Forks. Some argue that doing so made each half of the party that much more vulnerable to an attack by unfriendly natives. The explorers just got lucky it never happened."

"What do you think?" Lottie asked.

"Piffle," Louis said with conviction. He struggled to catch his breath on the uphill trail. "Sure, there was luck involved. But luck favors the bold. Personally, I would frog-march all of those do-nothings, second-guessers, and armchair explorers right out of their cozy ivory-tower sinecures for challenging the quality of Lewis's command."

Raul sighed. "We'd better get frog-marching toward Great Falls. Route 287 can be awful slow going."

Back in the SUV, Louis noted that they had now nearly completed a giant circle that began a few days before on the Beaverhead. But it had been well worth it, he added. He turned halfway around and made a suggestive gesture with his eyebrows.

"You silly!" Lottie cackled, dismissing him with a wave.

At State Highway 287, Louis explained, they would peel off and head north, gradually bending westward on 287. They would cross the Missouri at Toston and again at Townsend, just before the river flowed into the first of numerous impoundments, Canyon Ferry Lake. Then they would lose the river again until near Helena and I-15.

After a pit stop for gas, Lottie cracked a Fanta and dove right back into the atlas, absorbed in tracing their route and interpreting the map's curious hieroglyphics. She hungered to know the land and the places Louis spoke of with such easy authority: Deer Lodge, Missoula, Dillon, Chico Hot Springs, Cascade, and Gallatin Gateway.

Lottie read aloud, "Anaconda."

"Anaconda-da-vida," Louis said absently.

"Too good," Raul conceded.

"Wow . . . so that's the famous Continental Divide!" Lottie traced it on the map with an index finger as it wandered down the Rockies.

They made good time, speeding north on 287 along the broad valley of the upper Missouri. The afternoon sun fell upon orderly crop fields and rangeland. Distant mountains were a permanent feature of the horizon, as were straight fence lines and small groves of trees along watercourses or spring seeps where ranchers invariably built their modest, single-story homes.

Louis and Raul began to discuss their plan for fishing the Missouri; soon they were talking hatches and tippet material and whether Pale Morning Dun emergers were fished more effectively right in the surface film or just below it; with strands of Z-lon representing a trailing shuck or without; with a clipped deer-hair post-style wing featuring hackle tied parachute style or a simple cul du canard feather wing, undressed.

Lottie leaned her head to the side and dozed off. Near Townsend, she woke to the sound of her name. Louis was pointing east toward a jumble of mountains, the Big Belt range.

"We're only about eight miles from the Lombard thrust fault," he said, as if the place were a popular tourist attraction. "The Lombard is the easternmost of the many thrust faults in the area."

"What does that mean?" asked Lottie.

"To many geologists, it means the eastern boundary of the northern Rocky Mountains. I'm not sure I would endorse that opinion, but there it is. Another ice cube, pardner?"

"Yes. Thank you, Louis," Raul said.

Louis unzipped the thermal plastic travel bag and removed a large ice cube from a Ziploc bag. He wrapped it tightly in transparent cling wrap and passed it to Raul, who alternately pressed the cube against either eyelid while watching the road with his free eye.

"What's that about?" Lottie asked.

"It's a wonderful trick we use to keep from falling asleep behind the wheel," Raul said. They had learned the technique from an English professor, Graham Cane, a feather-throwing friend from back in the day on the Fork. An all-day pot smoker, the professor was always drowsy and found that the ice cubes helped enormously, in the car or even on the water.

Louis said they soon would be passing White Sulphur Springs, near the notorious Confederate Gulch, where at one time the gravel was so rich in gold that a single pan sometimes yielded as much as $1,000 worth of the precious ore—this when gold was worth less than $20 an ounce. He told how almost all the gold—about $16 *million* worth in 1860s money—was taken from a two-acre area called the Montana Bar.

In the years of the westward migration following the Civil War, the population of Confederate Gulch soared as high as ten thousand, a large portion of which could be located on any given Saturday night in the gaudy bars of Diamond City. But the boom was furious—and fast. By

1870, the gold was gone, and Diamond City was a ghost town with just two hundred miserable souls hanging on.

Lottie searched the map, looking for the names she heard the men bandying about. They soon arced away from the shores of Canyon Ferry, heading for Helena. It was dinnertime. They pulled over to eat at a roadside picnic table, where they were washed over by the periodic *whooooofff* of passing trucks.

The hours spent driving at high speed had left them all a bit punchy; they didn't talk much, not even Louis. Even Little Jack's relentless begging elicited little banter.

North of Helena, the landscape began to change. Rangeland stretched back from the road on either side, rising until it melded into steep pitches dotted with pines, aspens, box elders, and eruptions of stone. The mountains weren't very high, but they were formed on a breathtaking scale, like preposterously large hills featuring high-elevation meadows and gentle, rounded tops—many of them capped with rock formations that were like the cherries on top of ice cream sundaes.

Soon they came to the exit for the Gates of the Mountains, the portion of the river where the Corps of Discovery, heading southwest from the Great Falls and traveling upriver on the Missouri, got their first inkling of the wonders that lay ahead in the Rocky Mountains. The Gates referred to a twisting, steep canyon of Madison limestone.

"Should I tell her, Raul?"

"By all means."

"Hey, what happened to Yova?" Lottie asked.

"Lottie. The diaries describe the Gates as a canyon cut through black rock. Probably volcanic shonkinite—not the white limestone that constitutes today's Gates."

"So?"

"Only this." Louis paused. "While paddle boats ferry gawking tourists to and fro in the area officially known as the Gates, the real Gates, we're reasonably certain, lie some twenty miles *downriver* from here—where the road crosses the Adel Mountains between Wolf Crick and Cascade."

Louis swiveled to see her reaction. Alarmed, he asked, "What's wrong?"

"Nothing!" Lottie dabbed at her tears with a sleeve. She forced a laugh. "Go on, finish your story."

Louis was perplexed. "Is this particular element in the saga of discovery disturbing to you in some way?"

"Oh-you, Louis. Forget it." She composed herself. She began toying with her topknot, winding strands around her index finger. "Tell me, I'm curious."

Louis described the Adels, a volcanic pile that just lay helter-skelter over Cretaceous sedimentary rocks typical of the high plains. Soon, he said, as they entered an area of teetering stone spires and canyons of dark shonkinite, she would see exactly what he meant.

Raul chimed in: "The sweetest thing about all this is our campsite, near Pelican Point. If Louis's reading of the diaries is correct, it's the exact place where the Corps of Discovery camped on July 17, 1804. On their way upriver."

"Yep. Just think, pardner. We'll be laying out our bedrolls there tonight."

"This job," Lottie blurted. "What if I hate it?"

For a moment, Louis had no idea what she was talking about. Then he said, "Don't worry. You'll fit in perfectly, with your progressive ideas on subjects like communication and exercise."

"Thanks for the support," Lottie replied. She was miffed at the whiff of condescension in his voice. "You don't even really care. But then, why should you?"

Louis and Raul exchanged an "uh-oh" look.

"I'm sorry," Lottie drawled. "I have to tell you—I'm just jealous. You're so footloose and free."

A short while later, she said, "Yova? What's a nimrod?"

Louis took the liberty to reply: "I believe the dictionary definition would be something on the order of 'enthusiastic hunter.' Wouldn't you say, pardner?"

Why was Louis suddenly paying so much more attention to Raul? Lottie wondered. He was distancing himself from her. Men were forever fleeing from their emotions that way. But she wasn't going to let that get her down. It was what it was.

"Nimrods," she said, somewhat harshly adding, "yeah, that's kind of accurate. You *are* nimrods."

"Perhaps you'll be able to escape those dim-witted children some evening this week and join us in camp for an elegant repast," Louis suggested. "We can prepare a leg of lamb in your honor."

"That might be nice," she replied.

"There's the Missouri," Raul declared.

"The Missourah! Hallelujah."

In the distance, the Missouri was a shining ribbon winding through golden meadows, its lush islands and banks lined with dense brush and trees with puffy, dark green heads. Lottie remembered the brown, seething river of that morning and remarked, "But—it looks so different. It's so clear and *gentle.*"

Raul explained how large reservoirs like Canyon Ferry and Holter Lake tamed and altered rivers. "Dams are a mixed blessing at the best of times. But the best thing—for us *nimrods*—is the way dams transform rivers into cold-water trout fisheries."

Raul explained how the steady flow of water released from a dam usually came from a valve down near the bottom of the headwall, where water on the reservoir side was sediment-free and frigid.

"I get it," Lottie interrupted. "And that's good for trout."

"You're learning," Louis said, pleasantly surprised.

A moment later, Lottie added, "I apologize, Yova. I can tell you didn't like being called a nimrod."

"It was a bit offensive. It's stereotyping. And I'm sorry for responding with sarcasm."

"What's wrong with stereotypes?" Louis asked. "All stereotypes are based in truth."

"Forget it," Raul said. "You wouldn't understand."

"He's just a nimrod," Lottie said.

"Amen to that," Raul replied good-naturedly.

They pulled off the highway at Craig, a dusty, forlorn-looking town right on the rail line along the river. It was a large block of featureless, one-story homes and trailers, all seemingly held together with a massive web of clotheslines, cables, wires, and satellite dishes.

"Say hello to your new hometown, Lottie. This is the closest vestige of civilization to where you're working."

On the short main street, they passed the combination gas pump, convenience store, and café. The most prosperous establishment, Louis explained, was the Fly Shop, a combination tackle shop, motel, and restaurant frequented by elite feather throwers. Behind the Fly Shop, beside the tracks along the river, was a tavern called Bar. It was a wooden building that had lost almost all vestiges of its original pea green paint.

Lottie was stunned. She was going to work at the ranch of a fabulously wealthy entrepreneur. She had expected the local town to be something more like Livingston.

"I've always approved of these little rail towns." Louis chuckled. "They have real character. More, actually, than you find anymore in the Yellowstone country. Round here, you half expect to see a gunfight on Main Street at high noon."

Gunfight! Lottie wanted to cry.

They slowed to a crawl, checking that no vehicle was approaching from the other side of the long, single-lane, steel bridge over the Missouri.

"The river looks to be in great shape," Louis said.

"Who are all those people?" Lottie asked as she looked downstream.

"Feather throwers," Louis said proudly. "The Missourah is a mecca."

Across the river, they followed the service road downstream. There appeared to be a drift boat every hundred yards or so. Anglers afoot were bunched together at the runs and pools that could be waded.

"Hey, look," Raul said, braking.

Up ahead, a dirt road peeled away to the right and wound its way back between two steep mountainsides. First, though, it passed under a giant archway made from the trunks of lodgepole pines. The legend on the cross member at the top said, "CB Ranch."

———

After negotiating several miles of winding dirt road, and stops at two rustic cabins that were discreet but obvious security checkpoints, the travelers pulled into a drive leading up to an enormous, stately log home artfully integrated into the hillside above the drive. As they pulled up to a parking area, three men popped to their feet off the porch railing above and came down the long, meandering path.

"Howdy, ma'am. Welcome to Crooked Butte Ranch. I'm Ollie—Old Ollie, they call me—and this here is Vern and that's Hank. We'll take your bags and such. Did you have a good trip?"

Louis and Raul got out of the War Pony to help Lottie get her things organized. They noticed a small wagon nearby, set on a miniature cog railway that ran uphill to the side of the house.

"There's Mr. Seebold now," Hank said. He gestured toward the porch and a figure in a white shirt, who waved. "Let me take you up to say howdy."

"Would you please hold Little Jack, Louis? I don't want to make a bad impression."

Louis felt silly holding the tiny dog as he engaged beefy Hank in a conversation about the Clearborn, the river that ran through Crooked Butte Ranch. Meanwhile, the other men transferred Lottie's gear to the mechanical luggage trolley.

"That about does it," Raul said. "You ma-ma-ma-ma-mind if we wait and say good-bye to our lady friend?"

"Sure thing, sir."

They had a pleasant conversation about fishing until Lottie came back down the path. She was beaming. "Mr. Seebold would like you to stay for a drink. He was very impressed with all you've done for me."

Raul and Louis exchanged glances.

"I reckon that would be nice," Louis said. "So long as we don't keep these here boys."

"Don't make no never mind to us," Vern said, stuffing a wad of Skoal into his cheek. He had to be pushing eighty; he was amazingly fit and spry. "We mostly wait on something to do."

The guests followed another of the wranglers up the path, which was lined with colorful flower beds. When Raul commented on them, the cowboy explained that they were *all* indigenous species, including some endangered ones that had been specially cultivated in the CB's block of greenhouses.

The porch looked out on the dramatic, open valley through which they'd just come, ascending to an impressive elevation. They could now see where the Clearborn flowed, across and well back from the road. It looked to be about the same size as Goat Creek.

Louis removed his legionnaire's hat and held it in both hands as he entered the house. Inside, Seebold stood by a great stone fireplace, talking on a cell phone. The room was enormous, with gigantic windows and a soaring cathedral ceiling. From it hung a chandelier made from intertwined elk antlers. Heavy Remington sculptures were positioned here and there amid the elegant furnishings. Almost an entire wall was taken up by a spectacular painting depicting a dramatic encounter at the base of the Rocky Mountains between colorfully dressed Indians and a ragtag band of white men.

Seebold hung up, looked at his watch, and went to greet his visitors. "Adolph Seebold," he said, extending a hand to Raul. "Thank you for getting Miss Moffo here in one piece. It sounds like you had quite the adventure."

Miss Moffo, Louis thought. The image of Lottie cupping her breasts and growling like a cat in the candlelight in the blue tent flashed through his mind. His face felt very hot.

Seebold, who was dressed in an immaculate white guyaberra shirt, khaki slacks, and slip-on Hush Puppies, was a slight, balding man with a neatly trimmed salt-and-pepper beard. He looked to be about seventy, but his pale blue eyes, behind owlish, wire-rimmed glasses, were clear and alert.

"B. Louis Traub. It's a pleasure to meet you, Adolph." Louis spoke forcefully, like a football captain at a coin toss. In a jocular aside, he added, "I'm of Jewish extraction, so forgive me if your name makes me somewhat, um, nervous."

Seebold took measure of Louis before he replied. "Actually, we're Jews ourselves, but I was Born Again, thanks to my wife. Adolph is a family tradition that goes back six generations—to well before the war. Most of my friends call me Dolph."

Louis bobbed his head and said agreeably, "Then Dolph it is."

Lottie winced and glanced at Raul.

A hefty woman in jeans and a western shirt appeared with a tray of assorted cheeses, introduced herself as Babette, and took drink orders. The only one who wanted anything from the bar built into one wall was Louis, who had already scoped out a bottle of aged Balvenie single malt. He requested it specifically.

Louis gestured toward the giant painting. "I approve of that Offerman you have hanging there, Dolph. I've always been partial to *Contact in the Crazy Mountains.* It's a magnificent painting and I'm, um, honored to see it, as it were, in the flesh."

"You know it?" Seebold asked.

"Yes, I know it well. I've always felt this particular canvas represents a facet of the rebellion . . ." Louis folded his hands and rolled his eyes skyward, searching for words. "Actually, the *apogee* of the rebellion against Europe launched by the Hudson River School. It's also Offerman's first real experiment with the sort of mystical realism articulated by his contemporary Blakelock."

"Well put," Seebold said, evidently impressed. "I've always been interested in the roots of abstract expressionism."

"I assume you'll agree, the floodgates were opened by Blakelock's *Buffalo by Moonlight?*"

"Indeed." Seebold briefly stroked the area right below his septum with two fingers, seemingly lost in thought. Then he muttered an apology and unhooked a two-way pager from his belt.

"Irena. Put me in for thirteen minutes on the call to Senator Yancy. Starting at 10:02 P.M." Seebold glanced at his watch. "And while I have you—you may as well write me in for the rest of the hour visiting with Miss Moffo and friends, Misters Traub and Mendoza. That will bring us right to ten P.M. Oh—and for tomorrow, book me an eleven A.M. call to Dr. Fernicola at the Museum of the West. That will be all for today, Irena. Good night."

"My secretary," Seebold explained. "I try to keep a strict schedule."

Babette returned with the drinks.

"That's quite a beverage," Louis said, staring at Seebold's drink. He leaned over and carved off a huge wad of Montrachet cheese. "Is it some sort of licorice?"

"It's a Japanese herbal cocktail. I like it for appetite control," Seebold said. "I don't do the hors d'oeuvres thing anymore." He set the pager on the coffee table, a giant, glass-topped shadow box containing a replica of a trout stream—right down to a beautifully carved, foot-long, wooden brown trout lurking among the colored pebbles.

"I keep a written record of how I spend my day," Seebold explained. "I started when I was thirteen, using a plain blue composition book. It's easier now that I employ someone to keep track for me. For some reason, people have always had trouble believing this. It was the one thing Letterman and Leno and all the rest asked about when I was on tour promoting my autobiography."

"Ah," Louis said, finally making the connection that had escaped him. *"And the Bull Shall Lie Down with the Bear."*

Seebold arched his eyebrows. "You've read my book?"

"Yes," Louis replied. This was a half-truth, for he'd only read a review and then gone scurrying to a local Barnes and Noble, where he sipped a latte and read selected passages without actually buying the book. "I, for one, was particularly impressed by your prognostications of a drastic shift in emphasis to nanotechnology in the chip-manufacturing sector. It's all come to pass, hasn't it?"

"Are you in the financial markets?" Seebold asked.

Raul leaned toward Lottie and whispered, "Louis has always dabbled in the market. He's quite knowledgeable."

But Louis averred, saying, "I have a few modest investments, Dolph. But I've had my heart broken too often by the street to make an occupation of it—if you know what I mean."

"Louis is a wordsmith, Mr. Seebold," Lottie exclaimed. "He has this wonderful website, Guardian of Grammar."

"Pshaw," Louis said.

Seebold cried, "You're joking!"

He stared at Louis in disbelief. "*You're* the Guardian of Grammar?"

Louis was holding a piece of Limburger the size of a golf ball perched on a tiny cracker.

"I stand unmasked," Louis said, popping the hunk of cheese in his mouth.

Seebold leaped from his chair.

"Why I've read your website for years—I'm your biggest fan! If it weren't for you, I would still be saying 'most unique' or sullying a perfectly good noun with the bastardized active verb, as in 'to access.' I wouldn't know the meaning of the Australian expression 'Bob's your uncle,' and I would still be using redundancies like 'fellow countryman'—not to mention outright oxymorons like 'giant shrimp.' I could go on forever. If it weren't for you, I wouldn't know the word *interstices,* and if it weren't for you, right now I'd be saying 'if it *wasn't* for you.' It was you who taught me the meaning of the hypothetical phrase."

Lottie had one of her speechless moments, head vibrating. Even Raul was impressed.

Seebold turned to them. "Do you appreciate what your friend here does? Do you have any inkling?"

"So-so-so-sort of," Raul said.

"Do you know about the whole theory about *Mel Tarto?*"

Lottie and Raul shrugged.

"Oh, that." Louis chuckled. "I'm flattered that you remember, Dolph. Say, do you mind if I freshen up my drink?"

"By all means." Seebold took a small bell from the coffee table and rang it. Babette immediately appeared. "But go ahead, Louis. Tell them."

Louis explained how he had once written a long essay on the ultimate linguistic achievement, blending impeccable logic with lovely sound. As an example, he had cited the Hungarian words for "bra," *mel tarto.* Louis told his readers that the literal translation of those words was "breast holder." He contrasted that precise, descriptive phrase with its opaque English equivalent—the single word *brassiere.*

Lottie listened to Louis, mouth agape.

Louis popped another hunk of Montrachet in his mouth and continued: "Mind you, there is no lascivious subtext here. My only point was that *mel tarto* is refreshingly clear. The phrase is highly phonetic. And it actually has a lovely lilt on the tongue. It represents language at its finest and most lyrical. Say it to yourself—*mel tarto.* Isn't it beautiful?"

"But you forgot the part about the crooner," Seebold interjected.

"Oh, I also suggested that the particular sound of those words was so lovely that they might be the name of a crooner—some romantic soul of Italian descent, like a Frank Sinatra. *Mel Tarto.*"

Seebold turned to Raul. "Isn't that great?"

"I've always kno-kno-kno-kno-known that Louis is a genius with language," Raul said. "But I probably take that aspect of his character for granted."

"Well, that settles it," Seebold declared. "You absolutely must stay tomorrow and fish our river."

Raul and Louis wanted to leap, punch the air, and cry, "Yessss!"

"Pardner?" Louis asked.

"I'd la-la-la-la-love to do that."

"Hear, hear, let's drink to that," Louis said, hoisting his Balvenie. "To the Clearborn. And to our host, the entrepreneur and author."

Seebold looked very pleased. He drained his black shake. Then he rang his bell and instructed Babette to fix up a light dinner for his guests. He returned to the subject of Louis's website, explaining that the qualities that he most appreciated, especially as an entrepreneur, were precision, accuracy, and the ability to see room for improvement where others did not—where others were content or complacent. In fact, his next book was going to be on that very subject.

"Louis," Lottie cried, "tell him about your idea for a new personal pronoun. Tell him about the *'om'* thing you're planning."

By the time Louis outlined the reasoning behind his pending campaign to create a new indefinite personal pronoun, it was well past ten. But Seebold, mesmerized, stayed on.

"Perhaps I'll refresh this," Louis said, rising and heading for the bar. "I see no need to disturb Babette."

The evening went on, and the guests enjoyed homemade black bean soup with freshly baked corn chips, as well as prosciutto and cheese sandwiches on olive sourdough bread.

Raul asked about the CB and its fishable waters. Seebold admitted that he wasn't much of a fisherman. But he believed that the Clearborn was the only stream on the property where either his guests or staff fished. He'd been told, though, that many of his other ranch properties had equally good—if not better—trout waters.

"I've got all the topo and tax maps over there," Seebold said, indicating an old-fashioned wooden newspaper rack by a desk in a far corner of the room. "You can pore over them if you're interested."

"Thank you," Raul said. "We might take you up on that."

"Good, then," Dolph said, rising. "It's after eleven and I'm well off schedule. Eat. Drink. When you're all ready to turn in, just ring the bell. Babette will show you to your rooms, and Old Ollie—by the way, that's what he prefers to be called, Old Ollie—will get your bags. Miss Moffo—I'll see you at seven?"

"Yes, sir. But, please—call me Lottie."

"Yes, Lottie. Good night."

When Seebold left, Louis and Raul high-fived. Louis went to pour himself a nightcap, while Raul went to the map rack and began flipping through maps hanging limply from oak rods. As he examined the maps, he carried on a conversation with Louis about the next day's fishing. Should they stay downstream, near the Missouri, where the fish were apt to be larger, or go up above, where the Clearborn was bound to be more scenic?

Lottie sat in the sofa, arms folded, while Louis examined paintings and chatted with Raul. Finally she sighed, popped to her feet, and shuffled off in a huff toward the hall leading to the kitchen.

"Where are you going?" Louis called.

Lottie ignored him and disappeared.

"You'd better pay a little attention to her," Raul advised.

"I'll make it up to her." Louis suppressed a belch. He realized that he had consumed quite a bit of scotch. "How often do we get a chance to fish the Clearborn, pardner?"

Babette and Lottie came back together. A moment later, Old Ollie appeared. "You boys can follow me when you're ready," he said. "Babette here will fix up your lady friend now."

As Lottie disappeared with Babette, Louis waved meekly.

Old Ollie sat down. After a few minutes, Raul realized that they were keeping him, so he reluctantly gave up his studies of the maps, and the men followed Old Ollie up a staircase.

Soon Louis and Raul lay in identical king-size beds under white down comforters that covered them like two feet of snow. Both men had showered and used the steam in the bathroom. They lay looking up at the high ceiling, feeling somewhat dazed by their good fortune.

"It's strange, isn't it?" Louis crossed his arms under his head. "We're just a couple of miles from our regular Missourah campsite, with all those stars. The crickets. The chill of the river bottom."

"It is," Raul replied. "But I suppose we'll be back there soon enough."

8

The light was just pink on the mountaintops when Raul opened his eyes the following morning. He lay in the bed closest to the sliding doors that opened onto a small balcony with a spectacular view. Although the room was elegant, Raul had slept fitfully because of Louis's thunderous snoring. He felt cranky.

Raul heard voices. He crawled out of bed, pulled on his fleece, and slipped outside. Down below, he saw Seebold, Lottie, and two children—the twin Seebold boys. The boys were huge, with blond hair as coarse and straight as straw. They lumbered around after a soccer ball, knocking each other over like a pair of bear cubs.

The door slid open behind Raul. "Mornin', pardner."

Hit by the fresh air, Louis thought better of going outside. He sat back on the bed, scratched his gut, and declared that he needed a cup of joe.

Hearing Seebold's voice, Louis chuckled. "A reviewer playfully suggested that Dolph's book ought to have a subtitle: *Unsolicited Advice on Just About Everything from the World's Most Egomaniacal Christian Entrepreneur.*"

Raul shrugged. "You seemed to like what he said about nano-technology."

They went back inside, showered, and made their way downstairs, following the sound of voices down a long hall and through swinging doors to a huge, light-filled room. At one end was a kitchen and at the other a dining area dominated by a giant table and some benches and storage chests.

"My domain," Babette called from behind the kitchen counter. Her cheeks were rosy, and she wore a bandanna over her permed gray hair. "This used to be the ranch mess—fed fifteen, twenty at a time. Coffee's already brewed—on the sideboard. With the juices."

Louis groaned and looked around. "I reckon the cowpokes weren't fed from that high-tech Viking range, though." He tried to engage Babette in a discussion of high-end kitchen appliances, but she couldn't have cared less. She muttered some platitude about cooking being hard work no matter how you cut it. Louis joined Raul by the coffee urn, drew a cup, and pronounced the blend satisfactory. He added, "I could get used to this."

Babette hollered over, asking whether they preferred eggs with home fries and bacon or pancakes.

Raul went for the pancakes. Louis asked for eggs over easy, fried in butter, not oil. He also instructed Babette to crisp up the potatoes and cautioned her against allowing the bacon to get crumbly.

Raul sipped his guava juice. Suddenly they heard banging and commotion in the hall.

"That's just Mr. Seebold and the twins, Biff and Buff," Babette said. "They adore their father. Don't look nothin' like him, though."

The swinging doors burst open; two boys rampaged through the room. Babette lit out after them, waving a spatula and hollering, "Settle down!"

Seebold and Lottie entered, deep in discussion.

"There's our gal now," Louis said, noting that Lottie had abandoned her sporty topknot in favor of a more conservative do, her hair forming a pyramid around her face.

Just then, a ceramic pot shattered on the floor.

"Boys!" Seebold thundered. The kids immediately came to a standstill. "Come over here. *Now.* You need to say hello to someone."

Seebold said, "They always act out when their mother stays at home in Los Angeles. She's not big on ranch life."

Biff and Buff, identically dressed, fell in like soldiers ordered to inspection. They stood with hands clasped in front of them, staring at their feet. They were still panting. The boys had cheeks so bulbous they appeared to be inflated with air, freckles, pale blue eyes, and thick lips. One of them had slightly more protuberant ears; it was about the only way to tell them apart.

Seebold spoke to the one with the outstanding ears: "Biff. Say hello to Mr. Traub and Mr. Mendoza. They're here to do some fishing."

"Hello," the boy said sullenly.

"Pleased to meet you," Louis replied. "Those are quite handsome lederhosen. How did you come by the name Biff?"

"My real name is Adolph Bifford Seebold the Fourth. That's how."

"Well. I'll be . . . My real name is Bonaparte Louis Traub. But folks call me Louis."

The boy looked up, momentarily seeming to connect. He mumbled, "Yes."

"Yes, *sir*," Seebold interjected.

"Sir," Biff repeated.

Raul was shocked to hear that the hefty lads were just twelve.

"Sir," Biff said again to Louis. "Will you take us fishing? We've never been."

"Is that right?"

"It's their mother," Seebold explained. "She doesn't want the boys around hooks and knives and things. They are—how should I put this?—accident prone."

Buff was no more forthcoming than Biff and, Louis noticed, mildly cross-eyed. His gaze seemed fixed on a point somewhere well behind the person with whom he was speaking. Buff's lederhosen were so tight that he had red chafe marks on the insides of his thighs. He held his fists balled up at his sides. He asked his father, "Can we go, sir?"

Babette set down the breakfasts.

"Remember—you have a session with Miss Moffo in fifteen minutes. It's your first one. Let's focus on that, shall we? Now git."

The boys smashed through the doors. Seebold told Lottie to stay and not to worry—Old Ollie or one of the other ranch hands would round up the boys and deliver them to the playroom for their first therapy session.

Seebold asked, "So what do you make of them, so far?"

Lottie spoke with authority about symbol recognition-and-transposition issues and emphasized that she fell in with the less traditional camp when it came to analyzing learning disorders like dyslexia. That is, she didn't believe such disorders were necessarily genetic. They could be the by-products of other circumstances, from traumas to developmental glitches and even environmental factors. "I have to tell you, I've grown skeptical of the hard-wired school. I tend to go for nurture over nature."

Seebold seemed pleased with her answer.

"I'll tell you what's irregular," Babette shouted. "You don't need to be no anchorman to see it's their size and their appetites. They each woofed down a double stack this morning, with half a dozen sweet sausages. And they ate up a pound of butter."

"You know, Babette may be onto something," Lottie suggested. "There's a growing body of evidence suggesting that LDs can be caused by metabolic irregularities that affect chemical production in the brain. The preliminary research is very promising."

"Are you saying my kids eat too much?" Seebold leaned back in his chair, stroking his septum. "That's *all* that's wrong with them?"

"Oh no, not at all. First of all, I'm not taking any position until I have a chance to observe and test them—in a nonintrusive way. The point is that there may be a chemical reason for their big appetites, and that may have other ramifications."

Louis, chewing on a piece of bacon, took all this in. He was proud of Lottie. She sounded quite authoritative at times. He also liked her hair worn down. He had a mental image of her bottom, the strap of her black thong mysteriously disappearing into the fold between her plump cheeks. He felt a surge of lust. Perhaps they could manage a midnight tryst.

"Louis?" The sound of Seebold's voice snapped him out of his reverie. "You were making strange grunting noises."

Seebold pulled out a chair. "One of my friends out here—actually, he's an employee and an advisor of sorts—is due to show up here around ten to take you fishing. He's a heck of a guide, I'm told."

Lottie excused herself to go finish unpacking.

"Are you ready, Mr. Seebold?" Babette asked. "The usual?"

"No, I'd like an egg-white omelet today. With a side of steamed broccoli."

Raul complimented Seebold on his shirt, an unusual multicolored garment made of numerous patches of denim. It was quite unlike anything Raul had ever seen. He asked Seebold to tell them more about his new book.

Seebold explained that the volume was about the blueprint for his own success—the quest for betterment. He told Raul to take a good look around the room. "Everything you see—everything—was someone's better idea of something else. Do you understand the implications of that?"

Raul felt uncomfortable. He had never tested well.

"Better yet . . . ," Seebold said, rising. "Excuse me."

"He does this all the time," Babette said, rolling her eyes.

Seebold returned shortly with a roll of toilet paper and stripped it all off. He inserted a pencil in the cardboard tube that remained and held either end. He asked Raul to pretend that this was a spent roll of toilet paper in the john in his own home. How would he remove it in order to load a fresh roll?

Raul shrugged, grabbed one edge of the tube, and slowly pulled. It pulled apart in a nice spiral.

"See," Seebold said. "But do not for one moment assume that the core tubes of toilet paper were always made to come apart so conveniently. For decades, people wrestled with these tubes—until someone bright enough hit upon the idea of making them in a way that incorporated this tearaway seam."

"I see," Raul said.

"That someone was me—it was my first big manufacturing hit," Seebold explained. "I patented the technique and sold it for royalties to all the big toilet paper producers. Then I had a remarkable idea. I envisioned the spiral as a *wrapping*. Guess how those twist-apart frozen biscuit cylinders appeared on the market?"

"Aha," Louis interjected. "So that explains why those biscuits taste like they're made of toilet paper." He chuckled at his own joke but ceased abruptly when Seebold shot him a cold look.

"Now," Seebold said, "toilet paper. TP. Flip the initials around." He put his hands together, fingers spread and lightly touching at the tips, and delicately rested his chin on them. "Do you see? Do you see what I mean?"

"I th-th-th-think I see," Raul said weakly.

"TP and PT. Toilet paper and—*paper towels*. A brave new world."

Seebold told of his forays in the paper towel market and went on to note other highlights of product evolution. He waxed poetic on zipper bags and plastic cable ties, which, in one stroke, rendered obsolete three venerated products: tape, string, and rubber bands.

"You're preaching to the choir here," Louis said emphatically, "Frankly, I don't know where Raul and I would be without cable ties."

Seebold ignored Louis and pointed to the kitchen cabinets. He noted the superior magnetic latches that kept the doors closed.

"Cup holders!" Raul cried.

"I don't think they meet Dolph's criteria," Louis objected, eager to get back on his host's good side. "I believe they're an invention, not a refinement."

"Louis is right," Seebold said. "But you see my point. Almost all of my entrepreneurial activities sprang from seeing how good things could be made better. My latest efforts have been in the tech field. One of my subsidiary companies recently developed the shirt-pocket hard drive."

"Interesting," Louis observed. "I assume you mean the Firestarter drive, developed by Divergent Emergent Technologies—the firm trading as DET?"

"Why yes, Louis. I'm impressed."

"I bought the stock at six in February," Louis confided smugly. "When I left New York, it was at sixty-five."

"Hold the stock," Seebold said. "But you didn't hear that from me."

"I haven't heard a thing. Did somebody say something?" Louis jovially cast furtive looks over his shoulders. "I've always had a few strong positions in the tech sector. But it was all in hardware. Luckily, I was barely affected by the collapse of the dotcoms."

"Now that's smart investing," Dolph said. "You get the upside of the tech trend, but with the buffer of traditional manufacturing."

"Yes, Dolph, that's the conventional logic. But I expect the growth of Chinese and Korean manufacturing sectors to create real problems in that regard."

Seebold, stroking his septum, contemplated this warning.

This conversation made Raul uncomfortable. He felt like a rube for investing his money conservatively in IRAs, Keoghs, and such—all of it, no less, in dismally performing "green" funds for the socially conscious. Now he suspected that Louis was laughing all the way to the bank like some high roller, despite his frequent denunciations of businessmen and developers and the potato-growing despoilers on the Fork.

Raul pondered how he had always cut Louis a little slack financially, assuming that his friend was artistically inclined and strapped for cash. He had never asked Louis to contribute to routine maintenance of the various vehicles that they had used over the years. Raul had even paid for the beaded seat covers that Louis urged him to purchase to keep their sweaty shirts from sticking to the seat backs on long drives in Big Sky Country.

What next? Was Seebold going to clap Louis on the back, suggesting that they drink a glass of port and smoke a cigar while they gloated over their Wall Street killings?

Raul's Ironfeather training kicked in, and he caught himself before he strayed too far down the path of negativity. What did he have to be resentful about? Raul's own business, Dent-A-Men, had enjoyed a pretty good little run. And Darby Wingo—as the great man himself freely admitted—certainly reaped rewards from founding the Ironfeather Society of Warriors, not to mention lavish royalties from his various writings.

He silently repeated the 8th Virilian Protocol, which addressed materialism: "The eagle was given many beautiful feathers, but not so many that it would be unable to fly. So it is for the warriors with the things of this world. Beware the surfeit." Nevertheless, Raul resolved to make Louis pay for the next scheduled maintenance on the War Pony—perhaps at the Jiffy Lube in Lewiston. It was only fair.

Raul's ruminations were interrupted by the sudden appearance of a lanky guy who was pale as an albino, with a square jaw, wire-rimmed glasses, and a white-blond Prince Valiant haircut.

"Hey, Dolph, what's shakin'?" he said, but he approached Babette, flashing a jack-o'-lantern grin. "Hold on here—let me get a little somethin' from my main squeeze."

"Chipper!" Seebold cried, jumping up. "You rapscallion!"

Louis did a double take. It was Dale Chippen all right. They had met a few years earlier at the New Jersey Somerset County Flyfishing Expo. Chippen manned a booth for Quake Lake mineral water and spent most of his time schmoozing with feather throwers like Ted Blinken, trying to generate buzz among the feather-throwing elites for Quake Lake. Somehow the brown-nosing Chippen had even cadged an invitation to a group dinner that Ted and Louis helped organize for the casting champion Joan Wulff.

Chippen hugged Babette and said, "I was out to the big city last week. I've got news for you, gorgeous. They don't make ladies like you anymore."

"Oh, stop." Babette giggled like a schoolgirl. Clearly Seebold wasn't the only one under Chippen's spell.

When Chippen finally turned to Louis and Raul, he said, "Sky? What a coincidence. It's been ages, man—since, what, the Somerset show? Wow. What brings you here?"

"I was about to ask you that same question." Louis was irritated by Chippen's familiar tone. "I was under the impression that you were in Trenton or some similar outpost along the turnpike of the so-called 'Garden State.'"

Chippen flashed his smile and explained that he had finally taken the plunge and moved to Montana. It was almost two years now. "And you're still in New York?"

"Yes," Louis admitted. "I have professional obligations unrelated to angling."

"These guys," Chippen said, addressing Dolph, "they are the Big Kahunas among fly fishermen. People all over the friggin' world know them."

Raul basked in the praise. Louis acknowledged it with a dip of his head.

Seebold explained how Louis and Raul had rescued Lottie and delivered her to Crooked Butte.

"What a saga," Chippen said. "Welcome to the CB."

"Tell me something, Dale," Louis said. "There's been considerable speculation about the alarmingly rapid spread of whirling disease in this upper Missourah watershed. Some have suggested that it may be accelerated by the ability of certain hosts—namely, the Trico—to act as, um, hyperefficient transmission media for the whirling disease spores."

"You know, I'm not sure about that," Chippen said evasively. "I haven't totally kept up with the latest science on that. We're not losing fish here, not so's you'd notice. In fact, I think you'll find out real soon just how great the fishing is."

"I see," Louis said in a tone expressing his disappointment with this reply. "Of course, the lost fish would be juveniles—as I'm sure you know. Mature fish are not affected by whirling disease. So nothing would be obvious—until the precipitous decline of fish in the ten-to-twelve-inch class, oh . . . next summer."

Seebold stroked his septum, looking troubled. "Is there something wrong with my river?"

Chippen began to say something about exaggerated threats, but Louis cut him off. He gave Seebold a brief history of whirling disease, which was caused by a mysterious deadly parasite. "The parasite causes deformities that can make tiny trout so crooked that they can only swim in circles. Hence the name *whirling* disease."

Seebold looked at Chippen. "Are we proactive on this?"

Chippen smiled weakly.

"I'm painting the picture here in broad strokes," Louis said. "I'd be happy to provide a more, um, substantial analysis at the appropriate time. One of the things we *don't* yet know is just how—or how rapidly—the infection spreads within a river or watershed. That's where the

Tricos of the Clearborn come in." Seebold looked at his watch and frowned, while Louis continued: "With all due respect, Dolph, permit me to suggest that you contemplate funding some sort of study on these critical spore transmission issues, right here on the Clearborn."

Raul glanced at Chippen, expecting to see smoke coming out of his ear holes.

"That sounds like an excellent idea," Seebold said. He popped to his feet and said that he needed to see Louis—alone. After that, they could throw their gear into the Suburban, and Chippen would take them fishing.

After the others filed out, Seebold said, "I've just now decided something. I'd like *you* to help me write and edit my new book, *The Boon of Betterment*. I'm sure I can make it worth your while."

Louis was shocked. He couldn't imagine an assignment he'd be less inclined to take on than serving as the literary waterboy to the world's most egomaniacal Christian entrepreneur.

Seebold plowed ahead. He was already late lining up a coauthor to fulfill his agreement with his publisher. But he just couldn't stomach the stream of sycophants jockeying for the job. Louis, a writer of great integrity and intelligence, would be perfect. In fact, Seebold said, he had already blocked out large chunks of time over the coming months to work on the book.

Louis listened, with a queasy feeling growing in his stomach. He could see it all too clearly—Seebold banging on his door at some ungodly hour of the morning, just so they could stick to some "sacred" schedule. He envisioned himself taking dictation like some vacuous secretary, ever at Seebold's beck and call. He would be constantly embroiled in petty confrontations over word choice—*ubiquitous!* No, *omnipresent!*—with the final decision always in Seebold's hands.

Of course, the project would allow Louis to do something he'd always wanted—stay in Montana for the fall to experience the copious blue-winged olive and midge hatches. But what good was that if he were deskbound, miserably dotting Seebold's *i*'s and crossing his *t*'s? It was sure to drive him nuts.

Louis saw no reason to jeopardize his good standing in the short term with his host, however. He said, "I'm genuinely flattered by this offer, Dolph. I'll certainly consider it."

"Good," Seebold said. His pale eyes danced as he clapped Louis on the back. He led him back to the great room, where Raul and Chippen were deep in conversation by the map rack.

"Don't let me hold you up," Seebold said.

It was time to go fishing. It was *showtime*.

Not far above the CB Ranch compound, the road became little more than a well-tended wagon track, and the Suburban, loaded with mountains of gear, made slow progress. The road wound through a broad valley that stretched on either side toward the base of plum-colored mountains with serrated tops.

Raul tried to engage Chippen in conversation, but Seebold's right-hand man seemed distracted.

A buck mule deer, bedded below a ponderosa pine, regarded them from the shade. He had a dark, immaculate coat and a thick body; his antlers, with eight points on each side, were still in velvet. They looked fake, like foam Mickey Mouse ears.

Two smaller bucks stopped browsing and lifted their heads to sniff as the Suburban passed. Then they resumed feeding. Some ponderous animals grazed at the foot of the mountains across the river valley. They were unmistakably buffalo—black cutouts, with massive shoulders and backs that sloped sharply to surprisingly slender hindquarters.

Farther on, Chippen said, "I'm glad you boys are hard-core. You don't need me to hold your hand, and I've got chores to do. So I'll just get you squared away on the river and then come back for you at dinnertime. How's that?"

"That'll work for us," Louis declared.

"Maybe we can all get out again tonight after supper," Chippen said. "Fish the spent wings."

The valley grew more rugged and spectacular, but they had yet to lay eyes on the river. It was always off to their left, its course marked by pale green willows and a few nearly black pines.

The dirt road improved again, and soon they were threading their way through a low mountain pass. Coming around a long bend, they surprised a black bear. It sat watching them on the high bank, coat glistening and rippling. Scrambling down, the bear mis-timed its getaway and, confused, briefly loped alongside the Suburban. Louis could have touched its moist, black nose.

Heading down once again in a sweeping turn, Chippen said, "We're almost there." He soon pulled over under a cluster of trees on high ground, about two hundred yards above where the river ran through the trees.

"Suit up, boys," Chippen said. "This is gonna rock your world."

Louis groaned and stretched when he got out. Raul remarked on the cacophony created by myriad birds flitting in and out of the trees and bushes. Their gear was all in the backseat of the overstuffed vehicle. Louis had even thought to throw in the large square of green Astroturf that they used as a mat for changing into waders.

Raul proudly showed Chippen various pleasing details of his brand-new Eagletech 5-weight rod, while Louis attached the reel to his rod and gave the stick a few firm shakes to make sure all was in good order. "Gentlemen?"

The men followed a faint trail, single file, through brambles and brush, to flat ground.

"Oh, my Lord," Raul said.

They stopped in their tracks. All along the river, funnel-shaped clouds that resembled miniature tornadoes hung over the water, reaching forty and fifty and sixty feet into the sky. They shimmered like fine mist from a sprinkler in the sunlight; it was the sun glinting on the minute wings of hundreds of thousands of insects, none larger than a fleck of pepper.

"Will you look at those Tricos," Louis said, shaking his head. His jowls jiggled as he declared, "It's *psycho Trico* time again, folks."

Chippen cracked a grin. "I thought you might appreciate this."

"It's in-ca-ca-credible," Raul said of the undulating mating swarms. "I've never seen Tricos so dense."

They dashed the last few yards to the river and clambered down to the pebbly beach. The river, sixty feet wide, was shallow and swift. At every indentation in the bank or break in the rough water, trout were poking their snouts through the film as they feasted on Tricos.

"You can get dialed in here if you want," Chippen said casually. "But you'll find more fish—and most of the big heads—up in the long glide."

"More fish," Raul thought.

Chippen pointed out a charred, half-dead ponderosa pine about a hundred yards upstream; it marked the beginning of the best water, which extended a mile or so up to a wooden bridge. "If you don't want to work your way up, you can wade across and take the path on the far bank. It's easy going. I'll pick you up at the upstream bridge at around six tonight."

Chippen left and the men began rigging up.

"Why do you dislike him so, Louis?"

"Raul, Yova—he's bad news. You know, he had the cojones to plant a bottle of that Quake Lake ripoff water at every setting at the dinner for Joan Wulff. It was a crass act of commercialization."

Raul didn't see that as too awful a crime. He mentioned that while Seebold and Louis were in conference, Chippen had picked his brain about their angling itinerary—and done so very aggressively.

"He's a weasel," Louis said. "At Somerset, he was always working someone, trying to get something out of them."

"Wouldn't that be 'out of *om?*'"

Louis laughed. "I stand corrected."

Downstream from where they stood, a fish rose and sipped in a Trico. The large trout created a bow wake on the glassy surface. Seeing it, the men grinned at each other, high-fived, and simultaneously cried, "Showtime!"

Minuscule flies were the order of the day, along with the finest of leaders and tippets. "I'm going with the Chernobyl Trike," Raul muttered, selecting a size 22 fly named for its fluorescent orange wing.

"Good choice," Louis surmised. "I reckon we've got a whole lot invested in that silly fly after all these years."

The first time Louis had used the outlandish fly, he fished rings around Raul. The experience was shocking for both men, as garish flies, especially tiny ones, were rarely successful. But Raul, a staunch traditionalist, still held out against using the orange-winged Chernobyl Trike until a fateful evening in 1992. Louis was simply hammering the fish, the visibility of the fluorescent orange wing helping him make the repeated precise casts and drifts that were the key to success during psycho Trico time.

Meanwhile, Raul strained so hard to find and track his realistic imitation in the vast drifting mat of insects on the water that he ended up back at camp that night with a cold compress on his eyes and a hot towel wrapped around the base of his neck. Worse yet, Raul was forced to endure Louis's whiskey-fuelled triumphalism. Raul finally tore the compress away, popped out of his recumbent attitude, and bitterly denounced his partner as an "insensitive, scorekeeping, know-it-all."

The tiff put a damper on the next few days, but the happy outcome—as Louis took pains to note whenever he told anyone the story—was that Raul finally saw the light about the Chernobyl Trike.

It was an easy wade across the thigh-deep pool. On the far bank, they followed a clear trail among moss-covered rocks, yellow-and-blue wildflowers, and thick grasses up as far as the burned pine.

The scene on the long, flat stretch before them was extraordinary. The transparent river had a gold tint and an unusual bottom composed of rocks mixed with long beds of dense, pale green weeds that reached almost to the surface. They slowed, altered, and braided up the current into forms that, taken together, were as varied and intertwined as the strands of a sleeping woman's hair.

Pods of fish, some containing a dozen or more trout, were grouped at almost every hint of structure or vagary in the current, eating Tricos.

"Think they're on the duns or spinners?" Raul asked, for he saw freshly hatched Tricos as well as the tiny corpses of expired insects.

"Mixed bag, I suspect—probably on a fish-to-fish basis. Anything at the banks?"

Raul said it was tough to see against the far bank because of the shadows. He would wade out alongside Louis to observe and help figure out what was going on.

Louis bent over, peering closely at insects floating in the surface film. He would start with that proven Trico imitation, the Griffith's Gnat. It was easier to see than most patterns because it was slightly larger, meant to imitate a cluster of Tricos glopped together.

A pod of fish was working within easy casting range. Louis stripped off the correct length of fly line, shaking it out through the tip-top so that it all lay on the water.

Going into a predatory crouch, Louis adjusted his legionnaire's hat and began to false-cast with a deliberate tick-tock motion. As he shot the last few feet of line, he added his trademark flourish with his free hand. He stooped even further and thrust his chin forward, jaw dangling open, as he struggled to follow the path of the fly. It drifted among the rising fish, untouched.

This was no surprise. Because of the abundance of insects, the fish had adopted a feeding rhythm, coming up repeatedly for as long as ten or fifteen seconds to sip in a number of insects before taking a brief break. Then they moved upstream a bit and gorged in another fifteen-second burst. It was like that, one binge after another, over and over.

A feather thrower had to time his cast and the subsequent drift so that the fly passed directly over the nose of fish when it was "up," gobbling Tricos. And you couldn't just throw into a pod of fish, even if they were stacked up, shoulder-to-shoulder. It was imperative to target a specific fish, or you never would get a take.

Fishing the psycho Tricos was like playing with one of those Cracker Jack box toys that challenge you to maneuver two tiny steel balls into indentations in a clown's eyes.

"Game on," Louis muttered, casting again.

After two dozen casts, Louis cried out, "There he is!"

The fish zipped across the river, somersaulted through the air as if someone had punted it, and spit out the fly.

"Nice fish," Raul remarked. "About fourteen inches. Looked like a rainbow."

Louis spotted a rising fish that might have been slightly larger and went to work on it. The fish was one of several feeding in a seam on the far edge of a skinny weed bed. It was impossible to get a good drift through the seam because of the current irregularities. Five, six times Louis cast, never quite satisfied with the drift.

They were interrupted by a commotion well downstream on the bank behind them. They turned, immediately fearing the worst—grizzly.

Then it was still, and Louis cast again.

"He's a tricky one," Louis muttered, fishing in his vest for a fly box. "This is going to take something a little more sophisticated than a Griffith's Gnat. He's feeding in irregular spurts, so I never get the same look twice. I almost want to try him with a flush-riding dun of some sort . . ."

Raul peered over his friend's shoulder into the fly box.

Louis settled on a cul de canard pattern.

Kerplunk!

The men nearly jumped out of their waders at the heavy splash up and across the stream. Raul watched, horrified, as bright blue monofilament line came tight just upstream of them and a flashing silver lure began chugging directly toward him. He danced out of the way, and it narrowly missed hooking and puncturing his waders.

"Hey! What gives?" Louis bellowed.

Raul turned to see the Seebold boys, still dressed in lederhosen, standing knee-deep in the water. He muttered, "Oh, no. We've got company."

Louis glared at the boys.

Buff, the heftier one, cranked the lure right up to the tip-top of the cheap, black spin-casting rod.

"Hold it!" Louis shouted. "Just hold on now."

It was too late. Using both hands, Buff unloaded a mighty cast. Both men ducked, and the lure whistled past their heads and landed like a mortar round.

When Buff started reeling, Louis grabbed the blue mono and, in a swift move, cut it with the nippers on his vest. As the boy reeled up the slack mono, Louis carefully retrieved the bit with the lure tied to it.

"We have to address this," he muttered, starting toward shore.

"Hey mister, why'd you do that?" Biff whined.

"These little rascals are trouble," Louis said under his breath. "We can't pussyfoot around."

At the last moment, the boys tried to flee, but Louis grabbed Buff by the scruff of the neck, and Raul collared Biff. They marched the boys to the bank, and Louis barked, "Now, sit!"

The boys obeyed, scowling. They were a mess, scratched legs scarlet from submersion in the frigid water. Their arms were dirty, and their lederhosen were thickly caked with mud. They were unwilling to look at the adults.

"How did you get way out here? Aren't you supposed to be with Miss Moffo?" Louis demanded.

"We hid in the back of the Suburban after breakfast," said Biff. "Under the tarps and horse blankets. We knew Chipper was going to take you. We just wanted to go fishin' too."

"Did Miss Moffo give you permission to do that?" Raul asked.

Biff glanced at his brother before he replied: "Not 'zacly."

"What did she say?" Louis asked.

Buff finally spoke: "She didn't say anything. On account of the duct tape we put on her mouth."

"*What?*"

The boys squirmed, and Buff protested, "We didn't do nothin' bad!"

"We can explain everything," Biff said, rising. "We like Miss Moffo. She seems real nice. But we knew she wasn't going to let us go fishing, not with Dad around." Using his hands for emphasis, the boy seemed sincere and innocent while pleading his case as shrewdly as a trial lawyer. "We both love fishin', so what could we do?"

"Yeah, what could we do?" Buff interjected. "So we roped her and hog-tied her right up to the chair."

"Buff!" Biff shouted.

Louis and Raul were stunned. Buff plowed on: "Then we put some tape on her mouth. We didn't do nothin' wrong, mister. Honest. We just wanted to go fishin'."

Biff tried to mollify the adults, insisting that they could explain. The boys apparently had offered to show Lottie how Comanche warriors, preparatory to scalping the squaws of settlers, tied them up in chairs. Lottie agreed to a reenactment of that gruesome ritual, but once the boys had tied and gagged her, they ran out and stowed away in the Suburban.

"One thing just led to another," Biff said in an imploring tone. "We know what we did was wrong, but that was just how it was."

"Well, young man," Louis said, studying Biff with folded arms. "Let me tell you something. I don't know where you lads got your ideas about Comanche ways. But I assure you, they are luridly inaccurate. A Comanche would never go through the trouble of tying someone up—man or woman. He acted swiftly, feeling neither pity nor remorse. Where on earth did you get such nonsense?"

"Vernon, sir," Biff said respectfully. "He's one of the wranglers. Him and Old Ollie look after the horses."

"Yeah," Buff said, parroting his brother. "They're wranglers."

"So you're interested in learning about native peoples and warfare?" Louis asked.

"*Yessir!*" the boys cried simultaneously.

"Wait here," Louis ordered. "Don't you move a muscle. My pardner and I need to hold a war council. You know what that is, don't you?"

"Yes," Biff said with gusto.

Louis took Raul aside, and they debated their options. Taking the boys home meant walking about ten miles in hot, cumbersome waders ill suited to traipsing through the Big Belt Mountains—much less battling a marauding grizzly. And neither Raul nor Louis relished the idea of being held responsible by Seebold for any misfortune that befell his children.

They had no choice but to wait it out. They could take turns fishing and baby-sitting until Chippen or someone else showed up. Who knew? Perhaps the rascals would grow bored fishing with their crude tackle and, after skipping stones and building little cairns on the riverbank, fall asleep in the sunshine.

Raul determined not to get stuck doing the baby-sitting while Louis fished. He was surprised when his partner said, "Why don't you explore some, go hang a few bank feeders? I'll follow upstream in a little bit with the boys, and we can trade off."

They returned to the twins, who sat in identical attitudes, head in hand. Louis outlined the deal. Hearing that they could stay, the boys simultaneously cried, *"Yes!"*

Raul waded out, pulled his fedora down to his eyebrows, and began working his way upstream. He watched the far bank like a hawk, holding his rod on his shoulder like a rifle. He shaded his eyes with his free hand.

"How come he ain't fishin'?" Buff asked.

"How come you boys don't speak proper English?"

"We like to talk like Vern and the other wranglers," Biff confessed. "Dad gets mad. I thought you was gonna tell us about the Comanches. They were bloodthirsty savages, right?"

"We're gonna be wranglers when we get growed," Buff blurted.

"The Comanches were among the worst," Louis said. "But they were hardly more savage than the Blackfeet—the natives who once roamed these very valleys and mountains. The Blackfeet made war on the Shoshones, the Nez Perces, the Crows, the Pawnees—heck, they made war on everyone, especially the tribes that migrated here to hunt buffalo. It was the Blackfeet who almost killed Meriwether Lewis, up in the Marias River country. You lads must know of Captain Lewis and the Corps of Discovery?"

"I think I heard of him," Biff said. "Didn't he write the Declaration of Independence?"

"Not quite, buck-o." Louis chuckled. "He was far more important than that."

Louis proceeded to tell the boys all about Jefferson, the Louisiana Purchase, and the Corps of Discovery's journey on the upper Missouri. He also delivered a moving and lengthy dissertation on the nobility of the Indians and the beauty of their ways before he satisfied the boys' thirst for tales of atrocities.

The boys sat transfixed as Louis vividly described how the Blackfeet and Comanches—the Lords of the Great Plains—disemboweled Mexicans, set settlers afire after taking their scalps, and visited even greater horrors on rival savages.

"You see, Buff," Biff explained, "I told you the teacher in school was wrong. The Indians didn't just sit around all day, singing songs and praying for peace. Right, Mr. Traub?"

Buff interrupted. "You still never told us why your friend ain't fishin'."

Raul was almost out of sight, way upstream, still with the rod on his shoulder. Louis told the boys that there were lots of different ways to fish and different reasons for fishing, but that basically none compared with the art and science of fly fishing. He explained how the trout rising in front of them were actually eating tiny insects on the surface. When trout were feeding that way, they locked in on the specific fly that was hatching and wouldn't bother eating anything else—not even a big, fat worm dangled before their noses. The only way to catch the trout was with an accurate imitation of the insect they were eating.

Louis removed his vest and fished out a small book with a beat-up plasticized cover, *Western Fly Hatches Demystified.* He flipped through the slender volume until he came to the section devoted to Tricos. He extended it toward Buff, who sheepishly passed: "You'd best give it to Biff, mister."

Biff took the book and slowly read out loud the basic description of the Trico and its life cycle, pausing between each word and keeping track of his place with his finger. He needed help only with Latin terminology and particularly hard words, like *subimago* and *thorax.*

"Excellent," Louis said. He made sure Buff also studied the picture of the Trico.

Louis plucked a drifting spinner out of the water. It looked like a tiny cross plastered to the tip of his index finger; the body was black, the wings transparent, and it had two long, wispy tails. He said to Biff, "I bet his pecker is even smaller than yours."

He opened one of his fly boxes, removed a Trico spinner, and held it next to the natural.

"Wow, mister," Biff said. "You sure got lots of flies."

"How come you still can't catch nothin'?" Buff asked.

As he tied on the spinner, Louis explained that Trico fishing was tricky; sometimes it took many tries to find the right fly. The boys crowded close, jostling and bombarding him with questions. With the fly tied to the gossamer tippet, Louis pointed out a rising fish. He waded out, with a boy at either side, providing a running commentary on positioning, casting, and the drift of the fly as he deliberated his first cast.

The boys, caught up in the drama, fell silent.

Louis cast and cast again. At the end of every drift, he speculated about what might have gone wrong with the presentation or float. Three times he thought everything was perfect—but still the fish ignored the fly. That, he knew, was par for the course when fishing the psycho Tricos. But Louis also knew the fish eventually would take the fly—if not on the fourth cast, then on the eighth or ninth or thirtieth— whenever the circumstances aligned properly.

Finally the fish rose to the fly. "There he is!"

The fish leaped half a dozen times and made the reel sing on two or three runs. The boys squealed at the spectacle. Buff got so excited that he tried to grab the line and haul the fish in, nearly causing Louis to lose his footing and fall in as he collared the boy. Soon, though, the lovely seventeen-inch trout was in the net.

"I want you to look closely, boys," Louis said with gravity. "You won't ever see anything more beautiful than this. Not even a girl—although it may take a few decades for you to work that out."

Louis held the trout gently, close to the surface, with water flowing over its head and gills. They admired the spotted olive back and the dramatic red stripe on the trout's side.

"*Salmo gairdneri*—in plain language, a rainbow trout. Your local native." Louis held the trout facing upstream until it regained enough strength to vanish with a flick of its powerful tail.

"Can I try, mister?" Buff pleaded. "Pleeeeease?"

Louis knew resistance was futile; the kids would just drive him mad. This was okay, though, because Louis already knew that the Clearborn in these upper reaches wasn't for him. It was not like the nearby Missouri or Silver Creek—a challenging river full of educated fish that took full measure of a man. The river was inhabited by unsophisticated fish, and the angling barely qualified as technical. Sure, it was a beautiful river and perfect for neophytes or wealthy bozos who needed to feel like great fishermen. But the Clearborn didn't hold fish that made you wake up in the middle of the night with the sweats like Missouri River fish did. There were no great white whales in the Clearborn.

And while Izaak Walton himself would have been unable to teach two impulsive children how to fish a hatch that routinely brought grown men to their knees, Louis had a plan. He switched to a giant, highly visible Humpy dry fly, with a tiny beadhead Prince nymph added as a dropper. One or the other of those flies always proved irresistible to unsophisticated fish on private water, even during a Trico hatch.

So, with Louis guiding each boy's hand through the casting stroke, Biff and Buff soon were catching trout and whooping and hollering. When Buff got his first one—an eleven-inch brown trout—he tried to make off with it. But Louis chased him down and prevailed upon the boy to release the fish. Most trout took the nymph, but occasionally a greedy fish pounced on the floater.

They passed about an hour and a half in the pool this way. Louis had just decided to go searching for Raul when he heard voices in the brush across the river. Moments later, Old Ollie's wrinkled face appeared out of the wall of brush on the far bank, the sun glinting on his wavy salt-and-pepper hair.

"Ollie!" the boys cried in unison.

Buff hollered, "I caught a trout, Ollie! I caught a trout!"

"I'm fixin' to tan your hide—the both of you!" Old Ollie shouted. "Howdy, Louis. Sorry about this. I come to fetch the boys home."

"We're okay," Louis called back. "In fact, we're having a ball."

It was cocktail time, and most of Seebold's company and staff were gathered on the rambling porch of the main house. Seebold, looking rather monkish in a caftan and espadrilles, sat with one of his boys on either side in a wide, swinging seat suspended from the ceiling. The kids were subdued.

Louis sipped a single malt while Raul savored Babette's homemade lemonade. Old Ollie and Vernon, who was gnarly as a piece of beef jerky and just as brown, sat with a few other wranglers on the railing. Now and then, one of them unloaded a graceful arc of tobacco juice out into thin air.

The declining sun left broad, orange smears across the treetops and mountainsides, and the air was sharp.

Louis held his glass up and shook it gently, examining the ice cubes. He asked if they came from a freezer.

"Where else?," Seebold answered. "Why?"

Louis hesitated. "May I make a suggestion, Dolph? I really approve of the way you've retained an, um, authentic, yet rustically elegant flavor here at the ranch. It's fabulous—no doubt about it. Along those lines, though, it also strikes me that you could use a genuine icehouse."

"Oh, really?" Seebold had been jotting in his day-by-minute diary. "Tell me more."

"I expect Old Ollie would know whereof I speak. Ollie?"

"Sir?"

"An icehouse," Louis said. "They must have had one here in past times."

"Lordy, it got burned, what—forty years ago? Vern?"

"I reckon," Vern said.

Louis turned back to Seebold. He explained that back in the day, ranches all had icehouses, filled with snow and giant blocks of river ice collected during the winter for various uses during the long, hot summer.

Louis rose. He was wearing just the black long johns that he put on under his neoprene waders. "Before I freshen this up . . . ," he said. "Wouldn't it be hip, Dolph, if the ice cube in this drink were actually a shard of Clearborn water?"

Seebold said that sounded like a terrific idea. He called to Vern and Ollie, "Fellows? What say you?"

"I reckon it would be all right," Vern said. "Less trouble to use a freezer, though."

Louis and Seebold exchanged a look of amusement at the old wrangler's attitude. Louis added, "Perhaps you could top it off with an attractive cupola and a weather vane in the shape of a trout. Some of the icehouses were both handsome and elaborate."

Inside, Louis poured more whiskey. He felt quite comfortable at the CB and relaxed in the company of Seebold. All in all, his host was a decent fellow—for a businessman. Louis saw no reason not to go to the kitchen to replenish the bowl of macadamia nuts. On his way, he bumped into Lottie in the hall. Her eyes were rimmed with red.

"Lottie! Where have you been? You look upset."

Lottie stood before him, hanging her head. He set his drink down and took hold of her shoulders. She sobbed and said, "I can't face Seebold, I just can't. I feel so irresponsible. He's probably going to fire me."

Louis didn't want to set her off; he hugged her as she lamented, "It's my first day on the job. I feel horrible."

"But they tied you up," Louis said. "They're crafty little savages. If anyone has a legitimate complaint, it's you."

"Do you mean that?" Lottie said, wiping away tears. "I feel so, so . . . humiliated."

"There's no reason for that. Seebold is the one who ought to be mortified."

"Thank God you found the boys out in that wilderness," Lottie said. "I can't imagine what might have happened if it weren't for my guardian angels. My mountain men. You and Raul—Yova."

Louis whispered, "I miss you at night, Little Squaw. Let's get together. Tonight. After everyone's gone to bed."

Lottie laughed and pushed him away, but playfully.

"Come on," Louis said, quickly assuring her that it would be all right. He could do no wrong in Dolph's eyes. "Which room are you in?"

Lottie hesitated, but then described the upstairs floor plan. There were three wings: one for family, one for guests, one for some of the live-in staff. She whispered, "I'm in the third room on the left, in the staff wing."

Louis grabbed Lottie; she melted into his arms as he kissed her hard. The swinging doors opened, and they quickly broke their embrace.

"Later, my love," Lottie whispered. "Come at two A.M."

Babette stood by, smiling, holding a tray of hors d'oeuvres.

Lottie cleared her throat. "Let's go outside, shall we?"

On the porch, Seebold ordered the boys to stand up. Biff was holding the book retelling the Lewis and Clark journey, *Undaunted Courage.*

As Lottie walked up, the boys said in unison, "We're sorry, Miss Moffo."

Lottie told them how worried she had been and asked them to promise never to run off again.

"We promise," Biff said.

Buff was a little more reluctant, but he finally parroted his brother's words.

"You know what it means to promise, right?" Lottie drawled. She put a hand on each of their shoulders and said, "So tell me—did you learn anything out there today?"

"Yes, ma'am!" Biff cried.

Seebold glanced at Raul, eyebrows arched. He was not accustomed to such enthusiasm from his boys—nor to such a nurturing yet direct attitude in their tutors or nannies, who had been either unctuous opportunists or sourpuss disciplinarians who made the boys withdraw and play even dumber than they actually were.

The boys told Lottie all about their adventure on the river. They clearly had loved every moment on the water with Louis.

Seebold looked at his watch; the allotted time for cocktails and bonding with his boys and guests had expired. He sounded a bit grumpy as he said, "Great. Well then. How about you boys run off for dinner now?"

"Nooohhhhh . . . ," the boys protested.

"Yes," Seebold said firmly.

"Dolph. May I interrupt?" Louis stepped to the center of the gathering. "I believe we can all see how, um, affected your young'uns were by their experience today. And I personally took note of how affected *you*— Dolph Seebold—were by the enthusiasm of your children." Louis paused. "Incidentally, note how the enterprising young Biff—never one for reading, from what I've gathered—scoured your library this afternoon and came up with this volume chronicling the Journey of Discovery."

Louis jiggled the cubes in his empty glass. "With that in mind, I propose that after dinner we stage an, um, entertainment of sorts in the great room. I propose to make a dramatic reading from *Undaunted Courage,* accompanied by contributions from anyone so willing. Perhaps Lottie would like to execute an interpretive dance, or Raul might deign to honor us by chanting some of the mystical Indian mantras with which he is so familiar."

The boys cried out, "Can we? Can we? Please, Daddy!"

Seebold acquiesced, much as it skewed his schedule. The boys would be allowed to stay up after dinner. They could join the adults in the great room—but only for an hour.

———

It was around nine P.M. and almost dark, but the air in the great room was cool, and various birds were squawking and jabbering away the remains of the day in the treetops. Louis stood in the center of the great room, holding open a copy of *Undaunted Courage.* Everyone, including the ranch hands, was seated and ready.

After making some opening remarks about the book, Louis set the scene: It was the morning of June 3, 1805, and Lewis and Clark, traveling on the Missouri, came to a fork in the river near present-day Fort Benton.

He began reading. One river came in from the right, or north, the other from the left, or southwest. Meriwether Lewis had to make sure the Corps of Discovery continued on the true Missouri, for their orders from President Thomas Jefferson were explicit: They were to explore the Missouri River and attempt to find a water route to the Pacific Ocean.

Hidatsa Indians had told the corps that the Missouri would bring them within a two-day portage of the mighty Columbia—and thus, eventually, the Pacific Ocean. But the Hidatsas had said nothing of any other large river after the Milk River, which the men had passed weeks earlier.

Therefore, Lewis and Clark were unsure of which river was the Missouri. The right fork was 200 yards wide; the left one, 372. The left was swifter, but the right fork was deeper. The right had the same turbid, muddy characteristics as the Missouri they had traveled up on, while the left was, according to Lewis's diary, "perfectly transparent."

Louis paused and glanced at the Seebold boys. They huddled close on either side of their father, dressed in white pajamas.

"Well, boys—which fork do you think Captain Lewis chose?"

"The right fork!" Biff cried. "The muddy one."

Buff parroted his brother.

Louis called for a show of hands. Lottie and Seebold voted with the boys; the others voted for the left, southwest fork.

When he finished counting, Louis said: "Well, guess what? Lewis's party—to a man—voted that the right fork was the Missouri." He turned to Biff. "Just like you, buck-o."

"Yaaay!" the boys cried.

"Not so fast," Louis interjected. "Captains Lewis and Clark happened to think otherwise." After grappling with the issue all day, Louis explained, the captains decided that a river as muddy as the right fork had to travel a great distance over the plains, while the left fork, with its transparent currents and colored stones, must come from the mythical Rocky Mountains—their destination.

"To quote from Lewis's journal," Louis said, without bothering to refer to the book, "Thus have our cogitating faculties been busily employed all day."

Louis glanced at the boys—they were hanging on his every word.

Because of this dilemma, Louis explained, Lewis wisely instructed Clark and most of the corps to take the left fork, while he took the right with six corpsmen. It was decided that each party would travel at least a day and a half upstream, trying to determine which river to follow.

Louis paused, took a sip of his after-dinner scotch, and picked up the book again. He began reading about Lewis's ascent of the right fork, but now he began to add dramatic inflections, gestures, and even a measure of pantomime. As he described the prickly pear bushes, whose thorns easily penetrated the men's leather moccasins and caused them no small amount of agony, Louis himself tiptoed and hopped around the room—much to the boys' amusement.

But a hush fell over the room as Louis gravely read how this was the most critical exploration Lewis ever made, and how he and his men were utterly alone and vulnerable, in country totally foreign and completely unknown except to the fierce and savage Blackfeet Indians.

Louis signaled to Raul, who took his cue and stood, arms dangling by his sides with the palms facing out. He softly sang the refrain from the native Song of Praise for the Great Spirit: "Wee-ohhh, Wee-oh-ho-wee-ho-way . . . Wee-ohhh, Wee-oh-ho-wee-ho-way."

"Daddy!" Buff cried in alarm. "He's an Injun!"

"Hush up; it's quite a beautiful song."

After a dramatic pause, Raul stepped forward and intoned: "Ah-hi-e, A-hi-e-oh-may."

In a stage whisper, Louis interpreted the Shoshone words and explained that the rough translation was "I am much pleased, I am much rejoiced."

Raul repeated the entire refrain and sang two whole verses of the Song of Praise for the Great Spirit, repeating the refrain after each one.

Louis resumed reading about how, despite the hardships and dangers of his exploration of the right fork, Lewis still found time to write descriptions of two birds unknown to science: the long-billed curlew and McCown's longspur. The following day, he made two more discoveries: Richardson's ground squirrel and the sage grouse.

"Even though the party had to camp that night in a driving rain," Louis read, "Lewis still had the time and will to note in his journal, 'The river bottoms form one immense garden of roses, now in full bloom.' Lottie?"

Lottie, who was standing by the entertainment center on the far side of the room, punched a button. The sweet strains of Vivaldi emanated through the great room as Lottie performed a dance, interpreting the music. She twirled and swirled, carving elaborate arabesques in the air with her arms. At times, she vigorously thrust her neck and chin forward, like a chicken pecking.

The children squealed with delight, and Seebold complimented Lottie on her rhythm. Louis, mindful of their imminent tryst, imagined doing it with Lottie doggie-style—the way the Comanches did it.

Louis then pointed out that whenever the Corps of Discovery had time or reason to celebrate, a corpsman name Cruzatte brought out his fiddle, and all the men danced. Sometimes they danced with the Indians, who took special delight in watching York, the giant, powerfully built black corpsman, pirouette around.

"Hell, I got a fiddle," Old Ollie exclaimed. He rose and vanished upstairs.

Louis read on. He soon came to the passage where Lewis and Private Windsor were traveling together on a very slippery, rain-soaked buffalo trail, high along a hundred-foot precipice. Lewis lost his footing and just barely managed to save himself with his espontoon.

"What's an espontoon?" Biff demanded.

Louis explained that it was a staff that Lewis took everywhere. It came in handy in many ways: as a poking instrument, a gun rest when Lewis desired to take a standing shot at an elk, or a club with which to menace wolves and grizzly bears—even Indians.

He returned to the tale. Windsor, who did not carry an espontoon, also lost his footing and found himself sliding toward the edge of the cliff.

All faces were eagerly turned to Louis to see what happened next. He set the book aside. He asked for a volunteer to play Windsor. Both boys jumped up. Louis chose Buff and led him to the overstuffed sofa.

He lifted Buff onto the sofa back and arranged his belly and limbs in roughly the same position in which poor Windsor found himself, hanging over the precipice.

Lewis was in a quandary. If he tried to descend the treacherous slope to get Windsor, he might easily lose his footing, begin an uncontrollable slide, and sweep both of them into the jaws of the canyon below.

But he remained cool. Lewis instructed Windsor to remove the knife from his belt sheath, using his right hand—the one hanging over the cliff. Then he told the private to carve a toehold in the face of the cliff.

Louis manipulated Buff's limbs to demonstrate how Windsor, establishing a foothold for his dangling leg, could now use both his arms to boost himself back over the edge of the cliff.

Acting out the mechanics, Buff rolled over the sofa back and onto the pillows.

It was getting late, so Louis wrapped up the history of Lewis's adventure. As it turned out, the southwest fork was indeed the Missouri. This allowed Lewis to name the river he had explored after his cousin Maria Wood. Louis read Lewis's diary entry pertaining to the naming of the

Marias: "It is true that the hue of the waters of this turbulent and troubled stream but illy comport with the pure celestial virtues and amiable qualifications of that lovely fair one . . ."

Louis closed the book, clasped his hands over his belly, and cast his eyes upward. He had an angelic expression as he continued from memory, his rich nasal voice wringing the maximum sentiment out of each word: "But on the other hand it is a noble river . . . in addition to which it passes through a rich fertile And one of the most beautifully picturesque countries that I ever beheld, through a wide expanse of which, innumerable herds of living anamals are seen, its borders garnished with one continued garden of roses, while its lofty and open forests are the habitation of miriads of the feathered tribes who salute the ear of the passing traveler with their wild and simple, yet sweet and cheerfull melody."

After a moment of silence, the adults burst into applause. Then Ollie began to fiddle a sprightly tune, and everyone got up to dance, including the boys, who pogoed around like mad while their father did the frug with Lottie, Raul twisted with Babette, and Louis looked on with pleasure.

When Old Ollie quit playing, they showered him with cheers and bravos. But the energized children were flying around the room. Lottie took advantage of the chaos to pull Seebold aside. "I want to do a non-intrusive test on a hunch," she said. "Please support me in this."

Seebold shrugged. "Of course."

Standing by the large oak desk, Lottie clapped loudly to get everyone's attention. She announced that she had a surprise—a contest for them all. She produced a handful of stubby, little pencils and a yellow legal pad, tearing off sheets and passing them around until everyone, including Babette and Old Ollie, had one.

Lottie explained that she wanted them to initial their sheets and listen and write down a few lines she was going to read. She would then award a special prize to the person whose penmanship most resembled that of the author, Captain Clark.

Predictably, the boys relished the idea of the contest and eagerly scratched and scrawled the words as Lottie read Clark's original journal entry: "We set out at the usial time and proceeded on with great difficuelty. I continue to be verry unwell—fever verry high. I am further afflictioned with the rageing fury of a Tumer on my anckle musle. Three men with Tumers went to shore and stayed out all night. One of them killed 2 buffalow, a part of which we made use of for brackfast."

"Can you ra-ra-ra-read that again?" Raul asked. "More slowly?"

After doing so, Lottie collected all the entries and promised to announce the winner in the morning over breakfast. The overtired boys raged for a determination on the spot, but their father quelled them with a few firm words.

"Tell you what, boys," Louis said. "Tomorrow we'll make espontoons—but only if you behave for Miss Moffo. We'll select our very own, from choice saplings down near yonder river. And we'll do the carving ourselves."

"Really?" the boys cried, looking at their father.

Seebold addressed Louis: "Can you and Raul stay another day or two? The boys would love it—so would I."

"What say, pardner? Can the Missourah wait another day?"

"I suppose," Raul said.

"Okay, boys," Seebold said. "You can make espontoons with Louis— as long as you keep your end of the bargain. Your word is as good as a written contract, boys. And when your mother calls—not a word about knives or fishhooks or anything like that."

Seebold looked at his watch. He needed to get on a call to Australia in precisely nine minutes. He told Babette that he would put the boys to bed, where Lottie would read to them, and marched everyone off to the family quarters.

Alone with Louis, Raul said, "Well, that was a long day."

"It was quite productive as well," Louis replied. He was over by the bar, pouring himself another drink. It was a few minutes after eleven. "I approve of this setup. It's quite comfortable."

"This is very odd," Raul muttered from over by the newspaper rack. "One of the maps is missing—rod and all. The one for High Meadow Ranch. I'm sure of it."

"So?" Louis asked, sipping his scotch.

"Chippen took it," Raul said with quiet conviction. "He seemed nervous this morning. He hovered around me when I was looking at the maps after breakfast. And you saw how distracted he was when he drove us out to fish. Chores. He said he had to go do some chores. I thought he was intimidated by you, but it wasn't that at all . . ."

Louis was thinking about Chippen too, but in a different context. He knew that in a scant few days, Lottie would soon be alone at the ranch—alone and vulnerable. That was when an opportunist and long-haired sexual predator like Chippen was most likely to pounce.

Louis had observed Chippen's easy, flirtatious way with Babette. He undoubtedly would try to seduce Lottie in the same suave manner. He would bide his time, waiting to strike—perhaps at a time when Lottie missed Louis so much that she fell prey to self-pity or sheer desperation, sitting alone, drinking shots of tequila, wondering . . .

Chippen would work on Lottie's desire to feel like a woman. He would present her with a single red rose or perhaps some poetry he claimed to have written, comparing her eyes to dark, limpid pools. He would do anything to convince Lottie that she might find comfort and solace in the arms of a stranger.

Louis thought, "Not so fast, buck-o."

"Louis!" Raul cried. "Get over here!"

Louis shook himself out of his reverie and scooted over to the desk, where Raul sat clicking the mouse like crazy, zooming in on a portion of a richly detailed map. His raspy voice was agitated. "I think we've hit pay dirt."

Raul had fiddled around and opened a program that contained the maps of all of Seebold's properties. They were numbered in a way that corresponded exactly to the maps in the rack. So even though the paper map of High Meadow Ranch was missing, a copy was still in the computer.

"Come on, baby . . . Aha!" Raul zoomed in on a fine blue line that represented a stream or river. The initials along the waterway were clear: L. G. C. Furthermore, the river was just a few miles long; it had a bridge over it at one point, and it twisted and turned every which way before it faded into a broad area identified by cartographic icons as marshland. The river was fully contained on the vast High Meadow Ranch, in a secluded basin nestled among towering mountains.

Louis examined the map, his own enthusiasm growing.

"Interesting," Louis said. "No, very interesting. Note how the river just appears and disappears on the map. It must be a spring creek of some sort, fed by runoff from the nearby mountains."

"Yes," Raul said. "Yes, yes, yes. The runoff goes underground and filters through some limestone buffers at the base of the mountains. It filters into the basin and pops out of a springhead a few miles away, full-blown."

"Correct," Louis said. "And look how close it is to the Blackfoot."

Indeed, the High Meadow property wasn't very far from the legendary Blackfoot River, near the town of Ovando, just west of the Continental Divide and south of the Lolo National Forest.

"You ha-ha-ha-have to admit, it's an area we never bother to explore."

"This is true," Louis replied.

"Ca-ca-ca-can it really be?" Raul whispered, awestruck. "Can it possibly be Little Gooseneck Creek?"

"Let's not jump to any conclusions," Louis exclaimed. "Let's not lose our heads over this just yet. But . . ." His voice trailed off. ". . . Oh my God."

Raul was hyperventilating, flapping his arms and taking great, big gulps of air.

"Get hold of yourself," Louis said.

Raul slumped back into a chair. His dark eyes danced. "Do you realize what this potentially means? Bank feeders. Giant, unmolested brown trout, lurking under cut banks and grassy fringes—sucking down hoppers and PMDs and spent caddis, undisturbed."

"What it means," Louis said, "is that you and I, B. Louis Traub and Raul Mendoza, will take our place among the icons of the sport. If we have indeed discovered the Little Goose, we're likely to be acknowledged as the greatest feather-throwing explorers since the great Joe Brooks traveled to Tierra del Fuego to fish the sea-run browns."

Louis realized he was jumping ahead. "Clearly, we need to continue developing our relationship with our new friend, Dolph. I'm reasonably certain that he would allow us to explore and fish any of his properties. And remember—he wants me to help him write his book. Raul—Yova—what's he going to do, say *no?*"

They exchanged a high five and simultaneously cried, "Yes!"

They continued scheming while Raul powered down the computer. As neither man was disposed to waste any more time fishing the picturesque Clearborn, Raul proposed to make a reconnaissance trip along the Missouri first thing after breakfast. He would check their campsite and research how the river was fishing, in case they wanted to throw some feathers while they laid the groundwork for their Little Goose expedition. Louis would stay behind, free to canoodle with Lottie, entertain the Seebold boys, and otherwise suck up to Dolph, with an eye to getting permission to visit the High Meadow property.

"Sounds like a plan," Louis said.

As they trudged off to bed, Louis told Raul about his planned rendezvous with Lottie. Raul weighed the intelligence and said gravely, "Be careful; a little poontang has wrecked many an otherwise great plan."

Louis promised to be extra careful. They continued talking as they prepared to turn in, until Raul put in his earplugs and almost immediately passed out.

Louis, though, found that lying down with the lights out made his head spin. He'd consumed a little more whiskey than he realized. He sat up, eyes wide open, to ride out the buzz. The Bob Dylan song "Lay, Lady, Lay" kept playing in his mind.

Each time Louis pushed the light button on his digital watch, he was disappointed by the agonizing creep of time. Finally, though, it was 1:50. He could start his stealthy advance to his lover. Standing up made Louis dizzy, however, so he got down on all fours. This minimized the chance that he would knock anything over and wake the entire house.

It was a short crawl down the hall to the T intersection where, turning right, he would soon be at Lottie's room. Louis covered the distance in less than five minutes and paused, still on his hands and knees, in front of the bedroom door.

"Jack," he thought. "What about Little Jack?" Surely the dog would raise an alarm when Louis pushed through the door. But there was nothing to be done about that now. Louis made his move.

Inside, he made out the vague outline of a bed. Ever so slowly, expecting at any moment to be set upon by Jack, he proceeded. Finally he reached the foot of the bed. Lottie was sound asleep, breathing quite heavily. He slid his hand up the bedpost and under the sheets. He got hold of her cool, delicate ankle.

"Is that you?"

It wasn't Lottie's voice; it was Old Ollie's.

"*Tarnation,* Vern—where you been?"

Louis froze. He scrambled toward the door on all fours and barely made the turn into the hall before a spell came on. In moments, he was sitting up with his eyes twitching and rolling in their sockets, his hands working like flippers.

The hall light flashed on.

It wasn't until Raul, still half asleep, finally appeared among Babette and the ranch hands and took charge, that the commotion began to die down.

———

Just an hour's drive from Crooked Butte Ranch, Nathan Nuckel fidgeted nervously in the lobby of the Best Western of Great Falls. It was a clean but nondescript place, with shiny, blond furniture and cutesy pink-and-blue-striped wallpaper.

Nuckel craned his neck and looked into the bar. The two local gals he'd been chatting with were still sitting there. Gina, the one he fancied—the one in the embroidered jean jacket—had just lit up another cigarette.

Was it worth going back in? Nuckel wondered. He had already gone for three whiskey sours at city prices—Great Falls prices—and

Gina showed no signs of having a special interest in him, even though she freely accepted his offer to buy her a drink.

Nuckel had excused himself to go use the facilities, hoping Gina would persuade her friend to leave. But it didn't happen. Perhaps these two smoking swingers just wanted to bilk him. Feeling duped, he thought, "What the hail, she already got her free danged drink." Also, Nuckel hated the smell of cigarettes, and this Gina was not a considerate smoker. She was a real addict, firing up one after another, sucking them hard and expelling prodigious clouds of smoke. The ashtray in front of her was overflowing with butts; the filter tips so heavily marked with her scarlet lipstick that they looked like tiny, freshly discarded tampons.

Nuckel sensed this was not exactly the right time to indulge in any hanky-panky with a stranger, even though it might result in him getting another pair of underpants for his collection. He considered himself enough of a connoisseur of both character and underpants to guess that Gina's would be peach-colored polyester, from the Helena Wal-Mart. "She's probably just a hoor," Nuckel thought. "I wouldn't be missing much."

The whiskey sour he'd also ordered while chatting with Gina and the other "hoor" had left him slightly buzzed. You didn't get AIDS or VD from fooling around collecting panties; it was just a spot of fun. But he had a big morning coming up, and he needed all his faculties in working order.

Nuckel knew he was closing on those danged bandits but fast. His investigations had paid off, and he had them pinned at Crooked Butte Ranch. It only figured that Kiick's desperadoes, on the run for so long now, would hole up at one of the many Montana properties gobbled up by that filthy-rich out-of-stater, Dolph Seebold.

Maybe there was some connection between them all, maybe not. Nuckel knew for a fact that Seebold barely set foot on most of his properties. With a little help from idle ranch hands or caretakers, each property was potentially a great base of operations for any kind of shady outfit.

Nuckel tried to suppress his resentment of Seebold. He reminded himself that he admired the gumption of folks who made it in the world—that's what America was all about. If a few things had gone a little differently for Nuckel himself, who knew? "Hail, there ain't no sense bellyachin', either," he thought.

Nuckel fingered his bolo tie. He was back in possession of his wits. What had he been thinking? He was not the kind of feller who went hooring around in the bars of Great Falls, no sirreeee. He jumped to his feet and hurried along the ground-floor corridor toward his room.

9

Lottie tapped a spoon on the side of her juice glass. Biff and Buff had pestered her throughout breakfast, and now it was time to announce the winner of the Captain Clark look-alike penmanship contest.

"I have to tell you," Lottie drawled. "It's really interesting. Almost everyone—especially *you,* boys—has handwriting that looks very much like that of Captain Clark. But the one whose *most* looks like it is— *Babette!*"

From her station in the kitchen, Babette shrieked and danced a little jig. "Well, I'll be—that's the first time in my life I won just about anything."

The boys clearly expected to win. They both looked deflated. Buff huffed, "That ain't fair."

"It most certainly is fair," Seebold said. "You have to be a good sport. You can't expect Miss Moffo—or anyone else—to bend the rules for you. Just because your name is Seebold."

"The lesson is to keep working on your handwriting," Lottie advised the boys. "Look how long it took Babette to win a prize."

"I'm *sixty-four,*" Babette interjected.

"You see," Lottie said, "sometimes you have to be very patient to make your dreams come true."

She shot Louis a smoldering glance. Earlier in the morning, when they had met on the stairs, she turned red and looked hurt. How could he just blow off their rendezvous like that? Louis hastily explained what had happened. She felt better and forgave him. Louis tried to pull her into a side pantry for a prebreakfast smooch, but her cooler head prevailed. They would have plenty of time for that in the afternoon on the expedition for espontoons.

"What's the prize?" Biff asked, trying to determine just how much effort he should put into feeling disappointed.

Lottie held up the prize. It was a glass globe full of fake snow and a miniature mountain landscape. It said, "Welcome to the Rockies."

"Can I see it?" Buff cried.

Babette let them examine the globe. The boys quickly lost interest in shaking it and turned their attention to the project lined up for later in the day, making espontoons. They still had half an hour before their therapy session with Lottie, so Seebold let them go outside in the custody of Old Ollie.

After they cleared out, Seebold said he would be delighted if his guests could stay at the ranch for a few more days. He hoped Louis might find time to perform another dramatic reading of *Undaunted Courage*.

"The boys love the wranglers," Seebold said. He glanced at Babette and lowered his voice so she wouldn't hear. "But I've never seen them quite respond the way they have to you—and all this Lewis and Clark stuff. It's all they talk about."

"What a generous offer, Dolph," Louis said. "I'd be embarrassed to turn it down. Raul?"

"Yes," Raul chimed. "Me too."

"I guess that's settled," Louis said quickly. "Dolph. On a related subject. You've undoubtedly heard me describe my fellow fly fishers as 'feather throwers' . . . In light of the whole lasso and casting thing, I've often pondered the obvious similarity between the words *wrangler* and *angler*. In your judgment, would it behoove me to explore this, um, preternatural similarity in a future essay?"

"Hmmmm . . ." Seebold stroked his septum. "It's an intriguing idea. That reminds me—do you remember the observations you posted on the expression 'mad as a hatter'?"

"Ahh . . . I believe that particular essay was entitled 'Lewis Carroll, Unplugged: How an Avuncular British Fantasist Shaped the Way We Think.'"

"It was the first time I saw the word *avuncular,*" Seebold said.

Raul tuned out the literary banter. He was feeling somewhat torn. The prospect of finding the Little Goose and staying at the ranch, with its wonderfully firm mattresses, stinky cheeses, and potpourri in the bathrooms, was tempting. But you also lost something when things were too cushy, Raul knew. He missed the hidden riverside campsite at Pelican Point. He missed drinking in the rich, alluvial scent of the Missouri in the morning, while he waited for the coffee to brew as the sun first hit the water. He missed watching the pink and gold and blue flecks of evening light dance on the gentle riffles.

Raul excused himself and went to gather his gear.

The Seebold boys were down by the bunkhouse near the parking area, playing horseshoes with half a dozen cowboys. After transferring his gear from the Suburban to the War Pony, Raul did a quick search to make sure the boys hadn't stowed away again. He prevailed upon the cowboys to help him unhitch and stash the drift boat. He was so sick of dealing with the boat that he jokingly said he'd sell it to the first one who came up with a reasonable offer.

Raul's first stop was the Fly Shop in Craig, where Jerry and Chris, the thirty-something trout bums who owned the place, greeted him warmly. They asked about Louis and told Raul that the river was fishing great. Caddis were hatching in massive numbers, starting in midafternoon. The PMDs were sporadic, but the Tricos were coming on in a big way.

Just the previous evening, Jim Range, a gifted feather thrower whom Raul knew from back in the day on the Fork, had released a whopping twenty-three-and-a-half-inch brown trout in an area called the Bull Pit. Chris knew this for sure; he was fishing right alongside Jim and crack guide Pete Cardinale at the time.

Word of Range's fish spread like wildfire, from drift boat to drift boat, wading angler to float tuber, up and down the river. There was no elaborate backstory, either—the monster fell for a size 16 no-hackle spent caddis with a Swiss-straw wing and a head consisting of two turns of rusty African goat hair.

"Big fish," Chris said. "*Stoopid* big fish."

Raul smiled broadly. "Thanks, guys. It's ga-ga-great to be back on the river."

Raul left the shop with a spring in his step and a plan. He would do some chores—drain the cooler, off-load some perishables, tank up—then he would check out the sweet spot right below their customary campsite. It was a run along an island with a terrific cut bank on the far side. Raul wanted to scout that, as well as a side channel farther down.

About an hour later, Raul was jouncing down a short, rutted track surrounded by dense willows and chokecherry bushes. At the end of this road was a small, overgrown meadow, unremarkable but for a curious fact: The clearing probably was the precise spot where the Corps of Discovery had camped on the night of July 17, 1804. The diaries explicitly described a towering rock spire on which a pair of eagles roosted, and Lewis and Clark subsequently named it Eagle Rock. The cliff was still there, although in an uncharacteristic act of heresy, Louis had renamed it "Tit Rock."

It still amazed Louis and Raul that they could casually camp on so historic and sacred a piece of ground without having to fill out forms, kiss some park ranger's butt, or pay out the wazoo.

There was no other vehicle, but as Raul pulled up to the shaded area on the riverbank, he saw a tent—an old, canvas army surplus job. There were also jeans, black sneakers, and various articles of men's clothing strewn here and there on the bushes, drying. A large, flimsy panel of clear plastic was loosely stretched above the fire ring, and litter lay all about.

Raul pulled the SUV over, uncertain what to do. He was sensitive about intruding on others who might be communing with nature.

A moment later, a head poked out of the pup tent. A scrawny teenage boy crawled out. He was in black jeans but barefoot and naked from the waist up. He had a flat, hard stomach and a tanned, hairless chest with pale strap marks where the suspenders of the heavy canvas chest waders hanging nearby had protected him from the sun. He had a box of Marlboros stuffed in his waistband.

"It's Pha-Pha-Pha-Pha-Phoenix, right? From the produce department."

The kid jammed his fists in his pockets. When he cracked an impudent smile, his eyes became slits. He was unmistakably an Indian. "Yeah . . . It was your friend reamed out my manager. Then you all gave me a ride home."

"Of course," Raul said. "I told you about our trip."

"Yeah. The way you talked about this place—*the legendary Missouri River*—got me fired up to go fishin' again," Phoenix said, as if dropping everything on a whim to light out for Montana were the most natural thing on earth. "I ain't been fishin' in a long time—leastways till now."

"What about your job?"

"That job sucked. I won't be missin' it—that's for *shit* sure."

"What about your parents?"

"Mom ain't never around a whole lot. She don't care what I do one way or the other."

Raul saw a thick, bright yellow spinning rod leaning against a tree. It had a glittering silver lure attached.

"You've been fishing with . . . *that?*"

"Yeah. I caught a couple, too." Phoenix beamed. His teeth were small and perfectly formed, like kernels of white corn. "I been using scented marshmallow bait mostly, and them silver thingamajigs."

Raul was stunned. He felt somewhat responsible for the boy having—what, *hitchhiked?*—all the way out to the Missouri. And for what? To dunk *scented marshamallow bait* in these holy waters, home to the most wonderful dry-fly fishing on the planet? It was a crime what negligence, poverty, a broken home—even simple parental indifference—did to kids. Raul knew; he knew only too well.

Trying to hide his emotions, Raul rasped, "I'll tell you what. You ca-ca-ca-ca-come along with me. Let me get us rigged up, and I'll show you things you never dreamed about—things it took me years and years to learn on my own. I'll show you what fishing is all about."

Phoenix eyed Raul shrewdly. "What's in it for you?"

"I ma-ma-ma-ma-may as well tell you the first thing about fly fishing right now. It isn't just about the fishing." Raul paused and then quoted the 6th Virilian Protocol: "Brotherhood is sacred, for the warrior who walks alone leaves no mark upon the land, and the wind soon carries away all trace of him."

Phoenix scratched his head but said nothing.

Raul asked, "What size shoe do you wear?"

"I guess an eight."

That was about the same as Louis, Raul knew, so waders and boots would be no problem. The men had duplicates and triplicates of everything. Raul patiently explained the rudiments of fly fishing as he hastily stuffed his own backup vest with odds and ends and rigged up a rod and reel.

This untrammeled enthusiasm put Phoenix on guard; growing up unsupervised, he knew all about overly friendly loners. But by the time they were geared up and walking the bank, teacher and protégé were developing an easy familiarity. Within an hour, Phoenix was casting a caddis dry fly at rising fish under Raul's watchful eye.

Granted, the trout were run-of-the-mill, foot-long, riffle-dwelling rainbows—the kind of trout any feather thrower could catch all day on the Missouri. But that was just fine with Raul. He took enormous pleasure from guiding Phoenix and getting him into fish.

The quest for bank feeders could wait.

———

"No, no, not here!" Lottie cried. She pushed Louis back, but as soon as she relented, he again pressed his lips on hers. He clutched one of her boobs and began wringing it like a sponge.

"Ouch!" She grappled with him; Louis lost his balance and rolled over on the blanket spread beneath the pale green ash tree.

"You brute," she said, laughing. "Listen to me—I need to keep an eye on the boys."

Louis sat up. Tufts of hair stuck out from his temples, and his glasses were akimbo. They had been making out on and off for about ten minutes while, well out of earshot, Biff and Buff selected and marked willow saplings that might make good espontoons.

Louis fished a Brazil nut out of the trail mix. Lottie removed her hair thingy, shook her head, and then gathered her hair into a new topknot. "I have to tell you," she drawled. "It's just as well you went to the wrong room. I would have been worried about getting caught."

Louis chuckled. "I don't think Dolph would be foolish enough to jeopardize my developing relationship with him. Not when he's desperate to get me on board as his writer."

"But this is about my job, not you. Men always blame the woman—we're all Monica Lewinskys."

Louis supposed she was right.

"I reckon I had a powerful hankerin' for you last night," he said, tamping some hair into place. "It's unfortunate the way it turned out."

"I was looking forward to holding you . . . I see Biff. Or is that Buff?"

"Buff. It must be all the talk about Indians, I reckon, but . . ." He hesitated. "I see us doing it, um, the *Comanche* way." He looked at Lottie to gauge her reaction. "You know, doggie-style."

Lottie exclaimed and smacked his arm. She scootched over and settled between his thick legs and leaned back against his chest. Louis wrapped his arms around her. They watched the boys.

"So, Buff," Louis said, "he's the dull one. An unfortunate specimen. Yet I feel a certain, um, affinity with him."

"You do?" Lottie swept his paws off her chest. She twirled around and sat facing him, cross-legged. "Are you serious?"

"Yes."

Lottie looked down at her hands, which were dismembering a pecan. "I didn't know if I should tell you this . . ." She paused. "Well, you know that handwriting game we played last night?"

Louis waited.

"Well, I have to tell you—it was a ruse. It was meant to identify certain, quote, *learning disabilities,* unquote. I did it to confirm a hunch I had."

"Which was?"

"Well, that Biff doesn't really *have* any learning disabilities. That he was just adopting them—out of solidarity with Buff. Twins often do that kind of thing."

"It's an interesting theory. It seems a mite far-fetched, if you don't mind my saying so."

"Well, get this. Biff's writing sample was impeccable. He spelled nearly every word correctly. There was no sign whatsoever of dyslexia—or anything like it."

When her voice trailed off, Louis asked, "But?"

Lottie seemed reluctant to continue.

Louis chuckled. "You're extra cute when you're nervous."

She blurted, "Well, you and Buff, you produced identical—and I mean *identical*—writing samples."

"So . . . ?" Louis dryly added, "Is that supposed to mean something?"

"It gets even more weird. You not only spelled the same words wrong, but the ones you screwed up were *exactly* the same words Captain Clark spelled wrong."

Louis said nothing.

"Louuuis? That's weird. Look at me . . ."

He obliged, with a shrug.

"Not just regular weird," she added. "It's deeply weird. I mean, *difficulty* with an *e* after the *u*? *Very* with two *r*'s?" She merely spelled out the next word: *"t-u-m-e-r?"*

"These things happen," Louis said reasonably. "They're honest mistakes. F. Scott Fitzgerald couldn't spell, and you can verify that. Granted, he doesn't hold a candle to Hemingway as a writer, but . . ."

"Louis! Tell me again. You're the Guardian of Grammar, right? I really need to hear this, Louis." Lottie sobbed. Her whole chest heaved as she succumbed to emotion. "I really need to know that you're who you say you are—not some disreputable mountain man, taking advantage of my trusting heart." She grabbed a paper towel and blew her nose. It was a long blast, so loud that the boys, who had been busy trying to push over a small, dead tree, looked up from their chore.

She continued, "Tell me you're not just using me until you're ready to ride off into the sunset."

Louis felt relieved. "This isn't really about my spelling, is it?" He took her in his arms and spoke deliberately: "Why, you're the only one for me, Little Squaw. I reckon you'd realize that by now."

Lottie's sobs subsided. She blew her nose again, less volubly. "Oh, do you really mean it?"

"Of course I mean it. It may also comfort you to know that while some find it ironic, I have trouble spelling. I am perhaps overreliant on spell-checking software, I admit. The technology has been a godsend for me."

"I suppose that's all right." Lottie laughed, feeling foolish. "I don't know why I get so emotional sometimes. I have to tell you, it just happens."

The boys, having finally pushed over the tree and snapped off most of its dry, thin limbs, started back toward Louis and Lottie.

Lottie was lost in thought. After a few moments, her face lit up. "Jeez, Louise, how could I not see it? How could I be so blind? Do you realize what all this means, Louis?"

"What?"

"Buff is seriously learning disabled. Right? He spells exactly like Captain Clark—and you."

Louis fidgeted.

"You were learning disabled too, Louis! You suffer from the same handicap as Clark before you, and Buff after. That's why, as a child, you shut down and retreated to your fantasy world of dissected frogs and insects and fish!

"That's why you just stared out the window at school. Your ex-wife is wrong, Louis, you aren't just 'a lazy sack of shit'—Oh no, far from it!—Louis, you were LD. Nobody ever caught it back then."

"Piffle!" Louis cried. He was both embarrassed and irritated. "Let's drop it."

"Of course," Lottie said. She sensed his deep discomfort. He had built up so many walls to protect himself, so much emotional insulation. Why tear it apart now? It all made sense to her; as a professional, she knew the psychic terrain like the back of her hand.

"Miss Moffo!" Biff cried. "We want to cut the trees now. Can we?"

"We're coming," Louis yelled, reaching for the hatchet he had brought along to fell timber for their espontoons.

Lottie knew instinctively that her theory was true. It had thrown Louis completely off balance. She had never seen him so vulnerable. She drew him close and gave him a short, fierce kiss.

"I want to do it Comanche-style, too," she murmured. "With you pulling my hair."

————

Raul didn't get back to Crooked Butte Ranch until after cocktail hour. He rushed up to the room to clean up and found Louis catching a brief nap.

After a quick shower, Raul woke Louis and briefed him on the morning's activities. He also told Louis about Jim Range's humongous trout. Louis asked for all the details and expressed some skepticism that a brown trout of that caliber would have been feeding on spent caddis in the Bull Pit during daylight hours. But that, he philosophically noted, was fishing.

Raul was frustrated by Louis's measured response. Under most circumstances, news of a fish like Range's would have led Louis into a frenzy of investigations and replenished enthusiasm. He might even have lobbied for running down to the Bull Pit after dinner, for Louis was not averse to the idea of catching the same fish as had another man twenty-four hours earlier.

"Louis, we need to talk," Raul said. "Actually, I need to sha-sha-sha-share my feelings about something."

Louis, who was thinking about Lottie, absently said, "What?"

"I want to go camp at our Pelican Point site. I miss the vibe from over there."

"We can't do that, Raul. We have to broach the subject of High Meadow Ranch after dinner. We could be on our way to the Little Goose by morning."

They discussed the issue. Raul admitted that he wanted to put off the hunt for the Little Goose for a day because he had already made a fishing date with Phoenix for the next morning. He felt there might be some Trico action on the Missouri.

"Trico, shmico," Louis said. "We're talking about finding Little Gooseneck Creek. What is it with you and this kid?"

"Nothing," Raul mumbled.

Babette rang the dinner bell for the second time; everyone would be waiting downstairs.

"It's ja-ja-ja-ja-just that . . . he reminds me of me. I feel I'm seeing a movie of my own life. The dysfunctional family. The retreat to sports. I didn't even tell you—Phoenix played legion ball. He made the all-star team at sha-sha-sha-sha-shortstop. They kicked him off for smoking."

"I thought you hated smoking," Louis said.

"Da-da-da-damnit, Bonaparte! That's not the point!"

They dropped the subject and went downstairs.

Although they were eating in the old mess, the long table was set with elegant silver and three heavy iron candelabra, each holding half a dozen candles the size of soup cans. Seebold stood waiting at the head of the table. He looked vaguely like the vocalist in a mariachi band in a black vest over a spotless white shirt with puffy sleeves.

He directed Louis to sit immediately to his right, while Raul was dispatched to the far end of the table, where he was to sit with some of the wranglers who periodically ate with the family. Biff and Buff also were allowed to eat with the adults, as a result of having behaved so well for Lottie that day. The boys clutched their new espontoons. They were dressed just like their dad.

The empty place next to Seebold was for Dale Chippen, who apparently was on the way back from spending the day in Missoula on ranch business. Louis burned to know what kind of business but bit his tongue.

Louis tried an appetizer. He remarked that he had never expected to be served curry puffs—no less such evenly browned, aromatic ones—on the Rocky Mountain front.

"You've probably all picked up on the fact that Dolph Seebold is an internationalist in his heart of hearts," Seebold said. "I try to reflect that at special gatherings. I've been known to drive Babette to distraction with my menu selections, but you'll find she executes them exquisitely."

"Thank you, Mr. Seebold," Babette called from behind the counter.

"Let's everybody start; there's no telling when Dale might show up."

"Boys, did you tell your father how you made your espontoons?" Louis asked.

The boy described in vivid detail how, under Louis's watchful eye, they had been involved in every phase of making the espontoons. And they were clearly proud of their work.

"The young braves did a good job," Louis remarked, turning to Seebold. "They've clearly inherited their father's patience. Not to mention his ability to focus on detail."

Raul wanted to gag.

Dolph acknowledged Louis's compliment and took the opportunity to wax philosophical on the importance of paying attention to detail in all things. He could see that level of particularity in Louis's ruminations on language and grammar no less than in his own activities as an investor and entrepreneur.

Then Dolph embarked on a long-winded and frequently self-referential monologue on wealth creation and the nature of capitalism. He announced that he had recently thought up something he called the Contribution Index. This was a mathematical formula Seebold had worked out by which, he claimed, it was possible to determine precisely how much of a contribution an individual made to society. It was based on the difference between the amount of wealth created by an individual, such as a Seebold or a Donald Trump, and how much—or little—of that wealth the individual actually burned through with no benefit to anyone but himself.

The Contribution Index was meant to demonstrate how someone who earns fifty times more than another person doesn't necessarily live fifty times better, and therefore represents a social and economic "profit margin."

Seebold pointed out that he did not live much better than, say, Raul Mendoza, founder of Dent-A-Men, a modestly successful niche business in a secondary marketplace, Seattle. He gestured toward Raul: "The proof is before your very eyes, ladies—*lady*—and gentlemen. This very night, Dent-A-Men Mendoza is eating the very same fine chicken paprikash and cucumber salad as Dolph Seebold."

Lottie and Raul exchanged glances.

Seebold stroked his septum and went on to explain what this meant in terms of the Contribution Index. Finally there was a way to quantify an important principle and truth: that *all* the wealth created, but not directly used, by the Trumps and Seebolds of the world was being redistributed in "real time." That is, it was being doled out to people ranging from stockbrokers to housekeepers to workers in factories in which Seebold and scores of others—like B. Louis Traub—invested.

Furthermore, that distribution in turn created ever more wealth as it was being used by others. Seebold provided a simple example from his own life. Just by stashing a few million surplus dollars in a local bank, Seebold enabled that bank to guarantee loans for erstwhile small-business entrepreneurs—say, the next Raul Mendoza looking to start the equivalent of Dent-A-Men in some place like Missoula.

"The whole point of the Contribution Index," Seebold said, "is to demonstrate the extent to which wealth that isn't dissipated grows exponentially—if it isn't removed from the system. And that's a big *if.*"

Seebold turned to Louis, who had been listening and nodding like a bobble-head doll in a car window. He said, "Louis and I will be articulating this theory further, and working out the actual numerical values of the index, in my book."

Louis winked at Raul, cooling down the slighted founder of Dent-A-Men.

"Excuse me, Mr. Seebold," Lottie said. "But when you talk about money being taken out of the system, what exactly do you mean?"

Seebold suggested they take the discussion into the great room, where they could also have their dessert and coffee. "We're having an excellent flan, made from the closely guarded recipe of Nando, head chef of the Hotel Excelsior in Bilbao."

"Hear, hear," Louis said, ready for a postdinner whiskey. "Shall we adjourn then?"

"Can we stay up, Daddy?" Biff asked. "Please? Miss Moffo said she would read to us from Lewis and Clark."

Seebold promised the boys ten additional minutes, which they greeted with a cheer. Everyone rose, thanking Babette. Some of the wranglers drifted out the back entrance, eager to get back to sitting the fence, wads of chaw stuffed in their cheeks.

"Bilbao," Louis said, walking with Seebold. "Isn't that where they recently unearthed *Bogman?*

"Bogman!" Biff cried, full of wonder. "Who's that?"

"One of our ancient ancestors," Louis replied. "Discovered—quite by happenstance—when the municipal government of Bilbao broke ground for the city's new National Brocade and Embroidery Museum. Bogman is the fossil of a human, apparently carrying some sort of leather pouch and hatchet. He's thought to be over fourteen *thousand* years old."

The guests all settled into comfortable seats. The boys ran to the sofa and sat on either side of Lottie. Biff pulled her face close and whispered, "Louis said he was going to talk to Dad, so he could take us fishing tomorrow. If you said it was okay."

"And what's become of Dale Chippen?" Louis asked.

"I wonder," Seebold said.

Babette came in, wheeling a large cart loaded with the flan and coffee.

"Tell us more about Bogman," Biff demanded.

"Yeah, the Bobman," Buff chimed.

"It's Bog, like frog," Biff said.

"Well, boys . . ." Louis was over at the bar, pouring himself a whiskey. "It appears that the scientists in the field keep pushing back the date for when man parted ways with his evolutionary predecessor—his long-lost brother, if you will—the ape. Family Pongidae."

Babette, passing out helpings of flan, loudly cleared her throat.

"If, as originally thought, we made the crucial evolutionary break with simians . . ."

"Not quite so fast now," Seebold said amiably. "You ought to inform the boys that this is all speculative. There isn't any conclusive evidence for evolution."

"How's that?" Louis said cordially. "The scientific evidence is, um, overwhelming."

Seebold began drumming his fingers on the arm of the sofa as Louis turned back to the boys. "I see from all those old 'Carl' books that you boys are fans of the rottweiler breed. Do you know why the rottweiler has those two tan dots above its eyes?"

"Why?"

"Once, far back in the mists of time, through pure coincidence or some sort of genetic mutation, a rotti was born with those markings. That particular canid enjoyed a survival advantage in mortal combat with other wild dogs, because those dots were easily confused with the dog's eyes . . . much like the dots found near the tails of some tropical fish will fool a shark into attacking the wrong end of the creature."

"That isn't evolution," Seebold interjected, sounding irritated. "That's *adaptation*. Nobody has ever shown that some mud-dwelling snail ever 'evolved' into, say, a hummingbird or a mouse."

"It's interesting that you bring that up, Dolph," Louis said. "Surely you saw the article that was published in the *New York Times* just a few weeks ago?" Louis paused, taking in his audience. "The architects of the human genome determined that humans and mice have—oh, correct me if I'm wrong, Dolph—about 70 percent identical DNA."

"I didn't see that article," Seebold snapped. He leaped to his feet. "Evolutionary theory rules the roost for just one reason: because it's science-based. Sure, if you rule out or prohibit the concept of creation, then some form of evolution *is* the model that seems to make the most sense. But it's still not a lot of sense. And how can you rule out creation, just because it can't be proved or disproved?"

"Indeed, *Of Mice and Men*," Louis remarked, chuckling. "The idea foisted on us by Catholic priests, rabbis, and other religious extremists— that we are biologically unrelated to creatures as visibly similar to us as, oh, marmosets, guenon baboons, and capuchins . . . Well, that's something that I, quite frankly, find preposterous."

"*Similar to* and *related to* are utterly different concepts." Seebold was almost screaming. His face was beet red, and the sleeves of his gaucho shirt billowed as he waved his arms in protest. "Why is there such dogged opposition in scientific circles to the theory of intelligent design? Why? Why? Why?"

"'Intelligence' strikes me as a curious word to use in any context relating to unenlightened papists and fundamentalists," Louis said calmly. "They're—"

"Get out!" Seebold's face was white as a sheet. He pointed toward the guest wing. "Pack your things right now and scram!"

"Daddy, no!" the boys shouted in unison.

They were interrupted by a loud banging on the door.

Everyone fell silent and looked at each other. Old Ollie gimped over. When he opened the door, two Montana state troopers stepped into the room. One had his hand lightly resting on his sidearm. He was lean and tall, with a pencil-thin mustache. He squinted at Louis. "You must be Traub. Who's Mendoza?"

"How dare you!" Seebold said to the troopers as Raul raised his hand.

"You two," the mustachioed trooper said, "stand over there. You're under arrest."

Louis and Raul looked at each other and simultaneously asked, "For what?"

"This is outrageous!" Seebold declared.

"These men are under arrest for being in possession of stolen property and transporting it across state lines with intent to sell. They're working for a ringleader from down Bozeman way, fella named Kiick."

"The drift boat," Louis said. Raul repeated his words.

Lottie fainted, hitting the floor with a heavy thud.

"Wow!" Biff said. "You're outlaws. Way cool!"

Babette ran over and tended to Lottie.

"We da-da-da-didn't do anything," Raul protested. He quickly explained how Bowen Kiick had practically forced the boat—ostensibly, his own—on them and then disappeared. The only reason they were still towing it around was because of the fly-fishing ethic—you never returned someone's gear broken.

"I'm sure the judge will love that story," the mustachioed trooper said. "By the way, according to the wranglers down below, you offered to *sell* them the boat earlier today."

Louis looked at Raul, who shrugged and said, "I was joking."

"That's some humor," the trooper said. "What do you take us for, North Dakotans?"

Raul turned to Louis and whispered, "I smell a rat."

"Chippen," Louis hissed.

"Chippen."

"What was that?" the trooper asked.

"Bear with us for a moment," Louis said reasonably. "I'm certain that when you hear the facts you'll, um, appreciate our dilemma and perhaps even share a laugh over it."

"Button it," said the other trooper, a hefty, freckled redhead named Billy.

Billy stepped forward, roughly spun Louis around, and cuffed him with fancy, new plastic manacles. Raul put up no resistance when it was his turn, as the tall trooper explained the legal details.

The arrest warrant had been issued in Lincoln. The troopers were going to transport the two criminals back to that town, which was a few hours' drive west, where they would appear before the judge for arraignment and a bail hearing the following day.

The reality of the situation was beginning to sink in to everyone.

Suddenly, Buff began to wail.

"He's innocent, he's innocent!" Lottie cried. She ran over, fell to her knees, and clutched Louis. "You're not taking him anywhere."

Billy looked at Seebold and said, "The girlfriends. Always the last to know."

As the troopers led the men away, Seebold called out, "Lincoln. Don't I know that name?"

Billy wearily reported, "It's the town where we finally caught Ted Kaczynski—that Unabomber fella."

10

The bars on the window of the cell where Louis and Raul had spent the night cast a dramatic shadow on the cold cement floor in the Lincoln town jail. The jailhouse was part of the Lincoln municipal building, which also housed the offices of the tax assessor, building inspector, and animal control officer.

Raul, unable to collect even his toilet articles when they were hauled off, had no earplugs. Louis's rumbling snores from the bunk above had frequently wakened him. He did gain a paltry measure of satisfaction when Louis complained about Raul's gas, which undoubtedly was caused by Babette's rich flan. But the gray woolen blanket on the bunk bed was itchy, and the pillowcase, though clean, smelled of hair pomade.

From the window of their cell, the men could see steep mountainsides carpeted with green-black spruce trees in the distance. It was a sharp contrast to the high prairie of the Missouri River country. They were on the west slope of the Continental Divide now, where even the air was different—moist and cool, unlike the dry, searing heat at the margin of the Great Plains.

"This is one thing that we've never experienced, pardner. Incarceration. I expect we'll go before a reasonable magistrate soon, and we'll clear all this up quickly. I presume each of us will be permitted to make our one allotted phone call this morning?"

"Do you think they'll be that strict? My father used to call us drunk from jail all the time . . ."

"Those were different times."

Incarceration and the family memories it stimulated put Raul in a pensive mood. He insisted that whomever they called, Phoenix would have to be informed. Raul knew exactly how it felt to be stood up for a fishing trip because of jail; his father had done it to him a million times.

Louis took his tin cup and banged on the bars of the cell. Soon a sheriff's deputy poked his head into the small, six-cell unit.

The deputy, a skinny little fellow named Hochenpfeffer, stole in cautiously. He maintained a safe distance, darting glances over each shoulder to make sure no funny business was going on. He said that later an escort of troopers would take them to the courthouse for arraignment.

"It's not real often that we get high-grade criminals like yourselves round here. In fact, you're our only prisoners at the moment. But that Ted fella, the Unabomber? He was in this selfsame cell when he was first apprehended. Course, we had nothing to do with it—that was all the feds."

The little deputy irritated Louis. "I must inform you that I know my rights as a U.S. citizen," he said. "This is a terrible miscarriage of justice. I insist that you immediately allow us to make our legally mandated telephone calls."

"You want to use the phone, mister?"

"Let me be clear," Louis continued in a menacing tone. "Should you participate in any conspiracy to violate my civil rights, I'll have no recourse but to seek legal help. Do the words American Civil Liberties Union ring a bell? I don't need to tell you the damage that a nasty, highly publicized civil rights battle might cause to the reputation of your nice, little town—not to mention its budget."

"Okay. Let me get the cordless." Hochenpfeffer hesitated. "You're some kind of lawyer, ain't you?"

"I take the fifth," Louis replied. "How soon can we go before the judge?"

"You're scheduled for noon. First thing."

While the deputy was gone, Louis and Raul made a plan. They would call Lottie. Louis had gleaned enough about her affairs to know that she had adequate cash reserves to bail them out. They could use their other call to make one last-ditch effort to find Bowen Kiick, sending an SOS through Amber at the Elkhorn. He was the one who could clear up this mess, but fast.

The deputy returned with the phone and retreated when Louis demanded privacy. He dialed the number for Crooked Butte.

"Louis?" Upon hearing his voice, Lottie cried, "How are you? How are they treating you?"

He allayed her fears about police brutality and homosexual rape, making a crack about already having a "prison wife" in Raul. He outlined their dilemma and asked Lottie to come bail them out.

"I can't just now," she said. "Mr. Seebold left early this morning, and Babette's gone too—to Helena. I'm at the house alone with the boys."

"Tarnation," Louis said, exasperated. "Where did Seebold go?"

"California," Lottie replied. "He's taking the jet for a noon meeting in Silicon Valley. Then he's flying to Missoula at the end of the day to meet that Dale Chippen. They're going to drive to this place, High Meadow Ranch, to sign contracts. Seebold's selling it."

"What?" Louis shouted, cutting her off. "They're going to sell the High Meadow Ranch property? *Today?*"

Raul looked at Louis. Their eyes narrowed, and they exclaimed in unison, *"Chippen!"*

Louis was beside himself. Raul crowded close to listen in as Lottie told them everything she knew.

Raul whispered, "Don't forget to remind her about Phoenix."

"Hold on, Lottie," Louis said. Then he held a quick powwow with Raul. Chippen must have discovered Little Gooseneck Creek and struck some kind of deal with the prospective buyer, double-crossing Seebold. He was now forcing Seebold's hand out of the well-founded fear that Louis and Raul would discover the Little Goose and find a way to scotch the deal. Which was exactly what they now had to do.

Louis got back on the phone. "Lottie? Trust me on this—throw the boys in the War Pony and get up here as fast as you can to bail us out. Bring your checkbook and cell phone."

Raul nudged him. Louis explained about Phoenix, then declared, "Godspeed, Lottie. Our fate is in your able hands."

Louis and Raul agreed that they needed more than ever to find Bowen—only he could vouch for their credibility in front of Seebold. Louis called the Elkhorn and—*bingo*—got Amber. He cut right to the chase, but she soon interrupted: "Bowen knows exactly where the Little Goose is. He was trying to buy it himself."

"What?"

Amber sighed. "You're his friends. . . He'll tell you all about it himself—if I can find him. He's laying low."

"He's the only one who can save us," Louis reminded her. "And *we're* the only ones who can save the Little Goose."

Louis, Raul, and Deputy Hochenpfeffer got a ride to the court-house from an attractive female rookie trooper named Mavis, who drove with the lights flashing and siren blaring. She refused to converse with the "criminals," pointing out that she took her job too seriously for that. She was part of the "thin blue line."

It was almost one in the afternoon; the time of the arraignment had been pushed back because Judge Bennie Sternoe had decided to take advantage of the "early bird tire-rotation special" offered by the Quik-Lube in Missoula.

They waited in the large, empty court chamber. It was a handsome room with dark wainscoting, cream-colored walls, and vibrant prints depicting lawmen of yore. Mavis and Hochenpfeffer discussed Judge Sternoe's decision to go with the Cooper tires over the Bridgestones while Louis and Raul talked between themselves.

Gradually, a handful of the usual snoops and fishwives drifted into the room, on the off chance that another notorious serial killer had been apprehended overnight. They got their hopes up when they espied Louis and Raul. One spectator, a youth in an ill-fitting suit with his tie askew, clutched a reporter's notebook.

Shortly after one P.M., an officer of the court entered and declared, "All rise."

Raul respectfully removed his fedora and put it over his heart; Louis grudgingly lifted his legionnaire's hat.

Judge Sternoe appeared to the scratchy sound of a recording of "God Bless America," wearing an elegant black robe. He looked to be about eighty, but he scampered spryly up some steps and took his seat in a commanding position, high above the ordinary citizens. He called the court to order and declared that everyone would now recite the Pledge of Allegiance.

"I am not in kindergarten," Louis whispered to Raul. "I refuse to place my hand over my heart and mouth tired, jingoistic platitudes."

"Shhhh," Raul hissed.

After the pledge, Judge Sternoe invited the court to join him in the Lord's Prayer.

"This is outrageous!" Louis sputtered. "What about the separation of church and state?"

"Did I hear someone say something?" Judge Sternoe asked, raising his eyebrows. They were thick and prominent, like a pair of silver-and-black wings.

Raul gave Louis a shot in the ribs with his elbow. They replied in unison, "No, sir."

After the Lord's Prayer, Judge Sternoe called for a moment of silence to honor the brave men and women who had given their lives fighting for the nation's freedom. Then His Honor removed his wristwatch and propped it up against the water pitcher, where he could see it easily. He pushed his reading glasses far down his nose and shuffled some papers on his desk, muttering as he quickly reviewed the charges against Louis and Raul. He asked the men to step forward.

Louis spoke first: "Before we proceed, your honor . . ."

"Quiet. Speak when you're spoken to. Is that clear?"

"Technically speaking—"

"Is that clear?" Sternoe thundered.

"Yes, Your Honor."

"Good, then. Let's proceed to the charges being brought against the defendants in the State of Montana versus Traub, Mendoza, et al."

Raul gulped. The gravity of the situation fully enveloped him.

The judge examined the arrest reports and paperwork, now and then uttering, "I see . . . ," or a pregnant, "Hmm . . ."

Finally he looked over his glasses and down at the two men standing before him. He chortled. "Well, it looks like you two footloose out-of-staters are being charged with grand theft and the interstate transport of stolen property with the intent to sell."

Raul nearly fainted. He was filled with an irrational dread that he was guilty. The entire court could hear the youth in the rumpled suit scratching on a pad with his pencil. The exact words used by Judge Sternoe echoed in Raul's mind, and he thought, "I knew it. This is what happens when you fly by the seat of the pants."

The judge suddenly leaned way back in his big, black, cushy chair, folded his hands across his stomach, and said, "So you decided to steal a boat and cross state lines with it?"

"Objection, your honor," Louis said, trying to sound lawyerly.

"One more time, and I'm going to hold you in contempt of court," Judge Sternoe warned.

The cub reporter scrawled more notes.

The judge picked up a sheaf of papers and muttered as he read: "Seattle and New York . . . From Dillon to West Yellowstone . . . Eagletech—now there's a great store for you . . . I see . . . So, which one of you goes by the alias Big Sky Bonaparte?"

"I do, your honor," Louis said, stepping forward. "I would hardly—"

"Just answer the question!"

"Yes, sir . . . I do, *Your Honor. Sir.*" Louis gesticulated but stopped short of saying anything more.

Judge Sternoe returned to his reading. "I see . . . A burned vehicle, now that's interesting . . . The Three Forks convenience store? Hmm . . . What's this about causing a riot at the Round Up Inn?"

"Yes, Your Honor," Trooper Mavis said.

"This is *very* impressive spadework. Is it yours?"

"No, Your Honor. It was mostly Mr. Nuckel. The private investigator."

Louis and Raul looked at each other. Nuckel? Who was Nuckel?

Judge Sternoe removed his glasses and peered at Deputy Hochen-pfeffer: "He's that old boy from over Butte way, I believe."

"I think that's right," the deputy said.

The judge became absorbed in the paperwork again, but he kept up his running commentary. "This is quite the résumé . . . Are we looking at some kind of gang operation? Didn't anyone ever tell you boys, loose lips sink ships?"

He closed the folder and leaned back, hands behind his head. "This case seems solid as Fort Knox," he said. "Now, it's almost your time to speak, Mr. Bonaparte. Or should I use your alias, *Big Sky* Traub?"

Louis relished the opportunity to defend himself. Raul, though, had pretty much given up. He stood there, utterly hangdog.

"So. How do the defendants—that's you, Mr. Mendoza, Mr. Traub—plead? Not guilty, no contest, or guilty?"

"Not guilty!" Louis cried. "Emphatically not guilty!"

The judge leaned forward and stared intently at Raul. "I seem to detect some indecision on your part, Mr. Mendoza."

Raul almost leaped out of his shoes. "Na-na-na-na-no. Louis speaks for both of us."

"I ought to remind you," Sternoe said philosophically, "either of you has the option of turning state's witness and considerably lessening your individual sentence. I've found that business about honor among thieves is Hollywood nonsense. Feel free to cut and run."

The judge let the offer sink in before he continued: "Then. Have the defendants retained an attorney to represent them?"

Louis plowed ahead, "Once you see the facts, your honor—"

"Answer my question! Yes or no?"

"No," Raul said, toying with the brim of his fedora.

Louis spoke: "We plan to represent ourselves. Should we . . ."

"*Thank you*, Mr. Traub. No reason we can't set a date for a speedy trial." Judge Sternoe took out a soiled, dog-eared pocket datebook and flipped through the pages. "We can do this in as little as ten days' time. Defendants?"

"Ta-ta-ta-ten days?"

"Keep it together, pardner. We'll beat this bum rap."

"This brings us to the matter of whether or not the state would be meeting its obligations to its citizens by releasing either of you before the trial. I'm obliged to inform you that this release could be on your own recognizance or through bail. Do you have any questions in that regard? Defendants?"

Louis thought for a moment; he had no questions, but he jumped at the chance to speak. "My friend here is a distinguished entrepreneur, and I myself have attained a measure of celebrity in the literary sphere. I suggest you release us on our own recognizance."

"Why would I do that?" Sternoe inquired. "Celebrity? A celebrity wouldn't wear those filthy jeans."

"Your Honor, with all due respect," Louis said. "We're also quite well known among the international community of serious fly fishers who either live or annually gather in this state." He groped for the names of famous Montana feather throwers he knew and began to rattle off their names: "Beau Turner, Pat Hemingway, Yvon Chouinard, Pat Barnes . . ."

"This has nothing to do with who you know," Judge Sternoe barked. "It's cash bail or the hoosegow for you."

"Cash bail," Louis muttered.

The judge weighed his options and declared, "All right then, bail is set at fifty thousand dollars for each defendant."

"Fifty thousand?" Raul repeated, incredulous.

"Mr. Mendoza," the judge growled.

Louis grabbed Raul's arm to keep him from passing out. He looked up at Judge Sternoe and asked, "Can we prevail upon you to have our say, albeit briefly?"

"You've had your talking time," the judge said, banging his gavel. "The next time you have your say will be during your trial."

Mavis and Hochenpfeffer put the cuffs back on the men and led them out. They were all hungry, so they went to a drive-through for hamburgers on the state, a routine perk for the lawmen.

At the drive-through window, Louis politely inquired whether there was a spending limit. Raul couldn't imagine eating. He ordered just a large strawberry milkshake.

When the party arrived back at the municipal building, Lottie and the Seebold boys were in the sherriff's office. They all leaped up, but the sight of the men in handcuffs stopped Lottie in her tracks.

"Lottie!"

The boys, wielding their new espontoons, cried Louis's name.

Mavis and Hochenpfeffer stopped.

"We're here to bail them out," Lottie said. "You can release them now."

"Forget it," Louis said. "Bail is set at a hundred thousand dollars. You're a yoga instructor, not a Wall Street despoiler."

"Oh my God!" Lottie cried. "What's the charge, murder?"

Hochenpfeffer looked at Mavis, who arched her eyebrows. They nudged the prisoners to get them moving again toward the security door. Hochenpfeffer reached into his shirt pocket for the white, plastic passkey that activated the fancy electronic lock and passed it over the sensor. There was a sharp *beep,* and the door swung open to the long corridor leading to the jail cells.

"We'll be right back," Hochenpfeffer said to Lottie. "I'll explain everything."

As the men disappeared through the door, Louis half turned and cried out, "Have faith, Lottie—justice will prevail!"

Raul flung his head back, shouting, "We didn't do it—we're innocent! *Innocent,* you hear?"

The mood in the small jail cell an hour later was bleak. Louis sat on the edge of the bunk, head in his hands. Raul stood near the window, ramrod straight, with his legs together and his arms outstretched to the sky beyond; he was chanting softly in a native tongue.

Louis feared for his partner's emotional health. He knew that Raul was a sensitive man who had carefully designed his life to eliminate traumas and unexpected surprises—good or bad.

"Seebold will bail us out; he needs me to write his book," Louis said. "It will all be okay, but by then it will be too late for us to keep control of the Little Goose."

Raul raised his arms over his head, slowly brought them together, and genuflected. Yoga exercises helped him relax.

Suddenly there was a commotion in the hall. Phoenix and the Seebold boys, dressed in their lederhosen, ran up to the cell and began to fumble with the door.

Flabbergasted, Raul cried, "Phoenix? What's going on?"

"Jailbreak," Phoenix replied insouciantly without looking up from his task—trying to find the right key to fit the lock on the cell. Biff helped Phoenix while Buff clutched the espontoons, watching.

"Yeah," Biff bragged. "We tied up the deputy. Miss Moffo's waiting in the car. Hurry up!"

"Yeah, hurry up," Buff echoed.

"Oh my God, oh God." Raul was hyperventilating; he could barely speak. "*You ta-ta-ta-tied up the deputy?* We'll get the chair!"

"I got it!" Biff cried.

"Yeah, we got it," Buff echoed.

Phoenix swung the door open.

"Freedom!" Louis shouted, dashing out.

Raul stood by the window, undecided. But when the others raced down the hall, he grabbed his fedora off the sill and bolted after them.

Phoenix whooped. The Seebold boys echoed his jubilant war cry.

As they barreled out and through the offices of the constable, Louis saw Hochenpfeffer. He was bound to a revolving wooden desk chair with layers of duct tape and endless coils of rope. His hair was mussed, and he had a rag stuffed in his mouth.

Raul, caught up in the moment, let loose a scream: "Hee-yah!"

They dashed through the foyer of the municipal building, startling some visitors and town workers. Lottie waited, holding open the door of the War Pony. They all dove in. Lottie slammed the car into drive and stomped the accelerator.

The Seebold boys were elated to be reunited with their heroes. Little Jack leaped into the backseat and proceeded to lick Louis's face.

Lincoln, Montana, faded into the rearview mirror long before Little Jack released his first malodorous bomb.

When the fugitives reached the unmarked dirt road off Route 200 that led to High Meadow Ranch, they breathed a sigh of relief. Based on Raul's recall of Seebold's map, they still had about thirty miles to go.

Lottie pulled over when they were out of sight of the blacktop, exhaled, and slumped back against the seat. Phoenix, who had been forbidden to smoke in the vehicle, got out to have a cigarette. The boys tumbled out, with Louis trailing them. Lottie and Raul got out, too, with Little Jack. She ordered the dog to go poopsy, then asked if Raul would mind taking over the driving; she wasn't terribly comfortable on dirt roads.

"I don't think that would be a good idea," replied Raul, still in a state of anxiety over what surely was a genuine criminal act. "I'm in no ca-ca-ca-condition to pilot a motor vehicle at the moment. But thank you for thinking of me. I'm sure Louis would be happy to take over from here."

Little Jack struggled, but produced nothing.

"Uh-oh," Lottie remarked. "More stomach troubles."

Raul expressed his concern over their jailbreak. It was a serious crime, and they had implicated juveniles—Phoenix and the Seebold boys.

"I have to tell you," Lottie said, "the jailbreak was all Phoenix's idea."

They glanced his way. Phoenix lounged on the hood of the War Pony, seemingly without a care in the world, sucking on a cigarette.

"We'd better go!" Louis called to them.

They piled in again, Phoenix flicking his burning cigarette into the sand by the roadside. Louis made him get back out to retrieve the butt, noting that littering was as uncool as starting forest fires. Louis pulled away.

"Watch it!" Lottie cried.

Louis jerked the wheel just in time to keep the War Pony from plunging over a six-foot bank. He promised to pay full attention to the road. Soon they began a slow but steady ascent. It was past four in the afternoon, and the landscape was gradually but dramatically changing. Each mile brought new vistas of forested slopes, meadows carpeted with wildflowers, handsome red cliffs, and small ponds gleaming blue-black in the afternoon light.

"This is a good omen, boys," Louis said. "Note the water-rich environment. These water holes are indicative of a loaded aquifer. In some manner that I don't fully understand, this particular area seems to be a veritable magnet for water."

The road meandered into a pass filled with abrupt, twisting turns.

"Let's see," Raul said. "If my memory serves, over this ridge we ought to drop down into an enormous basin."

Sure enough, after another series of S-turns, they crested the ridge. Lottie caught her breath audibly, and the men uttered short exclamations of amazement at the spectacular sight that lay before them—a broad, dazzlingly green valley, surrounded by a semicircle of distant sawtoothed mountains.

"That, way off there, ought to be the great swamp," Raul said. "So we should be coming up on a left turn that leads over toward the base of those mountains."

"And Little Gooseneck Crick," Louis said.

"And the Little Goose," Raul echoed.

"Somebody's been on this road lately," Phoenix said. "Them's fresh tracks. They look like truck tires."

"Thank you, Phoenix, that's a very useful observation," Raul said.

"Man, I feel like a smoke," Phoenix added. "What's so special about this Goose Creek, anyways?"

"It's a spring creek," Raul replied. "The rarest and purest kind of river there is." He explained the difference between a freestone river, which depended mostly on melted snow and rain, and a spring creek, which usually came bubbling up out of the underground aquifer.

Louis took over, telling how the water in a spring creek was always cold and rich in minerals from being buffered underground by limestone.

"Miss Moffo," Biff whined. "Jack just laid a big fart."

They all lowered the windows.

"Okay, left up here," Raul said.

They figured they ought to hit the Little Goose about two miles farther on. Louis and Raul struggled to retain their composure. Nobody else in the SUV had any real appreciation of what they were about to find.

"There it is!" Buff cried. "I see it! I see it!"

Sure enough, there was water on the left. But it was almost at a standstill, black as old motor oil and hidden behind a tall screen of cattails. It looked more like a canal in the Everglades than a Rocky Mountain trout stream.

Biff hollered, "I want to go fishing!"

Louis and Raul were puzzled, but they went around a sharp bend and there it was—the Little Goose in all its glory.

The men knew they'd hit pay dirt. The river was about eighty feet wide, a liquid black mirror sliding along without so much as a gurgle. The only imperfection was the myriad dimples of rising trout, pocking the surface like raindrops. An assortment of birds strafed the surface, picking insects off at their leisure. Now and then, one would maneuver into a tight turn and briefly carve a silver slash on the surface with the tip of a wing.

"It looks black," said Biff, who'd imagined that the Little Goose would be like the Clearborn. "It's dirty."

Louis explained that, on the contrary, the water was as clean and transparent as any on earth. It only appeared black because it truly reflected the composition of the bottom—in this case, the dark, loamy soil and gravel spewed out by spectacular volcanic eruptions millions of years ago.

"Cool," Phoenix said.

"Yeah, cool," Buff echoed.

"You watch," Raul said. "The river will look turquoise when we get to some weed beds." He added, "The bridge that appears on the map—it ought to be just up ahead."

They came to the bridge, and Louis pulled over. They all got out. They had clear views up and down the river. Large mayflies—brown drakes, perhaps—were hatching in droves, and trout were gorging on them as far as the eye could see.

"Oh my Lord," Raul whispered, regarding the perpendicular banks. In many places, lush vegetation bent from its own weight and touched the surface of the river. Fish were feeding everywhere, leaving heavy swirls and bow wakes. Some even thrashed or wallowed halfway up into the weeds.

"Can we please go fishing?" Biff whined.

"No, Biff," Louis explained. "This isn't a place where we're allowed to fish."

Louis looked at Raul. Raul looked at Louis. The reality dawned on them simultaneously. They were actually with a Seebold—two Seebolds, in fact. Why *couldn't* they fish?

The men made a mad dash back to the War Pony and began tearing into their gear. Louis and Raul were men possessed.

"Jeez, Louise," Lottie said of the confusion. She turned to Phoenix. "Are they going fishing—*now?*"

Phoenix boosted himself up on the hood of the War Pony and, unfazed, fired up a smoke. He sat cross-legged, contemplating the river with his head cocked, a smile brightening his entire face. He said, "It sure is a beautiful spot. Kind of peaceful."

Buff began to cry. Louis took him by the shoulders and looked him right in the eye. "Uncle Louis and Uncle Raul have to go first, Buff. We have to make sure there are no snakes or poisonous bugs in the water."

Louis left the boy and, holding his legionnaire's hat to keep it from flying off, ran after Raul. They stood for a moment atop the steep, eroded bank leading down to the river. Linking arms, they slid and tumbled together, in an avalanche of stones and dirt, down to the water's edge.

Lottie kicked off her clogs and climbed onto the hood. Hugging her knees, she sat beside Phoenix. Little Jack wandered in a circle, whimpering, and lay down.

Louis and Raul were standing shoulder-to-shoulder, peering into a fly box. Lottie could see from their gesticulations that they were arguing over which fly to choose.

"They're good men," Lottie mused. "I have to tell you, though, they're a different breed."

"They sure know about fly fishin'," Phoenix said. He giggled. "Raul learned me a lot yesterday. Hey, did you notice? Raul hasn't been stutterin'—not since we busted him out of jail."

"I hadn't noticed," Lottie confessed.

"Maybe we cured him."

Before Lottie could evaluate this claim, a black Suburban appeared at the top of the steep hill just beyond the bridge. Two men jumped out and quickly scanned Louis and Raul with binoculars. They immediately got back in the car, threw it in gear, and barreled down to the bridge.

———

Louis stood by the large windows in a cabin perched on a bluff above Little Gooseneck Creek. A couple of ranch hands had politely but firmly escorted Louis and Raul into the cabin and instructed them to wait. They warned that there was no place to go if they busted out. Having recognized the Seebold boys, the ranch hands whisked them away, together with Lottie and Phoenix.

The cabin was part of the High Meadow Ranch compound of squat, simple buildings mostly made of dark logs with contrasting gray chinking. The compound occupied high ground overlooking the river valley, and Louis could only salivate at the Little Goose meandering in typical spring-creek fashion in the distance below. It was close, but too far off to tell if fish were still rising.

The western sky was dappled with lavender and orange puffs of cloud, and the mountain peaks were already the color of plums as dusk advanced.

"Well, we got to wade the Little Goose, if not exactly fish it," Raul said.

"Yes, that probably qualifies as an honor of sorts," Louis said.

The interior of the cabin was spartan, with half a dozen bunk beds positioned along the walls; Louis easily imagined a rowdy bunch of cowpokes hunkered down, blowing smoke rings as they lay in their bunks at the end of another long day spent driving cattle. In fact, Louis thought he could still detect the unpleasant odor of cigarette smoke in the unfinished wooden walls.

Louis examined one of the primitive propane light fixtures on the wall. He turned the black porcelain knob, and propane entered the light with a hiss. "This is hip, Raul. Look at this handsomely machined gas valve."

"We've got more important things to focus on," Raul replied. A moment later, he added, "I'm sorry, Louis. I didn't mean to be brusque."

While Louis looked out the window, two more vehicles passed. They were headed for the main ranch house, about a hundred yards farther up along the bluff. That, Louis assumed, was where the rest of their party had been taken.

"Those brown drakes were intense." Raul sighed heavily. "I've never seen such a heavy hatch—at least not of bugs that large. It was like giant Tricos carpeting the water."

"Indeed," Louis said. "I'm confident we'll get another shot at them—once we get all this straightened out with Dolph."

"I'm sure those were the same weird drakes we encountered on the Red Rock," Raul said, reviving the in-stream dispute that had been cut short when they were busted. "They had the same yellow underbelly and the same bulbous abdomen. You had to notice that."

Louis would not budge from his original position: The fly on the Little Goose was *Ephemera simulans,* the same brown drake that they knew from the Fork.

"The Centennial Valley is an environment much like this one," Raul argued, listing the similarities between the Red Rock River and Little Gooseneck Creek. Both were located in high-country basins. They were unspoiled ecosystems, off-limits to the public and far less likely to have been altered by invasive species or the loss of native species, including highly sensitive mayflies.

"That's just conjecture," Louis sniffed.

A single, loud knock interrupted their debate.

A cowboy poked his head in the door. "You all best follow me on up to the big house now."

They walked the dirt path in the dark, toward the intense white glow of the propane lamps on the outside of the main house. It had a covered, partially screened pavilion attached on one side, with enough tables and chairs to seat about fifty people for a barbecue. Inside the screened portion, seven or eight men were seated around a large table covered with maps, papers, and legal documents. They included Seebold, Chippen, and Bowen Kiick, who leaped to his feet and exclaimed, "Sky! Raul!"

"Bowen?" Louis was perplexed.

Bowen ran over and shared a Shoshone embrace with each of his friends. "I'm sorry guys," he said. "From the bottom of my black, no-good-ass heart, I sincerely and humbly apologize."

"You mean you knew about the Little Goose all along?" Louis asked.

"Come," Seebold interjected. He was wearing a pale yellow Nehru jacket, with a bit of dark green embroidery around the stand-up collar, and matching trousers. "Sit. I'd like to hear all of this."

The men did as they were told.

"This here is Nate Nuckelhead or something," Bowen said. "He's a private eye. Been trailing me, not you, all this while."

"Nuckel's the name." The private eye nodded. "But name calling never did make no never mind to me."

"But why you?" Raul asked Bowen.

The snaggle-toothed angler looked scornfully at Nuckel. "Go ahead—tell 'em."

"I was retained to investigate Mr. Kiick's activities and locate him for the authorities. There were warrants out for his arrest for failure to make child-support payments. To three different women."

"One of them was my former wife," Bowen protested, as if that somehow lessened his offense.

"One moment," Louis said. "Just who were you retained by? Surely the state cannot afford to retain, um, private investigators for this sort of thing."

"That would be confidential information, sir," Nuckel said. "But I can tell you that in the course of what appeared to be an otherwise routine investigation, I learned that Mr. Kiick had stolen a boat. At first I thought all of you were traveling together. Then I figured you were part of some kind of out-of-state ring of bandits."

"Was the boat stolen?" Seebold asked Bowen.

"Not exactly," Bowen said.

Seebold arched his eyebrows. "How *'not exactly'* exactly?"

Louis glanced at Chippen, who sat there with a smug smile.

"It was my boat," Bowen said. "I sold it to that shithead Aronoff."

"Joel Aronoff," Louis interjected. He leaned toward Seebold and confidentially added, "The trout-fishing entrepreneur who developed the first waders with a Sans-a-belt feature built in. I don't underestimate the needs of children, Dolph, legitimate or otherwise. But I know what that boat meant to Bowen and what it must have taken for him to sell it."

"Thanks, Sky," Bowen said. He turned to Seebold and explained that when he heard from Louis and Raul, his old friends from back in the day on the Fork, he felt obliged to organize the Beaverhead float. As Aronoff had gone down to fish the PMDs on the upper Snake in Wyoming, Bowen figured there was no harm in "borrowing" his old boat back for a day.

Bowen turned to Louis and Raul. "I'm sorry I never showed up for the float. But when I rolled into Amber's after our reunion dinner, I got a tip that this Nuckelhead here had been nosing around the way up from Bozeman, hard on my trail. I decided I'd better disappear."

"But I don't understand," Raul said. "Why would you have sold your boat? I can't imagine you doing that."

"That's where things get complicated." Bowen took a deep breath. "I sold the boat and I'm behind on my child-support because I was try-ing to raise enough money to put a deposit on this property. I wanted to buy High Meadow Ranch and Little Gooseneck Creek and ensure that it would never fall into the wrong hands—the hands of, as my good buddy Sky here likes to say, 'the despoilers.'"

Louis nodded at this acknowledgment. They heard the crunch of tires on gravel from the driveway, followed by the slamming of car doors.

Bowen went on: "True, I come from old money that was once big money but now is mostly tired, small money. I liquidated all my assets, borrowed from the family, tried to scrape together every cent so I could make an offer on this place. I thought I had it, too."

"So what happened, Dolph?" Louis asked.

"We had a better offer," Seebold replied with a shrug. "At the eleventh hour. It was just business."

"A better offer," Louis repeated softly. He tore off his legionnaire's cap and leaped to his feet, startling the lawyers. He glared at Chippen, but Seebold's unctuous confidant was a cool customer. "A better offer? I see! And pray tell, just where might this better offer have come from?"

Louis waited for his rhetorical question to register with everyone. He clasped his hands behind his back and paced the floor like a prosecuting attorney. He looked up at the ceiling as he continued: "Just who might have had a good reason to put together a better offer? Who had a lot to *gain* if the L'il Goose didn't fall into the hands of a dedicated, ardent conservationist—a stand-up guy and true friend and lover of trout? Any idea—Dolph? Mr. Nuckel?"

Nobody spoke. Louis broke the silence: "Dale Chippen. That's who."

The men around the table murmured and shifted in their seats. A ranch hand came in through the screen door, holding his ten-gallon hat, and announced: "Mr. Seebold. Mr. Kantarian and his associates are here."

Four men, three of them clutching briefcases, entered the room. Kantarian, the empty-handed one, approached Seebold and greeted him cordially but briefly. He was tan and fit, with gleaming white teeth. He looked very businesslike, dressed in gold-buckled loafers, immaculate blue jeans, and the safari jacket once favored by television producers. "Sorry," he said, "we were delayed flying in. But we're ready to go. Just a few minor questions."

"I have a major question," Louis interrupted.

For the first time since he arrived, Kantarian noticed the portly feather thrower with the raccoon tan, greasy jeans, and stubbly jowls. His expression was disdainful.

"Mister, Mister—Kevorkian," Louis said.

"It's Kantarian."

"My apologies, sir. Mr. Kantarian, is it? In any event, I think Mr. Seebold has a right to know what you plan to do with this ranch."

"I appreciate your opinion, but I think you're wrong about that," Kantarian replied smoothly.

Seebold said nothing.

"He most certainly does. What if I were to tell him?"

"You can tell him anything you want," Kantarian said, sounding irritated. "I'm exercising an option to buy. In fact, I'm doing it a full forty-eight hours before the option expires. Gentlemen—shall we?"

"You can't do this, Dolph." Louis was upset. "They're going to drain the greatest undiscovered trout river in the world and sell it off as a designer mineral water. Something called Quake Lake. Chippen works for them on the side—he set you up!"

It was so quiet you could have heard a size 20 Trico spinner drop.

Chippen looked uncomfortable. He squirmed in his seat, twirling a hank of his white-blond hair in a knot around his finger.

"Let me get this right." Seebold was as pale as his raja outfit. "You advised me to sell this property on the grounds that it was mostly swamp—and you work for the man who's buying it?"

"No way, man," Chippen protested. "What do you take me for, anyway?"

"A no-good, dirty, double-crossing rat," Louis interjected, lunging at Chippen. But Bowen caught Louis in a bear hug, restraining him.

"Oh, why don't you get a life already!" Chippen snapped. He turned to Seebold and cracked his jack-o'-lantern grin. "It's true that I worked for Quake Lake. But it was years ago and just briefly. I never even met Mr. Kantarian until tonight."

"Don't sell, Dolph. You can still back out!" Louis cried.

"I'm afraid I can't do that," Seebold said. He had regained his composure; the color was returning to his face. "I would violate every principle of ethical business if I tried to do that."

"Business!" Louis shouted. "The fate of the last great trout stream on earth hangs in the balance. This isn't about business!"

Seebold fingered the embroidery on his collar, undeterred.

Raul slumped back in his chair, realizing it was a lost cause. Nothing could prevent Kantarian from exercising his option. Seebold was being honest. He had simply been outfoxed, and he was man enough to cowboy up and get on with it.

"There are many fine trout streams on earth," Seebold said wearily. "I happen to own some of them."

"Now what the hail is that?" one of the wranglers said.

They all turned and saw a stream of bright headlights well down the road below. The vehicles appeared to be barreling right along.

"Are we expecting anyone else?" Seebold asked.

"We're not." Kantarian turned to Chippen. "What's going on?"

Within moments, the motorcade pulled over on the same bridge where Louis and Raul had been apprehended. Blue strobe lights flashed in the night.

Everyone ran out to the bluff.

"We'd better get down there," a wrangler said.

The dull whap of an approaching helicopter added to the chaos.

"Looks like the friggin' cavalry has arrived," Bowen remarked.

Louis grabbed Seebold by the sleeve. "Don't give an inch! Let's investigate."

They rushed to various vehicles and descended on the bridge, which was looking like the site of some horrific traffic accident. State troopers and game wardens in gray felt hats and dark green uniforms had cordoned off the road, while others had hooked up lamps to portable generators, flooding the bridge and Little Goose with harsh white light. Men were stringing yellow police tape from the bridge to the nearby bushes and fence posts, cordoning off the entire area.

Louis recognized the man directing the operation with a bullhorn. It was Digby Epps, a federal biologist and skilled feather thrower, one of the old crew from back in the day on the Fork.

Louis, Raul, and Seebold rushed toward Epps. The helicopter overhead was kicking up a massive dust storm, shining its powerful crime lights on the river. It was trailing some kind of seine through the air, which was full of brown drake spinners.

"Digby!" Louis shouted.

"Sky!" Epps replied. "Congratulations." Epps turned and barked more instructions. "I want all those sample vials date- and time-coded."

Bowen joined them. The men strained to hear each other over the noise of the chopper. Kantarian and Dale Chippen soon joined the crowd growing around Epps.

"It looks like you've done it, Louis. Hot damn, I never thought it possible," Epps said with undisguised admiration. "You've discovered a previously unknown species of mayfly."

"We did?"

"Whoa!" Epps leaped back as a state vehicle sped by. He turned to Louis and explained that a few days earlier, he had gotten a phone call from Ted Blinken. Ted claimed to have stumbled onto a fly unknown to science—he had even checked it out with one of the entomologists at the university in Bozeman. Among other things, the brown drake-like insect had twelve rather than the obligatory ten segmentations in the abdomen. All signs indicated it was a unique, heretofore unknown, mayfly.

"But how did you find us?" Raul asked.

"It wasn't easy," Epps said. "Ted said Bowen might know where you were. I finally got hold of him early this morning."

Louis and Raul looked at their snaggle-toothed friend, who winked.

Epps continued: "Bowen wouldn't tell me where to find you, and now I know why. You not only found a new species, you found the Little Goose. I admit—you and Bowen were probably the last three people on earth who still believed the Little Goose actually existed. My hat's off to you."

"He knew too," Louis said, jerking his thumb toward Chippen.

"What does all this mean?" Seebold asked.

"For starters, sir, we'll be obliged to shut down the river," Epps said politely. "I'm sorry about that, but I believe this is now an endangered species issue. That means the federal government has to get involved. And you know how it is with the federales. It could take months, perhaps even years, to complete due diligence on this. They will determine to what extent, if any, this rare new mayfly is endangered and deal with the implications that may rise from that."

Louis, Raul, and Bowen exchanged glances. They simultaneously turned to Kantarian, who had already pulled Seebold to the side. The two big shots were surrounded by their lawyers.

After a few moments, Seebold declared, "Deal's off. Everybody's going home now. The ranch remains in my hands."

Louis turned to Chippen, pointed at the dumbstruck conniver, and thundered: "Who knows what tangled webs we weave, when first we practice to deceive."

Seebold marched over to Chippen. He said in a low, seething voice, "Get out of my sight, you worm."

Chippen melted into the night.

"Nuckelhead!" Bowen called. "So tell us, what was Chippen's deal—why did he hire you?"

Nuckel strolled over. He shrugged. He knew he'd be lucky to get his legitimate expenses out of Chippen, now that the whole deal had fallen apart. "Chippen wanted you out of the picture—completely. He brought Kantarian in as a buyer. I think he wanted to get hold of the fishing rights. But he was always afraid you might get the best of him."

"But there wouldn't have been anything left of the river for Chippen to fish," Raul said. "Not after Quake Lake took the water."

Nuckel explained that the drawdown station for the mineral-water business would have been built almost a mile below the giant spring where the Little Goose originated—leaving plenty of room upstream for up to twenty anglers per day. Chippen figured that at a going rate of three hundred bucks per rod per day, it added up to serious money.

"They would have gotten it, too," Louis observed, "from the high rollers in the 'River Runs Through It' crowd."

"No doubt," Raul agreed. "Imagine, twenty anglers a day running up and down the fragile banks. It would have been an ecological disaster."

"Hmmm . . ." Louis thought aloud. "If indeed we did discover a mayfly previously unknown to science, what would it be called?"

Nuckel wandered off.

Seebold, still talking with Epps, seemed intrigued by the environmental issues at play. Nearby, the frantic activity began to subside into the methodical tempo of scientists at work.

"*Ephemerella Mendoza-Traub,*" Louis said. He savored the sound of the Latin name. "It's got a nice ring, doesn't it? I like it. I like the sound of that just fine."

―――――――

Caw-caw-caw; caw-caw-caw . . .

The magpie landed heavily on top of a young willow growing out of the bank along the Missouri River; the pale green limb swayed precariously under the bird's weight. Undeterred, the magpie declared it another Montana morning: *Caw-caw-caw* . . .

Daylight was just breaking over the Missouri River campsite at Tit Rock.

Caw-caw-caw . . .

Eventually heavy shafts of light penetrated the trees, dropping in bars across the camp. Beyond a barrier of brush, the river flowed along, its surface silver and black, with streamers of mist rising and immediately dissipating.

A host of other birds joined the magpie, vocalizing.

The campsite was like a village, with three vehicles and Bowen's McKenzie boat forming a protective semicircle around four tents. The camp mess and various chairs were strewn about under a scraggly pine. The Seebold boys, in Raul's one-man tent, were already awake and wrestling, causing the tent to tremble and shake.

Nearby, Raul and Phoenix shared the roomy army surplus tent. While tidying it up and whipping it into habitable shape, Raul had discovered that the tent had a mesh panel in its roof, covered by a flap that could be folded back to allow the occupants to lie staring at the stars.

Caw-caw-caw . . . *caw-caw-caw* . . . *CAW!*

The previous night, Raul and Phoenix had done just that, watching the stars as they talked about caddis and mayflies, baseball, dentistry. Raul was heartened to learn that Phoenix had not lost interest in playing ball, for he felt he had a lot to offer a gifted young player in the way of coaching. He looked forward to returning to Seattle in a few weeks' time. True, it would be too late in the summer to get Phoenix into organized youth ball. But they could certainly register in the Ironfeather Mentoring Program. He had always wanted to be a nurture warrior.

The blue tent, so often wracked by tremors, vibrations, and gastronomically inspired upheavals, was perfectly still. Louis and Lottie had both fallen into the deep, uninterrupted slumber of exhausted lovers after a night of passion. They had done it Comanche style, with Louis pulling Lottie's hair.

Only Bowen's well-worn tent was empty. He was already up, brewing coffee on a camp stove on his folded-down tailgate. It was chilly where he stood in the shade, chin buried in his canvas chore coat, lost in thought. His wild blond hair stuck out every which way from under his gimme cap. The hat was embroidered with the image of an Alaskan king salmon and the legend "Spawn till You Die."

Caw-caw-caw . . . caw-caw-caw . . .

Bowen glanced at the magpie and considered flinging a stick to scare it off. He took his mug and strolled over to the drift boat.

The epoxy binding the crude tin patch to the handsome wood had cured and seemed to be holding. The boat would be crowded with Louis, Lottie, and the Seebold boys, but this wasn't going to be a serious feather-throwing expedition today. It was going to be just fun.

Bowen was surprised to hear that Louis and Raul were splitting up. It was hard to imagine. Their partnership was like a successful marriage—not that he knew anything about that, he cheerfully conceded.

He walked over to stand in a patch of sunlight and heard stirring in the blue tent. Someone fumbled with the zippered door. In a moment, Lottie popped her head out, looked around, and wriggled out. She had found a way to apply makeup, including two spots of rouge on her cheeks, and gather her topknot.

Lottie wrapped both arms around herself to stay warm in her fleece and duck-walked across the campsite to the War Pony. She opened the door to let Little Jack out. Pointing toward the woods at the far end of the camp, she commanded, "Go make poopsy."

"Coffee?" Bowen asked.

"I'd love some."

They walked back to the truck; Lottie boosted herself up on the tailgate, holding the mug Bowen gave her with both hands. She smelled the aroma of the rich blend. "Yummm . . . you guys sure know your coffees."

"We do the basics pretty well," Bowen admitted. "We think we have our priorities straight. But basically we're just a bunch of fuck-ups, trying to keep some wonder in our lives."

"I never imagined you could get that from fishing," Lottie said. "It's fascinating."

"*Weird* might be the better word. Makes the day go by, though."

After an awkward silence, Bowen said, "I'm glad Sky decided to stay and write the book for Seebold. It's a good opportunity."

"I have to tell you, I never even heard of his website until we met. Do you really think this could be Louis's big break?"

"Actually, I was talking about the fishing opportunity. The blue-winged olives start to happen in September, and the river's empty by then." Bowen sipped his coffee. "You should check out the website, though. Sky doesn't get anywhere near the exposure he deserves. He's amazing, in that bombastic and infuriating way we know and love. Check the archives at the site and look up his definitive essay on Hemingway, 'Rebel Without a Clause.' It's a classic."

The flap of the olive army tent opened, and Phoenix emerged, stretching and yawning.

Little Jack trotted over, sniffed Bowen's shoe, and then ran off to the blue tent, where he sat down and whimpered.

"He really loves Louis," Lottie said. "Sky, I mean."

"Dogs know a stand-up guy when they see one."

After a while, Lottie asked, "So what's next for you?"

"For starters, I can make my child-support payments now. Beyond that, I don't know. Seebold and I are supposed to talk about me being caretaker up there at the Little Goose. Just to keep an eye on the place while the feds and God knows who all else are running around."

"Why not?" Lottie asked.

"My girl down in Dillon wouldn't like it much. Not that there's anything new in that. But I am getting a little too old for the lonesome life."

"Any of you guys seen that map, that road map?" Phoenix asked.

"Want some coffee?" Bowen flipped open a box of cigarettes and extended it toward Phoenix.

"Sure." Phoenix fished out a smoke.

"You should have socks and shoes on," Lottie said. "The ground is very cold."

Phoenix grinned at her, showing his corn-kernel teeth. "I ain't cold."

Lottie shuffled off to get the road atlas. While she was gone, Louis poked his head out of the blue tent. He groaned, grabbed Little Jack, and vanished back inside.

"So, where you heading?" Bowen asked, flicking his lighter for Phoenix.

Phoenix shrugged. "Silver Creek. I think it's in Idaho somewheres?"

Lottie came back. She put the atlas down on the tailgate, opened to the two-page spread of Montana.

"Seebold seems to run a pretty tight ship," Bowen said to Lottie. "I'm surprised he let you bring the kids down here for the night."

"I have to tell you, it's all because of Louis— and Lewis and Clark. He's never seen his kids respond to *anything* quite like this."

"Look, there's like nobody here," Phoenix said, pointing to the eastern part of Montana, below Fort Peck Lake. "It's just a whole lotta white space."

"No trout, either," Bowen said.

"Is that the reason?" Lottie asked.

"No." Bowen laughed.

The Seebold kids came tumbling out of the tent with a big ruckus. Their faces were already smeared with the remains of the enormous chocolate bars Babette had slipped into their daypacks—treats intended for the float trip. They brandished their espontoons as they ran down toward the river.

"Careful!" Lottie shouted. "Don't go far before breakfast."

Raul emerged from his tent, his fedora already in place, wearing a blue calico shirt and jeans.

Louis also appeared, groaning. "Mornin' pardner."

"Morning," Raul replied. "Sleep well?"

Louis yawned and stretched. He reached into one of the many pockets in his rumpled tan fishing shirt and fumbled for his glasses. Taking off his legionnaire's cap, he put both of his sets of glasses in it. He fell into step with Raul, heading for the water container perched on their camp table.

"Wow," Lottie said.

Bowen and Phoenix turned to her. She had taken over the atlas. "Look at the western border of Montana. It's amazing—it's like a profile."

The two men studied the map.

"It's unbelievable," Lottie said. "Doesn't it look *exactly* like Richard Nixon?"

"Who's that?" Phoenix asked.

The Seebold boys appeared, flecked with mud, brandishing their espontoons. They ran over and started pestering Louis and Raul.

"Listen up, folks!" Louis called to the group gathered by Bowen's truck. "My pardner has made a most generous offer. Given the arduous day that lies ahead for some of us on the Missourah, including these two rascals"—Louis made a gesture acknowledging the muddy boys—"Raul here has offered to fry us up a breakfast worthy of the name. Anyone for one-eyed Connollys speak now—or forever hold your peace."

The group collectively cried, "Yes!"

Little Jack, showing unexpected energy, leaped up on the camp table and barked twice. It was another fine Montana morning, like so many that Louis and Raul had known together. Flies would soon be hatching, heavy-bellied, colorful trout would soon be rising. Soon enough, it would be *showtime!*

That was the thing about Montana, as Louis and Raul knew full well. Each night, after they carefully stashed their fishing vests in the corner of the tent and turned in, the world would be remade. In the morning, it would be new again, full of promise and beckoning.

For feather throwers and select other pilgrims, it had always been thus, and it would always remain thus in the Beaverhead country and beyond. It would always be a glorious and unending Journey of Discovery, taken at a pace slightly swifter than geological time; a sojourn full of big heads and good whiskey and chokecherry bushes and battles with despoilers; a voyage full of mayflies and bank feeders and glittering riffles, with thick funnels of Tricos, twisting, undulating, and shimmering, rising like smoke or prayers, one after another, into the Big Sky.